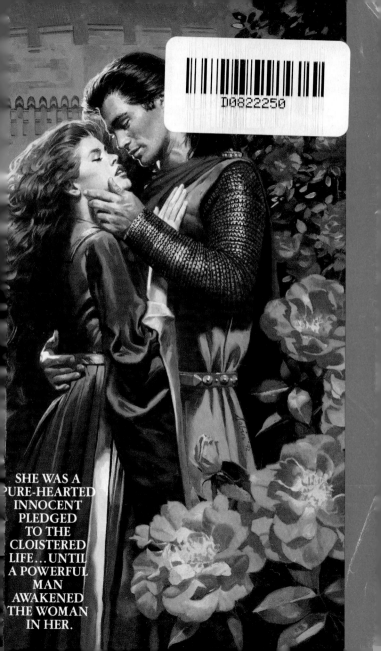

SHE WAS A
PURE-HEARTED
INNOCENT
PLEDGED
TO THE
CLOISTERED
LIFE...UNTIL
A POWERFUL
MAN
AWAKENED
THE WOMAN
IN HER.

D0822250

HIS EYES RAKED HER WITH A FURIOUS THOROUGHNESS, CAUSING HER TO STEP BACK IN DISMAY.

"You," he began in a voice hoarse with emotion. "You would *never* make a nun. No, quite the contrary."

"I *will* make a good nun. 'Tis only because you—"

"Because I what? I'll tell you. 'Tis only because I am the one who has forced you from the rigid mold you try so hard to fit yourself to. 'Tis only because I forced you to let down your guard a little. Now you're terrified by the feelings that have been unleashed in you."

She shook from the force of his words—and the force of his direct stare. Despite the distance between them, she felt overwhelmed by him. His gaze. His voice. His very essence seemed to surround her until that was all there was.

"Do you want me to admit I am terrified?" she answered him in a voice filled with pain. "Very well then, I am terrified. Do you want me to admit that you . . . that you have made me feel . . . things that I've never felt before?" She took a shaky breath, but her eyes held with his. " 'Tis all true. But even with that, you are still wrong about me. I *will* make a good nun."

Behind her the fire glowed, backlighting her every curve through the thin kirtle, but she could not know that. She knew only that Rylan's stare darkened, and she trembled in response, feeling as if he actually touched her with his eyes.

MY GALLANT ENEMY

"A love story of old to thrill and delight. Much intrigue and an awesome, arrogant, but lovable hero and the lady who turned his heart upside down."

—*Affaire de Coeur*

"Sensitive, realistic and passionate, *My Gallant Enemy* is a delicious medieval love story. Rexanne Becnel is sure to take her place in the ranks of well-loved medieval romance writers."

—*Romantic Times*

REXANNE BECNEL

A Dove At Midnight

A Dell Book

Published by
Dell Publishing
a division of
Bantam Doubleday Dell Publishing Group, Inc.
1540 Broadway
New York, New York 10036

ISBN: 0-440-20911-0

Printed in the United States of America

Published simultaneously in Canada

June 1993

10 9 8 7 6 5 4 3 2 1

RAD

For Dot and Al,
who have so lovingly
made me a part of their family

The Sparrow dismayed, the Raven undone
   upon the Sunne's demise;
The Blackbird flown, the Falcon fled
   when late the Moone doth rise.
Full measure of the Night shall fall,
   too still and without Light.
Yet in that darkest Hour comes
   to me a Dove at Midnight.

                   —Anonymous

Prologue

There would be trouble tonight at Oxwich. Joanna sensed it instinctively. It was there in her mother's strained features. It was there in the subdued mutterings and grim expressions of the maids who tended the chambers in the female wing of the castle.

Normally life at Oxwich Castle proceeded peacefully enough. But every few weeks an odd tension would grip her mother and extend itself throughout the castle, and Joanna, young as she was, knew what was to come. In the evening her mother, the Lady Harriet, would dismiss everyone from the great hall and greet her husband alone. Joanna never knew what was said, but afterward her mother always fled to her chamber in tears, while her father would drink himself into a rage before storming off to places unknown. He would be surly for days while her mother would take to her bed. Everyone else would step very lightly during those dismal days, careful not to anger the master, Sir Aslin. As for Joanna, she would stay far out of her father's way, for he seemed to despise the very sight of her at those times.

Though she was only nine years old, Joanna knew she must not hate her father for his harsh behavior. The priest had scolded her severely the one time she had confessed her childish feelings toward her parent. Yet as much as she tried to love and respect her father, she was hard-pressed to muster any warm feelings for him, especially now when it was all beginning once again.

A worried frown darkened Joanna's innocent face as she arose from her play, clutching her new kitten. "Mama," she called hesitantly as her mother glided past. "Mama," she repeated with a quiver of fear in her voice.

But Lady Harriet was preoccupied and did not hear her only child. She just drifted about the hall, sending the servants to tasks elsewhere, fluttering her hands nervously, but never raising her soft voice. Like some beautiful swan she was, the little girl thought wistfully. Beautiful and dignified, yet somehow withdrawn.

But swans didn't weep, and tonight her mother would most assuredly weep. It was that knowledge which spurred Joanna on. "Mama," she persisted, tugging on her mother's pearl-gray linen gown. "Please, won't you wait a moment and talk to me?"

When she finally turned to her child, Lady Harriet's face was pale, and the fine lines around her mouth were more pronounced than usual. "Perhaps later, dear," she said with an absent pat on her daughter's head. "Perhaps later. Presently I must prepare for your father." Her voice trembled slightly. "Go along now." Then she moved away, and an icy finger of fear stabbed at Joanna's heart. The kitten in her arms squirmed as the child's grip unconsciously tightened. But Joanna was oblivious to her beloved pet. All she could think of was her beautiful, sad mother. Why must it be like this? Why? Yet even her childish anger could not overcome her thickening fear.

In rising panic she whirled and ran up the narrow

stone stairs that led to the women's chambers. She would go to her mother's room and wait for her there. Eventually her mother must come. Once her parents were finished with their mysterious conversation her mother would come, and this time perhaps everything would be all right.

Joanna's wavy locks flowed behind her in tangled excess as she hastened up the twisting stairs. Her green eyes were dark with worry and fear and then, when she reached her mother's chamber, doubt. She should not be there, she told herself, trying to be brave. She should go to her own wall chamber as she always did. But before she could make up her mind, the kitten finally wriggled free. Mewing her complaint, the disgruntled kitten slipped under Lady Harriet's high bed.

"Come back here, Lady Minnou," Joanna cried in frustration. She dropped to her knees to peer under the bed. "Come back here," she pleaded in a voice that wavered with her suppressed emotions. When the kitten only licked her paw, however, and stared resentfully at her, Joanna inched her way under the bed. She was completely under the wood-and-rope frame before she reached her pet, but once she had it in hand, she did not back out at once. Instead, she curled around the kitten, creating a warm dark nest where they both could hide, at least for a little while.

"It's all right now, my baby. You just go to sleep," the little girl whispered in a broken voice as she rested her head on one of her arms and curled the other protectively about her charge. Then in a sweet shaky voice, she began to sing.

"Be not 'A' too amorous, 'B' too bold, 'C' too cruel, nor 'D' too dull. Be not 'E' too errant, 'F' too fierce, 'G' too gamboling, nor 'H' too hasty. Be not . . ."

Her voice trailed off once, then rose back to the reassuring cadence of her nursery song. But it was not overlong before she faded off again, retreating from her unhappiness into the blessed comfort of sleep. Then there was nothing to be heard but the faint purring of the kitten and the shallow breathing of the sleeping child.

The light was much dimmed in the chamber when a creaking movement above her awakened Joanna. The kitten still rested in her arms, but there was another sound, as if someone wept. In one unhappy moment her mind cleared and she remembered her mother. She started to squirm out from her warm hideaway, but the pounding of rapid footsteps and the abrupt slam of the chamber door caused her to shrink back in fear. Above her the bed groaned as if her mother arose.

"So you hide here from your failure."

Joanna cringed at the cruel yet familiar tone in her father's voice, and any thought of revealing her presence vanished at once.

"How fitting that you run to your bed, when 'tis *there* your failure lies! Christ's blood! Why am I so cursed as to have a barren wife—useless thing that you are!"

"I beg you, husband," her mother's voice came, soft and faltering. "There will be another month, and another. When my courses are run—"

"And how many months have you said the self-same thing?" he shouted furiously. "How many *years* have passed since your girl-child was born, with no others to follow? Soon you will be too old—perhaps you already are. Shall I be left with no son to pass my name and holdings to? By God, I will not have it!"

"Joanna is your child too," Lady Harriet whispered. "Would it be so awful if—"

"Is she?" the caustic reply came. "Yes, you would have me believe that. You make a cuckold of me, then think to foist off Roget's spawn as mine. Even now you hope to see him when we go to London. Only he will not be there this time." He laughed, but it was a cold, dark sound with no trace of mirth in it. "He met his match at Gaillard. Some Frenchman's blade sent him to the devil! Now, my sweet *whoring* wife, you must play your whore's role only for me!"

Joanna heard her mother's cry of anguish, and then the ropes and mattress creaked as her father threw her mother and himself upon the bed. In terror the child curled into a tight ball, crushing the kitten to her. Alarmed, the startled kitten struggled to be released, but Joanna would not let it go despite the scratches she suffered. Though the pet cried out plaintively, the unhappy sounds so close above them drowned it out.

"Aslin! Do not! I beg you!"

"Be still and do as you're told, woman!"

"But I am not clean . . . I am not clean now," Lady Harriet whimpered as the bed began to shudder rhythmically.

"Then I'll get a devil from you. But one way or another, I *will* have my son!"

There was no talking after that—only the ominous thudding of the bed—but that terrified Joanna even more. She clasped the kitten in a near stranglehold as she clenched her eyes shut and tried to blot out the ugly thudding—the endless thudding. Tears leaked from between her lashes, and her small body trembled in childish anguish. Her mother . . . Her mother . . .

Then the movement of the bed ceased and she could hear only her father's harsh breathing and her mother's heartbroken weeping.

"Every night, Harriet. Every day and every night if that is what it takes to have my heir."

Then he left with a violent slam of the door.

For a long time there was no sound. Her mother lay still on the bed above her; even her weeping had quieted. Yet Joanna could not move from her dark hiding place. How she hated her father in that moment—he who was so cold to her and cruel to her mother. Why must he always make her cry?

Then her mother rose from the bed and on silent feet moved across the room. Joanna wiped at her tearstained face, and as she did, the kitten finally escaped her too-tight embrace. It scampered out from under the bed, mewing plaintively and rubbing itself against Lady Harriet's skirts.

"Oh, my love . . . 'Tis too hard for me," the woman whispered softly, as if explaining to the disgruntled kitten. "I cannot bear it if you are gone . . ." She trailed off, but the despondent flatness of her tone frightened Joanna even more than the words did. In a panic she began to back out from her narrow confines.

"Mama," she cried as she struggled out from under the bed. "Mama!" She sobbed, choking on the word. But when she stood up her mother was not there.

Lady Minnou sat on the window seat, staring out an opened window, sitting so still she appeared almost a statue. Joanna tried to wipe the last blurry tears away, yet they rose again in freshening fear.

"Mama, where are you?" A tremor of foreboding washed over her as her eyes darted about. "Where are you?"

She rushed to the window, startling the kitten away in her alarm. Outside the narrow opening, the sky was a pale mauve blue, laced with high floating clouds. A flock of grebes flew into the wind, wheeling and turning as they made their way toward the fens. Yet the peaceful afternoon scene was in that moment morbid and threatening.

Joanna looked down and something inside her died.

There in the dry moat she saw her mother sprawled in obscene repose. She lay still, as a bird at rest might, her dress ruffling like plumes in the gentle wind. And yet there was no peace in her stillness.

Joanna lurched back from the window. "Mama!" Her despairing sob pierced the air. "Mama!"

But there was no answer to her cry. Despite her bitter tears, she knew there would never be.

1

Castle Manning, England
Summer, A.D. 1209

Sir Rylan Kempe, Lord of Blaecston, strode unannounced into the great hall of Castle Manning, but his
entrance was noticed at once. Sir Evan Thorndyke, Lord
of Manning, was mildly surprised. Rylan took every opportunity provided publicly to oppose King John and his
careless treatment of his subjects, particularly his stran-
gling taxes and his obsessive need to control his barons'
every move. As a result, Rylan had become more cautious about visiting his friends, especially those who
managed to keep up a friendly relationship with the
king.

Several of the lords who gambled at dice now that the
meal was done raised their brows at Kempe's entrance.
His politics were well known, and although most of
them might affect to deplore him when at the royal
court, privately they lauded his courage and sense of
honor.

The ladies also remarked on his approach, for Sir Rylan Kempe was nothing if not impressive. Tall and well
formed, he had earned his reputation in the lists as well
as in the battles for Normandy. He was known as a bold
and fearless fighter, and it was said that his disgust with

his king sprang from John's abhorrent leadership, which had resulted in England's complete loss of Normandy to King Philip of France. It was whispered as well that Kempe's near death at Valognes was just as responsible for his enduring resentment toward the king. However, no one had ever been known to broach that idea to Rylan Kempe directly.

But no matter why he opposed King John, the very fact that he so openly displayed that opposition only increased his reputation for unswerving valor. He was a man to both fear and respect.

His hair, which he wore unfashionably long, added to that image, for it gave his already dark countenance a decidedly dangerous cast. More than one man had been struck silent when Rylan Kempe turned his piercing stare on him. The ladies at court and elsewhere much discussed why his arrogant disregard of fashion nonetheless increased his appeal. But no matter their opinion, Sir Rylan did not seem in the least concerned. He could be incredibly gallant or ruthlessly determined where women were concerned. And although he had a wide reputation for leaving women in his wake, that did not lessen his attractiveness. He was unmarried and very rich. Even were he as ugly as sin, he would still be considered an outstanding match. However, he seemed in no hurry to take a bride.

After a slight pause, the buzz of conversation resumed in the hall. Sir Rylan received a goblet of red wine from one of the serving lads, nodded politely to one or two acquaintances, and then made his way directly to where Sir Evan sat at the high table. With only a sharp glance Rylan dismissed the man who had thought to speak to Evan, and without preamble he pulled a chair out and seated himself.

"Had I recalled you were entertaining," Rylan said, "I would not have bothered myself to seek you out."

"I'll admit I am more than a little surprised to see you here. Is something amiss? No, I can see something is. Shall we adjourn to discuss it more in private?"

"I'd like nothing better, but there is your reputation to maintain as a supporter of our liege lord," Rylan answered sardonically.

"Yes, there is that," Evan agreed with a rueful smile. "However, fewer and fewer barons support the man, much to your credit—though you surely know that. The king would not be unduly alarmed should I be visited by one of his foes; after all, he has so many. Why, you could no doubt discuss whatever it is that presently disturbs you before this entire company and not fear to have it repeated in John Lackland's ear."

Rylan shot him a mocking look. "We shall see whether you hold to that sentiment after you hear what news I bring."

As they left together—the one man so dark and menacing in bearing, the other redheaded and affable—the whispering began again, but neither of them showed the least concern. Gossip was a given among the nobles, but more so in these unsettled times of King John. Uncertainty bred unease, and for the past few years no one could be trusted. It was only now, when John's policies were wreaking havoc on everyone without exception, that the barons were beginning to unite. The king knew it, and as a result, his politics had become even more divisive. But it could not go on forever, Rylan thought. More and more the king was referred to snidely as John "Softsword," and not only for his poor military leadership. The man was ineffectual at everything; England would soon be in ruins if no one forced him to mend his ways.

"Now, what is afoot?" Evan asked as soon as the door closed behind them. "After declining my invitation to the summer solstice feasting, you show up unannounced with lowered brow and thunder in your eyes. 'Twould take a lackwit not to implicate our good king in your black mood."

"Aye, you know our liege well. Only this time he has not yet caused any trouble. That does him no credit, however, for I am certain it is only because he has not yet heard the news. Or if he has, he has not yet devised a way to put that news to his best use." He rubbed his brow restlessly. "Or perhaps he does not know about her."

"Her?" Evan gave Rylan an impatient look. "Pray tell, who is 'her'? And what precisely is this all about?"

"Ring for ale and I shall begin, for we have a long night of it ahead, Evan. A long night."

Once they were well fixed with ale, a wedge of cheese, and a loaf of bread between them, Evan settled back. Rylan drank and then paced before sitting down as well.

"Aslin is dead. His wife and son also, so I am told."

"Preston? Aslin Preston, Lord of Oxwich? By damn, but that is a surprise. But how?"

"A fever, they say. At least a dozen more of his people are lost also."

"Well, I am sorry of that. Not that he was any friend to me, but he was of no harm either. But now that he is gone—and his one heir as well—that is something to consider. Who stands next to inherit Oxwich?"

"That is what has me so bedeviled! No man is so close to the family as to have a strong claim. That means John may set any lackey of his choosing at Oxwich, directly in the midst of Yorkshire! God's blood, but I will not have it! He will overset all my work to bind the lords of that area together. Bad enough that all of England is in turmoil, but we in Yorkshire are beginning slowly to come together. We've a lords' council to put an end to all the unnecessary suspicion and accusations. But John sees any attempt at peacemaking without him as an attack on the crown. By God, but he will plant some fool at Oxwich and the entire countryside will be cast to the devil!"

Rylan had risen to pace once more during his tirade, while Evan watched him thoughtfully. "You have a plan, I suspect. You did not come to me for advice but for approval. Am I right?"

This insightful comment drew a smile at last from Rylan's dark face. "I have come by a useful bit of information—one that I hope the king does not have. At least not yet. But eventually he will find out. It behooves me, therefore, to act swiftly."

"By damn, will you be out with it then?"

"Aslin Preston has another heir."

"Another heir? A bastard, I presume. And an infant."

"No, a daughter older than his boy. He was married once before. There was some nasty business about the first wife's death. And there was a daughter, only she has not been at Oxwich in near a half-score years."

"Is she wed?"

"No."

It was a clear answer, and the one Evan would have hoped for. Yet the inflection in Rylan's voice alerted him. "There is more that you have not said."

Once more Rylan's grin was out in full force, lighting up his harsh face and softening its often menacing cast. "That is why I so enjoy your company, Evan. I need say only half of what I'm thinking—you divine the rest quite on your own."

"Go on with it. What is the problem with the maid? Is she malformed? Or an idiot that no one will have?"

Rylan sighed. "If only it were that simple. The unfortunate truth is that she is a nun. Or at least she plans to take the veil as soon as she is of age. Because her father refused to provide her with a dowry, no order would take her save the Gilbertines."

"Quite fortuitous, wouldn't you say?"

"Perhaps. However, in the case of Aslin Preston, 'twas more than likely due to a tight fist than any foresight on his part."

"Be that as it may, are you certain then that she has not already assumed the veil? There are severe penalties for leaving any order of nuns, even the Gilbertines."

"Do you forget the papal interdict so easily? Even if she *has* taken up the veil, the church will not honor it until Pope Innocent and John come to an agreement."

"So you mean to search her out, carry her back to her home castle, and somehow convince her that your choice of a husband for her is best. By the by, who *do* you have in mind for her?"

Rylan shrugged. "Any number of game fellows will do, assuming she's not *too* dreadful on the eyes. Perhaps even you." He grinned. "Oxwich is a fine little castle, with good fields and a well-populated village."

"Perhaps you should consider her for yourself," Evan replied with a disgruntled scowl.

"I've another wench in mind, thank you. With far more important properties even than Oxwich." Rylan drank deeply of his ale, then banged his pewter goblet down on the table. "And the Lady Marilyn is at least a known quantity. Unlike Aslin's little nun."

"Lady Marilyn?" Evan started forward. "Egbert Crosley's girl?"

"Aye, the same," Rylan admitted as he poured himself more to drink. "But save yourself any congratulations for another day. My agreement with her father is not yet common knowledge, and anyway, *she* is not a part of this discussion."

"No," Evan agreed, although reluctantly. "The king shall be apoplectic when he learns of it, though, for he has worked diligently to join Egbert's properties to those of one of his own supporters. When he learns that you and Crosley conspire to circumvent his authority . . ." Evan shrugged. "Well then, has Preston's daughter a name?"

"Joanna. Lady Joanna Preston, late of St. Theresa's Priory, but soon to be mistress of Oxwich. I've no doubt she will be well pleased to find herself an heiress once more."

Evan was quiet a moment. "When you marry Lady Marilyn you will control enough estates that John may not ignore you any longer. And if your plan works and you find a husband for Lady Joanna, all of Yorkshire will be firmly set against him. That is, assuming the chit goes along with you."

"She will. 'Tis clear her father sent her to the priory once he had got himself a son. Now she's to inherit. Why should she not go along?"

"John will not stand idly by, you know. He'll fight you for her, especially after learning he has lost Lady Marilyn to you. He will want to marry this Lady Joanna to a man of his own choosing. After all, she is rightfully a ward of the court. 'Tis the king's place to make a match for her, not yours."

"Perhaps, but once the deed is done and she is safely

ensconced in Oxwich Castle, with a babe growing in her
belly and a determined husband to defend the place, it
will be much too late for John to do more than rant and
rave. I ride tomorrow to St. Theresa's to get the maiden,
and I'll hold her at Blaecston until the marriage is well
consummated. John dares not attack me in mine own
castle. He has no allies in Yorkshire to support him and
he knows it."

"Do your allies know what you plot?"

Rylan laughed out loud. It was clear he enjoyed the
game he was embarking upon. "They all agree that we
must have one of our own at Oxwich. They will not balk
at my means once the girl is in my hands."

Evan let loose a great sigh. "All right, Rylan. It appears you have it all planned, very likely to the exact
hour at which this marriage shall take place. What is it
you want of me?"

"No more than the usual, my friend. Keep a close ear
to John's court. They move to Ely soon, not seven
leagues from here. 'Twould be only proper for you to do
him honor. Be alert for any rumors. Keep him appeased
as best you can. But once the bird is loose—and eventually he *will* hear of it—then send word to me at once."

"You shall be at Blaecston?"

"Once I see the deed done I shall be at Blaecston,
tending my sheep and seeing to my fields."

"And plotting against John."

Rylan lifted his goblet. "And plotting against John."

King John fixed the Bishop of Ely with the most imperious of his stares. "As long as she has not taken the
final vows, the church will not interfere. We are correct
in our assumption, are we not?"

The bishop nodded so eagerly that his fat jowls

quivered in obscene ripples. "Of course, your Highness. Of course. The good sisters of St. Theresa's are ever eager to bend to the royal will. If this maiden has not yet taken up the veil . . ." He trailed off as his king's stare grew colder and shifted his gaze uneasily to the queen, searching for some aid in that quarter.

With a small, very feline stretch, Isabel bestowed the full force of her smile on the bishop, then turned to her husband and placed her hand upon his arm.

"If she has taken up the veil, then we can claim her lands by royal decree."

King John frowned. "'Tis messier that way. 'Twill be far easier if I can simply wed her to someone of my choosing."

"So it would." She practically purred the words. "However, we do at least have other options."

"Kempe will challenge me if I claim the lands from the priory."

Isabel sighed and rubbed his arm reassuringly, though the bishop could have sworn impatience was the stronger of her emotions.

"Instead of fretting endlessly on this matter, simply send someone to fetch her. Now," she added.

The king nodded. "All right. So be it. See it done," he snapped at the man who ever trailed him, awaiting his least command. As the fellow scurried away, however, John rose to pace anew.

"How long shall it take?" he asked in a voice as petulant as ever.

"If the weather holds, no more than a week," Isabel answered. "Come, John," she added. "No good comes of this pacing."

The king whirled and the furious expression on his face caused the bishop to shrink back in alarm. But Isabel's poised features did not alter in the least. As always, the bishop wondered at her aplomb.

"Kempe will be after her." John swore. "He is just the shifty sort of snake who would steal her from the priory and wed her to someone against my will. He cannot be trusted!"

Isabel waved the bishop away, and he left the royal couple gladly. He counted the queen a great ally. The king, however, was too unpredictable for comfort. God pity Rylan Kempe if he crossed the king in this matter.

As for Preston's daughter, the stout bishop did not spare her a thought. She would do as duty bade. If not duty to God, then duty to her king.

2

Joanna knelt on the cold granite. Her posture was humble, her head was meekly bent, and her hands were clenched together, her fingers twisted almost painfully. To all appearances she was immersed in devout prayer as became an aspirant to the Gilbertine Order. Even the prioress gave a curt nod of approval to see the intractable Joanna at her prayers.

Yet Joanna struggled inside. More than anything else she sought an inner peace, a calm that might sustain her when one of her moods came upon her. But she found no solace in prayer. Her soul resisted, as if the devil had taken root within her breast. The prayers she knew by rote were so much muddle in her head, and when she searched for her own words, they would not come.

You are not one to judge your betters, she silently chastised herself. *Or even your equals.*

How she longed to shift her weight. Her left leg was cramping, yet she stubbornly stayed as she was. *Who are you to think your sin any less than hers?* she reviled herself. *You who are so proud?* Yet the fact was, she had spied one of the other aspirants meeting a man near the small pond in the woods, and she had judged the woman at once.

Joanna had been collecting arrowroot in the damp places beyond the pond when she had seen Winna and the fowler, and she could not help but stare. How they had clung together—their bodies pressed close, their mouths seeking each other's. How familiarly they had touched each other, then sunk down in the thick ferns where she could not see any more of them.

She had not *wanted* to see any more. Indeed, she had been repulsed and horrified, and she had not lingered in that place a moment longer. But on her hurried return to the priory she had recalled the scene over and over again. That Winna was a shameless hussy! Yet Joanna knew it was not her place to judge another. That was only for the heavenly Father to do. Through the prioress He would have his penance from Winna. Joanna should concern herself more with a penance for her own pride in judging another when such was not her place to do.

Yet her sin was not limited to pride, and that was what preyed most sorely upon her mind. When she had seen Winna with that man, she had become unaccountably angry. She had tried to pretend it was a righteous anger that Winna could betray the other Gilbertine sisters and aspirants by consorting with a man. How could she! Yet quite perversely, Joanna had also felt a disturbing desire to know more. What had they done in the deep bed of ferns? Why had Winna gone to that man so willingly?

A long-ago memory of her mother weeping and her father's cruel tone and furious accusations came back to her as she wrestled with her conflicting emotions, and it restored her righteous anger. Men hurt women. Winna might not know that yet, but eventually she would find out. Perhaps that would be God's way of punishing her for her sin.

Then Joanna made a devout sign of the cross in atonement for daring to impose her own human need for justice on a matter that lay only between Winna and her Lord.

She stayed upon her knees on the ancient stone floor until the bells rang for the afternoon chapter reading. But even after she joined the other aspirants in the chapel, sitting across the aisle from the white-garbed sisters, she feared her prayers fell short of cleansing her of her sinful feelings.

It was true that she no longer was angry at Winna. That emotion was ill-placed. Nor did she judge the woman for her weakness. After all, she herself had her own weaknesses that seemed to defy mending. Her temper, her quick tongue. Her propensity to judge others. Yet try as she might, Joanna could not rid herself of her unseemly curiosity. What had Winna and the fowler done together in the woods? And when would they do it again?

When they all knelt at the prioress's signal, Joanna's knees protested their renewed abuse, and a faint groan of pain escaped her lips.

"Shh" came the quick censure from, of all people, Winna herself. Joanna frowned down at her own clasped hands, trying hard to restrain her freshening anger.

". . . and beg His forgiveness for our sins—both those sins known to us as well as the many unknown. Pitiful creatures that we are, it is only the good Lord's love of us that confers any dignity upon us," the prioress intoned in her familiar low monotone.

Once more Joanna was overcome with guilt and vowed, as she seemed to do now on almost a daily basis, that she would keep her troublesome thoughts under control. She would not be proud. She would not be contrary. She would not judge others. Yet as they lingered at

their prayers, celebrating only portions of the mass since
the sacraments were now forbidden in England, Joanna
felt a sinking desperation. She feared that even after five
years at the priory she would never make a good nun,
humble and meek, content with quiet days of prayer and
endless labor at embroidery. It was what she wanted,
but . . .

Of their own volition her thoughts strayed back to the
little scene she had witnessed in the forest, and she
sighed disconsolately. Sister was right, she *was* one of
God's most pitiful creatures.

Visitors at St. Theresa's Priory were rare. Joanna had
often thought it due as much to the priory's lonely situation on a promontory that pointed into the German Sea
as to the spare accommodations associated with all of the
Gilbertine houses. No well-dowered priory, this. St.
Theresa's was peopled primarily with the castoffs of so-
ciety: women fallen on hard times with nowhere else to
turn; reformed prostitutes from Durham and York and
Lincoln; the occasional widow, unwilling to be sold by
her liege lord into another marriage. And others like
herself—daughters of lesser lords. By and large they all
shared one trait in common—a lack of funds—and this
accounted for the priory's dire situation. Yet that was as
their founder, Gilbert of Sempringham, would have had
it, and so it was that the Gilbertines drew those women
whom the Cistercians, Cluniacs, and White Ladies
would not accept into their holy orders.

The aspirants and sisters at St. Theresa's labored long
and hard to sustain the priory and, therefore, themselves.
Their embroidery graced many an English church as
well as grand castle halls. Fine stitching was their bread
and sustenance, and twice monthly the cart left with

their goods for York. Prayer, stitching, and the garden-
ing necessary to provide for the kitchens formed the sum
total of life at the priory, and by and large she and the
others were content with their lot. Their choices outside
the priory were grim.

Yet precisely because of this solitary existence, visitors
were a rare treat and cause for great excitement. Thus
everyone buzzed with curiosity when, during one morning's reading, the prioress was interrupted by a messenger. After hurriedly completing her sermon, Sister
Edithe announced to the curious congregation that a
group of travelers approached down the stony track that
led to St. Theresa's.

As they filed out from the chapel, an uncommon ani-
mation gripped the whole of St. Theresa's populace. In a
flurry of activity, the priory was hastily prepared for its
visitors. The stone steps were swept by the younger
girls. Tables were dragged out for an early supper while
the cooks hastened to the kitchens. From the tower
above the chapel one of the nuns marked the company's
progress down the narrow route.

They had made the turn past Norse Beck. They filed
down the narrows that edged Christa's Spout, where a
clear stream of water fell past the chalk-white cliff. They
came now up through the moor!

Joanna was as filled with anticipation as the others,
and as eager to glimpse a new face, hear a different
voice, and learn news from elsewhere. For the moment,
at least, she forgot her determined rejection of the outside world. Here was a reprieve from the dull and repeti-
tive life at St. Theresa's for a little while.

The men who rode into the unfortified yard of the
priory were an awe-inspiring lot. Though they wore neither armor nor mail and flew only one pennant—a black

field dominated by a white circle and a bloodred eagle—
they were nonetheless unmistakably men of war. There
was that aura about them that spoke of strength and
daring and even menace, should circumstances demand
it.

Yet as Joanna watched, only one face within a crowd of
observers, her eyes were drawn to the man who led the
band, and a prickle of alarm rippled up her spine.

Though all of the men appeared impressive, especially
to women unaccustomed to men of war, the leader of the
group was the most formidable of all. It was not his
height nor his breadth of shoulder and chest that marked
him apart from the rest. The fair-haired giant who rode
at his right surpassed him on both those counts. It was
more in his bearing, so erect, so composed, as if he possessed a power—an authority—that no one dared cross.

The typical arrogance of a nobleman, Joanna thought,
only tenfold. But though she felt an instant dislike toward him, she still could not pull her eyes away. He sat
tall and easy in his saddle, at one with the proud steed he
rode. His garb was simple and dark: a short leather tunic
above deep-green hose and tall gray boots. A cape was
flung back over one of his shoulders, held by a dark
glittering brooch. His only concession to the chivalric
style was the fine girdle that circled his waist, leather
worked with gold and silver, and encrusted with jewels
that winked in the thin sunlight.

He was every inch a lord of the realm, yet as Joanna
followed his progress, she was put more in mind of a
marauding Dane than a gallant from the court of King
John. He was too watchful; he sat too still upon his
mount. Then there was the unorthodox length of his
hair, worn well past his shoulders, as if he were a Vandal

of old. Indeed, he most assuredly looked the part, and she shivered in apprehension.

He let his eyes slide slowly across the yard, as if he searched for some unnamed thing, and Joanna felt certain nothing escaped his discerning scrutiny. As his gaze passed over the little group where she stood, she shrank back, suddenly fearful of his presence at St. Theresa's. This boded ill, she thought in a sudden, unwarranted panic. At once she regretted her foolish longing for some break in the monotonous life in the priory. *Send him away*, she silently prayed as he dismounted before Sister Edithe and made a courteous bow. *Oh, please, sweet mother Mary. Send him away from this place.*

"I hope there's news of York," she heard a whisper behind her.

"If they're up from London, p'rhaps they've word of Scunthorpe. I've no word from me mum . . ."

"Sure as anything they ain't come from the bishop."

The chatter picked up as Sister Edithe led the man toward the main hall, and the remainder of his fellows began to dismount. The several steeds and two sumpter animals that were lightly loaded were led to the sheds—meager housing for such fine beasts. But then, St. Theresa's had few horses—there was no need save for the delivery cart. Still, it was not the housing of the horses that troubled Joanna as the women in the yard began slowly to disperse. That man had come here for a reason. She was certain of it. The priory was too remote for it to be otherwise. He did not look to be a messenger from the Gilbertine Order. Therefore, it must be something else.

"Such a fine group of men. 'Tis enough to make a body forget the troubles a man can cause a woman," a sultry voice remarked. When Joanna identified the speaker as Winna, still staring after the men who now followed their lord to the hall, she frowned.

"'Tis best to avoid visitors, and thereby avoid the temptations of the world," Joanna replied curtly, quoting from a recent sermon she had heard.

"Are *you* tempted?" Winna asked in a deliberately provoking tone. "Best be forewarned, then. Men are a hard habit to renounce."

"And *you* quite clearly have not rid yourself of the habit," Joanna snapped in irritation.

"And methinks you are too curious by half about that selfsame habit," Winna drawled out knowingly. "I wonder why?"

Joanna's temper rose in quick response, but she determinedly squelched her sharp retort. Winna judged everyone by her own standard of loose morals. For a moment Joanna worried that Winna might have seen her watching in the woods after all. But she dismissed that as unlikely. Her real concern should be whether she *was* too curious about these men—about men in general. She marshaled her emotions, cloaking herself in an icy calm.

"You make a mockery of yourself—and this place—by your unseemly remarks."

"I am here because I must be. Piety I will leave in the hands of those better suited to it. Like yourself," Winna added archly. "But then, perhaps piety is not precisely to your liking either, despite the prim demeanor you affect. I've always wondered, Joanna, why *you* are in this place. Why hide yourself among us when you've a home and title? Why hide from the pleasures you might claim as your birthright?"

Joanna had no answer to give, and as she stalked angrily away from Winna's mocking laughter, she was caught between a terrible fury and a sudden dejection. Her place at St. Theresa's was no one's concern but her own, she fumed. No one's! But Winna's cruel taunt had opened up memories that, once unearthed, were always hard to bury.

The Priory of St. Theresa's had been home to her since she had arrived at the tender age of twelve. Certainly it was more her home than the castle of her birth. For three long years—from the time her mother had died until her father's second wife had so proudly presented him with a son—her father had ignored her completely, rarely even condescending to acknowledge her presence. Joanna had pleaded continually to be sent away to a convent school. Anything to escape from Oxwich. But her father had been adamant in his refusal. Only the birth of a worthwhile heir had softened his stance. Or perhaps it was Lady Mertice's impatience with her difficult stepdaughter that had swayed him. Whatever the reason, Joanna had come to St. Theresa's gladly, hoping to find solace and to escape the bitter memories at Oxwich. But she had not succeeded. Not really. And now, for whatever unknown reason, the day's unexpected visitors heightened that realization.

Joanna stayed away from the main hall during the meal. She did not want to see or hear any more of the strangers who supped with them—especially the man with the long dark hair. Instead she begged a bowl of cabbage soup and a piece of brown bread from the cook in exchange for a promise to help clean up after the meal.

It was as she was rinsing the collected spoons and wooden cups in a vat of warm water that the summons came.

"Sis-sister Edithe wishes to see me?" she stammered in dismay.

"Aye. She said you were to make yourself presentable and come at once," the older nun answered in the subdued tones common to all the Gilbertine sisters.

"Presentable?" As Joanna wiped her hands dry, then rolled her sleeves down, her mind turned in disjointed thought. The prioress seldom called one of the aspirants —those girls and women who had not yet taken up the veil—to her private chamber unless an infraction of the house rules was involved. A serious infraction. Try as she could, Joanna could not recall any recent behavior on her part that might result in such a summons.

She had watched Winna and the fowler, she recalled. And she had not shared that information as was required. But how could Sister Edithe have heard of that? Neither the fowler nor Winna had seen her; she was sure of that.

Sorely troubled, she smoothed back several of her mahogany curls which had come loose at her temples, tucking them beneath the white *couvrechef* that held the rest of her unruly hair back. Her dress was wrinkled and well worn, but then, that was true of most of the women at St. Theresa's. The gray wool was plain and serviceable, and it suited her well enough. There was little she could do to make herself more presentable other than to pull her cord girdle snug and distribute the bulky gathers of fabric at her waist more evenly. As a last effort she splashed a bit of cold water on her cheeks to cool their rosy warmth. Then with her head lowered as befitted an aspirant to the Gilbertine Order, she made her way silently to Sister Edithe's chamber.

She had not been to Sister's offices in several months —not since she'd been caught staring off into the wooded distance when she should have been busily working on one of the green damask altar cloths for Bishop Milford of St. John's. The entire populace of St. Theresa's had been thrown into weeks of frantic embroidering to complete that order at the time. Sister had chided her for her too-frequent, thoughtless preoccupation. She was selfish to let her mind wander when everyone else labored so diligently to prepare the intricate altar cloths, she had come to understand. Bishop Milford was an important man; his church was one of the most beautiful of God's houses, and she should feel honored to contribute her efforts to such a grand project.

Joanna had been duly chastised and appropriately repentant, and she had been careful to put only her best effort into the green damask—and careful as well not to harbor any personal pride in her handiwork. If the work was fine and even, and surpassing anything she had done before, it was to God's credit, not her own.

Now, however, Joanna did not know what she had done wrong. Her hesitant knock was answered at once, and at the soft command to enter she pushed the door open. A cat darted through, startling her, then slipped away on silent feet. Joanna couldn't prevent a shiver of intense dislike. It was Sister Edithe's one weakness, this fondness for cats. But Joanna did not share it at all. Far from it. Cats ever reminded her of Oxwich and that one terrible night. Though her reaction was illogical, she couldn't help herself.

"Joanna," Sister Edithe said with a slight dip of her head, drawing Joanna's attention back to the matter at hand. Her unsmiling countenance revealed nothing. "You were not at dinner."

"No . . . no. I was in the kitchens."

"Is this your day to work in the kitchens?" Then Sis-

ter waved the question away in an uncharacteristic gesture of distraction. "Well, never mind. That is of no
consequence. There is news for you."

"News?" A cold stab of fear went through Joanna.
The last news she'd had was three years previously. Her
father had flatly denied her petition for a dowry so that
she might more quickly be allowed to take up the veil. At
the time she had been terrified that he meant to wed her
off, but as time had gone by, that fear had lessened.
Since then there had been no further contact between
them, so what—

"Lord Blaecston has come quite out of his way to
speak with you," Sister went on, clearly flustered. "He
insists that he be allowed a private audience with you."

Joanna was too disconcerted to reply. Lord Blaecston?
He must be the man who led the visitors. The intimidating one.

"If you will walk with me, Lady Joanna, I have news
from Oxwich."

Joanna whirled around at the unexpected voice. Quiet
and low-pitched, it had a dark quality. Much like the
man, she thought a little wildly as she stared at the window niche behind her. There, silhouetted by the sun's
late offering through the thin hide window covering, he
stood at easy attention, seeming to dwarf the otherwise
commodious chamber.

"Will you walk with me?" he repeated, offering his
arm to her while she stood there staring, not saying a
word. But Joanna was too numb to answer. She had been
right, the thought echoed in her mind. She had been
right that he boded ill for her.

Sir Edithe broke the lengthening silence. "You see, 'tis
as I said, milord. There is no news so private that our
young women will not share with their sisters in the

Gilbertine way." The prioress rose from her chair with a new air of composure. "Whatever you have to reveal, go ahead and say it now. There are no secrets at St. Theresa's, only the goodwill of us all under the guidance of our bishop and, of course, our heavenly Father."

Lord Blaecston appeared completely unaffected by the good sister's subtle rebuke. He just kept his disturbing gaze on Joanna as if he might bend her to his will with only his eyes.

They were such dark eyes, Joanna noted unwillingly as their gazes remained locked—the midnight blue of the night sky. And so compelling. He seemed almost to command her in his steady scrutiny of her. Then his gaze slipped down a little, flicking over her almost measuringly before it returned to meet her gaze, and a slow warmth washed over her. She'd never suffered such an assessing look from any man before. Never. Yet she recognized innately what it meant. He'd looked at her as if she were a woman—as if she could play the woman to his man. Had she not been so uncertain of the message he carried—had he not stood there so maddeningly calm as he regarded her—her temper would have flared at his ill-mannered arrogance. Sister was right to be annoyed with his request for a private discourse with her.

Yet there was something else in his stare. Something that unsettled her. She knew, without understanding how, that for now, at least, she must yield to his silent command.

Her eyes darted apologetically to Sister Edithe, then quickly returned to the man. "We can go to the Grotto of St. Theresa. I will hear your news there." Then, fearing Sister's censure, she hurried from the chamber.

"You *are* Lady Joanna—Joanna Preston of Oxwich?" he asked as he followed her down the narrow stone steps. In the dim stairwell, lit only obliquely from a high window, his voice was a cold echo, disembodied words raining down on her from above.

"I *was* Lady Joanna of Oxwich," she corrected him sharply, hiding her fear in a show of anger. "Now I am only Joanna."

"Not *Sister* Joanna?"

She turned to face him when they reached the main hall. "Had I a dowry to commend me, I would indeed be Sister Joanna by now. But I endure the delay as best I can until my twentieth birthday. Then I shall accept the veil and assume my place in the Gilbertine Order."

Although he made no reply and only offered her his arm once more, Joanna felt a distinct quiver of unease. He knew something that could change everything. She saw it in the way he studied her. If he bore word from Oxwich, then he was a messenger of her father's, and it followed that any message from Sir Aslin Preston must be unpleasant to her.

Again her old fear overwhelmed her and her green eyes widened. Perhaps this time her father *did* send word that she must return to Oxwich! Perhaps this time he *had* arranged a marriage for her—one that would work to his advantage, of course. Ignoring the man's arm once more, she whirled around and hurried to the grotto, trying hard to quell her rising panic. First she must have the news, she told herself, for she might be incorrect in her speculation. First the news, then she would decide what she must do. But she would sooner die than give herself into marriage with any man of her father's choosing!

The grotto was set within a towering stand of cedar trees. A simple stone arch built from smooth river rocks stood within the dense shade; a stone bench was set directly before it. In the recess formed by the open-fronted dome stood a marble statue of St. Theresa. She stared out at her audience with sightless eyes, a white lady with white robes and fixed, white eyes. Normally Joanna found the grotto a peaceful escape, as it was intended to be—a place to pray or meditate, or simply be alone. But today it offered her no relief, for the presence of the man who had followed her there overwhelmed any other mood.

She pressed one hand to her stomach as she drew a deep steadying breath. Then she turned to face him. "Now, pray, give me my news. Then leave me in peace."

His expression revealed nothing, nor did he appear in the least inclined to hurry with his message. "Allow me first to introduce myself properly. I am Rylan Kempe, Lord of Blaecston." He gave her a courtly bow, even though she did not extend her hand.

"You are a friend of my father's." The contempt in her voice was clear, despite her effort to be civil.

"My castle is not too distant from Oxwich," he admitted after the briefest hesitation.

"You carry my father's message. I would hear it now."

Again the pause, but this time there was a look of curiosity in his face. When he spoke his tone was more gentle.

"I beg you, seat yourself first, Lady Joanna."

"Just Joanna," she corrected him once more, irritated beyond reason that he could be pleasant and cordial while she was so consumed with fear.

"Joanna," he conceded with a faint smile, which immediately caused her to regret correcting him. Despite her panic, there was something in the way he said her name, some warm thread of intimacy that she sensed was wholly improper.

"Please be done with this delay, Lord Blaecston. Just give me my news!"

"The news I carry is not *from* your father, Joanna. Rather, it is news *of* him. Of his death."

If he said anything further, Joanna did not hear it. Her father was dead! The man she had feared and hated—and desperately wanted to love. The man who had never had more than a passing glance for her.

She sat down abruptly on the stone bench, not seeing the statue of St. Theresa and no longer aware of the tall man who watched her. Her father was dead, yet instead of relief and satisfaction, that knowledge only brought back chilling memories of the day her mother died.

How many times had she relived it? How many nights had she been torn from sleep by the nightmares that tortured her? She remembered her father's arcane accusations, which she had never understood. She recalled a kitten in her arms, scratching her. She still carried a white mark on her wrist from it. She remembered the image of a bird as she had stared out the narrow window. Yet the most vivid memory, the one that turned her to stone and made every awful moment of that day real once more, was the silence. After only a brief murmur—words that Joanna did not clearly remember—her gentle, beautiful mother had gone to her death without a sound. No cries. No prayers. No words for a child left behind. There had just been silence.

Only later had Joanna's anger come, and not directed solely at her father. Her beloved mother had abandoned her and left her all alone to roam the cold empty halls of Oxwich. She had struggled for years with feelings of both desperate longing and helpless fury at her absent mother.

A violent tremor suddenly shook Joanna, and with a

choking sound she bowed her head. At once an arm came around her shoulder and she was gently pulled against a solid chest. She had forgotten the man entirely, yet for a moment, at least, she was glad he was there. She was glad for some human comfort. More than anything she longed to surrender herself to another's care, to put herself for once into someone else's safekeeping.

"I'm sorry, Joanna," he murmured, rubbing her arm a little awkwardly. "I'm sorry to bear this sad news to you."

At once she stiffened. Her father's death was *not* sad news to her. She felt nothing for him at all. It was her mother she mourned, she told herself. Though she shuddered yet with her sobs, she pulled away from the man. She wiped her eyes with the back of one hand as she tried to steady her breathing.

"You need not apologize, Lord Blaecston. 'Twould have reached me by another, if not yourself," she managed to say. "Please—" Her voice caught in her throat. "Please accept my thanks for coming so far out of your way to relay this news to me."

"As your father's neighbor—albeit a somewhat distant one—I did only my duty. 'Twas no trouble at all."

Joanna stood up. She was uncomfortable sitting so near him and felt awkward now to have accepted this stranger's comfort.

"You will want to be on your way, of course. Please do not linger on my account. I would remain here awhile longer to pray." She moved toward the pale marble figure of St. Theresa, wondering how she might in good conscience pray when her soul struggled so with feelings of anger, vengeance, and resentment.

"There is more, milady."

She stopped at his quiet words. "I am not 'milady.'"

It was an automatic response, almost absentminded, for his serious tone sent new tremors of fear through her. *How could there be anything more?*

This time he came to her, turning her to face him with a hand on each of her shoulders. "Your father fell ill to a fever that spread throughout Oxwich. Serfs, nobles, and servants—none were entirely spared. Your father died. So did his wife who was with child, and his young son."

"Little Eldon as well?" Despite the fact that she'd last seen her half brother as a babe in arms, Joanna was horrified to think that he was dead. And Lady Mertice, big with child taken also. She shook her head in disbelief.

"Your entire family was lost," he quietly confirmed. "Word has been slow to spread because the village priest placed an order of closure on the castle."

He lowered his face until it was level with hers and stared intently at her tear-streaked face. "The dead are buried. The rest are recovered. But Oxwich is without either lord or lady, and you are now its rightful heir."

Joanna heard his words but after the shock of his other revelations, this last one was too much. She could not respond as she stared into his shadowed face. She? Heiress to Oxwich? It was ludicrous! It was beyond belief!

Without warning she began to laugh at such an impossibly ironic situation.

Lord Blaecston's brow lowered at her unseemly mirth, and she felt his hands tighten on her arms. Yet she could not stop her hysterical reaction to his words. *She* would inherit Oxwich—a woman unworthy of such an inheritance? Hadn't her father deplored just such a possibility? Hadn't he made her mother's life a hell on earth and driven her to desperation in his demands for a more fitting heir—a son? Her saintly mother had sinned against her church and her God when she had made that profane leap to her death. Though the priests had deemed it an accident and buried her as was proper, Joanna had always known the truth. Her father had accused her mother of some inexplicable shortcomings, but Joanna knew those were not her mother's great failing. Her mother's true sin had been to take her life—and to abandon a child who had needed her so much. And now her father's cruelty was proven all for naught, for the daughter he'd judged so unfitting was to gain Oxwich after all. Only she didn't want it.

Tears stung her eyes anew as she drew a shaky breath. On her face was a grim parody of a smile. "Forgive me sir, I am . . . I am taken aback."

"So it would seem," he remarked coolly. "Laughter was hardly the reaction I expected from such sad news."

Joanna jerked out of his grasp as if he had struck her. "You do not understand—" Then she broke off, unwilling to share any of her pain with this stranger and unable, in any case, to give words to her feelings. "Thank you for the diligent execution of your duty, Lord Blaecston. As I said, however, I should now like to be alone." She stared at him aloofly. "Unless, of course, there's something else."

Joanna did not flinch beneath the hard stare he gave her. But at that moment her original assessment of him was reinforced. Although he had comforted her in her first shocked reaction to his news, there was no trace of kindness on his face now.

His brow was wide, his face lean with a straight, proud nose. He would be a handsome man, the aberrant thought came to her, if he would smile. But his expression was fierce now, and it made his strong face harsh and an already intimidating demeanor menacing. In the deep shadows cast by the cedars he was tall, dark, and intense. Not a man easily dismissed.

Then his gaze flicked over her once more with that impudent awareness she'd sensed so briefly in Sister Edithe's chamber, and her caution wavered under her instinctive outrage at his intentional rudeness. Before she could respond with an appropriately cutting remark, his lips curved up in a taunting smile.

"Never may it be said that I kept a troubled soul from her prayers. When you are ready to depart for Oxwich I am at your service. However, we must leave no later than the day after tomorrow."

"Depart for Oxwich!" Joanna stared at him as if he were quite mad. Then her expression became bitter. "I have *no* intention of returning to Oxwich Castle." She lifted her chin and stared at him, conscious of the enormous sense of relief that simple statement gave her.

"I'll never return there," she added as she purposefully shed the last of her ties to her old home. "If you came here with the thought to return me to my father's house, I thank you for the kindness you intended. But it is my plan to take up the veil. My father's death and that of his heir do not change that whatsoever."

It was his turn to stare at her dumbfounded, and Joanna's mouth lifted in a faint smile. "I know this is not what you expected, Lord Blaecston. No doubt you thought to find me eager to return to Oxwich. To be mistress there." She shrugged, then took a deep breath. "I do not know who should be next in line. There must be a cousin or . . . or someone. And even if there is not, the king will undoubtedly have someone deserving of such a grant."

It was her final words that brought Lord Blaecston from his silence. But though his words were cool and reserved, she sensed that she had somehow angered him greatly.

"I think it is too soon for you to make such a decision. Perhaps after your prayers you will be more composed."

"'Tis my intention to become a sister of the Gilbertine Order, Lord Blaecston. Oxwich ceased to be my concern five years ago."

"Your commitment here is not final, and your duty to Oxwich and your family is clear."

"You are wrong in that. I *have* no duty to Oxwich," she snapped at his unemotional words. Then she calmed herself. "'Tis true that my vows are not yet taken. But my decision is made." Once more she smiled at him. "Now, if you will leave me to my prayers."

The tension that gripped him was obvious as he towered over her, and she felt a momentary twinge of panic. But then he bowed, a brief perfunctory display of manners.

"As you would have it, Lady Joanna. However, I would discuss this matter with you once more on the morrow, if you would be so kind."

"I shall not change my mind."

His gaze narrowed. "Even though Oxwich go to the vilest of the king's lackeys?"

"King John and his lackeys are not my concern. Just as Oxwich is not yours," she answered. Then her hard-won composure slipped and her voice trembled with emotion. "I would not care even should the king level Oxwich Castle to the ground!"

For another long moment their eyes clashed across the tense span of the little clearing. Then he nodded curtly, turned, and left her to her unhappy prayers.

* * *

A scowl darkened Rylan's brow when he vaulted over the stonework fence and into the horse pen. He strode toward the small group of war-horses without hesitation, unfazed when most of them shied away, for the one horse he sought did not move. He leaped onto the animal's back, then with only his knees he began to put the steed through its paces around the inner perimeter of the compound. Over and over they made the rounds, at a trot, at a canter, and at a death-defying gallop, given the moderate size of the pen.

The lowering sun had touched the horizon and glinted gold off the dark-forested hills to the west before Rylan and his destrier ceased their determined exertions. Though the air was crisp in the breeze off the sea, both man and beast were damp with sweat from their drills. Around and around the irregularly shaped enclosure he walked, leading his horse as he went.

By the time his destrier had cooled down, Rylan's mood was much lightened, considering the black temper he'd been in after his discourse with Lady Joanna Preston. That difficult minx had in one easy breath upset his well-laid plan, and in so doing had thought herself finished with the subject. But she sorely underestimated him if she thought he would so easily allow Oxwich—and thereby Yorkshire—to slip into John Lackland's corrupt hands. The king had cost him his father and two brothers in the wars with France for Normandy. His mother had not survived even a month when the news of the slaughter at Valognes had reached her.

He had thought he would also die from his wounds. Only his bitterness had sustained him. That and his vow to see England wrested from John's incompetent hands. Yorkshire at least stood firm now against the king. And his own coming marriage to Lady Marilyn would strike a serious blow to John, for John thought to wed Egbert's sole heir to his own cousin Robert of Short.

Yes, everything was coming together. There was no way he would allow this slip of a girl to ruin everything.

He rubbed his destrier's velvety muzzle absently as he considered Oxwich's reluctant heiress. She had been adamant about becoming a nun and forsaking her inheritance, he was convinced of that. He'd thought that after five years in the dreary surrounds of St. Theresa's she would be eager to leave. Then when she'd laughed so uncontrollably, he'd been sure of it. But her laughter had been hysteria, not delight. She had vowed to stay at the priory and, moreover, had displayed a considerable temper—especially when he'd let his gaze rake her entire body.

He chuckled at the memory of her outraged expression. No doubt she had not encountered many men, tucked away as she was at the tip of Flamborough Head, for if she had, she would most certainly be familiar with such glances. She was a comely one—no argument on that point—with wide brow and clear green eyes and skin as fair as a babe's. He would find no resistance from either of the gallants he was considering for her. One look at those thick lashes and her long curling hair, and they would draw swords against one another for her hand. Though her clothes were rough and plain, Rylan had an experienced enough eye to have noticed the narrow waist and generous thrust of her breasts against the coarse wool bodice of her tunic.

The only difficulty Lady Joanna would present to her future husband was her ready temper. But then, once she was wed, that would not be *his* concern, Rylan decided.

With a firm pat on his horse's withers, he sent the

animal back to the others. Then he turned toward one of his men who waited patiently for him beside the stone wall.

"Trouble?" the man asked as he unfurled his huge body from its relaxed position.

"Only a change of plans," Rylan answered. "Nothing more than that. It seems our meek little dove does not wish to claim Oxwich, Kell. She prefers the life of a nun."

"Some do."

"Some do, yes. But she's been here since she was a child. She knows nothing of the outside world. Once she tastes the freedom—and the power—she'll have as a mistress of her own castle, I warrant she'll change her tune."

At the taciturn Norseman's raised brow, Rylan became more serious. "No matter her wishes, she *must* marry to ensure Oxwich is kept free of the king's spider web. I have no doubt she will one day thank me, but I don't presume to think it shall happen in the next few days."

"She's not yet a nun?"

"Not yet, which is our good fortune, else she'd be hounded all her days for marrying. Not even Father Govan would dare marry a nun, no matter how much gold I rained on him. As it is, it shall be difficult enough gaining her verbal consent."

"Withholding food will work," Kell retorted with the flat assurance of one who knows. His unemotional suggestion brought a slight frown to Rylan's brow.

"I hope not to need such measures as that." Then he glanced around the priory yard, grown long in shadows as the sun withdrew. "I'll speak to her tomorrow, though I doubt she is likely to change her mind. Meanwhile I've a plan in mind that will allow us to take her quietly. We will be well away before any alarm can sound. And once I have her in my custody, there will be nothing our *good* king can do about it."

3

"The gentleman wishes to speak with you," Winna informed Joanna the next morning. Curiosity—and a trace of belligerence—colored her voice, and it irritated Joanna at once.

"I am occupied, as you can clearly see," she replied, refusing to look up from her closework. Yet despite her attempt to concentrate on the silver and gold threads she was working with two needles on a rich burgundy panel of Tartaryn cloth, she promptly pricked her finger. "Sweet mother—" she muttered. Then she jerked her eyes up to the still-waiting Winna.

"I said I was occupied. Did you not hear?"

"I heard," Winna answered smugly. "Though methinks you are quite the fool to ignore such a man as he." With a last arch look she smoothed the coarse fabric of her gown and sauntered from the room, clearly well pleased with herself.

That woman! Joanna fumed as she sucked the tip of her finger. She was a hussy and quite unashamed of it! Yet Joanna knew at the same time that it was not Winna or her unseemly behavior that had her so unsettled. It was that man.

The whole of the previous night she had lain in her cot, unable to sleep, recalling over and over her brief yet emotional audience with him. She had set him straight, she reassured herself. She had made it perfectly clear that Oxwich was no longer her concern and that the king could grant it to the devil himself if he were so inclined and she would not care at all. Yet she had the distinct feeling that Lord Blaecston had no intention of letting the subject go so easily.

In grim silence she railed at her father who once more plagued her. *Are you to haunt me in your death even as you tormented me during your lifetime?*

With a resigned sigh she let her embroidery fall to her lap. Her father was dead. The news had taken her completely by surprise, yet beyond her initial shock she felt nothing. No sorrow. No anger. She only felt empty, as if she'd been drained of all ability to feel. She was empty and adrift with nothing to anchor her any longer.

Yet that was not precisely true, she told herself. She had St. Theresa's Priory. It was her home now, the place she wanted to be. No one could force her to leave now and she should take comfort in that.

But even that could not ease the ache that suddenly welled up within her chest. Though it went against all logic, she was overwhelmed with acute loneliness. Not since her mother—

Joanna shook her head, refusing to allow that memory to surface. She had been lonely then, yes. She had hoped to die herself in the dark days that followed her mother's death. But the news of her father's passing did not begin to affect her so, she vowed. She was sorry for his second wife, and for his little son Eldon. But as for him . . .

Joanna rose from the workbench and moved restlessly toward the windows of the carrel. Sister Edithe had allowed her the seclusion of the prayer carrel for her work today so that she might mourn her loss in private. Instead, however, her thoughts had tumbled disjointedly, snatching at fragments of her childhood which she had firmly suppressed for many long years. And now Winna had come with a summons from that man.

At the thought of Sir Rylan Kempe, Joanna's mind found a focus. How appropriate that word of her father's death be conveyed to her by such a man as Lord Blaecston. Like most of his kind, he was arrogant and condescending. He even had the gall to think she should bother herself with his petty politics! How like her father he was, she decided bitterly. How alike *all* men were. The man beckoned and the woman was expected always to leap at his call.

Only she did not have to leap any longer. Neither her father nor the overbearing Lord Blaecston could force her to do anything at all. For the first time in her life she was truly her own woman, free to make her own choices.

And she chose St. Theresa's.

Joanna looked up through the high window of the carrel. All she could see beyond the stone frame was the tops of the trees and the sky beyond. That same sky arched over Oxwich, she thought. And beyond Oxwich Castle, the whole of England and even farther. There were days she wished to search out the end of the sky, to find that mythical place where the blue of the heavens touched the green of the earth. The birds that glided over the priory and on, out to sea or else inland, could no doubt tell much of the world had they but the tongues to speak on it. Yet despite her frequent yearnings, she knew it was only childish daydreams. The wide-reaching sky captivated with its ever-changing colors and exquisite cloud forms, but a person could not cling to the sky like she might cling to a sturdy stone or the solid earth. In the simple buildings of the priory she had found security. She would never risk losing that, no matter how appealing the outside world might sometimes appear.

On that firm note she folded her embroidery into an oak-split basket and wove the two needles into a cross at one corner of the cloth. She might as well face the determined Lord Blaecston and be done with him once and for all. Perhaps this time when she again declined his offer of passage to Oxwich he would believe her.

When Joanna came into the priory yard, she was unprepared for what met her eyes. Winna, ever bold where male visitors were concerned, was standing beside Lord Blaecston, her face turned prettily up to his.

". . . Alas, but she refused your summons, my lord. It tries my soul to see you so rebuffed, however, so I hope you will accept my humble company in her stead." Winna averted her face as she made a little curtsey and in so doing spied Joanna. She promptly slanted a smug smile at Joanna, but when she straightened up, her attention was focused entirely on the tall man before her. "St. Theresa's houses several inspiring relics that you may care to see. They are kept in a basement tomb. Where a person may find absolute privacy for his contemplations," she added in a huskier tone.

Joanna did not hear his response to Winna, for his face was tilted away, but when Winna stepped nearer him, Joanna was certain he had encouraged her. Winna would surely not contemplate the same familiarities with this man as she'd shared with the fowler! Armed with righteous indignation that the pair of them could be so bold within the very priory walls, she charged forward.

"Thank you for informing me that Lord Blaecston

awaited me," she said to Winna, trying to sound civil
and failing completely. At Winna's haughty glare, however, Joanna's temper nearly boiled over. Had the girl no
self-respect? she wondered furiously. It should not fall to
her to protect the hussy from her own foolish actions.

"Ah, Lady Joanna," Lord Blaecston said as he turned
toward her. When he saw her frowning countenance, his
glance shot briefly to Winna, but then he turned his full
attention on Joanna, smiling faintly as he did so. "I'm
most pleased you can join me. Winna had informed me
that you were previously occupied . . ." He trailed off,
leaving his words a question in the air as his gaze held
with her own.

"I . . . I *was* occupied," she answered, trying hard to
muster her suddenly unsettled emotions. It occurred to
Joanna most uncomfortably that Winna's bold behavior
would not have concerned her had it been directed toward some other man, but she determinedly quashed
that notion. As an aspirant to the veil, it behooved her to
care for the behavior of everyone in the order. Sister
demanded that they reveal any sin they might witness in
order that they all might better achieve that perfect state
of grace. Her anger at Winna's behavior was part of her
duty, she told herself. Somewhat better composed, she
faced Lord Blaecston.

"Your friend had offered to show me the priory's
relics," he began. "Now that you are here, however, perhaps we can have our talk and see the relics at the same
time." His well-formed lips curved up a little further,
clearly mocking her as they did so. "If you'll excuse us,"
he said to Winna with a short dismissing bow.

He did not spare Winna a parting glance as she
flounced away. Joanna, however, watched her departure
with unwarranted interest as her own composure fled.

Now that she was alone with the man, what was she to do with him? Something in her balked completely at the thought of taking him down the narrow stairs to where the bone of St. Theresa's left thumb and a scrap of leather from her sandal were interred. The idea of being alone with him twisted her stomach in a nervous knot. Even speaking privately to him in full view of the yard was having a most disturbing impact on her.

"Well?" he prodded. "Take my arm, Joanna, and be my guide to the wonders of St. Theresa's."

"You are not in the least interested in our relics," she snapped as he offered her his arm.

"Never think such a thing," he replied with a grin, lifting one hand to his chest in mock horror. "Do you question my faith?"

"Your faith?" Joanna stared at his sardonic expression and arrogant carriage, and her opinion of him crystallized. "I believe you are one who can live just as easily under his Holiness Pope Innocent's interdict against celebrating the sacraments in England as you lived before he made that ruling," she retorted. But though she meant it as the worst sort of insult, he only grinned.

"I was baptized in the faith long before the interdict, and I expect not to require extreme unction until long after Innocent's interdict is lifted. In the meantime, like any good Christian, I abide by my pope's ruling."

Joanna's back stiffened at such a casual dismissal of the other sacraments. Christian indeed! But it was not her intent to argue points of religion with this man—this blasphemer—she reminded herself. He had summoned her to encourage her to assume responsibility for Oxwich. She had only to hear him out and turn him down once more. Then he would be on his way and she would not be bothered by him again.

"You summoned me for a reason, Lord Blaecston. Please speak your piece. I've other matters awaiting my attention," she said with a forced air of bored indifference.

"Ah, yes, your embroidery." He nodded gravely as if he considered needlework of paramount importance, but Joanna knew he mocked her yet again. It took all her willpower to prevent a mighty outburst of anger. But though she waited in determined silence for him to begin, he seemed equally determined not to be pushed. As her gaze clashed angrily with his, her stomach tightened in some innate recognition of him. He spoke quietly. He moved calmly and without any hint of threat. Yet she knew in her woman's soul that he was a man to be wary of. For a long moment she stared into his lean face, seeing the barbarian length of his dark hair and noting the deep sapphire color of his eyes. Then, unable to bear such intense scrutiny one moment longer, she glanced away, toward the open yard beyond him.

It was only then that he spoke, as if he knew he'd won some battle with her. But to her surprise, his voice was deep and sincere, with no trace of triumph in it.

"I would like to restate my case to you, Lady Joanna, regarding the demesne of Oxwich which title now lays with you. Do not speak," he hastened to add when she turned at once to face him. "Hear me out, I ask. Just hear me out."

Once more their gazes met. This time, however, Joanna did not let herself be drawn into another silent battle. She could afford to be gracious, she told herself. She could politely hear him out—hear all the ridiculous reasons he would put forth in an effort to sway her—for she knew they would be in vain. He would reason and she would turn him down. It was as simple as that.

At her nod of assent he smiled. "Let us walk anon as we talk." Then he took her elbow and steered her away from the yard.

Joanna was at first dismayed. His hand held her arm so confidently; he guided her toward the open gate so effortlessly. But she beat down the flutter of alarm that rose in her stomach at the warm strength of his touch. It was only for a little while, she reminded herself. Once she made it clear she would not abandon the Gilbertines, he would leave her alone. No doubt he would depart in disgust, she imagined smugly. For it was unlikely he would accept his defeat very graciously.

They walked in silence past the unguarded gate and down the dusty road. Far to the right the sound of the ever-constant sea carried across the open moor. Day and night the waves waged their endless battle with the chalk cliffs, battering them yet receiving only a fragment of gain. Though the sea stretched forever and the tides seldom relented, the towering cliffs never gave way. So might this man beat at her defenses, she thought fancifully. But like the ancient cliffs, she would ultimately persevere. And she would remain at St. Theresa's long after he had departed.

"You've been here many years," he began, turning to look down at her.

"Yes, and it's my home now," Joanna answered. She stepped away from him on the pretext of picking up a broken piece of gray chalk and pocketing it, but her true purpose was to free herself from his disturbing grasp.

"'Tis a beautiful place."

At that surprising statement Joanna straightened up and stared at him. With the wind at his back and his long dark hair ruffling in the strong gusts, he seemed strangely in his element. The stark land and bright sky beyond him lent his silhouette an even more powerful aura, as if he might tame the wind if he so desired. By contrast, she felt almost buffeted by the sea breeze. It whipped the free ends of her hair and tugged the hem of her skirt against her ankles as if it would pull her whither it would.

"Yes, it is a beautiful place," she agreed. "Flamborough Head is wild and alone, and the priory is safe and private."

"So that you will be undisturbed in your endless stitching?" His dark brow lifted in question as he eyed her speculatively. "I should not have thought that would be the goal of a young well-born woman like yourself."

Joanna stared at him suspiciously. "What other choices does a noblewoman have?"

"To be mistress of your own demesne would surely provide you more challenge—and more reward—than the quiet seclusion of this place."

"But I would never truly *be* mistress of Oxwich. My eventual husband would become Lord of Oxwich. I would only be his wife. There's a great difference between the two," she added bitterly.

His expression did not alter save for a slight narrowing of his eyes. "Your husband would indeed be Lord of Oxwich, but that is to the good, Joanna. A man labors long to improve his estates and protect his family and his people. As his helpmate you would have the respect of all, and rule a fine household in any fashion you wished."

"In any fashion my *husband* would wish," Joanna countered, recalling her mother's quaking fear of her own husband. "I do not need a husband, for I have everything I need here. I come and go as I please. I have my duties and, of course, my prayers. But I wander these moors and the woodlands near the fens at will. 'Tis all I want from life."

She turned away from him abruptly and faced back toward the priory, at its gray squat buildings perched on the barren promontory. Why had this man come to upset the fragile peace she'd found here? Why must he pry and prod at the painful wounds that still lay so near the surface of her mind?

Then he moved to block her view of St. Theresa's and addressed her in a warm and sincere voice. "You need not fear the man who would be your husband, Lady Joanna. A man would be a fool to do other than please a bride of such surpassing beauty." His eyes slipped over her and the warmth in their deep-blue depths unexpectedly heated her wherever they passed.

"You have only to smile upon him to have your way— to offer of your sweetness to gain whatever you might desire."

Joanna's eyes widened at his surprising words and her heart began an unsteady rhythm in her chest. Yet despite the sudden rush of warmth over her, she knew his words were wholly improper—as was his bold gaze. Added to that, he spoke on behalf of another, as-yet unspecified man. That knowledge, however, did nothing to calm the disturbing knot in her stomach.

"All I desire," she began nervously. "All I desire is to be left alone. Nothing you can say—"

"What of children?" he interrupted. "A woman's fondest desire is a full nursery. Do you forsake that so easily? For once you take up the veil, you shun that part of your life forever."

Joanna lifted her chin and tried bravely to ignore the lump in her throat. What good had it done her mother, that desire for children? She'd wanted a son above all things, yet God had not seen fit to send her one. Instead she'd suffered the abuse of her husband until she could endure it no more. And now, even though the idea of a babe of her own was sweet, Joanna shook off the possibility. Wanting a thing—even praying for it night and day—did not ensure its deliverance. She could bear witness to that, although she was convinced this Rylan Kempe could never understand it.

With a slow shaky breath she stared up into his impatient face. "I shun it all—children, a husband, and especially Oxwich Castle."

The air between them was fraught with tension at her angry words. Yet to his credit, Sir Rylan did not respond in equal anger. Even in her tumultuous state, Joanna saw fire leap in his eyes. When he spoke, however, his voice was quiet and steady.

"'Tis plain I have upset you, and that was hardly my intention. But I am hard-pressed to understand your fear of Oxwich—for that is what you feel, is it not? But why?"

"I fear nothing," Joanna snapped, even more unsettled by his calm in the face of her emotional turmoil. "I simply do not wish to . . . to change my plans."

"There's more to it than that, Lady Joanna."

"My reasons are my own!" she cried.

She saw his jaw clench. "And what of your duty to Oxwich? No matter what your feelings for the place, you have a duty to Oxwich and to England to continue your family line."

"My family line?" she scoffed. "It may die out with me as far as I am concerned. Another will gladly take my place at Oxwich. Besides, this is none of your concern. Why should you care who is lord at Oxwich?"

He stiffened at that. "Oxwich, like all the estates in

Yorkshire, has long stood fast against King John's excesses. I will not let it fall into his hands."

"'Tis none of your affair who shall be lord at Oxwich!"

"If I am to be loyal to my country, then it must become my affair."

Joanna stared at him, trying hard to control the tremble in her voice. "'Tis clear you mislike the king and would thwart him in this, but do not think to disguise it as loyalty when it is clearly greed!"

His eyes narrowed at that and she knew she angered him greatly. But she could not care. She met his ferocious glare with one of her own. When he finally spoke his voice was cold as ice.

"No matter how you deny it, milady, the fact remains immutable. 'Tis your duty to protect Oxwich now, just as your father did."

"My duty!" she cried in frustration. "My duty is not to Oxwich but only to . . . only to God. Oxwich will thrive under another, and England is not likely to fall at my absence!" Her chest heaved with emotion and she stared at him through eyes blurred now with tears.

"You or the king—I care not who lays a claim to that unholy place. For all I care, you may both go to the devil, and Oxwich with you!"

4

The men from Blaecston left well after midday. Joanna heard them even though she had secreted herself once more in the prayer carrel. Both the horse's whinnies and snorts and the men's shouts as they assembled and made ready to depart pierced the still depths of the secluded chamber. Despite her sincere attention to her prayers, she was time and again distracted.

Rylan Kempe—he of the disquieting news and compelling stare—was leaving St. Theresa's. Yet his absence would not be complete. She knew already that he would haunt her for many a day, for even now his words continued to divert her from her prayers. Duty to Oxwich, he had said. Duty to the villagers. Yet she had no duty to either castle or folk, she told herself. Oxwich was a hated place. The people would not even know her, and surely would not care who should be their overlord, so long as they were protected in their labors and not pressed too hard for their manorial services. No, she shirked no duties when she clung to St. Theresa's. Besides, she reasoned as she shifted her knees on the cold stone floor, duty to God came before any other duty.

But what of children? a deep voice seemed to mock her.

With a resigned sigh Joanna got to her feet. She rubbed her knees absently as she pondered that one troublesome point. What of children?

If there was an acceptable way to have a baby without the necessity of a husband she would most certainly embrace it, for something in her longed for a child of her own. How she would love a baby; how she would happily tend its every need. It would never want for love or comfort but would grow up happy and smiling, and always content.

She crossed her arms, wrapping them tightly around her as she let her imagination wander. She would love a child of her own above all things. And such a child would love her back as well. The very thought of it brought a warmth to her heart. But as she recalled where she was—and why—that warm glow congealed into a cold lump in her throat. Her arms fell to her sides as she faced the reality she had chosen for herself. There would be no children for her, because there would be no husband. Her comfort must be found in God's love. Surely His love would be far more fulfilling than any other kind.

Still, that belief did little to lift Joanna's spirits as she heard the clatter of horse's hooves outside. Lord Blaecston and his men were leaving, taking with them her last claim to the outside world. Though she tried her utmost to rejoice in their departure, it was all she could do not to cry.

When Joanna left the quiet row of prayer carrels it was time for the evening chapter reading. But her mood was too bleak and her soul too troubled to seek any comfort amidst the restless shuffling of the Priory's entire populace. She had missed supper, but she did not care about that either. The wind had increased considerably, roaring in from the sea in angry blasts, yet the very violence of it seemed almost comforting. She felt angry and aimless herself, filled with energy but with nowhere to direct it.

To the east, extending far across the German Sea, the sky grew darker and darker. But to the west the sun still showed weakly through the cloud layer. During midsummer the twilight lingered a long while, and Joanna knew the darkness would not become absolute for several hours. As she remained still, staring to the west with the wind thrusting against her back, the chapel bells rang compline. A few latecomers scurried up the three steps and through the wide portal, but then she was alone. Standing there in the empty priory yard, she let her gaze sweep around her, taking in the dusty grounds and the plain buildings.

Rain would settle the dust, she thought absently, although the roof leak in the chapel would surely be worsened should a storm come. Then she turned to face the wind and lifted her eyes to the lowering sky. Leak or no, a fierce rainstorm was exactly what she wished for. Let it blow and storm until all of England cowed from the fury of it. Let the rains come so long and hard that the entire world was washed clean—or else washed away.

Unable to understand or control her careening emotions, Joanna tore the *couvrechef* from her head. As the square of linen caught in the wind and flew up and away, she shook her head hard, letting her long curls and ringlets fly freely around her face. Then, with no destination in mind, only the overwhelming need to be somewhere else, she hurried toward the gate and the windswept moors beyond the confines of the religious enclave.

Joanna did not follow the narrow cart track away from the priory. Instead, she headed toward the cliffs that lined the coast. Far below was the sea, beating impotently against the chalk deposits. The high tides seemed intent on devouring the cliffs, as if they hungered to take over the land. Joanna leaned out dangerously beyond the rocky edge, but she was not afraid. The wind pushed at her so hard that she felt she could have jumped out into space and still have been thrust back onto the solid earth beneath her feet.

If only the wind had pushed her mother back.

That thought brought her immediately upright, and a shiver ran up her spine. At once she turned and walked stiffly away from the sheer cliffs, back to the gently rolling moors.

How could her mother have found the courage to make such a leap? the perverse thought tortured her. And how could she have been so cowardly as to abandon the rest of her own life?

I don't want to think about that, Joanna told herself as the wind half carried her forward, whipping her waist-length hair and long skirt before her. *I only want to take a walk in the quiet woods and find some measure of peace there.*

Clinging to that solitary thought, Joanna let the wind blow her along, through the tall grasses and prickly heather, past the cart track and almost to Christa's Spout before she veered toward the woods. Already her hair was tangled beyond redemption and her face was warm with exertion, but slowly she recovered some modicum of composure. The clouds loomed dark and low and she knew the trees might not be safe should there be any lightning, but until she heard the warning thunder she would not worry about it. She would walk until it rained, she decided fancifully. Would God let her go until for-

ever, or would He send a downpour to direct her back to
the priory? A part of her wanted to ridicule such a foolish thought, yet another part of her needed an answer,
and God seemed the only one available.

Rylan spied Joanna as she left the priory. After he and
his men had ridden beyond view of St. Theresa's, they
had doubled back, clinging to the forest to remain un-
seen. Now they camped on a little knoll that provided a
clear view of the priory. When Kell had notified him
that a solitary figure of a woman walked across the moor,
he had been unsure at first whether it was his quarry.
Then when she'd headed directly toward the sheer cliffs,
he'd felt a moment of sickening fear. It was Joanna. She
strode so purposefully for the cliffs. Was she going to
cast herself over the edge? Rumor had it her mother had
flung herself in the same manner to her own death. He
had leaped up in alarm, prepared to ride to her rescue
even though he knew he could never reach her in time.
But to his enormous relief, she had stopped and then
turned away from the cliffs, angling toward the very
place where he and his men lay in wait.

Her hair whipped before her like a shimmering sail.
Her skirts flared out as well, snapping and tangling in
her feet, exposing brief flashes of bare leg. Up to now
she had appeared a pale slender woman, garbed in
shapeless gray with only her translucent complexion and
huge green eyes to commend her. Now she was a face-
less creature, all long wild hair and shapely legs. As fast
as his relief for her safety came, another unexpected
emotion tumbled directly behind it. Some fellow—of his
own choosing—would be a very happy man come his
wedding night. Some lusty young buck would have those

long pale legs wrap around his waist and would bury his hands and face within that silken mass of hair.

A sudden heat rose in him at the thought of her that way, and although he knew it a madness, he could not at once suppress it. She was a complete innocent—how could she not be? And yet he knew with a certainty he could not explain that she would be passionate beyond all logic. Perhaps it was her ready temper. Perhaps the way she blushed or simply the way she embraced the wild winds. But whatever, he knew it was so. Only he would not be the one to find out firsthand.

With a low oath he jerked his eyes away from her and forcibly quelled the rush of blood that tightened his loins. This was no time for his mind to be wandering in such a direction. Yet as he turned back once more to follow her progress—as he saw her hold her hair away from her brow with one careless motion—he knew he would hold a meaningful talk with the man she wed. He must at least ensure that she be treated gently and carefully on her wedding night. He owed her that much.

"'Tis too easy," Kell grumbled from behind him.

"Better this than my plan to steal back into the priory tonight to abduct her," Rylan replied. "Save your Viking instincts for another day, Kell. And another target," he added as his eyes remained fixed on Joanna.

When she steered a little south of them, pushed by the slant of the wind, he made a decision. "Stay here with the others. I would confront our reluctant bride alone."

At Kell's short, knowing laugh, Rylan's brow lowered. "She's an innocent young girl. Keep your base thoughts to yourself."

"If she's *that* innocent, how shall *you* know what to do with her?" Then the normally silent Kell walked off, laughing still at his own humor.

Rylan did not dwell on Kell's wry comment, for he knew that innocent maidens were indeed foreign territory for him. He leaned more toward married noblewomen, well versed in pleasing a man and satisfied with an occasional tryst. For that very reason he dreaded his coming union with the young Lady Marilyn Crosley. Virgins were not in his line. But as he settled into his saddle, he was reminded once more that the virgin who roamed the moor just beyond had managed to rouse more than merely his casual interest.

By the Rood, but he had been too long without a woman if he was lusting after young girls now. And a novice in a religious order, no less. Once he returned to Blaecston he would remedy that situation at once.

Within the protective cover of the woods, he made his way down to a spot beyond where Joanna would most likely reach the treeline. There he dismounted and tied his horse, then leaned back against an elm tree to wait. He kept his gaze on Joanna, watching as she futilely attempted to subdue her hair, then stood a little straighter when she reached down and pulled the hem of her skirt up to tuck securely into her rope girdle. She walked much easier through the thick growth in the meadow then, but he did not care at all about that. As she hurried along, his eyes were drawn to her well-formed legs. The slender ankles and shapely calves. The dimpled knees. She wore no hose, he noted, and once more an unwonted heat suffused him.

"Christ and bedamned!" he swore under his breath. Had the girl no sense of propriety at all? Bad enough to wander fields and forests unprotected, but displaying herself this way was unforgivable!

As tense as if he faced a foe in battle, Rylan crept silently nearer. Her face was hidden still, as much by her hair whipping in the wind at her back, as by the fact that her face was averted.

Another reckless mistake, he fumed. She was walking into a dark forest without the least care to be certain it was safe. She worried more that she might trip than that some evildoer might be lurking about!

Rylan's assumption was indeed correct. As Joanna made her way through the thick profusion of heathers and field grasses, she was making very certain not to trip. The wind was blowing so hard at her back that she could barely slow her pace enough to keep her feet before her. Just a little farther, she thought as she glimpsed the trees ahead from the corner of her eye. She tried and failed to catch her hair in her hand, then stumbled over a stone and nearly fell. Out of breath, she glanced up as the trees loomed before her, but instead of feeling relief, a sudden spurt of terror jolted her. In the shadows of the forest a tall form lay in wait!

Joanna did not pause to think. It was a man and he had not called out to her as she had approached. She needed no more than that to be filled with alarm. In an instant she whirled, and as if the devil pursued her, she fled toward the priory and safety.

"Damnation!"

The man's curse carried to her ears, redoubling Joanna's fear. He *had* been waiting for her! Now he was certain to follow!

She ran as fast as she could—as she'd never run before. But the wind was against her now, holding her back no matter how fast she ran. She felt the scratch of heather against her skin. Her heart pounded thunderously in her chest, and she feared her lungs would collapse with her effort. But still she struggled forward.

Then she heard him closing on her, and before she could veer out of his grasp, he had her.

A steely arm came around her waist. In one terrifying moment she was lifted from her feet and pulled against a hard chest. Though she fought him and kicked in a wild panic, twisting desperately to be free, he would not relent in his hold.

"No!" she cried, arching back in his clasp. Her head cracked hard against him and she saw stars, but his grip did loosen slightly, and she instinctively slid down his tall frame. She was almost away but as he grabbed wildly for her, she lost her balance. With a shrill scream she tumbled to the earth, and before she could collect her senses to scramble away, he flung himself on top of her.

Joanna's breath left her with a long *whoosh*. The man pressed her heavily into the hard earth and despite her overwhelming fear, she could not catch her breath either to scream or struggle. Her hair fell across her face and tangled in the grasses as her cheek pressed into the ground.

I am going to die, she thought as useless tears stung her eyes. *I am going to die here, all alone at the hands of this vile monster*.

When he shifted his weight her chest filled at once with blessed air, but she was no less caught in his remorseless grasp.

"Christ and bedamned!" he swore viciously. Then he twisted her beneath him so that they lay face to face.

Joanna felt every granite-hard muscle in the man's body, for he lay directly upon her in the most intimate manner imaginable. Despite her wish not to display her fear, two huge tears leaked out from between her tightly clenched lashes, and her body shuddered in dread of what was surely to come. Then a rough palm pushed her hopelessly tangled hair back from her face. Though she flinched from his touch, he gripped her chin between his thumb and forefinger and forced her to face him.

"Open your eyes, Joanna. Open your eyes."

Overcome as she was by paralyzing fear, Joanna neither recognized his voice nor responded to his command. Then he brushed her tears away, first from one eye and then the other with the gentlest of motions, and despite her horror, she opened her eyes.

The face that met hers was not that of a monster, yet it struck just as much terror into her heart.

"You!" she cried, though her voice was choked with tears.

"Yes, me," he replied grimly. "Though it could just as easily be some fiend with murder in his heart—or worse."

"Get off me," she muttered, twisting against the heated weight of him.

But her restless movement seemed perversely to fit them more closely together. One of his legs slid between her own, and even though he propped himself up on one elbow, she was more securely than ever pinned beneath him. With a renewed sting of tears in her eyes, she glared up at him.

"Get off me, you disgusting oaf! You vile beast! You . . . You . . ."

"My, my, but our little nun has a considerable temper. And such a vocabulary. Surely such is not condoned in the hallowed halls of St. Theresa's."

"You may not excuse your wretched behavior by pretending my anger is not warranted!" She shoved at his chest, then glowered at him when it proved to no avail. "Is it your way to skulk around attacking women, *Sir* Rylan?"

Up until then his expression had been an odd mixture of triumph mingled with surprise, as if he were pleased to have trapped her, yet somehow still taken aback by it all. But her scathing accusation immediately drew his face into a frown.

"Is it your way to stroll the fields with your dress raised indecently high, displaying your legs for anyone to see?" His hand moved down to grasp her leg, gripping the bare flesh of her knee to prove his point.

"I was trying to reach the trees. Before the rains came!" She stared up at him with wide green eyes. "Let me up. And take your hand off my leg," she added in a shakier tone.

Rylan's hand was slow to leave her leg and even when it did, it was to finger the impossible tangles of her hair. Above them the wind still whipped the tall grasses and prickly heather, but pressed to the earth as they were, the impending storm seemed to surround them yet still not quite touch them. His dark hair lifted around his face, flying in the strong gusts. But he seemed oblivious to it. He only stared down at her with that same perplexed expression as he coiled one of her ringlets around his finger.

As the moment stretched out almost unbearably between them, Joanna felt an involuntary current of heat well up inside her. From the deepest recesses of her belly it surged outward, warming her blood and causing her skin to flush a rosy pink. For an instant she wasn't afraid —at least not in the same way she had been. A fragmented memory of Winna and the fowler flashed through her mind, but those two were swiftly forgotten as she stared up into the midnight blue of his eyes. He seemed to be devouring her with his dark inscrutable stare, and her heart's pace sped up even more. Then his head lowered and she gasped.

"What—what are you doing?" she cried, trying her best to hold him back. Against her hands she could feel the pounding of his heart, and it seemed a dreadfully intimate discovery.

At her words he stopped, but his face was so near hers she could feel the warmth of his breath and the brush of his hair. Then he pulled back and a scowl replaced his previously unfathomable expression.

"What I'm doing," he muttered in a voice gone low and husky, "is taking you to Blaecston." He rolled off her and took a harsh breath. "Once you leave the oppressive surroundings of that priory you'll change your mind about being a nun."

"I'll never change my mind!" She lunged away from him, but he had her in a moment, with one hand around her wrist. Though she jerked her arm frantically, his hold was implacable.

"Don't make it harder than it has to be, Joanna," he warned as he sat up.

Joanna rose to a crouch, leaning as far away from him as their outstretched arms would allow. "What you are suggesting is unthinkable," she vowed furiously. "You cannot just abduct me this way. I won't go! I won't!"

"Oh, you'll go, all right. And one day when you are well wed with a babe in arms, you shall thank me for saving you from that miserable place, my little gray dove."

She stared at his face, seeing the hard determination there, and sudden despair overwhelmed her. "You may drag me away from here," she whispered, stricken anew by unwanted tears, "but you will never succeed in this.

I'll not marry some minion of yours. I'd sooner fling myself in the sea!"

His brow lowered at her softly worded vow and his eyes burned into hers. "And risk the fires of hell? I think not." His hand tightened almost painfully on her wrist as he rose to his feet. Then, ignoring her furious struggles, he dragged her relentlessly toward his waiting horse.

5

Joanna rode stiffly, trying hard to avoid any contact with her captor. She was seated sideways before him, balanced most precariously with her bottom nestled between his thighs and her two legs resting over one of his. Under the circumstances any attempt to lean away from him was hopeless, yet her fury would not allow her to react in any other manner. How dare he treat her this way! How dare he lay in wait for her, hunting her down and dragging her off like some prize hart!

She gasped as the horse lurched down a sharp incline and her balance was threatened. Rylan's arm tightened around her, preventing her from falling, yet she could not feel an ounce of gratitude toward him. If not for him she wouldn't be perched on this frightening animal, terrified for her very life. If not for him she wouldn't be riding through the forests while a storm threatened.

As the horse resumed its steady pace, Joanna pulled away from Rylan, unwilling to rest against his chest no matter how sturdy it was. But he clearly had other ideas. His arm tightened, keeping her pressed against him, and his head lowered nearer to her ear.

"Relax, milady. This struggle is useless, as is your anger."

"'Tis your blunt-witted plan that is useless. Do you truly think to change my mind in this fashion? By stealing me away from the life I choose?"

"You have chosen that life without ever knowing what other life is open to you. I seek only to make you aware of the alternatives."

"You waste your time then, for I shall never change my mind. And you will have to return me to St. Theresa's once your hateful plan is undone."

He pushed a tendril of knotted hair from her cheek. "You shall never return to St. Theresa's, Joanna. Accept that fact and we shall deal very well together."

"I should as lief deal with a murderer!" she cried in a voice that shook as much from fury as it did from fear.

"We shall see," he answered coolly. "We shall soon see."

When they reached the place where his men waited, Joanna was thrown into a new quandary. How was she to manage amid this hard-eyed group? They were, to a man, all clearly veterans of many a battle, and though they stared at her with an odd mixture of curiosity and discomfort, she held out no hope that they might intercede on her behalf. Rylan's command over his men was subtle yet unmistakable. Even the blond giant who looked second to no man in physical prowess seemed content with his lord's wicked ways. Should he or any of the others feel a twinge of guilt or sympathy for her poor treatment, she was depressingly certain they would still not come to her aid.

"Rouse yourself, my boys. We've many leagues to go," Rylan called, all the while keeping a snug hold on her.

"Shall I prepare one of the packhorses to take your

. . . our . . . ahem, to take a rider?" one grizzled soldier finished, with a sidelong glance at Joanna's rigid
face.

"For now she shall ride with me. Once we've gone a
distance perhaps I shall give her her own mount."

"I prefer to ride alone," Joanna snapped. Though she
had never once ridden a horse herself and was, indeed,
rather frightened of the large animals, she nonetheless
would gladly ride anything in order to be free of the
smug Sir Rylan's grasp.

"Your preferences are not being considered today," he
replied softly, for her ears only. Then, at her gasp of
outrage, he shifted her on his lap as if to emphasize how
at his mercy she was. To his men he winked. "Let us
make haste, for the heavens threaten to open up on us,
and I do not relish riding in the rain."

Yet ride in the rain they did, for no sooner did they
break through the other side of the woods than the lowering clouds spilled over. The wind had dropped considerably and the rain fell in thick heavy drops—at times in
veritable sheets of water.

Joanna was heartened by the rain. Surely they would
stop now, and perhaps she would find a way to escape.
However, save for a brief pause in the meager protection
of a clump of oaks, the band did not stop. Rylan re-
trieved a tightly woven *chape à pluie* from one of the
packhorses and flung it over his shoulders. Then, still
keeping her seated sideways across his lap, he pulled her
into his arms, wrapped her securely within the folds of
the voluminous cloak, and started forward once more.

Joanna was much too furious with him to appreciate
his attempted kindness. The rain was not likely to ruin
her life—only he could do that! Yet struggle as she might
to be free, the confining cape held her well. She was like

a poor insect, caught up in a web, she fumed. Though she was warm in the dark protectiveness of his embrace, what she really wanted was to be set free.

"Be still," she heard him mutter as her pointed elbow met with his ribs.

"I cannot see!" she snapped, and poked him even more sharply.

"By damn, woman—" The cloak parted and rain pelted her face. "If you would rather be soaked to the skin you need only say the word!"

"I would rather be set free!"

He did not answer her angry words, but only bent forward against the fierce onslaught of rain. A deep hood sheltered his face, but Joanna was no longer so protected. Although the cape still covered her body, her head projected through the open front, and the rain swiftly drenched her face and hair. Before them, barely visible through the downpour, she saw one rider. The others she assumed trailed them. Beyond that she could see very little. The rain obscured field and forest alike, revealing only the bit of stony track they now traversed at such a perilous pace.

She ducked her head against the sting of the pelting rain, then was surprised when he hunched one shoulder and brought the cloak up to cover her head, but without covering her face. Joanna shivered as a cold droplet ran down her neck from her now-soaked hair. Yet as icy as it was, she was well aware of his constant warmth. Beneath the enveloping cloak the heat of their two bodies, coupled with the horse's exertion, had created a remarkable warmth. Though she still sat stiffly across his legs, her body moved in rhythm with the horse, rocking in tempo with Rylan's. His arms remained clasped securely around her waist, and despite her best effort to maintain whatever distance she could between them, her weary muscles were slowly overcome. She slumped unwittingly against him, succumbing to an exhaustion caused by both the emotional trauma of the past days and the physical exertion of the past hour. Her back curved almost imperceptibly against his chest, and her shoulders leaned ever so slightly against his encircling arm. Though she now gripped the open ends of the cloak in her own hands, she held the fabric tight against the merciless rain.

"Relax and get some rest," he murmured very close to her right ear.

At once she jumped. "I'm not tired," she stated scathingly, though she knew it was a lie.

He shrugged. "Have it as you will, Joanna. We've a long ride ahead of us. Eventually you will wish you'd taken me up on this offer."

"Where are you taking me?" she demanded, not fooled for a moment by his affectation of concern for her well-being. "And what do you truly expect to gain by this shameful deed?"

For a moment he did not answer. Through her wet lashes she saw his jaw clench, then he turned a quick look upon her. "You may have abdicated any responsibility for your people—for your country. But I have not done so."

"You cannot think to hide your crime beneath such lofty ideals as that," she countered bitterly. "I am but one noblewoman in a land of many more. Oxwich is but one stronghold—and not so magnificent a one as to influence the fate of the entire kingdom. No, Lord Blaecston—Lord Black Heart!—you delude yourself if you expect me to believe so poor a tale as that."

"I do not expect a maid to understand the complexities of state," he clipped out.

"Oh, but I understand very well, and this has nothing to do with the 'complexities of state.' Like most men of your ilk, you hide your greed and cruelty beneath the claim of a greater good. Only those of us who suffer for it know the truth!" Once more her elbow found his midriff, but before she could feel the least satisfaction for it he jerked her hard against him.

"Have a care, mistress, or else you may find yourself tied upon a packhorse, hind end uppermost as we enter Blaecston Castle."

Oh, how Joanna wished to poke him once again, for it was clear it angered him enormously. But that very anger of his gave her caution. She did not doubt his threat for a moment. A man who would kidnap an innocent woman from a priory was capable of anything, and though she hated to accede to even the mildest of his demands, she knew that in this case, at least, she must.

"You are holding me too tight," she muttered, facing obdurately into the unrelenting rain.

His arm slackened a bit, but before she could rejoice in her meager victory, his hand splayed wide open at her waist so that she could feel the firm pressure of each of his separate fingers.

"I can be very accommodating, Lady Joanna. As gallant and courtly as the next man." His hand slid slowly up her stomach until his thumb just touched the underside of her breasts, and she gasped at the intimacy of his touch. Then he bent nearer until his lips almost touched her ear. "But cross me and you will find me to be a veritable devil." He paused as if to let his words sink in, then relaxed his hand on her waist. "I suggest you settle back for the ride, milady. For you and I have many hours yet to spend in one another's company."

With heart pounding and her breath shallow and fast, Joanna could do nothing but comply. But she fervently prayed that God would smite him with a bolt of lightning from above!

They rode well into the night. Although Joanna was angry and scared, and her every muscle ached with fatigue, she did not say one word to her hated captor. They rode in silence, moving together in rhythm to the destrier's tireless gait. They shared the cape—and each other's body heat—but nothing else. Joanna's thoughts were dark and bitter, unlike his, which she was certain were smug and gloating. She imagined the horse rearing and dumping him off so that she might ride away. She pictured his men turning on him in anger that he could treat a woman so terribly. She even envisioned that she might pull his own sword on him—that she could thrust it through his black heart. Then she immediately regretted that last wicked thought. *Thou shalt not kill*, the commandment rose in her mind. She knew her vengeful thoughts were still a sin, no matter how wretchedly he treated her, but that knowledge only fired her anger higher. Was she denied even that meager outlet for her frustration?

By the time they stopped, the rain had ceased and the air was still. Great puddles glinted in the wan moonlight which broke through the high clouds, and all around them she heard the unsteady dripping from the trees.

"A brief rest, my boys. Then up before light. I would make Blaecston before sunset tomorrow," Rylan said as he loosened the cloak from around them. When he flung it back Joanna leaned away from him, dismayed anew by the intimacy of their long ride. Her every muscle was stiff and sore, but she was not about to reveal as much to him.

"Allow me," he said as he released the reins. Then before she could respond, he caught her about the waist and lowered her to the ground.

If she could have, Joanna would have run off right then. After all, she had no other real plan for making good her escape from her hard-hearted captor. But she had not counted on the effects of the long ride. When she reached the ground, her legs nearly folded beneath her. Had Rylan not lifted his leg over the horse's withers and slid down to steady her, she would have collapsed in the mud.

"I've got you," he said as one of his arms encircled her waist. "Don't worry, you'll be all right in a minute. Just walk a little ways with me."

"I don't need any help from you!" she snapped, trying to jerk out of his too-familiar embrace.

"'Tis clear you do, Lady Joanna, so why not be gracious and accept it?" He urged her forward, forcing her to limp along on legs that were at once both painfully sensitive and awkwardly numb. They walked across a dark clearing toward the low shadows of a clump of elder shrubs, him with an arm snug around her waist and her half leaning on him despite her best effort not to. All about them the other men dismounted and prepared their meager camp. The horses were hobbled so that they could graze and yet not wander off. The huge blond man drew a stash of kindling from one of the packs and swiftly started a small fire with the dry wood. Bread, cheese, raisins, almonds, and several flasks of wine appeared, and by the time Joanna was able to walk unassisted, the camp was very well organized.

These men had spent many a night in the field together, she realized, feeling even more glum than before. They were very likely Sir Rylan's best men, and she was a fool to think even one of them might feel enough pity for her to help her escape. No, she was completely on her own in that.

"Better?" Rylan asked when she pulled away from him.

"Better?" she mocked bitterly. "Hardly. But if you mean 'can I walk alone?' it's clear I can." She faced him across the darkness. "Now what?"

Though she could barely see him, Joanna heard the amusement in his voice. "Now we eat and sleep. Come along."

"Wait!" Joanna squeaked as he came toward her. She was afraid all over again. "Where am I to sleep—where will you be?"

"I'll be right beside you, Joanna. Don't worry. I'll keep you safe."

"Safe!" she cried, furious at his deliberate taunt. "I'd be safer in a nest of vipers than ever I could be with the likes of you!"

"You wound me." He laughed. Then he caught her by the arm and she knew he would not be crossed in this matter. Yet still she resisted.

"Wait! I—I need to be alone."

"No." He pulled her along, back toward the small campsite.

"But . . . But you don't understand. I have to—I mean—"

"Oh." He halted when he finally understood. "Yes. Well . . ." He looked around, then gestured. "Those bushes. I'll wait for you here."

Joanna jerked her arm angrily from his slackened hold. He was the vilest, most disgusting man that had ever lived! To make her plead and explain to him that she needed to—to have some privacy! What did he think she was, some clay doll with no feelings or needs of her own?

"Not too far," he warned as she stormed away from him.

"Not too far," she muttered under her breath. Had he no shred of decency within him at all that he would deny her some seclusion under the circumstances? But the answer to that was more than obvious. He was clearly possessed of no morals whatsoever. He was selfish—and a bully of the worst sort.

She stooped behind what she thought must be a thicket of hollies, judging by the prickly leaves she felt with her hand, then squinted back toward him. The small flames of the campfire cast only a meager light in the clearing, but it was enough to silhouette him. He was watching for her, but then the giant blond—Kell—came up to him, and Rylan was momentarily distracted.

"Hornsea is beyond the next hill," she heard the man say.

"Then we are best hidden here," Rylan replied. "The sheriff there wavers yet between King John and the Yorkshire barons. We'll skirt the town before dawn."

They continued in low murmurs, but Joanna heard no more. She was too elated by what she'd overheard. If she could only get to this town. Perhaps she could appeal to this sheriff at Hornsea for help.

She crouched down and looked stealthily around her, straining all her senses to find some escape. The air was cool and damp, redolent of leaves and forest mold. Dripping still sounded, giving the woods an unusual liveliness for such a late hour. Then, far off in the distance, she heard a rushing sound, not the wind but . . . but the sea. They were paralleling the coast and still near the sea. If she could just get away, she was certain she could find her way home.

Joanna felt a jolt of confidence at that knowledge. She peeked carefully around the bush. He was still there, but now he was accepting a cup of wine from one of the other men. If she was going to flee it must be now, she told herself. It must be now.

Joanna pulled her skirts high and threw them over one arm. She had no care for decorum as she crept deeper into the woods, careful to keep the thick holly bushes between her and Rylan. A low-hanging cedar bough caught her full across the face, wetting her and tangling in her hair, but she stifled any cry of alarm or pain. She would most willingly suffer any hardship to escape him.

When she was deep enough into the woods that the trees nearly blocked any light from the campfire, she began to feel a glimmer of hope. She straightened up from her cramped crouch and took a shaky breath. Now what? she wondered as she stared into the darkness around her. Then she heard a furious curse, "Christ and bedamned!" and her indecision fled. To the sea, she thought wildly as she plunged on toward the distant sound of waves. To the sea! Anything to escape the godless heathen who pursued her!

Joanna did not get far. On the one hand she seemed to run forever—past the wet grasping branches of the forest understory, tripping over roots, stumbling through the pitch black unknown. Yet for all her efforts, the sounds of the sea seemed to get no closer. Then she heard the thunderous crashing of her pursuer, and her flight became even more panic-driven. She was completely unmindful of which direction she went, so long as he did not catch her. But it was all for naught. Like a

giant cat, well able to stalk his quarry in the darkest
night, he found her and, with one mighty lunge, caught
her trailing skirt.

"No!" she screamed, even as she tripped and landed in
the mud, skidding on her hands and knees.

"Yes," he countered grimly. He grabbed her arm and
jerked her to her feet, then pulled her around to face
him, holding her immobile with one unforgiving hand
on each of her shoulders. "Understand this, woman.
One more rash move like this and I will make you very
sorry you ever crossed me."

"I'm already very sorry! Sorry I ever laid eyes on such
a vile, loathsome blackguard as you!" she screamed in
utter frustration. Unable to shake off his steely grasp,
she kicked at him, landing one sharp jab on his shin that
hurt her foot as much as it probably hurt him. But that
only increased his ire, for with an indecipherable oath he
lifted her up and flung her over his shoulder.

The breath left Joanna with a hard grunt as his solid
shoulder thrust into her stomach. When he lurched
around, then started forward at an angry, ground-eating
pace, she could only hang there, upside down and totally
disoriented with her hair streaming down to blind her.

"Let me down!" she cried when she caught her
breath. She pounded furiously against his back, kicking
and twisting though she feared to be dropped upon her
head.

"Be still!" he thundered, then punctuated his words
with a sharp slap on her derriere.

If she had been angry before, that humiliating gesture
positively undid her. With a determination borne of
murderous outrage, Joanna found the projecting hilt of
his sword and yanked it partially from its scabbard. At
once she was flopped upright. As the sword fell from her

startled fingers, he slid her down in front of him, sandwiching her arms between them.

"I warned you," he growled in a voice black with menace.

"Another threat?" she sneered, although she was shaking with fear. "What worse can you do that you have not *already* done? Perhaps you shall beat me now," she spat out contemptuously as she struggled against his grasp.

"By damn but I am sorely tempted!"

Joanna gasped in fear at the dangerous threat in his low voice. She suddenly regretted her foolish effort to escape him, for it seemed he would indeed punish her cruelly for it. She strained back from him, but her breasts still pressed against his chest. She stared up at his darkened face, truly frightened now for what he might do.

"I doubt a beating would do any more than intensify your resolve," he continued. Then his gaze slid down to her mouth and a slight grin lifted his lips. "So fair and yet so stubborn. But perhaps there is a better way to prove to you the futility of fighting me."

Without warning his hands pulled her higher so that her toes barely touched the ground and she was hopelessly off-balance. In the same motion he bent down and before she even understood what he was about, his mouth had captured her own.

No! her mind cried out in silent dissent. But it was far too late to stop him. Like the marauding Vandal she had compared him to, he swooped down upon her and carried her away in that kiss, totally impervious to her feeble opposition.

Terror and fury fought impotently for supremacy as he pressed his kiss upon her. His body was hard and unyielding as he bent her backward in his arms, pressing his advantage unmercifully. His lips moved over hers intimately, dominating her and causing her head to spin. His tongue crept out to slide along the clenched seam of her lips. Then one of his hands moved down to cup her derriere and when she gasped in shock, his tongue delved deeply into the recesses of her mouth.

It was that which was her undoing. Fear and anger had been sufficient emotions to steel her to his unwelcome advances. But the unexpected stroke of his tongue within her mouth sent those emotions skittering off into a thousand different directions. She was under a new form of siege, one she had absolutely no knowledge of—and no defense against—and she did not know what to do. She was not aware that his grip on her changed. She was wholly unconscious of the softening of his lips and the new awareness that went through him. She only knew that no one had ever kissed her before and that now she understood about Winna.

His mouth slanted across hers, fiercely seeking a new reaction from her. His tongue slid in and then out, caressing her sensitive inner lips in the most sensuous manner imaginable. No longer fighting him, Joanna accepted the exquisite stroke in a daze as all her senses began to clamor. Some remnant bit of caution warned her, yet that tiny voice could not begin to compete with the myriad sensations that besieged her. Her heart thundered; her blood rushed to her head at a dizzying rate, then seemed immediately to rush away to settle somewhere in her lower stomach. Warmth radiated up through her and a sudden sensitivity overwhelmed her. In an instant she was acutely aware of every place he touched her, and a new form of fear took root in her.

His hand moved from her derriere up to the nape of

her neck while his other pressed her intimately close. When his mouth moved from her lips to her cheek, and then to her ear, she was trembling in his arms.

"Sweet, sweet Joanna," he murmured hoarsely in her ear as he gasped for breath. "I would have more of this sweetness . . ."

He found her mouth once more, but gently this time, exploring and enticing her. His tongue stroked the corners of her mouth; his teeth tugged at her full lower lip. Then when a faint moan escaped her, he kissed her deeply once more, finding her unschooled tongue with his own and eliciting such frightening feelings from her that she jerked back in alarm.

In the dark, dripping forest they stood that way. His arms were still around her, but they no longer kissed. His steady stare, however, seemed almost as intimate as everything that had gone before, and Joanna averted her eyes in utter confusion as he lowered her feet to the ground.

Dear God, but this was madness! Yet there was a warmth in her belly that belied the horror she felt. When she backed out of his embrace, trembling with inexplicable emotions, he let her go. For an instant longer they stared at each other in silence. Then, appalled by what had just passed between them, Joanna turned and fled toward the faintly flickering fire.

6

Joanna lay on a thick bed of leaves, wrapped in the *chape à pluie*. It was still dark; the fire had been banked and only the pale mauve on the eastern horizon gave a hint of the impending dawn. Around her the faint stirrings of the forest sounded—some small creature scurried beyond the trees; an owl swooped low with an almost-silent rush of wind through its outstretched wings; the erratic breeze shook drops from the trees. But Joanna hardly noticed those sounds. Instead she concentrated on the steady breathing of the men who slept in the small clearing. That, and the distant sounds of the sea.

Somehow the presence of the sea seemed a salvation. The sea could direct her home, even if she had to walk up the coast alone. And then there was Isle Sacré.

In the long hours of the night, unable to sleep and unable to escape the watchful gaze of the guard, she had struggled to find a way to elude her horrible captor. Although she was certain she could find her way back to St. Theresa's, she knew it would be almost impossible to avoid being hunted down once more. She needed a safe place to hide. They would naturally expect her to flee to

Hornsea. But what if she were to seek refuge on Isle Sacré?

She had only been there once, and that was so long ago she had almost forgotten about the small island retreat. But she remembered that it was near the village of Hornsea. If only she could manage to escape and then sneak out to the island when the tide was out. Once the tide came in, he would never be able to find her. It was unlikely he would know of the little island and the safe passage to be had only at low tide. And even if the tide wasn't out, she would rather take her chance with the sea than with the devil who threatened her now.

At the thought of him she turned her head sharply away. How she hated him. How she thoroughly despised him. He was cruel and vile. A wretch of the worst sort with absolutely no feelings whatsoever.

Yet what incredible feelings he had roused in her.

A small cry of anguish escaped her at that painful admission. No matter how desperately she wished to deny it, she could not pretend otherwise. He had kissed her and she had responded. Like the devil, he had lured her with the temptations of the flesh—the temptations she'd heard so much about but never understood. And like one of the fallen angels, she had followed his wicked lead.

"Oh, God," she pleaded in a faint whisper. "Please help me. Help me . . ."

As if in answer—or more properly, denial—an arm came across her stomach and a hand curved around her waist, and she was immediately pulled against the chest of the very man she sought to escape.

"No!" she cried as she jerked violently away from his drowsy grasp. She scrambled to her feet in a panic, all her fears galvanized by his one electrifying touch. Without regard to her path, she stumbled back, tripping over someone's outstretched feet and nearly treading in the smoldering fire. Had it not been for Rylan's lightning reaction, her skirt might have caught fire in the hot embers.

But Joanna did not see his sudden hold on her as a blessing. It was more a damnation, for once again she was in his clutches with no chance for escape.

"Keep your hands off of me!" she shouted, unconcerned that she sounded like a shrew in the quiet of the forest dawn. But no matter how hard she jerked against the hand that held her wrist, he would not relent.

"Behave yourself," he growled, as he pushed his long hair back from his brow.

Around them the men were stirring, roused by the commotion in their midst. But Joanna's attention was focused solely on the man who still held her fast. Across the meager distance of their outstretched arms she glared at him, willing every bit of her hatred for him into her expression. But she could not ignore the warm strength of his hand, nor the sudden increase in her pulse. Unaware she did so, her eyes slipped from his sleep-flushed face down to his lips. They were full, well-shaped lips, she thought. Not nearly so rigid and hard as she would have guessed. Then she stiffened in horror as she realized how reprehensible such thoughts were.

It was at that moment he let go of her then arched his back and stretched. "Good morning, Lady Joanna," he said in an excessively polite tone, meant, she was certain, only to mock her. "I hope you were able to rest, despite our mean accommodations."

Joanna could not answer. She averted her eyes from his too-discerning ones and only stood there, trembling in the cool morning air. Around her the other men sat up, donning their boots and gathering their few possessions. One man stirred the fire and added more wood, but she did not move from her place.

She was undone, the thought echoed back and forth in her mind. She was undone and in the most unimaginable manner. A painful shudder ripped through her, and in self-preservation she turned away from him. Who would have thought she could turn out like Winna, she who had never cared for men—who had indeed spurned them all, and willingly? Yet let but one of them touch her—let but the most wicked of them kiss her!—and she had succumbed. She shook her head in abject misery, unwilling to believe it, yet unable as well to deny the truth. Last night this arrogant black-hearted knight had kissed her, and like a pitiful wooden palisade, her defenses had gone up in a fiery inferno. Even now the memory of his lips on hers conjured up that same coiling heat in her belly.

Joanna took a sharp breath, willing away the tears that lay so near the surface of her eyes. She had never wanted a man. She still did not, at least not in her heart and soul. Yet her body seemed to have a will of its own in this one instance. Slowly she turned her head to see him, forcing herself to be calm. Whatever she felt, he need not know, she told herself. Everyone made mistakes—people were sinners all, and she was no better or worse than the rest. Her most serious mistake had been believing that she was immune to the temptations of the flesh. God had punished her for her pride and had shown her the error of her ways. But now she knew, and now she repented. If she prayed hard enough and denied these wicked feelings, surely God would approve.

Her spirits lifted a fraction as she contemplated her circumstances. God often tested His people, and this was undoubtedly her test. God tempted her and waited to see if she could resist the temptation to sin. It was up to her to prove she could. And as she glanced around her, she knew that, more than ever, escape was the only way.

"There's bread and raisins, milady," one of the men offered her in a reasonably friendly manner.

"Thank you, no." Joanna scanned the clearing with a new, more observant gaze. "Is there a place where I may wash?"

"I'll fetch you some water," he answered, clearly eager to placate her.

Joanna shot a glare toward Rylan who was watching her as he fastened his sword belt around his waist. "I shall need a moment of privacy as well," she stated, a note of challenge in her voice.

Rylan's mouth lifted in an almost imperceptible grin, but Joanna was instantly aware of his mocking intent, and her jaw clenched furiously. Somehow she would make him pay for this humiliation!

"Kell. My Lady Joanna requires a few moments of privacy. Guard her well, for I would not have her lost in these thick woods."

Joanna did not wait for the big Norseman to respond, but turned and strode imperiously from Sir Rylan's amused presence. Clod! she fumed as her pulse beat an angry tattoo in her head. Cretin! Any hope she had for escape disappeared when the giant Kell appeared at her side. Though he was silent and not so prone to provoking her, his very presence nonetheless infuriated her. She made a hasty toilette while he waited at a little distance, his back turned. Then she quickly studied the forest around her.

"Is there a stream?" she addressed him in a stiff voice.

"Down this knoll." He gestured to her right.

Joanna did not wait for his permission. She would have a good washing, whether Rylan Kempe liked it or not. This brute guard of his could do no worse to her than his master had done. Indeed, as she strode angrily down the hill through the wet underbrush of the still-shadowy forest, she almost wished he would try to stop her, for in her present mood she would not have hesitated to turn her consuming fury upon him.

But Kell did not stop her. He only followed silently behind her, too near for her to try to escape. When they reached the stream, Joanna paused, one hand against a young oak. What was probably a quiet little beck under most circumstances was today a rushing flood. Yesterday's rains had swollen it into a fierce torrent, and from the looks of the overcast dawn sky, it would be replenished in the same manner again today.

Joanna eyed the flooded stream carefully, trying to judge whether she could safely cross it. But even if she did, she thought glumly, the giant behind her would just as quickly follow her. Unless she could somehow disarm him.

But that seemed completely ludicrous, she decided as she slanted him a look. He was far too big and brawny for her puny strength. Dismayed by her dire predicament, Joanna sighed, then moved nearer the water. At least she could bathe her face and hands, she told herself in resignation.

"Be careful," Kell warned as she stepped onto a tree trunk that projected out into the frothing stream.

"Why? Because I might get hurt?" she replied curtly. "You'll forgive me if I doubt the sincerity of your concern."

She sent a contemptuous glance back over her shoulder, but her expression changed when she saw him. He was not looking at her but at the rushing water. And he had a worried frown on his face.

"Of course," she added as her pulse began to race with sudden hope, "since your Lord Blaecston is going to all these pains to capture me, you no doubt would come to my aid if I *were* to fall in the water."

The big man's face blanched. He looked briefly at her then back at the rushing water. "Back up," he warned her, taking a step back himself. "'Tis not safe—"

Joanna did not linger to hear the remainder of his words. It was not safe for one who could not swim. However, she could. With a bravery borne of desperation, she flung herself out into the stream, almost certain he was too frightened of the water to come after her. She did not even try to keep her head above water, but only curled up tightly and let the flooded beck carry her away, hoping all along that he would think her drowned—and hoping as well that that did not happen.

When she finally surfaced, spitting and gasping for breath, she was freezing cold, tangled in her skirts and her matted hair. A small branch caught against her as she struggled to keep her head above water in the wild current, swimming as best she could at an angle toward the bank. Beneath a dense canopy of trees the water dragged her along, under overhanging branches and past boulders and tree trunks. Despite her headlong trip down the roiling beck, with every bend and twist of the streambed she nonetheless rejoiced, for she had escaped. She had escaped!

When Joanna at last dragged herself from the water she was trembling from both exhaustion and the cold, but she could not have been more jubilant. The stream was shallower here, and wider. Just beyond her it pushed out of the trees and across a wide grassy meadow before cutting through the dunes to the sea. She gasped for breath as she steadied herself against a willow sapling.

Then, unable to trust her shaky legs, she lowered herself to the ground to rest. She was unbearably cold from her icy swim, and she'd suffered innumerable bumps and scrapes. But Joanna gladly ignored those discomforts. She could hardly believe her reckless plan had worked so well.

What a blessing that the man Kell was so frightened of water. Who would ever have guessed it? For a moment she felt a pang of sympathy for him. Rylan Kempe would be enraged to find out she had escaped from him. She certainly hoped he didn't punish poor Kell. But that was not her concern, she decided. The Norseman would have to fend for himself against Sir Rylan—just as she had been forced to do.

Somewhat restored by her brief rest, Joanna looked around. She knew it would not be long before they came searching for her. She must hide herself quickly if she hoped not to be recaptured. With an effort she scrambled up the grassy bank and started up a little rise. There was no sign of any town or village nearby, but she knew she was near the sea. Instead of searching out the sheriff at Hornsea, she might be safer making her way directly to Isle Sacré. She could cut through the woods, careful to avoid being seen. Once the tide was low enough, she would dash across the sandy spit of land and hide herself on the wooded island. Only when she was certain Lord Blaecston and his men had departed would she venture back to the mainland to begin the trek home to St. Theresa's.

When they didn't find her, they would probably imagine that she had been washed out to sea and drowned, she thought with considerable glee. But her elation was squelched when she heard the first distant sounds of pursuit. As she scurried up the hill, searching desperately for a hiding place, she recognized one of the voices.

". . . until she is found—not before! And a gold coin to the man who brings her to me!"

Joanna was so unnerved by the dark threat in Rylan's voice that she struck her shin painfully on a fallen log. "Christ and bedamned!" she muttered as tears of pain started in her eyes, then she immediately cringed at such a profanity. Those were his words, taken directly from his blasphemous lips. How was it they had sprung so readily to her own?

But Joanna had no time to dwell on that unpleasant thought, for the crashing of horses through the underbrush gave evidence that her pursuers were drawing ever nearer. Searching wildly for a hiding place, she spied a gaping hole at the base of the very tree she had stumbled over. The roots lifted above the space like gnarled fingers warding off any threat, and though Joanna normally would have been too squeamish to secrete herself into such a dark, dirty place, she had no time to hesitate. She backed into the hole, her now-bare feet and legs sliding in the wet mud. Then when she was as far down as she could fit, she drew several nearby branches and piles of leaves over her. Though her heart was pounding like a drum, she tried not to think of snakes or worms but only resigned herself to wait.

It wasn't long. In a matter of minutes she heard horses moving slowly through the wooded area nearer the streambed.

"I'll take this hill," one man called to the others.

Joanna's heart nearly sank at his words. He would find her—she knew he would!

But then, as if in answer to her unsaid prayers, it began to rain. At first the droplets caught in the high branches of the trees, but before long the big drops were plummeting through, filling the forest with sound and movement, and thereby providing her with another layer of protection.

She heard a foul oath—something about the king and women in general—but it was muffled by the storm, and she felt her first glimmer of hope. They might search all morning for her, but she suddenly was certain they would not find her. Not now.

The search moved past her and then beyond, out to the meadow and farther into the woods, judging by what she could hear. Slowly her heart ceased its thundering and her breathing became more normal. But as the pressing fear of capture wore off, Joanna became more and more conscious of her dank hiding place. Rainwater flowed in a steady rivulet through the mud and down her left leg. Something moved at her elbow and she jumped, willing herself to believe it only more of the runoff rain. But she knew she could not stay where she was much longer.

Then there was a sudden scurrying sound just behind her head, and when she turned to see she let out a short scream.

The poor hare who sought its burrow was far more frightened than she, and it dashed madly away from the wide-eyed creature who'd taken over its home. However, Joanna could not concern herself with the terrified rabbit. In a rush all her worst imaginings rose to torture her, and she was certain a nest of snakes squirmed around her legs. With a cry of terror she lurched up from her hideout, scrabbling with hands and knees to escape. Then she crouched trembling behind the log and stared wildly around her, fearing the worst.

But as she huddled there, with the rain beating down

on her, her panic slowly abated. All around her the forest was a vague misty place, hidden by the gray curtains of rain. After her dunking in the beck—and her mud bath in that dreadful hole—she found the rain almost pleasant, but she knew its protection would not last forever. Crouching low and glancing nervously from side to side, she began her nerve-wracking escape. From tree to tree and shrub to shrub she scurried, straining her senses for any sign of Sir Rylan and his men. But luck was with her —God was with her, she amended apologetically. God was with her and she would prevail.

At the edge of the forest she halted. Before her a salt meadow stretched toward the dunes, the grasses slowly thinning in the face of the invasive sand. Beyond the dunes was the sea and her sanctuary. Isle Sacré and safety were so near.

She looked off to her left for the place where the stream must give out to the sea. No doubt those men searched for her there. But she could see nothing through the pounding rain, and though that worried her, it also reassured her. They could not see her any better than she could see them, and the rain would surely wash away any trail she left in the sand. She took a tremulous breath. The time to go was now, she told herself. She might never have a better opportunity.

Joanna did not look left or right when she began to run. In one hand she held her soggy skirts; the other she used to balance her headlong flight. Across the salt-grass meadow she dashed, ignoring the cutting sting of the long blades of grass against her legs. As the thick undergrowth gave way to firmly packed sand, she increased her speed, certain someone must have spied her by now. When she reached the first dune she was gasping for breath. Up the low swell of the dune she clambered, trying hard to ignore the painful stitch in her side. Then she reached the crest and tumbled behind one dune and into the embrace of several others.

Joanna lay where she fell, completely winded by her mad dash. The rain pelted her face but she did not turn away from it. Her chest heaved from her exertion; her legs trembled. But she could do nothing but lie there, letting the endless rain wash the sand and grit from her.

Dawn was fully upon the land when she finally peered between the dunes. Although the rain had eased a bit, everything nonetheless appeared gray and obscure. The sea lay just a short distance beyond her, choppy and angry, but thankfully at low tide. Then, as she squinted desperately toward the horizon, she saw the dark shadowy mound that was the island. It was so close! she realized with an enormous sense of relief. Just a short distance down the shore, then across the sand causeway.

But Joanna knew there was not much time. The wind was steadily strengthening, promising a storm that would outdo the previous day's. The causeway would not remain above water for long, if indeed it was dry even now.

Renewed by the very nearness of sanctuary, she stole between two dunes, then glanced up the beach toward the stream. Still no one in sight. This was her chance. Steeling herself for one last dash to freedom, she lifted her skirts once more, fixed her eyes on the little island, and broke away from the dunes.

The sand nearer the water was hard and she ran much easier there. Plus, the waves would immediately wash away her footprints, she thought with satisfaction.

As she neared the narrow spit of land that linked the island to the mainland, Joanna knew she had waited almost too late. Already the tide was beginning to eat away at the causeway, inching in with every foaming wave. But she would make it, she told herself. She would make it. In the strong wind her hair streamed behind her like a pennant and her skirts billowed like the sails of a Viking ship. Then the rain eased a little and Joanna had her first clear glimpse of Isle Sacré.

It would be close, the grim realization hit her. She might have to wade the last part through the waves. But even if she had to swim, she would do it. If not, she would surely fall prey to Sir Rylan once more. And that she refused to do.

Once she was near enough, Joanna cut across the ankle-deep waves toward the narrow causeway. The early-morning sky was dark and ominous, and the sea was quickly building to an angry froth. The tide was coming in much faster than was normal due to the storm, and Joanna suddenly had second thoughts about her madcap flight to Isle Sacré. Perhaps if she'd stayed hidden beneath the tree roots . . .

Her pace slowed somewhat in the face of the daunting task she'd set herself, but her momentary doubt was interrupted by a distant shout. When she turned toward the voice, however, her efforts were renewed, for there far down the beach, astride his tall destrier, was Sir Rylan! He stood up in the stirrups, staring toward her, then his horse surged forward, signaling his recognition of her.

Joanna's heart leaped into her throat. She was undone! Yet even that thought could not force her to give up. With a cry that mingled fear and anger, she doubled her efforts, dashing furiously toward the island. The water dragged at her ankles, the wind flew in her face—her chest heaved with her painful effort—but she refused to give up. She could make the island. She knew she could!

Once she was on the narrow causeway, she chanced a glance back. Already he was half the way to her, leaning low over his mount's neck and urging it on. She stumbled and for a moment almost fell, but through sheer determination she righted herself. She would not be caught by him—not again! She would never let him use her for his own political gain. Not him nor anyone else!

But even as she fled his dogged pursuit, Joanna could see the sea encroaching upon the causeway. Then the sea closed in, swallowing the narrow spit that led to the island, and her heart truly sank. Through the ankle-deep waves she continued, her legs aching and her lungs about to burst. The waves licked higher, to her knees, then buffeting her thighs. When the water caught at her raised skirts she nearly floundered. But the island was so near she could not give up.

In a final act of desperation she flung herself forward, determined to swim the remaining distance. And for a few strokes, at least, she nearly succeeded. But then she heard the sharp whinny of the horse behind her and at once a hand caught her trailing skirts.

"No—"

Her cry was drowned out as her head went under the water. Though she twisted violently against his hold, he had her as securely as a fish upon a hook. When she surfaced, sputtering and gasping for air, she was immediately pushed under by another giant wave.

"Christ and bedamned!" She heard his oath as he forcibly dragged her out of the water. Then, with his other hand looped around her waist, he pulled her up and across his lap.

Another wave struck them, hitting Joanna fully in the face while she yet coughed and spit salt water. The horse reared in fright and Joanna nearly tumbled back into the

sea, but Rylan had as firm a hold on her as he had on his
horse. With a fierce curse he drove the horse forward.
Joanna could do no more than hang there, limp and
bedraggled, as tears ran down her face.

7

Sliding off the horse like a lifeless doll, Joanna landed in a muddy puddle. For several seconds she could do no more than lie there, laboring over every breath, thankful she was beyond the deadly grasp of the angry sea. The past few minutes had been frightening beyond all experience, and she had been certain she would die, sucked under by the huge merciless waves and down to a watery grave.

Perhaps it would have been best, she thought morosely as she heard Rylan dismount. Considering the future he planned for her, death could certainly be no worse. At least dead she would be in heaven with her mother.

Only her mother was not in heaven, she reminded herself harshly. At least not according to the teachings of the church.

Still shaking, she raised herself to a sitting position and pushed her matted hair out of her face. The rain beat down in erratic bursts, stinging her cheeks; the wind howled around her and the waves tore angrily against the shore. But she nonetheless *was* glad to be alive.

At her movement, Rylan turned a furious glare on her, although he still held his horse's head low against his chest in an effort to keep the snorting animal calm.

"I should have tied you across a packhorse—"

He broke off his threat when his horse jerked back, startled anew by his master's angry tone. Joanna looked away, as upset with him as she was with the sudden tears that sprang to her eyes. Dear God, but what was she to do now?

Then her vision cleared and her back stiffened as she realized where she was—where they were. It was not the mainland he'd dragged her to, but the island! Around them the sea rose in a violent display, exactly as she'd hoped. But instead of providing her a sanctuary from Sir Rylan and his band of heartless men, it had become a prison, trapping her there alone with the very man she sought to escape.

With a cry of absolute fury she leaped to her feet and stared wildly about her. Far across the dangerous waves she saw the narrow beach with the dunes and forests beyond. Then she turned toward her captor, so consumed by her fury that she could hardly express herself.

"You—" A fit of trembling halted her words and she had to fight for control. "I wish to God the sea had taken you!" Then, before he could reply, she whirled and fled.

She didn't go very far. The island was not big, and besides, she was too exhausted. As she leaned hopelessly against a gnarled salt oak, clinging to the trunk for support, she grew even angrier as she recognized why he had not bothered to prevent her flight this time. She had no place to escape to; the island was too small for her to remain hidden very long. She was trapped there with him, and unless a miracle came along, her fate seemed to be sealed.

She took several deep breaths, trying to still her trembling and regain her strength. A sudden streak of lightning split the dark sky, followed almost immediately by a clap of thunder. Joanna jumped in alarm, then felt a smug satisfaction when she heard the horse squeal, followed by a string of vile curses from Rylan. Perhaps, if she was very lucky, his horse would trample him to death. Or drag him back into the sea. Or—

But luck was not with her, as events of the past few days had already proven. For she saw Rylan swing up onto the animal's back and, through sheer strength of will, urge the terrified horse away from the raging sea and toward the sheltering interior of the little island.

Joanna stayed a long time under the weatherbeaten oak, staring unseeingly across the lashing waves to the far shore. To the north, not so very far, was St. Theresa's, and she wondered what they thought of her disappearance. Did they link it to Sir Rylan? She sighed, slowly regaining her breath. Right now they were no doubt at the morning chapter reading. Soon they would receive the instructions for the day's activities. Then they would share the morning meal and go off to their tasks. Oh, how she wished she were there right now! How content she would be at her stitching. Never would she drift into idle daydreams of the world beyond her ken. She had seen enough to know it was not for her. Yet it now seemed she was doomed to a life in that very world.

She wiped at her eye as a tear trickled down her cheek and sniffed back any further hint of tears. Crying did no good—she'd learned that lesson many years before. Yet she was hard-pressed to stifle the anguished sob that caught in her throat. She was cold, soaked to the skin, and the prisoner of a ruthless blackguard. Her future was indeed bleak, but she would never let *him* see her despair.

With that firm resolve her only comfort, she peered around her with reluctant curiosity. The sea continued to rise; the wind roared across the little island, bending trees and bushes low with its fury, and pushing the rain in almost horizontal sheets before it. Protected by the wide trunk of the oak, Joanna stared out at the storm and felt an odd kinship with it. *Howl for me*, she thought. *Cry and moan and beat the world down.*

Then from the corner of her eye she detected a movement, and her gaze sharpened. Across the churning stretch of water and farther down the opposite shore several riders appeared. They were hunched against the storm and struggling to control their unhappy horses.

Rylan's henchmen, she realized at once. Were they looking only for her, or had they realized that their erstwhile leader was missing as well? In an instinctive move of self-preservation she eased herself behind the tree. Though the wind buffeted her there and the huge raindrops stung her back and arms, she did not care. She only watched the men as they continued up the beach.

There were three—and she singled out the last one as Kell. Slowly they moved nearer the place where the causeway lay, covered now by the sea. Did they know the Isle Sacré? she wondered. Would they suspect that she and Rylan were there? Apparently not, she realized minutes later as they continued past, sparing the island only a cursory glance. And if they did not know, she reasoned, their search might take them elsewhere so that, by the time the storm departed and the tide receded, she might still have a chance to escape. Of course, there was still Rylan, she thought sourly. But he was just one man and he could not stay alert forever.

Fortified by that knowledge, she looked back over her shoulder toward the dark growth of oaks and willows that covered the island. He was there somewhere with his horse, and eventually she would have to deal with him. But for now she would stay out of his way. Let him wonder where she was and what she was up to, she decided. Besides, he was so angry right now, there was no telling what he might do. One angry blow from his hand would very likely kill her.

But as she sought a quiet secluded place to hide, Joanna knew that, more than his angry blow, she feared the violent passion he'd shown her last night. Both his and her own.

She made her way cautiously down a narrow trail littered with leaves and branches. She knew there was a retreat house and a small chapel on the island. Also a rather large cemetery. Isle Sacré had been considered hallowed ground since before recorded memory. The cemetery was an odd rambling affair with markers that ranged from crude stones to carved masterpieces, as well as mature specimen trees planted in memoriam. The graves were the final resting places of all manner of folk, from the most common to titled nobility. But they all had in common a distinct trait. They had each lived saintly lives—pious, sacrificing, and good. And though they were not recognized by the church as saints, those whose lives they'd touched honored them by this choice of a resting place.

When Joanna reached the broad clearing that marked the cemetery, she made a fervent sign of the cross and lowered herself to her knees. *Help me find a way,* she prayed to the souls whose bodies reposed beyond her. *Intercede with the Lord for me and show me the path I must take*. Then she pushed her wet hair behind her shoulders and looked around.

There was still no sign of the beastly Lord Blaecston. Would to God the wind had blown him away! But she held out no hope for that. She shivered at a particularly harsh blast of wind. More than anything she needed to find shelter—to dry her clothes and rest until the rain stopped. Then she would have to find something to eat.

Although she did not know precisely where it was, after only a short search she discovered the chapel. It was set on the seaward side of the island, on a rise that provided a generous view and was protected from the weather only by three towering elms. The Holy Trinity, she remembered the trees being called. The biggest was the Father, the seaward one was the Son, and the third – the broadest branching of the three—was the Holy Ghost.

Bending low against the thrust of the unrestrained storm, holding her skirts in one hand and her hair with the other, she fought her way toward the chapel, then nearly collapsed when she reached the sturdy back wall. She was trembling from the chill bite of the wind as well as from her exhaustion. Too much had happened to her in the past two days. Yet Joanna knew she must not give in to the despair that threatened to overwhelm her. So far the storm had aided her. If not for the wind and rain, she would by now be entrapped in that horrid man's castle.

Blaecston, she fumed. Black fortress indeed! Where else would one expect such a black-hearted rogue knight to dwell?

As the wind howled and the three elms groaned and creaked in the powerful blasts, Joanna summoned the very last of her energy. Around the corner of the chapel she edged, closing her eyes to the biting strength of the storm. With head bent low and her hand against the mud infill of the cruckwork structure, she felt her way to the chapel door.

But instead of providing her entrance to her sanctuary, the simple wood door became one more obstacle. For the wind held it firmly closed, and no matter how she tugged at it, it was far too heavy.

"By the blood of St. Theresa!" she cried in frustration as she edged the door open only to have it slam closed again at a particularly strong gust of wind.

"Allow me."

Joanna gasped in alarm as a strong hand closed over hers. With one jerk Rylan forced the door open, sheltering her from the wind with his tall frame as he did so.

Joanna was too panicked by his sudden appearance to react. She only stood there, sandwiched between him and the stout door frame, staring up at him with her mouth agape. Then she realized his hand still covered hers, and all her battered emotions came alive.

"Get away from me, you . . . you huge oaf!" She tried to yank her hand from beneath his to no avail.

"Don't be a fool!" he bit back. With one foot he propped the door open. Then he grabbed her elbow, pushed her past the doorway, and followed her inside.

The door slammed with an ominous thud, and for a moment everything was black. Joanna was conscious of his hand still gripping her arm; that, and the fierce pounding of her heart. Sweet Mary, was nothing to ever go right for her again?

As her eyes slowly adjusted to the small chapel, she realized that four high windows made of rare glass panes instead of thin scraped hides did admit some light. But her quick glance around the holy place did not promise any escape. Once more she was in his vile clutches.

But to her surprise it was Rylan who released her arm, almost as if he could not bear to touch her. Joanna, however, did not pause to ponder his reaction. She only scurried away from him, backing around the simple slab altar so that there was something between her and her hateful captor.

She watched with wary eyes as he moved leisurely around the dim chapel. But though his movements were casual, she could not mistake his tension. His eyes were sharp and narrow, and she was certain he fought to slow his breathing. Then he turned to face her and she took an involuntary step backward. Oh, he was tense, all right. He was filled with a fury that was barely contained. When he crossed the small space with three long strides, then placed both hands on the altar and leaned forward over it, she resolved to be extremely cautious with her words, for he appeared fully capable of murdering her.

"You, madame, are the most bothersome wench I've ever had the displeasure to meet!"

"Me!" Joanna's vow of caution flew right out of her head at his harsh words. "Me! Why you—you—"

"I have had more than enough of your willfulness. 'Tis clear now why your father sent you to that priory. Had he been forced to deal with you on a daily basis, he would no doubt have been moved to throttle you!"

At the mention of her father, Joanna's fury turned to an icy rage. "As ever, you speak of things far beyond your knowledge. Only a foolish woman, with neither heart nor brains to commend her, would consent to your foul plan without dissent."

"You call running off into the forest at night—when

any number of beasts are out—mere dissent? You call flinging yourself into a raging flood and trying to swim a storm-plagued sea mere dissent?" he bellowed. "Of all the foolishness—" He broke off and forced himself to lean back from the altar. But his glittering stare never left her face. "God preserve me from the madness of women!"

Joanna laughed, a shrill unnatural sound in such a holy place. She was perilously close to hysteria, pushed beyond endurance by the glowering man who pursued her so doggedly.

"As I wish to God He would rescue me from the sordid likes of men like you!" Unwelcome tears started in her eyes and she whirled away from him, refusing to let him see any weakness in her. Spying a niche with a statue of the Virgin Mary in it, she fell to her knees before it, bowed her head, and began fervently to pray.

Strike him dead. Drown him in the sea. Cast him blind and dumb! Just please, please preserve me from the arrogance and madness of all men.

Her tears splashed on her tightly clasped hands but she dared not wipe them away, for then he would know she wept. She heard the howling of the storm—the steady pounding of the rain against the roof and the constant roar of the sea. The wind rattled the windows and seemed to tear at the sturdy little chapel. But within there was silence.

Joanna had no idea how long she remained on her knees before the unlit niche. But she was aware of the puddle forming around her legs from her soaked gown, and she felt the steady drip of water from her hair and trailing sleeves. Then he exhaled—a loud disgusted sigh —and moved around the altar to her side.

"Come along, Lady Joanna—"

"Don't touch me! Not ever again!" she shouted as she jerked away from his strong grasp.

"Not ever?" he mocked even as he caught her elbow once more. "That's rather impractical. We've a fire to build and clothes to dry. If we work together it will be much easier."

"'Tis not my wish to make things 'easier' for you," she spat.

"No, I did not imagine it was," he replied in an unexpectedly calm voice. "But nonetheless, you will do as I say."

The very moderation of his tone in the face of her absolute fury was the most devastating blow he could have dealt her, for it drove home to Joanna like nothing else could that her wishes meant nothing to him at all. He would have his way, no matter how she protested or what she did. It was such a bitter realization that all the fight drained from her, to be replaced by a weariness that went bone-deep. She could no longer run; she was unable even to fight his adamant grip on her arm. She simply did not have the strength.

When he pulled her away from the niche, she followed unresistingly. She was only vaguely aware that he now seemed somewhat at a loss. Like an aggravating dog chasing passing carts, he didn't seem to know precisely what to do with her now that he'd caught her. How appropriate, Joanna thought with an inward grimace.

But he was not at a loss for long. Keeping his hand firmly around her wrist, he peered out through the thick panes of glass.

"As soon as the rain eases we shall make our way to a cottage I found very near here. There's a fireplace and a small amount of wood. Perhaps we'll find some food as well, for it appears your reckless flight has stranded us both for the duration of the storm."

Joanna refused to look at him, although she knew he had turned to stare at her. She kept her gaze fixed on the yellowed image of the trees beyond the window, following their swaying movement in the storm's onslaught. Yet she could not suppress the odd shiver that went through her—almost as if he were caressing her and not simply studying her. Like a heated finger his eyes slid down from her stubborn profile and tightly clenched jaw to her jutting chin and stiff posture. His hand shifted slightly on her wrist and her heart began to beat faster as his gaze moved lower. She cringed inside when she realized how her soaked gown clung to her breasts and outlined her thighs and derriere.

Oh, but he was the vilest man on earth, she thought, sending him a furious glare. But no matter what he did, she would manage to thwart him. She would never accept some lackey of Rylan Kempe's as her husband. And somehow—somehow!—she would find a way to escape the grim future he planned for her.

When they left the chapel, Rylan kept his left hand on her wrist and his right arm around her shoulders. Joanna neither wanted nor appreciated his supposed effort to protect her from the storm, for she knew it was just a disguise for his true intent. He wanted only to prevent her from running away from him again.

As if she had anyplace to go, she silently fumed.

Across the cemetery they ran, past newer graves mounded with broken chalk and ancient ones covered now with yellow clematis and wild honeysuckle, until they reached a sheltering grove of birch trees. There stood another cruck structure, a small cottage built of great bent tree trunks filled in with mud and plaster. A chimney protruded from its thatched roof, and a small porch projected beyond the huge bent oak timbers at the gable ends. Rylan yanked the door open, pushed her in before him, then slammed the door on the howling gale outside. Both of them stood on the hard-swept dirt floor, gasping for breath for the first few minutes.

Joanna's eyes swept the small neat cottage—anything to avoid looking at him. The one time she'd been on the island, she'd only been thirteen. She and the rest of the youngest aspirants had slept in or under the wagons they'd come in. For a week they'd worked in the cemetery and the chapel, clearing and cleaning and generally putting things to right. The three sisters who had accompanied them had slept in this cottage, but Joanna had not even set foot inside it. Now she saw that it was a very plain affair, but nonetheless comfortable. And reasonably clean, as if someone had been there recently.

Maybe those same persons would return when the storm subsided.

Her momentary hopefulness was dashed when she heard a protesting screech. Turning, she saw Rylan with his shoulder against a tall oak cupboard, pushing it before the door.

"God send a pox upon you," Joanna muttered as her green eyes glittered furiously.

Rylan only smirked. "Do you beseech God—or the devil?" He straightened up and eyed his handiwork then sent her a faint yet clearly gloating smile. "With our every confrontation I cannot help but be reassured that my original assessment of you was correct. You do not belong in any holy order."

"I do!" Joanna broke off and turned away from him. She would not be baited by the likes of him. And she would certainly not lower herself to argue with him.

A shiver went through her. Goose bumps rose on her skin and she wrapped her hands around her cold arms. At once Rylan reacted.

"Strip off your wet garments while I build a fire. You'll be warm very shortly."

Joanna, however, did not respond, at least not out loud. Let him build his fire, she thought disagreeably. And let *him* strip off his own wet clothes. She was not about to bare herself before one such as him. Then her eyes sharpened on him as he knelt in front of the hearth, laying the wood for a fire. His shoulders were wide, straining the fabric of his shirt and leather tunic. His braies and hose clung indecently to his legs and thighs, and even showed the hard shape of his buttocks. Joanna took a sharp breath and had to force her eyes away from him. No, she gulped, changing her mind at once. Don't let him get it in his head to strip off his clothes, for that would be disastrous.

As if he heard her very thoughts, he shifted to the left so he could better see her. "I said remove your wet gown, Joanna. You can drape it over the mantel once the fire is going."

"I . . . I'd rather keep it on," she muttered, then was immediately disgusted at the meekness in her own voice.

He rocked back on one heel, staring at her as he squatted before the hearth. "No doubt you hope to make yourself ill and thereby avoid your duty to marry. But it won't work, Joanna. It won't work. Sick or well, you *will* become a bride, and mistress of Oxwich as well."

"I'll never do as you ask!" she cried, absolutely furious with his matter-of-fact tone.

"Then I shall do it for you." He stood up and in two quick strides towered above her. Before she could even react he spun her around, pushed her long length of hair over her shoulder, and began to unlace the neckline of her gown, all the while holding her in place with one unyielding hand on her arm.

"Don't you dare—Oh! Remove your vile hands from me! No!"

As if her struggles were no more than the irritating buzzing of an inconsequential fly, Rylan ignored both her words and her flailing arms. His fingers swiftly worked the wet laces free. Only when she twisted suddenly—and the gown ripped sharply—did he pause.

"Continue to fight me," his voice came, close to her ear, "and your gown will be ripped completely to rags. Is that what you want?"

"I don't care about this gown! And I hate you!"

"I'm sure you do. However, that changes nothing. This gown *shall* come off."

At such a self-assured statement, despair once again overwhelmed Joanna. "You are a vile and . . . and lecherous oaf!"

"Lecherous?" He turned her to face him, holding her at arm's length with a hand on each of her shoulders. His midnight gaze ran swiftly over her—critically, she assumed, for he seemed not to miss even one aspect of her totally bedraggled appearance. Then he stepped back from her and turned abruptly toward the cold hearth.

"God preserve me from virgins," he muttered, as if to himself. Then he fixed his glittering gaze on her once more. "Remove your wet clothes, woman. There are blankets on the bed to cover yourself. And Joanna," he added caustically. "Lest you work yourself into a lather over my 'lecherous ways,' keep in mind that your value as a bride lies as much in your innocence as it does with your properties. Your virginity is more than safe with me."

He stared at her another long moment, then, with a dismissive gesture, turned his attention back to building the fire.

Joanna stood where she was, trembling as much from her turbulent emotions as she did from the cold. Safe? She was safe with *him?* Oh, she fumed impotently, he was truly the most despicable man on God's green earth. To treat her this way! To speak so snidely, and of such personal things!

Despite her outrage, however, she felt a small reluctant reassurance at his avowed disinterest in her feminine charms. Purity of a bride was indeed important to a bridegroom. As long as he believed he would succeed in his reprehensible plan to marry her off, he would surely not defile her. That, of course, did not mean she wished to undress before him. Hardly! But she did not feel so immediately threatened.

"Could you at least wait outside?" she ventured, her voice still belligerent.

He sent her a scathing look. "No, I could not. However, I assure you, milady, that I will *somehow* manage to curb my base nature. Your state of dress—or undress—is of no interest to me beyond your safety and good health."

Joanna could barely squelch her fury when she finally acquiesced. She stomped over to the bed and yanked the coarse wool blanket up, then with swift jerky movements used it to form a crude screen between the tall cupboard and the wooden window latch. In the narrow corner she hurriedly shrugged out of her pitiful gown, keeping only her thin linen kirtle on. With a wary eye on Rylan's back, she then wrapped the blanket around her shoulders and knotted it as best she could under her chin. Using one hand to hold the front of her makeshift cloak closed, she then picked up her gown with the other and draped it over the tall cupboard, all the while keeping a watchful notice of Rylan's every move.

To her relief—and undeniable confusion—he suddenly seemed completely unconcerned about her, for he never once stole a glance toward her. No doubt it was because of the heavy cupboard that blocked the door. He knew she could not escape; therefore he was no longer concerned about what she did.

She couldn't have been more wrong. As Rylan crouched before the hearth, doggedly striking flint to steel, it occurred to him that this storm had better pass quickly or else he would indeed have to step outside the cottage. Yon Lady Joanna was a shrew and a virago—a termagant by anyone's standards. Yet she was fair and soft and possessed of the most remarkable green eyes he'd ever looked into. And in that wet clinging gown . . .

He missed the steel and struck his thumb with the sharp flint chip. "Christ and bedamned," he swore ferociously.

It was not the pain in his hand that troubled him, however, but another more invasive ache. One that he knew he'd be a long time recovering from.

8

Hunched before the fire, Joanna deliberately kept her complete attention on the soup just beginning to thicken in the iron pot. She was finally warm. Indeed, the heavy wool blanket was uncomfortably hot and itchy, and awkward to maneuver in as well. Still, she was not about to shed it in favor of only her sheer linen kirtle. Not with that vile man so nearby.

Rylan sat across the room from her, sprawled on a simple wooden stool. After building the fire, he'd arranged a length of hemp rope across one corner of the cottage, then draped her gown as well as his shirt, tunic, braies, and hose upon it. Now he sat, bare-chested and bare-legged, with a linen sheet wrapped loosely about his hips. Ill-mannered brute that he was, he'd not sought any privacy at all when he'd disrobed. He'd only peeled his drenched garments from his body, then had the gall to snort derisively at her gasp of dismay.

She had spun away from the sight, of course, but not quick enough to avoid seeing his unclothed chest. With one shrug he had lifted both shirt and tunic and tugged them over his head. Now as she stared fixedly at the bubbling soup, she could still envision that chest. Wide and tan it had been, with a growth of dark hair between his flat male nipples and a long, curving scar along his ribs. Up till now she'd thought of him as her rock-hard captor with muscles of iron and a will of steel—not quite human, perhaps. For some perverse reason, however, the sight of that scar had altered that conception. It had reminded her that he was only a man.

Very much a man—the wayward thought struck her—with short curling hairs on his chest and nipples that were a small taut version of her own. The very thought of his chest stirred the most unwelcome heat low in her stomach.

Oh, she was truly sister to Winna now, Joanna bemoaned. For she was consumed with wicked thoughts and unable to chase them away. In agitation she licked her dry lips, but that too brought wanton memories of the fierce kiss he'd forced upon her. Had it been only last night?

Joanna tucked a long curling strand of hair behind her ear then reached forward to stir the soup. But her thoughts remained stubbornly focused on the man across the room, despite her every wish to wipe him from her mind. Three days ago she'd not even heard of Rylan Kempe. Certainly she did not recall any mention of him or Blaecston when she was a child. But now—in two days' time—he'd turned her world upside down. First with his disturbing news from Oxwich. Then with his cruel kidnapping. And finally with his kiss.

A shiver raced through her and she sighed in resignation. What was to become of her now? Though she tried to recall her happy life at St. Theresa's, her mind constantly rebelled and inevitably returned once more to Rylan Kempe. The days—and years—before he'd arrived at St. Theresa's now seemed only a blur in her head, neither good nor bad, just quiet and uneventful. In the past two days, however, her emotions had veered from fury to terror, from frustration to elation. From sorrow to . . . to . . .

To the urge to commit murder, she added as she caught his movement from the corner of her eye.

Aye, she could easily be moved to murder, she decided as she kept her wary gaze slanted upon him. Given the chance she would gladly crown him with a heavy log from the woodpile, or season his soup with daffodil root. It was simply her misfortune that neither of those alternatives was viable.

A stab of guilt struck her at such a truly wicked thought, but Joanna struggled to ignore it and scowled at the concoction of cabbage, carrots, and onion that steamed in the pot. She was vitally aware, despite her studied nonchalance, of his every move. Since he'd discovered a small cellar and brought up the makings for a meal, she'd occupied herself with preparing the food while he'd sat idly by, watching her quite rudely.

"Is it ready?" he asked as he brought three more logs nearer the hearth from the stack behind the plank door.

"No," Joanna replied curtly, refusing even to glance at him. Then her jaw tightened and she could not restrain her temper. "Not everything in the kingdom jumps when you speak."

She was just congratulating herself for having silenced him for once when his finger ran down her back. She jumped forward in alarm, even as his taunting voice whispered near her ear. "Not everything, no. But you certainly do."

Joanna scooted sideways, trying to put some safe distance between them while her heart pounded in confusion. Rylan, however, only grinned at her discomfiture, then picked up the wooden ladle and stirred the soup.

"Needs salt," he informed her after testing the broth. "And any other spices you might find."

"Witch seed," Joanna muttered, glaring at his broad gleaming back. Yes, witch seed or deadman's bells would be just the thing for such a wretch as he.

"Witch seed?" He laughed out loud at her barely discernible threat. "What a wicked idea from such a near saint as you would have the world believe you are. Tell me, my bloodthirsty little dove. What shall it take for you to admit that the nunnery was not for you?"

"Even Saint Theresa herself would have been tempted to poison such a lowly vermin as you!" she cried in utter frustration. "My fury—my 'bloodthirsty' thoughts—are only natural, for I am no saint. I am only a woman—"

"Yes, my very point," he interrupted her disjointed tirade. "You are only a woman and you do not understand what is best for you."

"What is best for *you*, you mean! I know precisely what is best for me. And Oxwich and some dull fellow you would choose for my husband are not it!"

For a long angry moment she stared at him, forgetting for an instant his lack of clothing and her own humiliating dishabille. Then his mocking smile faded and his gaze became more earnest.

"Would you be more amenable if I let you select your husband? From several I would suggest," he added hastily.

"No!" she cried, maddened by his insulting suggestion. She spun on her heel, unable to deal even a moment longer with this man who toyed with her life without the least concern for her feelings. Yet though she stalked the length of the little cottage, the limitations of her prison only caused her anger to burn hotter. She was trapped with him and she saw no way out. Like the wind that howled and moaned without, her anger was all sound and fury now, but in the long run it would prove to be completely ineffectual. This island would withstand the storm's fury and Rylan Kempe would persevere against her.

It was that which brought tears stinging to her eyes. She was so intent on hiding them from his gaze, however, that she did not hear what he said.

"Tell me, Joanna," he repeated in an infuriatingly calm voice. "I want to know why you so dread being taken to wife."

She turned her face away as he approached her side. "'Tis . . . 'tis not your concern," she muttered, stifling a little sob.

"I'd say that, given the circumstances, it is very much my concern."

She turned her head sharply to peer up at him. "Why is that? Do you mean you would reconsider?"

He stared down into her cautiously hopeful face. "I mean that I could help allay your fears did I but know precisely what they were."

Joanna's expression fell, then closed against him in anger. "Your unfailing conceit never ceases to amaze me," she spat. But before she could slip beyond his grasp, he caught her in his adamant grip.

"My unfailing conceit? And what of your senseless resistance? You condemn an institution created by God —a man and a woman married, with the mandate to go forth and be fruitful—yet you refuse to justify yourself. And lest you think to pretend to a piety you do not possess, keep in mind that I have already tasted of your passion, Joanna." He jerked her fully against him so that her blanket parted and only her thin kirtle separated his naked chest from her own. "Deny it all you want, my icy little nun. But I know there is a fire in you—one both you and your husband shall relish burning within."

For an instant longer they stood thus, pressed together in an odd sort of embrace, his body heat meeting her own with a sizzling awareness. His eyes were dark as they bored into hers, lit only by the golden flickering from the fireplace, and for a moment Joanna thought he meant to kiss her once more. Her entire body stiffened in anticipation—in horror and dread, she tried to tell herself. Yet when he stepped back from her she felt an unbidden shiver of disappointment.

No, never that! She denied the feeling as she scurried to the most distant corner she could find. Yet once more the truth was painfully obvious. Unable to help herself, she stared at him, her eyes wide and frightened. He stirred something in her. Something wicked and sinful. And what seemed almost as terrible, he was well aware of it. Despite her vow to shun the outside world and the temptations of the flesh, he used those very temptations to weaken her resolve.

Her eyes followed him as he crossed once more to the thick-paned window to peer out at the storm. His dark hair gleamed with golden highlights and the fire glinted off his bare shoulders and arms. Then her eyes slid down the wide-muscled curve of his back to his lean buttocks outlined by the sheet that circled his hips. A forbidden knot of warmth curled in her belly, and she forced her eyes to move down to his knees and calves, only to note the dark hairs so liberally sprinkled there. Oh, he was truly a devil. She shuddered, turning her eyes away from him. He was the devil sent to tempt her, and saints preserve her, she was tempted!

He looked over at her and caught her staring once more, but Joanna lowered her eyes in renewed confusion. He must not know, she warned herself as she nervously fingered the hem of her still-wet gown dangling beside her. He must not know how profoundly he affected her. That base and wicked part of her nature must be firmly buried beneath the anger and outrage she felt.

Yet even as she resolved to appear immune to his potent masculine appeal, her eyes stole up to peer at him once more, and she knew it was the hardest task she'd ever set for herself.

When her stomach let out a small grumble of hunger, she moved back to the fire. But in her agitation she stirred the soup so vigorously that it splashed against her wrist. "Christ and bedamned," she muttered in annoyance, then looked up in shock, horrified by the words she'd just uttered.

"Christ and bedamned?" His taunting voice rang across the uncomfortably quiet room. "Christ and bedamned? If I did not know better, my Lady Joanna, I would think you succumbing already to the failings of the rest of us mere mortals. But you would not do that, would you?" He laughed then, keeping his astute gaze locked with hers. "She curses like a hardened fighting man; she parades around in a blanket and her undergarment; and she kisses with passionate abandon." His voice grew husky as he stared at her, and her hand unconsciously tightened on the blanket as he went on. "Surely not the makings of a nun."

Joanna was too shocked by his words—and too undone by the sudden knot deep in her belly—to respond. Dear God, how could she be so careless? How could she be so recklessly drawn to him?

"I . . . I did not," she protested weakly. But even as

she forced her gaze away from him, she knew her denial was untrue. She *had* kissed him with passionate abandon last night. She had not meant to, but she had nonetheless done so. Then, just minutes ago when he'd pulled her against him, she had been disconcerted when he'd thrust her away. Like a devil he drew her, tempting her to sin. Yet she knew she already sinned merely by the lust she felt.

And he knew. He knew.

There was a long silence before he spoke again. "Is the soup ready?"

Unwilling to meet his eyes, she reached forward nervously, for all intents and purposes concentrating on the soup. Yet her studied indifference to him only seemed to amuse him, she realized as she peered at him from beneath her long sheltering lashes.

"'Tis edible," she finally muttered, but only because to ignore him seemed pointless under the circumstances.

"Then serve the meal."

Joanna's head jerked around at that arrogant command. "If you wish to eat, you'd best plan to serve yourself."

"No, I think not." He relaxed back in his chair, his bare legs stretched out before him, crossed at the ankles, and his fingers laced and resting contentedly on his stomach. "It occurs to me, Joanna, that you have no training whatsoever in the wifely arts. Since I have taken it upon myself to find you a suitable husband, it behooves me to make sure he will find you a suitable wife."

"I'll make no man a suitable wife, so you may save yourself the effort," she snapped.

"Oh, it will be no effort. After all, I've little else to do as we wait out the storm. Now, let's start with the serving of the meal. 'Tis your duty as chatelaine of Oxwich to see your husband and his retainers well fed and served as befits each one's appropriate station."

Joanna stared at him furiously. "They may starve for all the care they'll receive from me. And so shall you."

He sighed, a long exaggerated sound, and gazed at her in mock resignation. "If you would just try it, you might find your role as a nobleman's wife most pleasing."

"More the fool you, if you believe such a thing."

"You found kissing rather pleasing."

"I did not!" Joanna cried. Despite her vehement denial, however, she could not ignore the thrill his dark words roused in her.

"Liar," he taunted. "I distinctly remember how your body went soft against mine. And how you opened your mouth and accepted the caress of my tongue."

The blood seemed to roar through Joanna's head, then coursed down in a heated rush to settle somewhere in her lower belly. It wasn't true, she wanted to throw back at him. It wasn't! She hadn't reacted that way at all.

Only she had, and just remembering it filled her with strange, forbidden feelings. For a moment the air in the room seethed, the undercurrent of emotions between them was so powerful. But before Joanna could collect her scattered wits and come up with a properly dampening retort, he was on his feet and towering over her. The firelight gleamed hotly on him, just as it also heated Joanna's skin. But the searing warmth she felt most acutely was centered deep within her nether regions. His eyes glittered as he stared down at her, and though she could have averted her gaze, she would then have been staring directly at that one portion of him that was so inadequately covered by the sheet. The very thought of his state of undress made her cheeks flame even hotter, so she kept her eyes on his face.

"I asked you before why you oppose the holy state of matrimony," he said quietly, all the while holding her gaze with his own. "But you did not give me an answer. Will you give me one now?"

"'Tis enough to know that I do." But Joanna's words did not have any bite to them. She was too unnerved by the gentleness of his voice. His arrogance she could deal with, and his taunts and insults as well. But this thread of concern in his voice . . .

A long moment passed between them, broken only by the futile howling of the wind and the hissing of the fire.

"Has this anything to do with your father?"

She turned abruptly away, refusing to answer. But he crouched down beside her and caught her chin in his hand and forced her to face him, clearly convinced he'd found his answer.

"Not all men are like your father, Joanna. They do not all mistreat their wives."

He watched her closely, clearly trying to gauge her reaction to his words and thereby find an answer to his query. But Joanna was too undone by his possessive touch and the compelling sound of his low-pitched voice to take any notice of what he actually said. She was going to suffocate if he did not release her, for she could not remember to breathe when he touched her so!

"Nor do they all mistreat their children," he continued.

At precisely that moment she leaned back from him, tearing her chin from his gentle grip. The fire behind her nearly singed her loosened hair, but she was more alarmed by the fire in her veins.

At her sudden reaction, Rylan sat back on his heels as well, his face going black with fury. "Did he mistreat you?" he demanded to know. "What was it? Did he beat you? Or—" He broke off abruptly and just stared at her.

Joanna realized at once that he had misconstrued her reaction to his touch as a reaction to his words. Though her father had never shown her any kindness, he could not be accused of physically harming her.

"He did not beat me," she corrected his hasty assumption. But his angry countenance only grew more grim.

"Did he—" He faltered in his words and Joanna looked at him in confusion. "Christ's blood! Did he touch you? You know—" He broke off once more as if he could not put words to what he meant. But when Joanna only stared at him blankly, not understanding at all what he was getting at, he finally exploded.

"Did he touch you, by damned! Like . . . like he should only touch his wife?"

Comprehension came then, as well as a fiery stain of color on her cheeks. Dear God, she thought. Was such a thing even possible? Yet judging from Rylan's fierce expression, it most certainly was.

"No!" she shouted. "He did . . . he did not do *that!* And you are quite beyond redemption to even suggest such a thing!"

Although his relief was obvious, he was nonetheless still irritated. "I am beyond redemption? Why, because you care for your father so dearly?"

He smiled grimly when her face reflected her answer to his gibe. "I thought not. But it only points up what is already clear. Your father has somehow soured you toward marriage. But it need not be as it was between your parents, Joanna. Not every man is the same."

"Do tell," she replied coolly. "In my experience—limited as it is," she threw in sarcastically, "men are arrogant, vain fools who care not a whit for the lives or feelings of their womenfolk. They manipulate and use both their wives and their daughters as a means to whatever ends suit them. My father did it to my mother." She raised her chin a notch and gave him her most condemning glare. "And you are trying to do it to me."

He had the good grace to look at least a trifle guilty, she thought, and she decided this was a good time to put a little distance between them. She rose to her feet with as much poise as she could muster, considering that she was sandwiched between him and the fire and hampered by the bulky blanket around her. But Rylan stopped her when he gathered a handful of the blanket where it circled her knees.

"You choose to see only the bad side of me—of men. But there is another side."

"Tell that to my mother," she snapped, yanking the blanket from his loose hold. When she stalked away, however, he rose and followed.

"What happened to your mother?" he asked, his tone quiet again, not demanding.

"She is dead, as you must surely know. She is none of your concern."

"But her daughter is my concern."

Joanna whirled to face him, dismayed to find him so near. "I am *not* your concern! My life is my own, to be lived as I see fit. Nothing you do changes that fact. You may present any number of your court gallants to me, but I shall send them all packing." She took a harsh breath and glared up at him, hoping her show of bravado would not fail her. "You cannot force me to say the marriage vow. You can drag me before the priest, but you cannot make me say the words."

To her enormous surprise, her words did not rouse him to anger. That alone was dismaying, but then he smiled at her—an odd, almost regretful smile—and every thought flew right out of her head.

He was too near. She knew instinctively that she had to get away. But before she could collect herself, it was too late.

"I'll not have to *make* you say the words, Joanna. I shall make you *want* to say them." Then his hand caught her chin and his mouth moved down to meet hers.

Had her wits been about her—had she been better prepared for the voluptuous feel of his lips against her own—she would have ended the kiss as soon as it began. After all, he did not hold her there by force. Only his finger beneath her up-tilted chin kept her in place. She had only to turn her head. Or take a step back.

But neither of those possibilities occurred to Joanna. Rylan's light touch on her chin kept her his captive as securely as the walls of a prison donjon might. And his lips . . .

Beneath the questing pressure of his lips she was undone. It was sweet yet forbidden; he burned her and yet filled her somehow with delight. He melted her very bones so that she thought she might dissolve into a puddle on the floor, yet he lifted her to unimaginable heights.

When his tongue stroked the seam of her lips she opened to him, seeking more of these wondrous feelings. But when his tongue slid within her mouth, caressing and teasing, mating with her own, the stakes suddenly increased. With a groan Rylan's arm came around her, crushing her to him so that they met thigh to thigh, belly to belly. As their tongues danced and dueled, creating an inferno of emotion, she strained toward him, arching in artless abandon.

The blanket fell away as her arms encircled his neck,

but Joanna was not aware of its absence. She knew only that she could not get enough of him and the way he made her feel. One of his hands held her head firmly while the other slid slowly down her back, past her waist and hips to curve around her derriere. At once Joanna felt a fiery surge deep in her belly. He pressed her hard against him until she was firmly held between the rigid pressure at his loins and the possessive caress of his fingers.

"Damnation!" he exclaimed as he struggled for his breath. But he did not give her a chance to object or even to catch a ragged breath of her own before he captured her lips once more. This time his kiss was ferocious, almost savage. He plundered her mouth recklessly, demanding that she respond.

And without hesitation, Joanna did respond. With every fiber of her feminine being she answered the age-old call of the virile man to his mate.

He lifted her high so that her feet left the floor, then slid his hand down one of her thighs, raising her knee until her leg curved around his hips. This time when his hand slid back to her derriere, his entire palm could press against that most private place between her legs.

Joanna gasped and pulled slightly back, dazed by the myriad emotions that beset her. She was dizzy and panting, unable to think. Then he tilted her back over his arm and moved his seductive lips down to her chin and neck, sliding his tongue in hot wet circles to the hollow of her throat, and even farther, over her collarbone and down to the upper swells of her breasts.

Unthinkingly she arched for more, consumed by the new feelings that bombarded her.

"Ah, woman. How you make me burn," he murmured the hot words against her breast. Then, as if it took a supreme exercise of will, he lifted his head and stared at her heavy-lidded eyes.

"I knew it would be thus," he whispered between ragged breaths. He released her raised leg and let her slide down against the hard length of his body until her feet touched the floor.

Still overcome by a riot of emotions, Joanna did not at once sense his withdrawal. Her hands clung to his neck and their thighs remained pressed intimately together. He kissed her lightly—regretfully—on the lips and reached up to disengage her hands. Then his avid gaze ran over her face, and he raised her hands to his mouth to press a hot kiss to each of her sensitive palms.

"There is more than even this, my sweet little nun." His voice came low and husky as his mouth moved to the soft flesh of her third finger and bit lightly at it. "But you must have a ring here before you taste that final pleasure."

Joanna froze in horror at his words. In a sickening rush she realized just how wantonly she had behaved. Was she mad?

She jerked back from him, nearly tripping on the forgotten blanket in her haste to retreat. Her hair flew in long ringlets about her shoulders and her arms wrapped protectively around her as she stumbled back. A vein throbbed wildly in her temple as her eyes darted about in desperation. But there was no place in the small cruck cottage where she could avoid his piercing gaze.

"You cannot hide from the truth, Joanna. No amount of denial will change the facts."

"You are a devil!" she cried. "The serpent come to unholy light!"

He laughed at that, but it was neither joyful nor triumphant. Then he turned his back on her and faced the fire. "Perhaps I am the devil—your personal devil, come to tempt you with the ways of the flesh." He halted and took a slow breath. "It may be, however, that I have been sent to guide you away from a life you are ill-suited to."

Joanna was too distraught to respond to his words. She was a sinner. A slave to her own dark passions. A creature no better than a dog in the streets. The undeniable fact of her depravity overwhelmed her. She glanced toward the man—the devil—who'd brought her to such a pass, but that only increased her guilt. For despite the fact that he stood before the hearth scantily clad, with flames that appeared to lick around his feet like the very fires of hell, she nonetheless drank in the sight. It was not hell she thought of as his wide shoulders gleamed in the golden light, but heaven. It was then she feared she was completely lost.

She whirled away from the sight of him, then scrambled toward the farthest corner of the chamber. There she huddled, crouching down with her arms around her knees, as a rabbit might seek to hide from a hungry fox. Only Joanna feared she had no hope of ever eluding the particular fox who had hunted her down, for he seemed driven to best her. He was strong and crafty, and possessed of no moral qualms whatsoever.

She had God on her side—or at least she'd *had* Him on her side. But this man . . . This man had the devil with him. For the first time in her young life she feared that the devil might be the stronger.

As if agreeing with her, the fire in the hearth hissed and popped, spitting and leaping wildly as some of the wind-driven rain worked its way down the chimney. Rylan squatted on his heels and used a length of oak heartwood to prod the logs and stifle the flames, so that only slow-smoldering embers remained. The room dimmed somewhat as he worked, but he was no less clearly silhouetted by the fire's glow.

He remained at his task far longer than was necessary, as if he were immersed in the fire—or else lost in thought. Then he took a breath, squared his shoulders, and stood up. As Joanna watched in increasing fear, he turned his attention once more to her.

Though she was settled in her corner, sitting on her bare feet with her hair pulled protectively before her chest and arms, she nonetheless felt the full force of his midnight-dark stare. She might as well have been naked beneath that too-perceptive gaze, she thought as a shiver ran through her. No doubt he now thought her completely in his power as well, judging by the arrogant expression on his face.

"You need not hide in that corner," he began. "Truth to be told, we have much to do before this storm abates."

"Much to do?" Joanna's heart leaped in her throat and a hundred dreadful possibilities suddenly clamored in her head.

"Yes, much to do. However, you have already shown yourself to be a fast learner. I have no doubt you shall grasp the remainder of your duties equally well."

"Equally well?" she echoed him once more, still not understanding his odd choice of words.

"You must learn your duties as a wife, Joanna. You've already shown yourself to be most adept—most passionate. I am confident your husband shall be well pleased with you in that regard. It now remains only for you to learn to wait upon him and cater to his needs."

Joanna listened in round-eyed horror to his words. She had proven herself most adept— Her husband would be well pleased— A wave of white-hot anger rushed over her. That and the undeniably bitter taste of disappointment. The anger she could deal with; it was an honest emotion and no more than the wretched Sir Rylan deserved. But the disappointment . . . Where did that come from?

Unfortunately Joanna recognized precisely where it came from. He'd kissed her and tempted her, and made her want that forbidden communion of the flesh. But he'd done it not out of a similar desire for her. No, he was far too self-serving and cruel to succumb to so human a failing as that. He'd done it only to make his point. He'd made her desire him just as her husband would do.

"Come prepare the meal," he was saying. "Serve me, but be pleasant about it, Joanna, as a wife should always be to her husband. I'll not countenance your ill temper."

"My ill temper is something you will have to accustom yourself to, *my lord*. And you are *not* my husband!"

His answer was to reach down, grab her arms, and abruptly yank her to her feet. "Do not push me, woman, for there is little that stands between you and the full brunt of my anger."

As terrified as she was of him, Joanna refused to acquiesce to his threats. "I shall be wife to no man of yours," she retorted as she struggled futilely against his grip.

"Christ and bedamned! Can't you see that you have already lost this ridiculous battle of yours? I need but pull you against me to prove you wrong. Is that it, Joanna? Are you trying to goad me into kissing you again—and more? For we both know it will take but the touch of our lips—the stroke of our tongues—to still your struggles and silence your arguments. Is that what you want of me?"

"No!" The cry tore from her, filled with an anguish that went to her soul. "No," she repeated in a trembling tone, as a mortifying flood of scarlet stained her cheeks and neck.

He let her go at once and stepped back, almost as if he were relieved by her sudden capitulation. They were still far too close for Joanna's comfort, however, she had her back to the corner and was trapped there by his imposing form. Consumed with fear, trembling with embarrassment, she could not meet his probing gaze. She stared instead at his chest but that too was unsettling, for the dark pattern of his swirling chest hair caused her stomach to tighten with a queer feeling.

She saw his chest fill as he took a slow, unsteady breath. Then he stepped aside and gestured toward the fire and the pot of soup.

"Serve the meal," he muttered in a tightly held voice. "And pray let us eat in peace."

9

Joanna could not enjoy a single bite of her meal. She was far too upset by Sir Rylan Kempe's hateful words to give even a thought to the savory broth and vegetables she now picked at.

Yet coupled with her justifiable fury at him, she felt another even more mystifying emotion. His words had been hateful, yes. But to her absolute dismay, they had been undeniably true. He *could* have stilled her struggles with just his kiss. Like a demon he exercised his unholy power on her, and she—frail sinner that she was—could not overcome it.

Once more the memory of her parents came to her: her mother's tears and weak defense, her father's anger and ultimate domination. She'd heard enough from the various women at St. Theresa's—many of them reformed prostitutes—to know what the word *rape* meant. She'd always found an odd solace in hating her father for raping her mother, for she knew it was that which had forced her mother to take her own life. But now Joanna was completely confused. Rape meant the woman was repulsed by what was happening to her, or so she'd always believed. But Joanna had not hated what Rylan did to her—at least not while he was doing it.

But then, perhaps she had not understood before and had simplified it too much. Perhaps what the man did was steal the woman's will from her, and only later when she was herself again was she sickened by what had occurred between them.

Yet even that line of reasoning had its flaws, for Joanna did not precisely feel sickened by his amorous attentions. Horrified, yes. And ashamed. But not exactly sickened and, unfortunately, not repulsed either.

She sent a baleful glare toward the man who had her so unsettled, but Rylan was unaffected. He sat across from her at the little table, filling himself with soup while she sat there, unable to force even one more bite. How she would enjoy tossing her bowl of soup in his spiteful face.

As if he read her very thoughts, Rylan glanced up and caught her staring.

"The soup is excellent, Joanna. I'm sure you shall easily take Oxwich's kitchens in hand." He paused as if awaiting some response then, when she only remained defiantly mute, continued. "I know as well that you will be able to oversee the sewing rooms, for St. Theresa's prides itself on its stitching. But tell me, how is your spinning? And also your weaving?"

At her determined silence he grinned and pushed back his empty wooden bowl. "Come now, milady. This reticence does you no credit, for we both know I can coax an answer from you." His eyes went from her narrowed glare to her pursed lips. Then for emphasis, he slid the side of one of his fingers back and forth along his lower lip.

"You devil!" she cried, forgetting that she meant to

ignore his taunts. She stood up, knocking her three-legged stool backward as she did so.

"Devil I may well be. However, I would nevertheless have your answer. Are you adept at spinning and weaving?"

As he watched her with no attempt whatsoever to hide the amusement on his face, Joanna fought hard to hold her emotions in check. She lifted her chin a notch and gave him her most haughty glare. She was not aware that her erect posture thrust her breasts forward against the thin linen of her kirtle and past the protection of her long curling hair. In the dimly lit cottage she appeared at once both innocent and seductive, angelic and yet tempting as well. His face lost its smug expression at the sight of her, but she thought it due only to her scathing words.

"If I thought my answer would dissuade you from your foul plans for me, I'd take pains to respond in a fashion most likely to displease you. However, since I doubt you care at all what housewifely skills I possess—indeed, you would force me into this marriage were I a drooling idiot with no skills whatsoever! —I see no need to answer you at all."

She swept away from the table with her nose in the air and her back as rigid as a pike staff. But inside she was shaking. He could force an answer from her if he decided to. He'd forced her to serve the meal, then to eat across the table from him as if they were sitting down to the most civil and proper of meals, without any animosity between them. While he'd eaten she'd had a brief reprieve from his hateful taunts. But now that he was replete, he was clearly ready to begin once more. Tense with impotent anger, she waited for his response to her reckless words, ready for anything.

But once again Rylan surprised her. Instead of bounding up in a fury, he let her stalk away, then forced her to wait for him to react. It was that wait that unnerved her even more. When he finally rose from the table, she jerked about in alarm, her affected poise totally destroyed.

"You're quite right, of course. I didn't think. Any one of your women may be assigned to oversee the spinning and the weaving. No doubt you could even dispense with your duties to preside over the kitchens and the serving room *if* your husband has other reasons to be pleased with you."

His hand strayed to his stomach and absently scratched the area just above the sheet that hung so low on his hips. "It is your responsibilities to your husband —for his personal comforts and pleasures—that are of primary importance." He grinned at her expression of consternation. "Since our time here shall be so short, 'tis best we deal with those responsibilities first."

Joanna's heart plummeted as he eyed her with ill-disguised glee. She was in for it now, she realized. He would show her no mercy at all, and should she oppose him, he would most certainly kiss her into compliance.

At the thought of him kissing her again, a rush of unwelcome heat moved up from the area of her belly. She took a step backward and wrapped her arms tightly about herself, desperately seeking some solution to her dilemma. But it was swiftly apparent there was none.

"Perhaps we should just follow a typical day's routine," he said, almost musingly. But Joanna knew this was anything but idle wondering. He meant to humiliate her in some new way. She watched warily as he touched his drying braies and then his chainse, which hung on the makeshift clothesline.

"Of course," he continued. He turned to her with a wide grin on his masculine face. "A wife must help her husband dress each day. Let us begin with that."

"No!" The word was out before Joanna could think. Her eyes grew huge as they fastened on his in disbelief. He could not be this hateful!

"Just imagine that I am your husband, Joanna, and it will not be so hard. I promise you, he shall be neither old nor ugly. You have my word on that."

"No," she repeated, shaking her head back and forth but never taking her eyes from him.

"Yes," he retorted. "Start with the hose, and then the braies and crossbanding. The shirt and tunic come after that. And then the boots and weapons."

"You . . . you can dress yourself."

"Of course I can, but that does not signify. I will not be the one dressing your husband. You will. Now come here."

Joanna was too undone by his insistent demand to do more than stutter in panic. "The . . . the . . . the clothes. They're not dry."

He grinned at her—a slashing white smile on his dark face—and her stomach lurched in a sudden feminine awareness of him. In that one moment—with that one confident grin—the true gravity of her situation was driven home to her. The heat in her belly, the frantic pounding of her heart, the damp palms and dry mouth— they might all be manifestations of fear. They might be, but they weren't. She lusted for this man. It was as simple and awful as that. She lusted after him. Her fear was not of him but of herself and her appalling loss of self-control.

That painful admission made Joanna's choice obvious. Better to acquiesce to his cruel demand than to let him force her. If she did not fight him, she could be done with the task as quickly as possible. If she resisted, he would kiss her until she gave in anyway, and she knew now that his kiss must at all costs be avoided.

"May I dress myself first?" she asked in a subdued voice.

His eyes narrowed slightly. Then he reached up to feel her heavy gown. "Your dress is still too wet."

Joanna stiffened. Her dress was too wet, but his clothes were not? Yet as she angrily snatched his light knitted hose from the line and his fine linen braies as well, she knew her own coarse gown would be a long time drying. Her linen kirtle at least was dry and no longer clung to her breasts and thighs. But she would not feel comfortable until she had her gown on again.

"As you wish," she snapped. She held his garments away from her, her arms stiff and her posture resentful.

"As you wish," he parroted her. "Ah, now there are words sure to keep any husband content." He sat down on a stool and crooked one finger at her. "Come closer, Joanna. We'll start with the hose."

Had she been an observer and not a participant in this little drama, Joanna might have laughed out loud at the scene. Her reluctance was more than evident in her lowered brow, her stiff carriage, and her snail-like progress toward him. His face reflected both surprise and triumph at her capitulation. To exacerbate the situation, each of them was so tense with a physical awareness of the other that the air fairly crackled with it.

Joanna halted before him, cognizant that she must kneel in order to help him into his hose. Yet that ignominy was easier to swallow than her fear of touching his bare skin. Feet, legs, arms—it did not matter where. She only knew she dreaded it.

She took a harsh breath, swallowed, then sank to her knees. Prayers should come naturally to her in that position, and she tried desperately to dredge up some holy words to get her through this ordeal. But nothing came. Her mind was empty of all else but his devastating presence. She lifted her gaze to his, unable to think what next to do.

"My left foot. Put my hose on my left foot," he instructed in a voice gone low and husky.

Obediently she gathered the knitted hose in her hands then held it open near his toes. He cooperated without words, only watching her bent head as she awkwardly tugged the hose up over his foot and around his heel, then up past his ankle and muscular calf to just above his knee. The dark hairs on his leg tickled the backs of her fingers and his warm skin was in marked contrast to her icy hands.

She leaned back on her heels, gasping for breath when the first leg was completed. Had she forgotten to breathe in her nervousness? Her eyes rose briefly to his then immediately fell to her lap, for his stare seemed to burn through her. She fiddled with the second hose, fighting to control her breathing and the fierce racing of her heart.

This time in her haste she pulled the knitted hose up so fast it twisted and pulled at his knee, bunching most awkwardly.

"Adjust it at the ankle first. Then smooth it up."

Joanna swallowed hard as a fit of trembling took her. She was too consumed with her own troubled thoughts to take any notice of his hoarse tone. She only knew she must somehow get him dressed, and the faster the better.

Unfortunately, in order to straighten his hose, she had

to circle his ankle with both her hands and slowly inch the garment into place. Against her palms she felt the warmth of his skin. From the bony strength of his ankle, up the muscular curve of his calf, to the hard protuberance of his knee, she was forced to smooth the uncooperative garment. Although she tried desperately to ignore the unsettling feelings that curled in her stomach, it was a useless effort. Her eyes, too, only made things worse, for in her effort to ignore his too-perceptive gaze, she had concentrated on what she was doing. But now as her hands fell away from his knees, her stare nonetheless remained there and even moved up along his well-formed thighs to where the piece of sheeting barely covered his loins.

"Sweet mother of God," she whispered, unaware she'd spoken aloud.

"Sweet . . ." he responded in an equally low and strangled voice. Then he exhaled noisily and she jerked into awareness.

"The braies—" He broke off and pointed to the garment in her lap. "The braies."

Joanna looked down at the braies, then up at him. His face was set in an odd expression, neither angry nor mocking, nor even complacent. He seemed almost in pain, she thought through her haze of confusion.

"The braies," he uttered one more time.

At last his words penetrated, as did the reality of what he asked. If encasing his calves in the wool hose was torture, how much worse would it be to draw his braies up past his hips and knot them at his waist? Joanna's face paled at the thought.

"The shirt," she gasped as she inched back from him then rose shakily to her feet. "The shirt is next."

"No, it should—"

"The shirt," she interrupted him, yanking it from the line. Before he could stand up, she circled him and, without allowing her courage any time to falter, threw the shirt over his head.

It was at best a rather haphazard method of dressing a man, but finesse was not uppermost on Joanna's mind. She knew only that she must see him dressed as speedily as possible. The long shirt would cover him . . . down there. Otherwise she would never get his braies on him and then he would kiss her . . . and then she would be lost.

"Damnation! You've got my hair," he growled, struggling to get his head through the neck hole as she pulled and tugged at the shirt, trying to align it properly. "Ouch!"

In an instant he grasped both of her wrists, holding her in place behind him, with each of her arms resting on his shoulders.

"You're not doing it right," he muttered, ignoring her struggles to be free of him. "And if you don't do it right, we'll just have to start over from the beginning."

That stilled her at once. But it seemed he was not through with his chastisement, for, with a soft chuckle, he began to pull her nearer him.

"Actually, Joanna, I hadn't thought that some men like a woman who is not too submissive. It could be that your stubborn resistance may fire your husband's ardor even more." With a final tug he pulled her up against him so that her stomach pressed against his back and her breasts pushed against his shoulders. He drew her arms down and crossed them over his chest, forcing her palms open against his lower ribs.

"I know it fires mine," he added so softly she hardly heard him. Then he moved his head back to rest upon her shoulder and nuzzled her neck and jaw. "You may dress me in any manner you wish. Or undress me as well," he murmured, nibbling at her ear.

Oh, help, Joanna pleaded silently as a hot wash of desire licked up from deep inside her.

"Like this," he continued. Then before she could react he slid her hands along the hard ridges of his bare stomach and chest.

Joanna could not move, she was so beset by a powerful mixture of desire, fear, and curiosity. His strong callused hand cupped her own and his fingers parted hers so that their hands were most intimately joined. Up and down, over the firm muscles of his belly and halfway up his chest he forced her to stroke. Warm skin, soft curling hairs, the uneven shape of his scar, and the rhythmic ridges of his finely honed torso—these she stroked and learned, and in truth, was not forced very hard to do so. Something blossomed deep within her, and she let out a soft sigh.

Rylan's grip tightened at that slight sound and his hands pulled both of hers to press fully across his flat male nipples. Then as abruptly as if he'd been doused with icy beck water, he loosed her hands and flung himself forward, away from her stupefied embrace. He stood up with his back to her, hastily thrust his arms into the billowing shirt, and yanked it down to cover himself. Only then did he turn to face her.

Joanna still stood behind the stool, sagging against the sturdy seat and afraid she could not stand on her own. Her legs were shaking; her bones were surely melting. She didn't want to think about what she'd just done— about the forbidden thrill he'd roused in her. Yet she could not just shrug it off, nor pretend to an anger she hardly felt. Thank God he'd pulled away, for she feared she never would have. Even now she was consumed with an indescribable yearning for him.

No, not him, she told herself. It was just that he was a man and she'd had no experience with men. If it hadn't been Rylan, it might have been anyone else. Yet that thought, meant to console, only made her feel worse. Was she like Winna now? A wanton woman panting after any man who came along?

She closed her eyes at that sickening thought. Dear God, what had this man reduced her to?

More than anything else, this new knowledge of herself made it imperative that she return to the priory. Once she took her vows—once she was safe within those walls, protected from the intrusion of any men—she would be all right. She would pray for God's forgiveness and dedicate her life to good works. Anything to erase this terrible sin of hers.

Through her misery Joanna heard him moving around, and when she looked again, he was lacing on his braies with remarkable haste. His face was shadowed in the firelight. Outside the rain beat sporadically at the thick yellow window glass, and the waves assaulted the shore with a roaring regularity. But inside all was as quiet as a tomb. She watched as he wrapped the cross-banding about his legs with jerky movements, then snatched his girdle and buckled it about his waist.

He behaved as if he were angry, she thought. Yet what had he to be angry about?

When he looked up at her, however, with his dark brows slanting together and his lips narrowed, she knew he was indeed in a fine temper.

"You," he began in a voice hoarse with emotion. "You would *never* make a nun." His eyes raked her with a furious thoroughness, causing her to step back in dismay. "No, quite the contrary."

His bitter words so mirrored her own fears that Joanna wanted to weep. Yet still she denied what he said.

"I *will* make a good nun. 'Tis only because you . . . because you . . ."

"Because I what? I'll tell you. 'Tis only because I am the one who has forced you from the rigid mold you try so hard to fit yourself to. 'Tis only because I forced you to let down your guard a little. Now you're terrified by the feelings that have been unleashed in you."

She shook from the force of his words—and the force of his direct stare. Despite the distance between them, she felt overwhelmed by him. His gaze. His voice. His very essence seemed to surround her until that was all there was.

"Do you want me to admit I am terrified?" she answered him in a voice filled with pain. "Very well then, I am terrified. Do you want me to admit that you . . . that you have made me feel . . . things that I've never felt before?" She took a shaky breath, but her eyes held with his. "'Tis all true. But even with that, you are still wrong about me. I *will* make a good nun. I have sinned, but—"

"Sinned! Christ and bedamned, woman. That was not a sin. The sin would be to resign yourself to that godforsaken priory!"

"Oh! How can you blaspheme so! God never forsakes His people, not even if they sin, so long as they repent. And I do repent! You should do so as well—"

She broke off at that ridiculous idea. He was hardly the sort to repent any of his foul actions. She stiffened her jaw. "I can see this gains me nothing with you."

"No, nothing. One day, however, you shall admit to me how wrong you are."

Her fingers tightened into fists. "You are a fool if you believe that!" Then she reconsidered her anger, knowing it was a useless weapon with him. Perhaps if she took a more reasonable approach.

Since he stood across the small space, fully clothed now except for his tunic, Joanna edged carefully toward her forgotten blanket. Behind her the fire glowed, backlighting her every curve through the thin kirtle, but she could not know that. She knew only that Rylan's stare darkened, and she trembled in response, feeling as if he actually touched her with his eyes.

When she reached the blanket she flung it over her shoulders then whirled once more to confront him, more secure with the heavy wool around her. If anything, however, his face was even grimmer than before, with that same expression of pain etched upon it. Still, she must not be concerned with *his* problems, she reminded herself. Her own were trouble enough; she did not care about his difficulties with the king.

But then again, maybe she should.

Joanna's heart leaped with sudden hope. If she could somehow devise a way for him to keep control of Oxwich without forcing an unwanted marriage on her, he might then leave her alone. He wanted Oxwich safe from the king; she was only a means to that end. But if his goal could be accomplished in some other manner, she could then be returned to St. Theresa's.

Clinging to that hope, she determinedly buried the tiny wave of disappointment she suddenly felt at the thought of actually living the remainder of her days at the priory. To admit to such feelings was to admit that he might be right about her. No, all she wanted was to return to her peaceful life at St. Theresa's. That was all she'd ever wanted, and nothing he had done or said could change that.

But she must do this right, she realized as her eyes searched out the cottage space. If she kept too much distance between them, she would look frightened. Too close was not good either. No, not good at all. She finally took a steadying breath, then moved toward him and seated herself most casually at the square table. She was conscious of his eyes following her, but when she looked up he was once more staring at the fire.

"Did you give this plan of yours lengthy consideration before deciding to abduct me?" she began without preamble.

He looked over at her. "'Twas not so complex a scheme as to require endless deliberations."

Joanna's jaw clenched in irritation at such an offhanded commandeering of her life, but she squelched the angry retort that bubbled to her lips. It was not her intent to argue with him this time.

"In your haste to secure Oxwich from the king, did you never consider that you might achieve your goal in another fashion?"

He stared at her a moment, then advanced toward the table and pulled out the stool opposite hers. Once seated, he folded his hands across his stomach and leaned back in his stool, lifting the forward leg off the floor in the process. "No, I did not consider any other idea. Marrying you to one of my own barons was the most obvious solution. It still is."

Joanna leaned back also, but not because she was relaxed and taking her ease. No, it was not that. Rather, she longed for the safety of some distance between them, and right now he was far too close for her comfort. Already her palms were sweating and she licked her dry lips nervously.

His stool came down with a thump. "Don't—" He broke off but his eyes remained locked on her mouth.

"Don't? Don't what?" She stared at him in confusion.

"Don't . . ." He took a harsh breath then stared up at the cruckwork beams above their heads. "Don't even try to talk me away from my plan. There's no other way."

"But I will most freely give you Oxwich!"

"You cannot."

"If it is mine, to be bartered away along with my hand in marriage, why can I not simply give it away?"

"It is yours, my innocent one, only at the pleasure of the king. It passes through your family, from father to son—or daughter in the rare case when no son remains. But you hold your demesne and maintain it for England. For your king."

"Then King John could very well disenfranchise me and the husband you force upon me." She smiled smugly at him at that clever deduction.

He raised one brow at her quick words. "In theory, perhaps. But in practice it is rarely done. Once you are wed, and you and your husband settled in Oxwich Castle, it will be almost impossible for King John to undo the deed. No lord, whether friendly or not to my cause, will want to support the king in deposing another lord— except in the case of gross treason. For such a move by the king makes every other lord's position more precarious as well. And John, softsword that he is, would never take it upon himself to challenge me or your husband. Yorkshire stands hard against our spineless fool of a king. 'Tis for that very reason your Oxwich is so important. So you see." He gave her a warm, wicked smile. "Your castle is the key to Yorkshire, and you are the key to the castle."

Joanna gaped at him, unable to believe that she could be so important a player in England's endless political intrigues. She was just one woman, the daughter of a lesser lord, at that. Yet if Rylan's words were fact . . .

She shook her head, not wanting to believe her cause was so hopeless. "I . . . I will not marry," she whispered, unaware of the tremor in her voice.

"You will."

"What if no man will have me?"

He grinned at that. "What man would refuse you?"

"You mean, what man would refuse *you*," she countered angrily. "Besides, if I am so important—if Oxwich is—why do you not offer for me yourself?"

The words popped out before she could halt them, and Joanna was aghast. He was the last man she would ever wed!

He clearly found the idea preposterous as well, for the amusement fled his face.

"I cannot," he clipped out, though his eyes bored into hers. Then he turned his gaze toward the fire. "I assure you, your husband shall be a most acceptable fellow. One who will be well pleased to have you to wife."

Joanna forced down the lump that had risen in her throat. "Then he'd best be well pleased with a shrew for a wife, for mark my words, I shall make his life a hell!"

"So you say now. But I—But he shall tame you, Joanna. He shall direct your angry passion into another direction. Another passion. You are fair and a virgin, with a fine demesne attached to your hand. 'Tis all any man could hope for in a wife. And lest you think to escape me once more, be forewarned that King John will treat you no better. At least I will find you a young man of honor. King John . . ." He did not finish but only shrugged.

Joanna stood up abruptly. With her two hands on the table she leaned forward, her eyes flashing with fury. The blanket slid down forgotten. Her waist-length hair lifted about her face, the mahogany streaked golden in the firelight.

"You have not enough honor yourself to identify that virtue in another!" Her glare did not waver although her strident tone trembled. "You think you have stolen the march in this game of yours, but I shall prove you wrong. The time shall come when you will regret ever having used me so poorly."

10

The idea came from nowhere. At first she thought it too ludicrous to even consider. But as the hours passed Joanna slowly came to see it as her last hope.

Outside the storm still battered the island. The rain came down in unremitting sheets and the wind gusted loud and strong around the solid cottage. She could not judge the passage of time at all, save for the occasional need to replenish the fire, for the sun was well concealed by the menacing storm clouds.

In such a grim surrounding did she sit silently before the fire, idle but for the nervous combing of her fingers through her long hair. Given enough time, the hopeless tangles had eventually come free. But her predicament was a far knottier problem, one not nearly so amenable to solution. No matter how she addressed it, the results came out the same each time: she was condemned, due solely to the castle of her birth, Oxwich. She despised that place above any other spot on the earth. Her father might have revered it—other men might consider it a prize to fight over. For her, however, it was a source of misery and torment. Hadn't her mother's suffering been caused by her father's obsession with an heir to Oxwich?

Wasn't her own mistreatment now at the hands of the arrogant Lord Blaecston due to the selfsame castle?

She sneaked a sidelong glance at Rylan who sat across the room, seemingly lost in thought. Over and over his words echoed in her mind until she wanted to scream. The irony was, he considered what he had said of her a compliment of the highest order—she was fair, and an heiress, and a virgin. Any man would be pleased to wed such a paragon of womanly attributes!

She tossed a bit of broken straw into the fire as she pondered his words, then watched the strand writhe as if in agony, turning first red and then black. The fact was, she could do nothing to change her appearance—if indeed she truly would be considered fair. She would not be surprised if his words had only been aimed at appeasing her. But she *was* heiress to Oxwich. Despite her wish to be free of the place, she seemed perversely encumbered with it for good. Those two factors she was unable to alter. But her virginity . . .

In went another length of straw, and in its tortuous writhings Joanna fancied her soul tormented in hell by the devil. What she contemplated was unforgivable!

No, she amended. God forgave his children everything if they but repented sincerely the deed. She struggled mightily with her conscience. If she were not a virgin she would not be deemed a suitable bride, for most assuredly no arrogant nobleman of the sort Lord Blaecston planned for her would want her then.

Yet she would also no longer be pure for her veiling ceremony.

Overcome with too many conflicting emotions, Joanna closed her eyes and rubbed her fingers against her temples. She need not be a maiden to take her vows with the Gilbertines. That she well knew. But she'd always thought her pure state would make up for her many other shortcomings. But now . . . now she would not even have the *chance* to take her vows unless she deliberately committed that one vile sin.

Could this really be happening to her? she wondered dejectedly. Could she truly be faced with two such unacceptable choices?

The presence of the man across the room unfortunately deemed it true. She could allow him to ruin her maidenly state, or else find herself wed to some oaf of his choosing, and condemned to a lifetime with the clod. She only had to remember her mother's long-suffering silence—and her ultimate choice—to make up her mind.

Without daring to think beyond the immediate present, she stood up, determined to go through with it at once before she could change her mind.

"So, does this mean you're done with sulking?" Rylan stared at her with an expression she could only describe as antagonistic.

"'Tis not likely you'd deal with the ruination of your life very easily!" Joanna regretted her tart reply at once. If her plan were to work she must first get him to kiss her, and he was hardly likely to do that if she were a shrew. With a grimace she forced down her fury.

"Anyway, I was not sulking. I was simply searching my mind for some way out of—some way to avoid the marriage you propose. I want nothing to do with Oxwich Castle, and least of all to live in it."

"And did you find a way?" he prodded in a voice that was dark and smooth.

He was mocking her, she fumed. Yet there was more in that low, amused voice than merely that. Had she not known better, she might have imagined that he mocked himself as well.

"I . . . No," she amended, afraid to reveal her desperate plot through some innocent slip of the tongue.

"No. I did not think you would."

At those smug words her resolve to maintain a calm mien at all costs flew right out of her head.

"Despicable vermin! Black-hearted swine! You think you are so smart. Well, I hope King John finds you out and spoils all your terrible plans!"

He rose from his chair as if a fire sparked beneath him, and Joanna stepped back in alarm. It passed fleetingly through her mind that mention of King John ever goaded him to fury. Then, seeing the look in his midnight-dark stare, she realized that she may have solved her problem after all. Each time he'd kissed her before he'd been in a towering rage. Why should this time be any different?

"You shall someday thank me, and very well, for my terrible plan," he said with a growl when he halted only inches from her.

It took all her courage to raise her chin, stare up into his unsmiling face, and goad him even further.

"Believe what you will, fool."

She saw a glimmer of amusement in his eyes, and for a moment she feared she'd miscalculated his reaction.

"A fool? I think not." His gaze grew warmer then, and his amusement altered to another emotion, one that sent a thrill of fear and anticipation through her. "You but cling to a vain hope, my passionate little dove. For the truth is clear. You were meant to be held by a man. Shall I demonstrate that fact once more?"

Before she could respond, his lips captured hers as he drew her nearer. In the first heady moments of their kiss Joanna tried to keep a perspective on what was happening. He was kissing her, although with a recognizable amount of restraint. Next he would move his hands up and down her back, perhaps all the way down to her derriere, as he did before.

At the thought of him touching her there, she gasped in remembered passion. At once his kiss changed. As her warm breath mingled with his, as her lips softened and allowed him entrance, a low groan of desire escaped his mouth. His arms tightened as if in reflex, and she was suddenly crushed against the full length of him.

"So sweet . . . so fiery," he murmured between the bold kisses he pressed upon her. "Like heaven. . . ." His tongue plunged deep into her mouth, as if he sought the essence of her. Then one of his hands did indeed move down to cup her derriere, and he pressed her intimately against the masculine glory of his rising passion.

Joanna melted against him, forgetting everything but the delicious feelings he was rousing in her. Oxwich was forgotten. King John faded from memory. Most especially did any thoughts of St. Theresa's or the Gilbertine Order flee her mind. As he held her and caressed her, she knew nothing but him and the way he made her feel. Her arms found their way to circle his neck. Her hands filled with his long waving hair.

How could this one part of him be so silken and soft, she wondered fragmentedly, while in every other fashion he was so hard and demanding?

His seeking mouth moved down from her lips to kiss and taste along her jaw to her neck, then up to her ear.

"Ah, woman." He breathed the heated words against her sensitive ear. "You are like heaven. . . ." Then he grasped her shoulders and roughly pushed her away to hold her at arm's length. "Like heaven," he repeated in a rough whisper. "Or else hell."

Joanna's breath came in harsh gasps, and for a silent

moment she stared up at him. She was too overcome by her intense reaction to him to disguise her emotions.

"Rylan," she murmured, unaware how desire shimmered within her eyes. Her hands moved up to grip his taut wrists, and her thumbs slid back and forth in agitation against the smooth spot where his pulse beat. "Rylan—" She shook her head in confusion.

He closed his eyes against her artless appeal, and a tortured expression crossed his face. "Get away from me," he ordered harshly.

But he did not release his hold on her, and even if he had, Joanna could not have done as he asked. Her hands slid up his forearm, reveling in the warm strength there. Her entire body burned to rub against him that way—to feel his hard form and coarse hairs against her softer yielding flesh.

As if he read her very thoughts and felt her very desires, Rylan groaned once more. Then he dragged her against him, buried his hands in the luxurious length of her hair, and forced her head up to his.

This kiss was not like the other. There was no restraint this time, no trace of caution or even control. His hands held her still before him, tangling almost painfully in her hair as his mouth crushed down upon hers. His tongue invaded her mouth fiercely and he tilted her back until she was held off balance in his arms.

She should have been terrified by his furious display of passion, and on one level, perhaps, she was, for he was like a warrior at battle. When he lay siege, it was to conquer his foe, and he was most assuredly conquering her. Her overriding emotion, however, was not fear but an intense yearning. Above all else she desired more of this battle he waged with her.

She arched, pressing her belly against him and yielding her softness to him. His tongue probed deep, sliding boldly within her mouth and sending tremors of excitement through her. She felt as if a fever gripped her, as if he stoked a fire within her, and with every sensuous caress of his tongue against her sensitive inner lips, the fire burned hotter.

What had begun as a last effort to gain back her freedom became, in his passionate embrace, something entirely new. She was gripped by a desire that drowned out all reason. Freedom was not what Joanna strained toward as she met his angry dominance with her own caresses and kisses. She answered his demands with pliancy. She succumbed to his urgency with unabashed acceptance. In the process, something altogether new blossomed between them.

His ardor was no less intense, yet what began in frustration and anger turned steadily more seductive. As he gained control, however, Joanna's grasp of the moment slid away. One thing only reigned in her mind, and that was the wondrous panic that filled her. The higher he brought her, the more she wanted.

Her thin kirtle was less than nothing between them, for it slid along her skin in the most sensual manner imaginable. His clothing, however, was still an obstacle to what she desired most of all.

In a state of mindless pleasure she ran her arms up his chest until her fingers met at the center slit of his neckline. Warm curls tickled her fingertips, and she tugged at the interfering fabric. Rylan needed no words to understand her plea. With hardly a break in their kiss, he shrugged out of the offending garment then pulled her once more against him.

"Oh, yes," she murmured as her breasts flattened against the pressure of his chest.

He bit at her lower lip, tugging with his teeth, then soothing the spot with his tongue. "You are a torment." His hands roamed possessively over her back and down to her derriere. "A witch . . ." He pulled her up hard against him and brought her legs off the ground to wrap about his hips. "A temptation I should resist . . ."

Joanna held on as he lifted her higher and slid his kisses down her throat and chest to the cleft between her breasts. She burned everywhere for him. For his touch. For his kisses. For his possession.

He pressed the side of his face to the fullness of her breasts, then moved his knowing lips to the tight points of her nipples.

"You were meant to be loved," he murmured as he turned his attention from one of her breasts to the other, leaving a round wet spot in his wake. "To be loved well and often."

Joanna's head fell forward. Her curling mahogany tresses made a curtain about them as she kissed the crown of his gleaming hair. "Then love me," she whispered, hardly aware of her words. She squeezed as close to him as she could, wanting him everywhere. "Love me."

In response he lay her down on the nearest of the beds. His movements were no longer abrupt and forceful, but they were no less determined. Joanna fell back onto the thinly padded pallet, still holding onto his neck. But he placed one knee on the bed beside her and pulled a little back, disengaging her hands from his neck. His breathing came hard and fast.

"Shall we go on?" he asked her hoarsely. His gaze moved from her eyes to her slightly parted, well-kissed lips, then farther down the length of her reclining body. There was such heat, such passion and desire in his eyes that Joanna felt it as distinctly as a touch. The pure physical pleasure of it made her shiver and arch helplessly beneath him.

"Yes," she whispered as she met his eyes with her own passion-filled gaze. In that one dark waiting moment, as he poised above her, she was oblivious to anything but him. He filled her vision with his perfect masculine beauty. He surrounded her with his potent virility. He made her want nothing but him.

She raised one hand to his face and touched his chin lightly. One finger strayed to his lips, and with a low growl he took it between his teeth. His tongue toyed with the end of her finger, flicking over the neatly rounded nail. Then in an agonizingly slow move, he sucked her finger deeper into his mouth, all the while absorbing her with his soul-searching gaze.

It was more than Joanna could deal with. Forgotten were her reasons for tempting him—for seducing him. Her eyes fell closed and her breathing came faster and more shallow. She was burning with heat. She shivered from the cold. No, not the cold. Never the cold.

He released her finger and twined one of his hands with hers. With his other he slid the hem of her kirtle up her thigh to her hip. When his hand moved farther, to curve around her waist, then slide down over her hip bone to spread over her concave belly, her eyes opened in surprise. He seemed to know exactly where she ached most. First her breasts, now this yearning deep inside. Yet how could he know?

His expression was intent as he watched her reaction, and when she moved restlessly beneath his touch he smiled as if he were well pleased. Then he drew her hand to the top of his braies and held her fingers to the warm skin at his waist. He rubbed his hand upon her belly while he moved her hand against his, then smiled when her trembling fingers began to move in an answering rhythm. Of their own accord two of Joanna's fingers slid beneath the tied waistband of his braies and moved hesitantly along the smooth skin there. He groaned softly and his eyes closed as his hand stilled upon her stomach. Emboldened by his response, Joanna moved her fingers toward his navel, brushing the dark spear of hair that grew there. This time he clutched her waist tightly with both his hands, dragging her down a little on the bed.

"Damnation!" he breathed the word harshly. Before Joanna could understand, he pushed her kirtle up past her hips and waist. He paused only a moment as he stared at her naked legs and her triangle of mahogany curls. Then he pushed the garment higher until her arms were freed from it and she was entirely bared to his view.

Joanna lay beneath his avid gaze, caught between shame and exultation. She was naked. No one had seen her so since she was a child. Yet he stared at her as if he would drink her in with his eyes, and she gloried in it.

Then he brought her hands to the top of his braies and once more taught her what he wanted.

As Joanna fumbled with the tie at his waist, Rylan lifted two long locks of her hair. He pulled them taut down to her waist, then slowly crossed them so that the two locks pulled across the peaks of her breasts.

"Oh!" Joanna's eyes flew up to his and she dropped the ribbon tie in her hand. His eyes were hungry as they moved from her flushed face to the dusky rose tips of her nipples, then up once more to her face. He moved the locks of hair again, and Joanna's senses jumped at the caress.

Like dry tinder prime for the spark, she leaped into flame under his expert touch. He teased but the taut ends of her breasts, and yet she ignited deep in her belly. His caress was light as a feather's touch, yet the impact shook her to her very soul.

The fires of heaven, she thought as she sank down into those dark pleasures. She burned and yet she had most assuredly found heaven. In the mindless throes of burgeoning desire, she writhed beneath the pull of her own hair over her breasts and arched ever nearer the source of her delicious torment. Her hands clutched and found his forearms. His skin was damp, as if he too burned. But she had no time to wonder at that, for no sooner did she encircle his wrists than he twisted his hands and quickly caught her hands in his. In a silent—urgent—demand, he brought her fingers once more to the top of his braies.

This time there was no dropping the ties. Though her fingers trembled mightily, she unfastened the knot, all the while dissolving beneath his searing gaze. As the braies loosened, he caught her hands once more and pressed her open palms to his taut stomach, while with his other hand he drew his braies down past the knee propped on the bed, then down his other leg and foot, which still remained on the floor. When at last he was free of his confining clothes he covered her hands with both of his, then slowly drew them up his hard-muscled chest.

Joanna lay still beneath him, yet she was far from calm or placid. She dared not look at his newly bared skin—that private male part of him. She knew it was somehow meant to be a foil for her softer feminine core. And yet the earlier press of its aroused state to her belly proved it was entirely unlike any part of her. Instead she focused on the sensuous feel of his overwarm skin beneath her palms. The precise texture, the crisp hairs, the small nubs of his nipples, the urgent pounding of his heart: all these she reveled in and found infinitely exciting.

"By damn," he whispered breathlessly. Swiftly he forced her arms above her head, then stretched out his full length upon her.

Joanna gasped, nearly swooning with the pure physical fulfillment of his hard weight pressing down upon her.

"Kiss me," he murmured as he nuzzled her ear and throat. "Give me every sweetness. . . ."

She turned her face up to his at once, eager for the consuming pleasure of his mouth on hers. He would dominate her with his seeking lips and she would succumb. As always, however, they would both triumph.

Yet this time there was more than the press of his lips and the thrusting possession of his tongue. This time his entire body pressed sensuously to hers. His chest fitted against hers; his belly cleaved to hers; and their loins met in exquisite intimacy. Then his thigh shifted to part her legs and he nestled his jutting manhood against the dark warmth of her nether regions.

Joanna writhed in mindless anticipation. Somehow she knew this was the way it was meant to be between a man and a woman. Between them. When his tongue began its erotic exploration of her mouth, as she opened her lips to him, so did she open her legs to the heated prodding of his arousal.

"Rylan." She gasped faintly against his lips. He lifted his head, but only a little, and stared into her heavy-lidded eyes. Then he seemed to focus more clearly, and she saw reality dawn upon his face.

"Christ! What am I doing?" He started to pull back, but Joanna was too immersed in the pleasure of the moment to allow him to stop. Not now. Not when he'd barely begun.

She slipped her wrists free of his slackened grasp. With one hand she circled his neck, drawing him back into their kiss. Her other hand she slid down his sweat-slicked back, along the ridge of his spine and lower, to the crevice where his hard buttocks curved.

He groaned against her mouth, still fighting the seductive pull of her young and willing body.

"Rylan. Rylan," she murmured between the tentative incursions of her tongue between his lips.

He released a last groan and then capitulated. Like a starving man he came to the feast she offered, devouring her with his mouth even as he pressed into her moist warmth. He was steady but unrelenting, filling her with a completeness that both terrified and thrilled her. A brief tearing pain marred the perfect pleasure, but he caught her startled cry in his kiss. He pulled one of her knees up and settled fully within her. Then he paused and focused on their kiss.

With excruciating thoroughness he used his lips and tongue to bring her pleasure. He devoured her mouth, thrusting his tongue boldly within, then drawing her un-schooled tongue out in an answering boldness. It was a dance of curiosity and discovery, a dance as old as time and yet new once more. He kissed her chin, her cheeks, her eyes. He breathed into her ear and bit softly at her lips.

Joanna might happily have expired from the sheer pleasure of his intimate caresses. It was only her desire to taste him in the same manner that prevented her from succumbing to the faintness threatening to overwhelm her. She nuzzled his prickly chin, then dodged his seeking lips as they sought to capture hers once more. She wanted to taste his neck. She wanted to bite at that projection on his throat, the lodging of Adam's apple that women did not possess.

It was not prickly, she discovered as she moved small kisses down his throat. He swallowed hard as he submitted to her exploration, and she smiled as the apple bobbed against her lips. Then her smile turned to a gasp as he moved upon her.

"Oh!" She stared up at him, surprise evident in her widened eyes and startled expression.

"Ohhh . . ." she breathed as he moved once more in the same fashion. This time her eyes fell closed as the sultry pleasure of it washed over her. He moved so slightly within her and yet . . . and yet . . .

Oh, God, surely the whole of England shook with the power of that one little movement. He pushed within her and then pulled slightly away. He slid his hard, unfamiliar maleness inside her, then tormentingly drew it out. In a fit of panic that he might pull entirely away and she would lose the vibrant warmth he filled her with, she too raised her hips, trying to keep him near.

The resultant thrust of his manhood deep into her brought a cry of shattering pleasure to her lips, and he drank it in with a crushing kiss. Once more he moved over her and she swiftly recognized the pattern. In and out he slid, torturing her with the perfect pleasure he wrought so easily. His tongue moved with equal hunger in her mouth, and Joanna felt certain she would swoon. The fiery delight from his mouth. The fierce pleasure from down there. Together those two sensations lifted her entire being to a new level of awareness. Her senses were bombarded with too much, and yet she was intensely attuned to everything. The rain blew an erratic tattoo on the roof and windows. The fire popped and the bed groaned. His skin tasted salty. His mouth tasted like nothing else she could describe. And his body moving above her and within her was a feeling—an exquisite voluptuousness—she could never have guessed possible.

He increased his rhythm and lifted his head. As she began to pant, responding to the accelerating wealth of sensations growing in her, he kept his midnight eyes locked on hers.

He was swallowing her whole, she thought as his hard body moved repeatedly over hers. His gaze consumed her. His body possessed her. She was lost to him. Lost forever to him.

Then an incredible tightness started deep inside her and her wide eyes turned dark with passion. She clutched frantically at his sweat-slicked back and, as if he knew what she felt, he moved ever faster. She arched up in panic-driven desire, then cried out as something seemed to burst within her.

He stroked on and on, drawing out her intense reaction until it was almost painful. She was flying. She was falling. He lifted her up. He crushed her down. Then he too tensed and, with a cry of his own, spilled his warmth deep inside her.

In the ensuing minutes Joanna's awareness of her surroundings abandoned her completely. She was warm and she was replete. These two were all she knew, and she wondered if this was, perhaps, heaven: complete contentment and a sense of absolute security.

Rylan shifted, rolling to his side but keeping her close with one brawny arm about her waist. Her head rested on his shoulder near his chest, and his heart beat a reassuring rhythm in her ear.

Like the rhythm from before, she fancied, and something warm curled in her belly at the thought. That only increased her sense of contentment, and with a huge sigh she relaxed against him. Nothing else of the world existed at that moment. Not the past nor the future.

It was enough for her that this unexpected present simply was. With another exhausted sigh she smiled and fell asleep.

11

Joanna dreamed of angels and saints. Though she well knew the teachings of her church, there were, nonetheless, certain impressions from her childhood that she'd never quite lost. Angels were always female, though there might be men among the saints. Those men were old and bearded, however, while the angels were always young and fair.

But a new angel came to her this night. He was dark—and a man. His eyes were deep and fiery and his smile was so beautiful as to nearly blind her. He burned her with his touch, and yet she longed for that fire. He reached out a hand to her and she did not hesitate to take it. Then he lifted her up, making her giddy with the sensation of flying. Up in soft wafts of sunshine. Higher until the clouds kissed her cheeks and neck with the lightest of caresses.

He was taking her to heaven, this mysterious dark angel. He did not speak but he beckoned her with his eyes and that beautiful smile. Oh, yes, he would bring her to heaven had she but the courage to follow him.

Joanna pressed her cheek into the curve of his hand. She sighed and relaxed as he drew her nearer. She was warm and filled with a contentment she'd never before experienced. Once more she sighed, then smiled as she felt an answering sigh from her angel. His breath tickled her ear. His chest pressed warmly against her back. His arm rested comfortably across her side, and his hand gently curved around her own.

Joanna twined her fingers with his as she flitted back and forth between her dream and reality. She was filled in both with a delicious languor that was unlike anything else she knew.

A smile curved her lips and she moved restlessly against him, wanting even more of these wondrous feelings. She knew there was more; he had showed her once before. . . .

Her mind cleared when he moved their entwined hands down the front of her. His fingers and her own moved slowly along her naked length, stroking lightly but very deliberately in an erotic exploration.

A short gasp brought Joanna fully awake, but the simultaneous lurch in her belly drove all thoughts from her mind. Their knuckles brushed once and then again over her left breast. They moved then into the valley between her breasts and up and across the right one to lightly tease her already rigid nipple.

Joanna was breathless as he orchestrated the joined movement of their hands. She felt the sensuous caress along her skin, yet also felt herself with her own hands.

She did not feel at all like him, the wicked thought came to her. She was soft where he was hard. She was smooth where his skin was covered with those intriguingly curly hairs.

Down along her ribs he continued his quest, and she found the indentation of her navel and the gentle rise of her hip bones. Then along the taut skin of her belly they went, to where the first crisp curls of her private place began.

Joanna was trembling in his embrace. She felt the heavy thudding of his heart against her back; she recognized the thrusting heat of his arousal.

A part of her knew what they were about. She sensed reality and remembered everything that had brought her to this moment. But mostly she ignored that reality, for she did not want to deal with the repercussions. She wanted her dream and she wanted her dark angel.

And she wanted this never to stop.

Over the cushioned Venus mound he pushed their hands. She stroked her curls with a strange new awareness. Her skin was damp, she realized as their hands moved between her thighs. She was damp all over, sensitive wherever they touched, and filled with an anticipation that was so acute it approached pain.

Then one of his knuckles parted her downy curls and moved to the apex where all her desire seemed to be centered. She sucked in her breath and tightened her legs. It was too much to bear. Too right. Too perfect. But the angel of her dreams—the sweet devil of her reality— seemed to know that she nonetheless wanted more. He straightened his hand and hers and guided her fingers back to that same place. She felt the soft folds part and found the sensitive peak that both cried out for and shrank away from their touch.

"Oh, please." She moaned as he led her with soft pressure to slide across that aroused nub. "Oh, I cannot. . . . You cannot. . . ."

He did not counter her protests with words, for it was unnecessary. He had only to continue his seductive caress to send all thought of denial from her mind. Her fingers and his own moved with a languid rhythm upon her, seeming to touch her most secret and innermost self. Joanna pressed back against him. Her legs moved restlessly, rubbing against his as a fire seemed to erupt within her.

She was hardly aware when his fingers took over the task entirely. One of her hands clutched at his smooth flank while her other found his arm and hand that curved under her head. Her fingers tightened on his as her other hand rubbed frantically against his hip, unconsciously mirroring his fiery stroking of her.

Both heaven and hell, she thought as her body quivered in indescribable pleasure. Her dark angel brought her to both heaven and hell.

Then she ceased to think at all. Her nails pressed in passionate agitation into his thigh and she arched hard against his hand. And as if he knew precisely how she felt, his touch moved even faster until she was crying out with mindless passion.

It was happening again—that reckless madness, that final abandon. So consumed was she in the overpowering sensations he roused in her, she was not aware of his own arousal. But before she could find that summit of pleasure he'd shown her before, he suddenly pulled away and, with an almost violent jerk, rolled her beneath him.

His arousal pressed against her belly. As she arched up to him mindlessly pleading her desires, he let his weight come fully upon her.

"Damn you, Joanna," he panted hoarsely in her ear. "And damn me for a fool."

She opened her eyes at his self-directed words and his almost bitter tone. But what she saw sucked the very breath from her. His fierce gaze devoured her. His eyes burned with a fire so intense she thought to perish in their depths. Then, with a low growl, he raised up over her and, before she could respond, he came into her.

Joanna knew nothing of time nor place as he took possession of her. Day or night. The cruck cottage, Isle Sacré—even England itself. All of these disappeared and only he remained real. The feathering ends of his hair falling against her face were real. The damp rub of his thighs against her own was real. The exquisite stroke of his manhood deep within her. . . . These alone were her reality, and she rose to him gladly.

She hardly recalled their previous joining. Instinct was her only guide as she slid her hands up his straining arms to slide across his shoulders and then tangle in his hair.

He leaned back, changing the angle of his approach and striking an even deeper chord within her.

"Rylan—" She gasped and arched her belly and breasts higher.

One of his hands cupped her cheek, then gently smoothed a long curling strand of hair back from her face. In the dim room their gazes met and clung, even as he continued the sultry rhythm between them. His eyes were dark as midnight; hers were as clear as sea-green water. Despite the complete intimacy their bodies' shared, it was the utter possession in his eyes that seemed too personal. In an agony of confusion Joanna closed her eyes and turned her face into his hand. She kissed his palm with lips and teeth and tongue, tasting the hard calluses and smoother indentations.

"'Tis too late to be shy, my little dove," he murmured. He lowered himself to his elbows so that they were belly to belly and breast to breast. He forced her to face him and for an instant more their eyes clung. "'Tis too late for far too many things."

Then his lips slanted across hers with a ferocious intensity. Like the very center of a wild and violent storm he plundered her mouth even as he stroked deeper and harder within her. They surged and fell together. Like the tide crashing upon the shore, they met in a magnificent struggle. And like the tide they rose ever higher until in a crescendo of physical desire and emotional anguish they were both consumed within the very storm they made.

He fell upon her slick and spent, gasping for breath. Joanna clasped him to her, welcoming his weight, reveling in the crushing nearness of him.

It *was* too late, the words echoed faintly in her mind. Too late to undo what they had done. Too late to go back to being the innocent virgin of before.

Yet even as her hazy thoughts considered that fact, it was not her imminent return to the priory that was uppermost in her mind. Her planned loss of her innocence was forgotten, for he had long ago driven the last vestiges of logic from her head. It was not her loss of innocence but her gain of knowledge that made it too late for her. For no matter how long she lived, no matter how pious and holy a path she trod, this moment of completeness between them would never leave her.

It would never leave her.

A streak of watery sunshine crept across Joanna's face. Her eyelids twitched in protest. She turned her face away and searched sleepily for the warmth that had cradled her through the night. When she did not find it, she curled up and pulled the coarse coverlet over her head, vaguely disappointed but unwilling to come fully awake in order to discover why.

The fire popped and hissed in the hearth, but other

than that, there was no sound. No wind. No rain. Not even the rushing waves upon the shore.

So the storm was finally spent, she thought in groggy remembrance. At once her eyes opened as lucidity returned. The storm . . . The island . . . Memory rushed over her and in an instant she recalled every detail. Then a log was tossed upon the fire and she jerked in violent reaction.

"'Twas no dream," a low voice remarked.

At the bitter quality of his tone, Joanna's heart began to pound. It took all her courage to pull the scratchy blanket down enough for her to peer at him. His eyes were fixed on her, and for a moment there were no words. Then he turned away and thrust another log within the hearth. "'Twas no dream. Better that it had been."

Joanna lay as still as stone upon the narrow bed, but inside her emotions were in total chaos. He was dressed, she noted as she stared at his back. His hose, braies, chainse, and tunic were all in place while she lay completely bare beneath the solitary blanket. Clearly he had no problem dressing himself, the angry thought came to her. But Joanna's anger was by far the lesser of her emotions. She was mortified by what had passed between them in the night. She was horrified at her own wanton behavior and his wickedness. But most of all she was hurt by his terse words.

She blinked back unbidden tears as she heard them once again. Best that it had been a dream. Last night had been a wonder to her, a slice of heaven on earth. Yet he wished it never had happened.

She stifled a sob as anger rushed in to rescue her. He should indeed wish it a dream, for it seemed her plan had worked better than she could have guessed. She was no longer a virgin. Now his selfish plot was ruined.

Yet even her anger was no proof against the niggling doubt that plagued her. If it was only her desperate straits that had prompted her to lay with him so, why had she not left his bed when the deed was done? Why had she lain with him again? Why had she let him guide her hand so—

With a strangled cry of dismay she jerked the blanket over her head. Dear God, dear God! She was truly lost now! For the most wicked shiver snaked through her at that memory, and her heart began madly to pound.

Oh, forgive me, she tried to pray. *I repent. I accept the guilt and beg—*

The prayer broke off despite the depths of her desperation. Try as she might, Joanna could not honestly plead for forgiveness. Not when her body yet quivered with remembered desire.

"Sweet Mother, help me," she murmured over and over again. "Sweet Mother of God, please help me."

At her whispered words, Rylan's footsteps sounded on the floor. The sharp screech of moving furniture was followed by the unexpected slam of the door against the frame. In the silence that followed, Joanna could hardly bring herself to peek beyond the limits of the bed.

He was gone. The fire burned brightly, her clothes yet hung on the makeshift line, but he was gone. For a moment she was once more overwhelmed by the most inappropriate feelings of disappointment, but she determinedly beat them back. She should thank her good fortune for this chance to cover her nakedness with clothing. It mattered less than nothing whether he regretted what had passed between them. Indeed, she should be well pleased with his disgruntled reaction, for it only verified what she already knew. Her value as a wife had been lost in that one act, and he had been thwarted.

On that firm note she rose from the bed, clutching the blanket to her chest. Her legs shook as she stood. The muscles of her thighs—and elsewhere—quivered from their unusual exertions, but she tried hard to ignore that. She searched hastily for her kirtle, but when she found it on the bed and snatched it up, her eyes met a sight much harder to ignore. There on the sheet was the proof of her sin—the fresh streak of her virgin's blood.

With a sharp intake of breath she whirled away from the sight. It didn't matter, she told herself. It didn't matter at all. But as she pulled the kirtle on with stiff, jerky movements, she knew in her heart that it mattered very much. She had lost her innocence to this man. She was a woman at his hands and she was forever changed. No matter his manipulations or her own scheme, she was forever changed.

She sighed desolately, unable to pretend any longer to a triumph she did not feel. Consumed with weariness, she pulled her gray gown from the line and slowly donned it. She had neither shoes nor hose, nor even a *couvrechef* to restrain her riot of curls. Forlorn and more uncertain than ever, she approached the door and opened it to the new morning light.

Outside all was wet and beaten down. Leaves and broken branches from the birch trees littered the yard before the cottage. Beyond her, near a small shed a tall elm had been uprooted and lay at a crooked angle, caught in the fork of a sturdy oak. The island had taken a severe lashing from the storm, yet now as the sky brightened and the sun pierced the high clouds that trailed the storm, Joanna knew it would recover. The wind had fled;

the sea would subside. Soon no sign of the storm's impact would remain.

Only *she* was forever changed by yesterday's storm.

As she pondered that indisputable fact, Joanna saw a movement at the shed. Rylan appeared, leading his much calmer horse, then loosened the rope halter so that the animal might feed. Joanna watched the two from the shadows of the cottage doorway, unwilling to face him just yet. With the distance between them she was better able to be objective in her study of him.

He was in many ways a most remarkable man. He was tall, well formed, and had all his teeth. Any woman would be attracted to his distinctively virile aura. He was also ruthless and unswerving in his goals, and if his temper was any indication, he was no doubt possessed of a violent streak. Yet he had in his unique fashion shown her more tenderness than she'd ever experienced before.

She frowned at that aberrant thought and forced herself to recall his selfishness and his arrogance instead. And what of his taunting jibes, and the way he'd forced himself upon her—

Joanna broke off at that. Although he *had* forced himself upon her at first—that kiss in the woods, and then later in the cottage—it was nonetheless she who had pushed him further. She'd goaded him to it and then urged him on when he would have halted.

A violent shiver shook her and she abruptly whirled away from the sight of him. But the inside of the cottage provided her no solace, for the disheveled bed seemed to taunt her with her own wickedness. With a small cry of despair she turned once more and fled both cottage and man. There was no escape from the feelings that plagued her, but she ran just the same.

It was the sea that stopped her. She'd run between the

thick-growing birches, through the slippery grasses onto the sandy beach. Now she stood there as gentle waves lapped at her ankles and stared east to the rising sun. The sea was calm—almost eerily so considering how violently it had heaved just hours before. Now it lay in lavender and gold swells, its deep green a canvas for the sun's brilliant colors. The sky was an unearthly hue—mauve and coral with streaks of aqua as well. The wind was gentle on her face and beyond the shore seabirds dipped and flew, their cries at once both eager and mournful.

She pushed her hair behind her shoulders and lifted her face into the crisp morning breeze. Somewhere beyond the endless stretch of the German Sea were the Danes and the Vikings—all the northern invaders she'd heard tales of. Yet those bloodthirsty marauders did not frighten her nearly so much as did facing the man who must soon seek her out.

The wind pressed her skirt against her legs and lifted her hair lightly about her face once more. Sighing in resignation, Joanna turned back toward the island. She stopped abruptly, however, when she spied Rylan. He was standing just beyond the narrow strip of beach, watching her silently with his hands thrust into the band of his leather girdle.

For a long unbearable moment their eyes met and clung. Only when Joanna turned her face away from his probing stare did he speak.

"The tide recedes. We shall shortly cross to the mainland."

There was a pause, then Joanna lifted her eyes to him once more. "Then what? Shall you return me to St. Theresa's now that your plan is undone?"

It was his turn to look away. "We ride to Blaecston, as before. Nothing has changed."

"Nothing has changed?" Joanna looked at him incredulously. "How can you say nothing has changed?" She started across the beach, intending, in her fury and hurt, to pass him and make her way to the causeway to wait for the tide to change. But he anticipated her move and stopped her with one hand.

"Much has changed, Joanna. I'll grant you that. However, we still make our way to my castle."

"To what end?" she cried, trying unsuccessfully to shake off his disturbing touch.

"So that I may determine how best to deal with you!" he snapped in sudden anger. He grabbed her other arm and gave her an abrupt shake. "Do not test my patience today, woman. Do not goad me or suffer me your interminable arguments. We go to Blaecston and there is no more to be said!"

He released her then and stalked away in a fury. Joanna was too disconcerted to reply or react at all. Between his unexpected pronouncement and his unwarranted anger, she did not know what to think. Her arms curved around herself, and her hands found the places where he had grasped her so tightly. Though she wished to despise him anew for his callous disregard of her wishes, at that moment all she felt was complete loneliness.

12

The sun beat down on Joanna's bare head. On the lee side of the island there was no breeze whatsoever, and her skin soon grew damp with the summer heat. But she remained where she was, perched upon a rock that jutted up from the sand, unwilling to seek relief in the shade as she stared blindly across to the English mainland.

She could swim the distance, she knew, for the sea was exceedingly calm. Yet that would be pointless, for her black-hearted captor kept a wary eye upon her. His horse was now saddled for the ride, and though the animal rolled its eyes at the gently lapping water, Joanna had no doubt its master would force it to cross if need be. Rylan Kempe was most adept at forcing others to do as he willed.

She heard the animal stamp once, and the swish of its long tail. Then came Rylan's voice, low and reassuring, and her nerve endings seemed to buzz in response. Her lips tightened as memories of their shared passion threatened to overwhelm her. *Don't be a fool!* she silently rebuked herself. The horse he gentled now meant far more to him than she did. She was only a means to an end for him, and she'd best keep that in mind. When he was hungry, he ate. When thirsty, he drank. When he was weary, he slept. And when he longed for a woman, he took one.

Yet that was not entirely true, and Joanna's innate honesty would not allow her to find comfort in such anger. She'd consciously enticed him, hoping—knowing —where it would lead. Her bare toes dug into the fine-grained sand and she shifted on the uncomfortable rock. He would have stopped had she but let him. Her fall from grace was by her own choice. She could not blame him for that.

But she could blame him for everything else, she decided spitefully as she caught his movement from the side of her eye. As he approached her, leaving his horse tethered to a fallen tree, she kept her eyes turned firmly toward the sea.

"We shall cross shortly," he began matter-of-factly. When she did not reply, his feet shifted slightly, making a scratchy sound in the wet sand. "You can ride in front of me as before."

"I'd rather walk," she spit out through clenched teeth.

"No doubt you would at the moment. But Blaecston is near ten leagues distance, and I would make haste—"

"And I would rather *not* make haste," she interrupted, turning an icily polite face toward him. "Of course, I do not expect you to consider my wishes. You have not done so up to now."

His face was stony. "Not your wishes, no. But I have ever had your well-being uppermost in my mind."

"Indeed. And how is my well-being served by what has happened? I am rudely severed from the life I want, to be thrust into a dreaded union with a man I do not know—nor care to know—" Her voice shook with sudden emotion. "And now I am ruined," she finished in a whisper.

Joanna stared once more toward the sea, blinking back the unwelcome tears that stung her eyes. Beside her she heard Rylan shift once more.

"All is not lost," he finally said rather gruffly. "If you would only—"

Joanna stood up, unable to listen to any more of his selfish reasoning. "All *is* lost, only you are too single-minded to recognize it. I am no longer the virgin your bridegroom seeks." She lifted her chin and took a deep breath, but still she could not look at him. "The causeway is nearly cleared. Shall we depart and see your game played out to its end?"

The silence that followed nearly broke her resolve to remain aloof and uncowed by him. She was trembling so hard she thought she might collapse when he let out a muttered oath.

"By the cross but I wish—" The rest was lost to her as he strode angrily to fetch his horse. She did not follow his progress with her eyes, but she was conscious of his every move.

When the horse and rider moved back to her side, she marched nearer the sea, gathering her skirts up in her arms as the gentle waves lapped at her ankles.

"You shall ride with me," he ordered, clearly impatient with her determined obstinance. When she only waded farther out on the shallow causeway, his temper snapped.

"Christ and bedamned, but I am truly accursed!" Then before she could evade him, he was beside her. With one easy movement, he snatched her up and planted her forcibly in front of him.

Joanna recognized the futility of struggle. But she was

wholly unable to make things easier for him. With a furious cry she twisted about in his arms, kicking and flailing until his horse half reared in fright and she nearly fell backward over his arm.

"Be still, woman!" he roared, clasping her tight with one arm as he fought to control his skittish destrier with the other. Then, before she could gain her balance to renew her fight, he kicked the high-strung animal into a full gallop across the watery passage to the far shore.

Joanna was certain she would fall and be trampled by the plunging beast. Through knee-deep water the animal charged as she clung frantically to Rylan's arm. When he jerked her hard against him she did not protest, and when his two arms finally circled her she leaned back against the security of his broad chest. One of his hands snaked around her waist, settling her bottom between his thighs. His harsh breath came in her ear.

"Gentleness holds no sway with you, does it, my little dove?" he muttered, turning his attention back to her now that he had mastered his horse. "You must be forced at every turn. Forced to acquiesce." His lips found her ear and he bit at the tip of her lobe almost painfully. "Forced to kiss before you relent."

Joanna's stomach tightened and her heart's pace doubled at his taunting words. In truth, she'd not had to be forced very hard. Even now her entire being leaped at his clever caress. She leaned forward to escape the seductive play of his mouth, but he leaned forward as well, and the horse responded by increasing its speed. She clung to the horse's mane as Rylan clung to her. Beneath her thighs she felt the mighty strength of the horse. But elsewhere was the heated press of Rylan's body. At her back, along her legs. Against her derriere. Tears stung her eyes and her hair flew behind them both like a pennant in the wind. But there was no escaping his touch nor the truth of his words. He pushed and she resisted. He pressed on and she fought back. But let him only force her a little further and she surrendered, and in her surrender found a form of glory.

Oh, but it was not glory. No, never that. What she had found in his arms had been a sin. The pleasure had been there, she could not deny it. But it was nonetheless sinful so long as it occurred outside the vows of marriage. Since she did not wish to marry anyone—and he clearly did not intend to marry *her*—the sin was more blatant than ever.

Her motivation had at least been pure, she reminded herself. Yet the man who held her so close seemed perversely unaffected by her clever plan. She'd been so certain that the loss of her virginity would destroy his selfish plot. But he seemed as ready as ever to proceed. Was he a complete madman?

She swiftly wiped away her tears with one hand while clinging to the horse's mane with the other. She was without any sort of plan as the destrier's long strides carried them nearer and nearer the mainland. When they galloped up onto the hard-packed shore, she only knew that she must continue to struggle against Rylan Kempe no matter what happened. No matter how weary she became or frustrated or downcast, she must never relent. To go along with his fiendish plot was to give herself up forever, and she would never do that. Never.

Rylan straightened in the saddle as he brought the big horse to a stiff-legged halt. But he kept his arm wrapped possessively around her, pulling her upright against him as well.

"Shall you be more cooperative now?" he asked in a low voice tinged with arrogance.

Though Joanna flinched at the silky resonance near her ear, she forced herself to remain calm. "Do not count upon it," she replied in her most contemptuous tone. "I shall be polite, if you so demand. I'll even cook your meals and mend your stockings—after all, I *am* a paragon of wifely virtue." Then she turned a scathing look upon him. "But cooperate in this mad scheme of yours? Hah! If I must trumpet my . . . my impure state to the entire world, so be it—"

"Don't be a little fool! That will gain you naught!" His dark eyes bored into hers across the span of mere inches.

Joanna's eyes darkened as well under his intense scrutiny and for a moment her resolve faltered. Though his eyes glittered now with anger, the heat within them was not unlike the passion she'd seen in them before. Then, even as she watched, she saw his eyes deepen almost to black and a fire leap somewhere within them.

His face lowered and for the space of two heartbeats her mind closed against all the reasons she must avoid his descending mouth. But before their lips could meet he groaned and swiftly pulled back. Before she could prevent it, a small gasp of disappointment escaped her.

As faint as it was, Joanna knew at once he'd heard the sound. His gaze moved from her eyes to her lips and then back again. Stifling a groan of dismay, she quickly averted her face, but she knew the damage was done. Despite her resolve she'd come perilously close to kissing him, and she knew only too well where that could lead.

The destrier pawed at the ground with one forefoot then tossed its head twice, pulling Rylan against Joanna. She heard a muttered curse. Then with a flick of Rylan's wrist the horse wheeled about and they started south down the beach.

"This is the wrong way," Joanna could not help but cry. She knew he had no intention to return her to St. Theresa's, but this southerly route suddenly seemed so final. "The wrong way," she repeated in a voice that threatened to fail her.

Rylan did not respond. He only sat behind her, hard and stiff, never yielding an inch as the destrier's long strides put more and more distance between her and the only home she knew.

They rode without stopping until well past noontide. The sun beat heavily upon them and the countryside fairly steamed as the soaked earth slowly dried out. They followed the coast until in the distance the smoke from numerous hearths signaled a village ahead. Again, without a word to her, Rylan guided the horse up a shallow outfall of water. The animal picked its way carefully up the beck, through a wet grassland, and then up onto a barely discernible track that followed the course of the water.

It was cooler in the shade of the towering beeches that lined the beck, and Joanna felt an undeniable relief. Between the hot summer sun and the uncomfortable warmth radiating from Rylan's body pressed up against hers, she was damp with perspiration. Still, she could take little delight from the cool forest. With every stride, with every change of scenery she was being dragged ever farther from St. Theresa's. With every passing minute he drew her relentlessly toward a future she refused to accept.

"I'm tired. And thirsty," she bit out as the horse splashed across a shallow span of water toward a clearer trail on the far bank.

"We'll stop soon," he replied, urging the horse on.

"There's no reason not to stop here," she persisted. But when she tried to twist loose from his arms, he tightened his grasp.

"Do not provoke me, Joanna," he growled in her ear. "We shall stop soon enough, when that village is sufficiently behind us. Until then I caution you to be quiet. And don't squirm," he added in an oddly strained tone.

Joanna, however, did not dwell on his tone. She was too uncomfortable herself to be concerned with his comfort. "I am parched from the heat and numb from sitting so long." Once more she wriggled, trying to ease the prickly numbness in her derriere.

"Christ and bedamned!" he exploded. In a trifling moment he hauled the horse to a stop, then abruptly slid backward over the animal's rump. Joanna gazed down at him in surprise, unable to fathom his sudden change of heart. Then just as quickly she realized that she was on the horse without him. Escape was within her reach. Her hand stole swiftly to the slackened reins but Rylan, unfortunately, was not so distracted as to overlook what she was doing. With a quick tug at her nearest ankle he threw her off balance. As she toppled from the high saddle, he caught her with an arm around her back and one beneath her knees.

"What ho, my peaceful little dove. Could it be you plot such violence as to abscond with my favorite steed?" He smirked at her and gave her a little toss so that she gasped and clutched at his neck. "But you would not do that, would you?"

"I would see you in hell—" Joanna broke off her blasphemous words and tried to wriggle free. But Rylan held her closer until she could hardly breathe. His face, however, was devoid of any humor, and his gaze burned hot as he stared at her.

"'Tis just such squirming I warned you of. Unless you would provoke me to—"

It was his turn to break off, but Joanna understood his meaning at once. Her eyes widened in consternation as she realized just *how* she provoked him.

His lips lifted in a parody of a smile. "I see you understand. Good. Now, have your drink of water," he said as he stood her upright. But before he released her he held her firm, frowning as all the while a muscle moved in his cheek. "I warn you not to attempt to escape me again, Joanna. I am only a man, and as such am subject to the failings of all men." Then with a meaningful look, he let loose her arms, turned on his heel, and stalked away from her.

Joanna was sorely perplexed as she stooped beside the sparkling beck and splashed the refreshing water onto her arms and neck. It was not Rylan's words that confused her, for she feared she knew precisely what he meant. Rather, it was her own perverse reaction that troubled her. He threatened her with his virile domination and instead of fear coiling in her stomach, it was something else entirely. Her heart pounded, her mouth was dry, and the fine hairs on her neck lifted. Yet it was not fear or anger that caused those responses. It was anticipation that had her atremble, and a fitful yearning that was wholly improper.

Joanna brought a palmful of water to cool her face and brow, although the heat that disturbed her most was not centered there. Once again she was beset by the unwelcome memory of their hours together in that cottage. That holy place!

She bit down on her lower lip to still its trembling

then sternly blinked back her shameful tears. She, who had been so proud, was now truly brought low. Only by sincere prayer and honest repentance could she ever redeem herself.

And yet honest repentance eluded her most unfairly. During their endless morning ride she'd tried vainly to pray for forgiveness, but always she'd been undone by the remembered feel of his hands on her. Of his body pressing down upon hers. Of the exquisite way he'd taken—

Joanna let out a short strangled cry. When Rylan turned a sharp glance on her, she quickly splashed another handful of water on her face, unmindful that she wet her long trailing hair and the bodice of her gown. She drank deeply of the refreshing water, then drank again. Anything to avoid facing the man who now rose from getting his own drink. When he straightened up, still watching her, she averted her face, letting her hair fall like a curtain between them.

"Let us be on our way. Come, I'll help you to mount."

Though Joanna wished more than anything to avoid rejoining him upon his destrier, as she sent a desperate glance around the dense woodland, she knew escape was out of the question. Yet as she moved reluctantly nearer him, she could not prevent a last stab at reasoning with him.

"I don't understand what you seek to gain by abducting me this way." She stopped just beyond the reach of his arms and gave him an accusing stare. "My value as a bride is lost." Her face colored but she went on. "There is nothing for it but to release me."

He stared at her steadily though his face was devoid of all emotion. "Your value as a bride is not so lost as you might think. And as for releasing you . . ." He smiled faintly, then looked down at the twig he held in his hand. "I'm afraid I cannot do that, milady. Honor demands—"

"Oh! Do not speak to me of honor when you have already proven yourself without the least honor whatsoever!" She sent him a withering glare then stood straighter and lifted her chin to a haughty angle. "Let us be on our way, Lord Black Heart!"

She marched past him to the horse, ignoring the animal's startled sidestep and flattened ears. "Come along then," she said sarcastically, still glowering at her beastly captor.

"Watch out—" In an instant he yanked her to him and out of reach of the horse's bared teeth.

"Let me go, you horrid man!"

"If I released you every time you demanded it, you would be lost, drowned, or else trampled by now," he muttered as he continued to hold her before him. " 'Tis clear you need someone to keep you sound of limb."

"Well, it certainly isn't you!" she cried furiously. "Before you made your unwelcome entrance into my life I had no need to fear any threats to my limbs!"

"No, of course not. You were such a meek and mild little dove that you had nothing to fear from anyone, or so you choose to believe. However, you have proven yourself to be more falcon than dove." He jerked her against him. "More sinner than saint."

"Oh!" Joanna gasped in sharp denial and shoved at his chest in outrage. " 'Tis you who are sinful and . . . and wicked—"

Her feeble tirade against him was halted by the sudden crashing thunder of hooves. She hardly had time to think before Rylan yanked his sword out and thrust her toward the still-skittish horse. But they had no time to mount. Even had they managed to get on the destrier,

they would still have been trapped, for a group of uni-
formed riders swept into the little clearing and in an
instant they were surrounded.

"What ho!" one man said with a gloating leer. "You
sport black, white, and red, the colors of Blaecston.
Name yourselves."

Joanna's heart thundered in fear. These men clearly
had the upper hand, and though they recognized Rylan's
colors, they seemed very little impressed by them. But
Rylan seemed equally unimpressed by the unfavorable
odds. Joanna felt the tension in his arm, but his voice
was cool and low.

"You sport the colors of John Lackland. Shall you
name yourself as well?"

The other riders darted glances toward their leader as
they awaited his answer to such a fearless response. But
though the fellow's eyes narrowed, he held any anger
well in check.

"Bless my soul, but if it ain't Lord Blaecston hisself.
And as unwise with his quick tongue as ever." He leaned
back in his saddle and smirked. "What do you so far
from home with no guard but only this wench?" Then
he gave a bawdy wink. "'E likely don't share with 'is own
men. But 'e'll share with us, I warrant you that."

He moved as if to dismount, but Rylan's menacingly
raised sword point slowed him.

"Touch her and you'll lose the hand that does the
deed."

There was an ugly silence. Joanna was suddenly sickened as she realized the man's intent. She clung to Rylan's arm as if it were her only salvation even as she
recognized the hopelessness of their circumstances. But
Rylan was clearly not resigned to their situation.

"You will have to kill me to get to her, and though you

think now there would be none to know, it will not take long for the truth to be out. Your king will hardly thank you when the wrath of his barons comes down hard upon him for the murder of one of their own. He will be forced by them to mete out a harsh punishment in order to assuage their fury." He gave the now-silent soldiers a faint, icy smile. "I suggest you all think on just who among you shall take the blame before you raise weapons against a lord of the realm."

The nervous shifting of several men in their saddles gave mute testimony to the effectiveness of his words, and Joanna felt a tiny glimmer of hope. But the captain of the group was reluctant to back down so easily.

"King John may not hold with killin' one o' his lords —no matter that the bloke speaks treason—but I wager 'e'll not bother hisself about a little sport with a comely maid such as this one."

"Try it and I vow it shall be the last act of your life," Rylan stated without inflection.

"Damnation, but it ain't like she's a noblewoman," the captain snapped in frustration. Then his gaze focused more closely on Joanna, taking in her plain priory garb. His eyes narrowed. "Who are you, girl? Give me your name."

Joanna glanced uneasily from the captain to Rylan. She felt Rylan grow even more tense, but she realized her true identity was the only protection she had. If she convinced them she was a noblewoman, they would not dare touch her.

"I am Joanna. Lady Joanna Preston."

The captain let out a loud burst of laughter at that announcement. "Lady Joanna of Oxwich? By God, what a stroke of good fortune!" At once he dismounted and swept her a wide bow. At her look of surprise he straightened. "King John sends 'is greetings and bids you join 'is court. We were on our way to St. Theresa's Priory to fetch you when we came upon you here."

Her instant relief was quickly replaced by cold anger. "You planned to rape me," she accused, sending him a furious glare now that her fears on that score had been somewhat eased.

"I . . . uh . . . If I'd known who you were . . ." He trailed off awkwardly.

Joanna's pulse still raced from the fright he'd given her, but she realized that they would not dare to harm her now. The king himself requested her presence.

Yet that knowledge brought her no particular comfort either. She looked up at Rylan's taut expression, then back at the captain. What a choice! Go with Rylan or with the king's men when both of them plotted the same unwelcome future for her. Or did they? Rylan planned to wed her to some stranger, but she realized that she could not be so sure of the king. She had only Rylan's word that King John plotted the same for her, but Rylan could just have been trying to scare her. Besides, the king would have to listen to reason when she explained that she was no longer a maiden.

She swallowed hard at that thought, then took a fortifying breath. "You will take me to the king?" she asked the captain.

"Don't do it," Rylan muttered. His grip tightened painfully on her arm.

Seeing how things lay, the captain pressed his advantage. "Unhand her, Blaecston. The king would not judge me harshly were I to skewer you on this lady's behalf."

As if on cue, the mounted riders drew their weapons. In the quiet glade the sound was sinister indeed. "Fact is," the man went on, "even if you turn 'er over to us willingly, who's to say that you didn't force our hand?"

In the chilling silence following that threat, Joanna's voice sounded thin and very young.

"I, for one."

Though she trembled with fear, this time it was not for herself. She had no reason to come to Rylan's aid. By anyone's logic he deserved whatever the scowling king's guard wished to mete out to him. Yet her reaction did not look to logic for its source. She would not see blood let on her account. Not Rylan's or anyone else's.

She felt Rylan's eyes on her, but she kept her gaze trained on the perplexed captain.

"Now, milady, this don't—"

"I mean what I say, Sir . . . Sir . . ." She gave him a meaningful look and he glanced away.

"Sir Peyton," he muttered.

"Sir Peyton. Yes, well, I will accompany you to court. However, I'm sure I would hear should anything befall Sir Rylan, and I'll make sure the other barons know who is responsible." Sensing that she'd won her battle of wills with Sir Peyton, she once more tried to pull away from Rylan's tight grip on her arm.

For a long moment he did not release her. She glanced up at him, wanting to be disdainful and triumphant, to flaunt her victory over him and gloat over his failed plan. But as her eyes met his, those emotions faded away. For that one endless moment she was filled only with regret. His eyes were dark. From anger or frustration or defeat, she could not tell, for of a sudden her eyes swam with ridiculous tears.

She felt his fingers slacken, and she pulled free of him. Turning away, she faced the captain, but in her mind's eye she still saw Rylan, tall and powerful, sword at the ready, face dark and fierce.

She was swiftly put on a horse with a lead rein to another soldier's mount. Then with a minimum of delay, they were off at a fast pace, leaving Rylan far behind. But though she rode away from him, Joanna could not leave behind the image of the man who had been both ruthless captor and masterful lover to her. She compressed her lips tightly as she clung to the hard saddle. He had come into her life without warning and was gone in the same abrupt manner. But she knew she would never be able to cast his memory entirely away.

13

Both horse and rider were in a lather when they crested the low hill that provided the first view of Blaecston Castle. But knowing his destination was so close at hand did not cause Rylan to slacken his pace. Rather, the proximity of his home spurred him to new haste.

All during the four-hour ride he'd been beset alternately by fury and frustration. He'd been so near to ensuring Yorkshire's solidity against the king. That, coupled with his own marriage to Sir Egbert Crosley's heir, would have struck England's fool of a king a harsh blow indeed. But now the Lady Joanna had fallen into the king's clutches. To make things even worse, he'd compromised the girl. Honor demanded that he make things right by marrying her. But that would ruin his own marriage plans—and political ones as well.

Not that the king would let Joanna marry him—not with Oxwich as the prize. At least King John did not know about his agreement with Sir Egbert. But the king's ignorance on that point brought no real ease to Rylan's mind. Joanna was still in the man's clutches because *he* had been so careless.

He thundered down the muddy track, unmindful of

the shepherds who waved at their lord's passing, then scratched their heads at his tearing pace. Rylan had one thought only on his mind, and that was to collect a contingent of his best men and make haste to the royal court now set up in Ely. He could salvage nothing by remaining at Blaecston. Indeed, he might very well gain no better by making straight for John's corrupt court either. But he had to try. Joanna would be no more than a pawn in the king's foul clutches, and although she'd been little more than that in his own care, he consoled himself with the thought that he, at least, had meant to see her happily settled.

But that self-serving logic did not sit as comfortably with him now as it had when he'd first conceived his plan. As he made his way up the hard-packed road that rose to his looming fortress, he was uncomfortably aware that she'd fought him every step of the way. She had not wanted marriage nor the home of her birth. But he'd nonetheless tried to force them both upon her.

He'd forced himself upon her as well.

"Christ and bedamned!" he muttered. Then he barreled across the narrow drawbridge and pulled his destrier to a clattering halt in the stony forecourt. In a trifling he flung himself down from the heaving animal and tossed the reins to a wide-eyed stableboy.

"Summon the captain of the guard," he barked to the first man who scurried up. "Prepare another horse and set out a meal. And ale," he added as he strode furiously toward the great hall.

The seneschal sat at a table poring over a parchment listing of the Blaecston holdings—arpents and chains, cropland and pasture—muttering to himself. When the lord of the demesne strode in unexpectedly, however, he leaped up from his seat, a ready welcome on his lips. But his quick smile of greeting faded when he spied Rylan's black expression.

"My . . . my lord. You are found. We had word that you were missing."

"Is Kell here?" Rylan snapped as he flung his dusty leather gloves on the broad tabletop.

"He yet directs the search for you, milord. He came here but briefly and then left with more men."

"Have him found. And all the others as well. Damn," he swore impatiently. "Everything conspires against me. Had it not been for that storm—"

He broke off his muttering as a serving girl hurried in with an ewer of ale in one hand and a heavy mug in the other. Rylan poured a full mug and quickly quaffed the cool refreshing liquid. He dismissed the girl with a heavy sigh, pulled out a high-backed chair, and lowered his weary frame into it. He filled the mug again, then finally looked over at the waiting seneschal.

"I travel to the king's court, Peter, with a full complement of men. If Kell appears before dawn he shall accompany me. If not—" He rubbed his sweaty brow. "If not then he can follow later, for I cannot wait on him. See to the horses and other supplies, will you. I'll need a small box of coins and whatever trappings you deem necessary for a visit to court."

"How long shall you be in London?"

Once more Rylan sighed. He stared into the cool depths of his ale, not really seeing the dark liquid or pale foam. "The king moves to Ely, so I am told. And as for how long, that is hard to say. Till my goal is met . . . or else truly lost." He took another long pull of the ale and in the silence Peter began to edge away, assuming he was dismissed. But Rylan came out of his dark thoughts.

"One other thing, Peter. Be sure each man is well

armed." He did not explain further despite the seneschal's clearly startled face. Indeed, after Peter left, Rylan was not sure himself what use a well-armed following
would be to him in the midst of the royal court. Again he
lifted the mug and downed the potent drink. Using force
to steal Joanna from under the king's nose would be
ludicrous and might cost him the support of the barons
he had worked so hard to gain. Besides that, it would be
nearly impossible to achieve. Yet as he thought about
Lady Joanna of Oxwich, he was consumed with a blind
need to get her back at any cost.

With a vicious curse he slammed one clenched fist
down on the solid table, unmindful of the pain it caused
him. How could a mere woman have ruined his plans so
easily? Yet to term her a mere woman was a disservice,
he realized. For she was unlike any woman he'd dealt
with before. He'd been surprised by everything having
to do with her from the first moment he'd laid eyes on
the Lady Joanna Preston.

She was supposed to have been a plain, unappealing
girl who would be eternally grateful for being rescued
from a boring life as a nun. She should have embraced
his idea wholeheartedly and willingly done her duty to
Oxwich and England by marrying as he dictated she
should. Yet from the first she'd been determined to
thwart him. She rejected his plan to find her a suitable
husband, refused to leave St. Theresa's, and had gone
so far as to laugh when he pointed out her duties to
her.

But worst of all, she was exquisitely beautiful.

Even in her unflattering gray gown, her fairness had
been undeniable, and then on the island with her hair
loose upon her shoulders like a magnificent bronze cape,

and clad only in her kirtle, she had inspired an all-consuming desire in him.

"Sweet Jesu," he muttered as blood rushed to his loins at the memory. He was a twice-damned fool to yet feel such a powerful desire for her soft womanly form. Wasn't it just such a reckless passion that had brought him to this pass? If he'd had his wits about him, she would never have escaped him in the first place. But his thinking had been clouded by the strong ache centered in his braies. Then, when he'd thought to keep some distance from her, she'd turned it to her advantage and escaped. Once the damage had been done and they'd been trapped together, she'd turned that to her advantage as well.

He exhaled noisily, willing away the taut arousal caused by the memory of Joanna. *Remember what a willful and devious little witch she is,* he told himself. He was unable to generate the anger he wanted, however, for overriding both his anger and the physical longing he felt was another even more unwelcome emotion.

Guilt.

Just three days ago she'd been an innocent maiden, content with her life and anticipating taking up the veil in the service of the Lord. Now she was without the home she desired—and without her maidenhead as well. At court she would be parlayed as a prize to win her king the most useful political union possible. Despite her loss of virginity, Rylan knew there were those men who would gladly overlook that single flaw in her in return for the freedom of access to her delectable young body.

His jaw tensed in fury at the thought, and he leaped so abruptly from his chair that it tumbled backward. John would not prevail in this, he vowed. If he himself must coerce every man who owed him—or feared him—he would find a way to stymie the king. He would see her settled as best he could no matter what happened.

It was the least he could do.

Joanna's legs buckled beneath her when she slid down from the cream-colored palfrey she'd ridden for so long. Had she not grabbed at the saddle, she might have collapsed in a heap. And in front of all these staring faces.

Yet at the moment Joanna did not care a fig for the round-eyed stares she was receiving. A bed was all she craved. A bath and a bed. As she clung trembling to the saddle, waiting for the aged maid who accompanied her to come, she almost laughed at the irony of it all. How long had she struggled at St. Theresa's to rid herself of her pride—to no avail, it often had seemed. Only now, when she was brought so unexpectedly to the court of King John and Queen Isabel, was she finally free of that cursed pride. She did not care what anyone saw, nor what they thought of her. Just give her a bed and leave her alone, and she would be content.

The bailey of the abbey at Ely was alive with people and fairly buzzing with talk as she was finally assisted by a sturdy young maid. It was someone new, she realized as she stumbled beside the girl. The old maid whose services had been purchased at Market Weighton had been needed for the three-day journey to Ely. A necessity for a noblewoman traveling among men. Likewise, so had the traveling cloak and rough clogs been obtained. She was now a ward of the king, she'd been told by Sir Peyton. It would not do for her to arrive at court with bare head and bare feet.

Not that she looked so grand even with those additions to her wardrobe. Even through her exhaustion Joanna could see that the people at court were dressed in a fashion far beyond her experience in recent years. Fine fabrics. Beautiful colors. She'd seen such goods used for altar cloths and bishop's robes, and she vaguely recalled her mother's fine gowns and tunics. But these were even finer, with jewels added, and furs and braided trims—a dazzling sight indeed. Or it would have been under differing circumstances. Now, however, the only thought that occurred to her at the sight of such a luxurious display was that if the clothes were fine, the beds must be as well. Fine linen sheets. A soft, overstuffed mattress . . .

"Take her to the ladies' quarters. She looks nigh on to dropping. A bath and a bed. Put her in with the new girl."

Joanna was too tired to even search out the source of that self-assured voice. She only trailed the maid up three steps and into a covered passageway. Like a sleepwalker she stumbled along until they reached a little solar where several women sat at their stitching and gossip.

"Milady Marilyn," the maid began with a swift curtsey. "Herself says I am to put Lady Joanna in with you."

A slender dark-haired girl rose from a large cushion on the floor, laying aside a hand tapestry frame and needle. She was dressed in an exquisite gown of rose pink Tavestocke with purfle, and adorned at the tightly back-laced waist and Magyar sleeve wrists with woven leather and silver bands. Her hair was loose upon her shoulders and, judging from her hesitant manner and shy greeting, Joanna thought her to be quite young.

"Lady Joanna." The girl curtsied slightly then gave the maid an imploring glance. "Would you have a bath prepared? In the antechamber, I think. If you will lay out a change of clothes for her, I'll help her with her bath."

The maid shifted from one foot to the other. "She came without any baggage," she said, glancing askance at Joanna, as if she doubted any true lady could travel without trunks and bags of clothing.

"No baggage?" The three other women in the solar had been listening to the conversation with the normal amount of curiosity. But when the maid revealed that the newcomer traveled without any baggage, they leaned nearer in undisguised interest.

"No baggage," a generously endowed blonde repeated. "Was she robbed?"

"I wouldn't know, milady," the maid answered earnestly.

Joanna straightened her posture. They spoke about her as if she were not even there. As if she were some new oddity with no mind nor will of her own.

"I was not robbed," she replied. Then her lips quirked in a self-mocking smile. "At least not as you imply."

Lady Marilyn hurried forward and took Joanna's arm. "Come along. 'Tis plain to see you are in sore need of your rest."

Then before the other women could protest and ply Joanna with further questions, she drew Joanna away from the solar and into a small chamber lit only from a narrow window set high in the stonework wall. Lady Marilyn called after the maid to bring the hard soap, not the soft, then closed the door. Joanna had slumped against a sturdy trunk and stared about rather blankly.

"Are you all right?" Marilyn ventured hesitantly as she peered at her curious guest.

Joanna sighed. "No, I am not all right, but that is not of your doing."

"A bath, a meal, and a good night's rest shall surely help—" Marilyn broke off as her new charge abruptly stood up and untied her cap. Joanna pushed her hood back and drew off the cloak. Then she stepped out of the ill-fitting wooden clogs.

As Joanna shook her tangled hair out and flexed her cramped toes, she too took stock of her new companion. Lady Marilyn appeared perhaps sixteen and painfully shy. She was rather petite with a figure in its first flowering. Her hair was dark and thick, falling in a heavy straight mass down her back. Her skin was pale—almost to an unearthly degree—and her eyes were an unusual shade of blue, almost green. Altogether quite comely. That is, she would be if she smiled. But the girl seemed so timid—her manner was so hesitant and her voice so subdued—that her good features were practically unnoticeable.

As the two of them stood there gazing uneasily at each other, Joanna realized that it was the younger girl who was clearly the more nervous of them both. That knowledge softened Joanna's taut features. Here was one person, at least, who would not bully her.

"I'm Joanna Preston." She pushed the thick length of her hair behind her shoulders and gave the girl a sincere smile. "I'm sorry you've been burdened with me."

"Oh, I don't mind," the girl said with a shy smile of her own. "I'm Marilyn Crosley. And I'm happy to share my chamber with you," she added when she saw Joanna's gaze move tentatively about the small space.

"Is this your home?"

Lady Marilyn's smile faded. "No. That is, not really. I've only been attached to the court since the Feast of St. Mark. My home is Lawton Castle near St. Albans." Her eyes touched upon Joanna's plain gray gown. "Where is your home?"

Joanna hesitated a moment, torn between giving the girl the answer she expected or one that would shock her and provide the very sort of gossip those other three women in the solar had sought. In the end she compromised. "I am born of Oxwich Castle. But these past several years since my mother's death I have resided at St. Theresa's Priory. At Flamborough Head."

"Oh." Lady Marilyn nodded. Then she pursed her lips and eyed Joanna more closely. "You shall wear a gown of mine—after you sleep, of course."

"That is most kind of you," Joanna replied. "But I cannot presume to use your clothes. I have this gown."

"It will not do," Marilyn retorted with what Joanna suspected was a rare streak of will. "But never mind that. Let us be off to your bath. Tomorrow we will decide on the rest."

Later Joanna could not recall much of what followed. She was bathed in a private antechamber before a small fire. The water was warm and fragrant—a luxury beyond describing. Her gown was taken away, but she did not notice for her arms and back were being scrubbed with a rough cloth, and her hair was being soaped with a delightfully sudsing soap. She might have succumbed to sleep right then and there, so relaxing were Marilyn's ministrations. But she was prompted to stand and was rinsed and then dried before being wrapped in a loose cloak. Down the hall once more she was guided, then her hair was combed free of any tangles and braided still wet into two plaits. In a fog she lay back on one of the beds, and after that she knew nothing. Marilyn came and went. A regally beautiful woman accompanied by two others looked in on her but did not stay. The evening progressed through the supper feasting and entertainments, then into quiet as the court sought its beds. Through the long night Joanna lay almost like one near death, still and unmoving, lost to sleep. The abbey bells rang compline, matins, and lauds, but she did not hear. Only when the morning chimes of prime pealed forth did she stir at all.

Her first conscious thought as she struggled up from the depths of her long sleep was that her bed was exceedingly soft. She was not at home, for the small walled chamber at Oxwich would not have sunlight streaming in.

Oxwich! Joanna's mind cleared at the thought of that place. Oxwich was not her home; St. Theresa's was. And this was not St. Theresa's either!

She sat up abruptly and stared around her. She was at Ely, she remembered. Sharing a chamber with a girl named Marilyn. At the moment, however, she was alone.

But then, she was well and truly alone now, and not just for the moment. No family. Not even the sisters from the priory. She was cast upon the whims of fate— no, upon the whims of the king. And all because of Oxwich.

Once again, as had been happening with more and more frequency, her thoughts veered to that hated castle. Oxwich—the bane of her existence. Oxwich—unhappy home of her youth. Oxwich—the cause of her current dilemma. Damn that place for the devil's abode it was!

Upset and frustrated, Joanna flung back the bed linens, then grimaced when she realized she was completely naked. At St. Theresa's they were instructed to sleep with their kirtles on, but she remembered now that most people did not wear clothing to bed. As a child at Oxwich she'd not done so either.

"Christ and bedamned!" she swore as once more she was reminded of Oxwich. But the words had no sooner left her lips than she recalled another even more troubling memory. Sir Rylan Kempe, Lord of Blaecston—Lord Black Heart—swore just so. How could she succumb to his bad habits?

But then, she knew she'd succumbed to more than merely his foul habit of taking the Lord's name in vain. As if to emphasize that fact, her body tingled with remembered passion. She looked down in dismay to see her nipples grow small and taut, and deep in her nether regions she felt a heated flutter.

A strangled cry escaped her lips and she searched the room wildly for her garments. When they were not to be found, she yanked a sheet from the bed and wound it haphazardly around herself. What was she to do now? she wondered despairingly. She was in a strange place with neither friends nor allies to turn to. And she was without any clothing!

At that very moment, as if she were a guardian angel sent to soothe Joanna's fears, Marilyn pushed open the heavy oak door and sidled into the room. Her arms were filled, as were the arms of the maid who followed her.

"Oh, you're awake." She smiled at Joanna as she gladly let the high stack of folded fabrics down on her own bed. "Put the tray on the window ledge," she instructed the maid. Then she turned to Joanna with a small expectant smile.

"The queen has sent all manner of gowns and tunics for your use," she announced with a sparkle in her eyes. "She said you are to break your fast and then dress so that you may be properly presented to her and the king."

Joanna swallowed hard as her despair deepened even further. "The . . . the king?" she stammered. "And the queen?"

"The queen especially has taken an interest in your situation."

"But—" Joanna shook her head in confusion. "But why? All I wish is to be returned to the priory."

At that the glow faded from Marilyn's face. Despite her own anguish, Joanna realized just how lovely the girl had been when she was animated. Marilyn signaled the maid to leave. Only when the door was closed did she turn a serious mien toward Joanna.

"I have learned some of your story during the long hours you rested, and I want you to know that I sympathize with your plight. Truly I do. But you must realize that when property must go through a daughter instead of a son, her choice may not be considered. Her father— oh, I am sorry. I know you have only recently lost your parent. But that is why the king has stepped in so quickly. You are now his ward and, as such, subject to his will." Then her voice became even gentler when she saw Joanna's downcast features. "I know this must be very difficult for you to accept. You've suffered so many losses in the recent weeks. But you must trust King John to do what is best for you."

"And you?" Joanna questioned bitterly. "Do you trust him to do what is best for you?"

"Oh. Well." Marilyn colored slightly. "My situation is somewhat different than your own."

"No doubt you have brothers to assume the transfer of your family's properties."

"No. No, I am my father's only child. But he, and not the king, shall choose my husband."

The sudden tremble and hesitance in Marilyn's voice registered in spite of Joanna's own misery. "Then why are you here at court?"

Marilyn took a shaky breath then began slowly to unfold the various garments she'd brought in. "The king would like to influence my father in his decision for me," she said as she shook out a lovely aqua gown made of the softest linen. "At King John's request I serve as a lady-in-waiting to Queen Isabel—as you undoubtedly will also—while the matter of my husband is discussed."

"Oh." Joanna stared at the pale girl as sympathy for Marilyn overwhelmed her own sense of desperation. "You do not yet know who the man shall be?"

Marilyn shook her head. "My father has been away from court these several weeks past, and that has angered the king, who would have me wed his distant cousin, Robert of Short. The king is annoyed, I can tell. But my father sends word that he shall visit me here. So . . ." She shrugged and forced a wan smile. "Perhaps I shall soon know."

Joanna frowned. She knew that she could not so complacently accept such a fate. And yet, what precisely could Marilyn do to avoid it? More to the point, what could *she* do to avoid the king's plans for her?

She clasped the sheet tighter around her chest as she searched her mind for any solution to her terrible situation. In the end, however, she realized that she could do nothing, at least not at the moment. Until she knew the king's disposition in the matter of Oxwich Castle, she would do best to tread lightly and wait. Heaving a sigh, Joanna looked resolutely at the solemn Marilyn.

"If there's no help for it, then I suppose I should break my fast and be off to greet the king."

Marilyn was clearly relieved by Joanna's practical response. As she raised up a fine Bissyn kirtle for Joanna's inspection then helped her don the wondrously soft garment, Joanna tried to take heart. What would be would be. Perhaps all was not so lost as it appeared. After all, Rylan might have been lying to her about the king in an attempt to discourage her escape. King John might happily take possession of Oxwich and send her back to St. Theresa's as she wished. And even if he were not immediately so inclined, once she revealed her unsuitability as a wife—

Joanna had to clench her jaw at the sudden tightness in her throat. Her unsuitability! Why was it that a woman was considered unsuitable but a man never was? No doubt Sir Rylan Kempe had bedded many a woman in the same fashion he had bedded her.

She trembled as the aqua gown was pulled down over her head, and Marilyn peered at her curiously.

"Are you cold?" She touched the back of her hand to Joanna's brow. "You've not become ill due to your journey, have you?"

Joanna swallowed hard then pulled the thick length of her hair out from the neckline of the gown. "I'm still a little weary, is all. And hungry." To dissuade Marilyn's concerned observance, Joanna reached for a white flour pastry from the tray and a small handful of raisins. Though her stomach was in a nervous knot and rebelled at the thought of food, she bravely forced it down.

"Good. Now here are a pair of summer stockings and indoor slippers. This ribbon will look lovely in your hair. Just let me pull two locks back from your brow . . ."

Joanna stood still while Marilyn fussed over her hair, tightened the side lacings of her gown, and settled a simply braided leather girdle upon her hips. Her mother had worn just such a girdle, Joanna recalled, though it had dangled keys on the trailing ends—the keys to Oxwich.

Once more she frowned as she was reminded of that loathsome place.

"Are you not pleased?" Marilyn exclaimed in a pained voice.

"What? Oh." Joanna buried her feelings and stared back at her reflection in the polished metal mirror Marilyn held before her. Her own face stared back at her, pale and serious, and for the first time Joanna really studied herself. There were no mirrors at St. Theresa's. The priory was too poor a place for such frivolities. Besides, Sister Edithe discouraged vanity among the women. But there was window glass in the chapel, and when cleaning the glass under certain conditions, a reflection could be seen. Likewise, the silver serving trays used for feast days provided some idea of one's visage. But this was the first time Joanna had been encouraged to examine her own appearance in a device made for that precise purpose.

Her hair was excessively curly, more so than anyone else she'd ever seen. But then, she'd known that. But she now saw that the waist-length curling tendrils sprang from a brow wide and unblemished. Her eyebrows were the same light mahogany color as her hair, but straight with only the faintest arch to them. Thick lashes framed her eyes, which were a clear shade of green. Her mouth was full, and staring at her lips she could not help but remember how sensitive they had been to the caress of Rylan's lips and tongue.

An unwelcome shiver coiled up from her belly. With a scowl she turned away from the mirrored steel.

"I'm ready," she muttered, not caring any longer about Marilyn's artful arrangement of her hair. What need had she to care for her appearance? It was not as if she sought a husband. Quite the contrary. "I'm ready," she repeated. "But I'd rather wear my own clothing."

"The queen sent your old tunic and kirtle to the seamstresses. She said they were to find some poor soul in need . . ."

Joanna did not reply to that. She could not. Somehow everything seemed so final. So decided. She'd not yet had her audience with the king, yet her fate seemed already settled.

Marilyn was silent after that. Joanna knew the other girl's situation was hardly better than her own: a father was no more likely to solicit his daughter's opinion than a king. Not when property was involved. But Joanna was not able to accept her fate so easily as Marilyn did. As they walked quietly down the hallway, then across an open yard to a covered portico, Joanna alternated between defiance and pure terror. First her father. Then Rylan Kempe. Now King John held her future at his whim. Neither of the first two men had considered her wishes. She did not hold out much hope that this third one would either.

But this time she at least had one weapon in her meager arsenal. She did not really wish to announce the loss of her purity, and she had decided to do so only if there seemed no other way. But if she must tarnish her reputation in order to protect herself, then so be it. She had fought her father. She had fought Lord Blaecston. If need be she would fight the king himself.

14

"They could have easily rid me of him. But no, they had to choose caution that day! The rogue yet remains free to torment me endlessly."

King John paced his privy chamber, his hands fluttering in agitation. Even his beard seemed to quiver with anger.

"'Twould have caused you all manner of trouble had a man of his rank been cut down by the king's men," the queen commented, never looking up from the fish-scale file she used on a jagged edge of her thumbnail.

"And who was to know or spread the tale?" the graying king snapped.

Isabel raised her dark eyes to her husband. She spoke patiently and without anger, as if to a peevish child. "For one thing, there are the guards themselves. *You* may trust them to keep such information secret, but I do not. It takes but one drunken braggart to speak his part in the deed and the wrath of the barons would come fully against you." She raised her nails for inspection, then when they met with her approval, tossed the fish scale into an embroidered basket. "There was also the girl.

You cannot forget that she would have been witness to such a deed as well."

"That fool Peyton could have sent someone back to do Blaecston in. She might never have known. And as for that, she is of no real value to me either. Oxwich is mine whether she lives or not."

At last Isabel's emotions flared. "Your complete lack of finesse will prove your undoing, mark my words. Killing Kempe or even the girl is no proper solution!" She took an angry breath and glared at him, but at his sullen expression, she relented. "There are ways and there are ways of dealing with the problem of Sir Rylan Kempe. He need not die to best serve your purposes."

"Serve my purposes? Hah!" the king fumed. "He is ever there to say me nay. To sway the barons against me. To pester me with his treasonous notions. And they *are* treason! 'Tis my divine right to rule England—not the right of that bloody crowd of barons!"

"Of course it is, my love," Isabel soothed. "But dealing harshly with him—having him killed—would only stir up the hornet's nest to an even angrier pitch. Far better to play with him, to torment him before the eyes of the entire court."

John's brows raised slightly and he ceased his endless pacing. "Isabel?" His petulant expression was slowly replaced by a crafty smile. "What deviousness do you plot in that beautiful head of yours?" He strode over to her and tilted her face up with one finger beneath her chin. "Come now, tell me all."

Isabel smiled, letting her full curving lips slide over her straight white teeth. "You have stolen Blaecston's little jewel. He must have hoped to marry her himself— the treasured centerpiece of his Yorkshire crown. He is not likely to stay long away from court if you flaunt her here. Added to that, she is a fair chit, and will attract many an eye. As her guardian, you must be very selective about a husband for her." Her smile grew wider. "Poor Blaecston shall be beside himself with frustration. For once you will have the means to torment him. To make him look the fool."

"I am not certain he meant to marry her. My spies have placed him in the company of Lord Santling and Lord Lawton—both men with only daughters and with considerably more property than the Preston girl."

Isabel shrugged. "Even if he meant to wed her to an ally of his own, it does not signify. He wanted her but *we* have her. That is sufficient to paint him the buffoon."

"But what if he does not come to court?"

"Trust me, milord. He shall come."

John thought on that. Then his eyes narrowed as he took in his wife's youthful appearance. "You seem to understand him very well, my dear."

Isabel laughed, a soft delighted tinkle. She took John's hand in hers and squeezed it as she stood up. "I do understand him," she murmured silkily. "Just as I understand you—as I understand all men. For a woman to wield power, that sort of understanding is a necessity. Sir Rylan has his pride. Your possession of Lady Joanna Preston has dented that pride, and he is desperate now to undo the damage. But desperation makes men reckless. We have only to play to that recklessness."

John stared at his queen—the child bride he'd flouted all political wisdom to possess. Were she not so devoted to him—or at least to his kingship—he would be dismayed at her brilliance. But she was his wife, and as he went so did she.

He cupped her face in his hands and planted a satisfied kiss on her unblemished brow.

"I trust you will take my new ward in hand, then. Outfit her suitably so that she will attract a following, especially among the men who mislike Blaecston and his ways."

"As you wish," Isabel answered, the picture of wifely duty and obedience.

"What of the other girl—Egbert Crosley's daughter?" John asked as the queen moved to depart. "I will not want our courtship of her father to suffer for the games we play with Kempe. Her lands are of even greater moment than Oxwich."

"'Tis already well in hand, my lord. I had Lady Joanna put into the Lady Marilyn's care. Our shy little mouse is even now playing mother to our little nun." She laughed once more and sent him a sparkling smile. "Suddenly our stay at this dull abbey looks promising indeed!"

Court was a dreadful bore. Joanna had been inordinately worried when she'd first followed Lady Marilyn into the queen's solar. There she had met several of the ladies-in-waiting as well as three matrons. She'd been kindly enough received by them all, but once her reticence had been noticed, the group had gone on as before, stitching and sharing idle chatter, only now and again breaking into giggles over some amusing bit of gossip.

She had sat nervously, awaiting she knew not what. But the time had crept by with no break in the monotonous routine, and now Joanna could contain her fidgeting no longer. "Shall the king ever come?" she whispered impatiently to Marilyn.

"The king?" Marilyn looked up from her handwork. "The king never enters the ladies' chambers. 'Tis the queen we await."

"Oh." Joanna pursed her lips. "But you said I was to be presented to the king."

Marilyn smiled in understanding, and once more Joanna noticed how pretty she could be. "I forgot how new all of this is to you. Poor dear, the royal court is terribly confusing. I remember how awkward I was. Even now I am ill at ease more often than not." She colored slightly, as if that admission did not come easily, and Joanna reached for her hand. Despite her misgivings at being thrust into the royal court, Joanna was certain she had at least one friend in the Lady Marilyn.

Marilyn smiled once more. "You shall soon get the rhythm of it. Whether the court is in London or travels about—as is more common—certain things remain the same. One approaches the king only at his command or at the express invitation of his first circle."

"His first circle?"

"His closest advisors. That is, the queen, his treasurer, Sir William of Ely, and his justiciar, Geoffrey Fitz Peter. We await the queen, whom we shall escort into the king's presence. She will tell you when to approach the king."

Joanna digested that for a moment. "I shall meet him among the company of others, then. Will I have no opportunity to speak privately with him?"

Marilyn's eyes widened in surprise. "Why would you *ever* wish to speak privately with him?" Then, when she realized the other women in the solar had paused at her shocked tone, she lowered her voice. "Why ever should you wish to do such a thing?"

Joanna stared intently at Marilyn, wondering how closely she should guard her words. When she noticed the curious glances she was receiving from the others, however, she squelched her need to confide in someone. Another time, perhaps, but not now.

"You have a father to decide your fate—a man who knows you well and whom you know well. But I must rely upon the king in the matter of my own future. I only thought it practical that he and I share some limited discourse on the matter."

Marilyn nodded at the logic in Joanna's words, yet her face still reflected doubt. "I would be completely unable to utter a word should he request a private audience with me, and under no circumstances would I request it myself." She stared at Joanna, a trace of wonder in her eyes. "You must be very brave."

Joanna only smiled. Not brave, she thought as they returned to their stitching. Not brave, just desperate.

A few minutes later there was a commotion in the hall. The door flew open and two footmen dressed in the purple and silver of royal service immediately flanked the door. A stern-faced matron entered the solar next, but Joanna's attention was drawn to the woman who followed her.

Queen Isabel was everything Joanna expected and more. As a child she'd heard of King John's beautiful bride, but the serene, elegant woman who smiled and nodded to the women all standing attendance on her was exquisite beyond imagining. No wonder the king had risked angering the powerful Lusignan family by taking Isabel of Angoulême to wife. No wonder all of France had been so furious to lose her.

For all Joanna's cynicism toward the holy state of matrimony and the limitations it placed on women, she could not help but be caught up in the sheer romance of it all. King John had risked much to wed this woman, and she looked supremely satisfied with the arrangement. If only it were always thus.

The queen waved one hand negligently, sending her women back to their sundry tasks, but her quick gaze swept the room, and when she spied Joanna she paused. "Lady Marilyn. Do bring your charge into my presence. I would speak with her awhile."

Marilyn gave Joanna's arm a quick tug before Joanna reacted. For a moment she felt a shiver of apprehension. The queen was as beautiful as any woman could hope to be. Yet she was still the queen and bound to seek her husband's best interest. The fact that she was a woman did not ensure she would be an ally. As Joanna approached Isabel, she bade herself keep that thought in mind.

"Good morrow, my queen," Marilyn murmured with a deep curtsey. After only the briefest hesitation Joanna followed suit. She was determined to do nothing that might appear the least improper while she curried royal favor. Though she was ignorant of court etiquette, she vowed to watch and learn so that no one could fault her manners.

"Good morrow, my queen," she echoed Marilyn's words softly.

The queen peered at her. Though her expression was pleasant—her face was fixed in a smile—her close scrutiny seemed more than a little assessing, as if she looked beyond Joanna's face to examine her innermost thoughts. Joanna swallowed nervously and clenched her hands together at her waist in an effort to still their trembling.

"You are quite lovely. Just as I thought you would be. Did I not guess well when I selected the dress? The size.

The length. The color for your complexion and eyes. Here, turn." She gestured with her hand.

Joanna did as she was told. Her eyes caught briefly with Marilyn's as she pivoted, but that one's face was carefully blank. When Joanna faced the queen once more, Isabel was smiling almost smugly.

"Who would have guessed such a bedraggled creature as you were but yesterday could be transformed into such a beauteous maiden?" She glanced over at her ladies-in-waiting who were all silently observing the queen and the new girl. "It makes one wonder how unpleasant might oneself appear without the benefit of fine garments, rich jewels, and the many beauty aids available."

At once there was a murmur of protest from the other women in the chamber.

"You would be fair, no matter what."

"Threadbare rags could never dim your luster, madame."

"Nothing could disguise your beauty, my queen."

Joanna marked well the queen's smile of pleasure. If that was the lay of the land, so be it. She would be meek and agreeable. She would flatter and fawn if that was necessary to gain the queen's goodwill. Anything so long as the queen—and consequently the king—looked with favor upon her request to return to St. Theresa's.

Having appraised herself of the newest girl's suitability, the queen began to circulate about the solar, granting a smile and brief comment to each of her ladies-in-waiting. She then seated herself on a richly upholstered chair and looked over her entourage with a speculative gaze.

"We shall seek the king's company shortly. I would have Matilda attend me. And Adele." Her polished nails drummed idly on the arm of her chair. Then she turned her gemlike gaze on Joanna. "You also, Lady Joanna. The king needs reminding of his duty to his newest ward."

Rylan strode down the wide stairs of the house he had taken in Ely. In the yard Kell stood with two horses. He was dressed for court, yet well armed with daggers in both boots and a short formal sword sheathed at his girdle.

"She is there," the Norseman informed his lord as he handed over the reins to Rylan's mount.

"I never doubted she would be." Rylan mounted without further comment, but his expression was grim and his shoulders were hunched tightly. Although he told himself it was ever thus when he confronted his careless and ineffectual king, he could not deny to himself that this time he was more tightly wrought than ever. Up to now he'd been the one to frustrate John—to prick his pride and thwart his devious plans. And it should have been so this time as well. His secret betrothal to Lady Marilyn Crosley would send John into a fit of apoplexy, and he should have been relishing that event enormously.

But his pleasure at such a coup was completely dampened, and all due to one slender young maiden.

No, it was not solely her doing. He who prided himself on anticipating and preparing for every possibility had sorely misjudged her reaction to being abducted. He'd considered the king's opposition but never hers. Now he was paying for his oversight. His jaw clenched convulsively as he realized once more the pleasure John would take in his predicament. He would no doubt taunt him unmercifully with Joanna's presence at court.

Still, there was some small consolation, he decided.

Joanna was sure to try the king's patience as completely as she had tested his own. Unfortunately, the king was not one to long tolerate obstinance.

As they cantered out of the yard, followed by two squires and four men-at-arms, Rylan knew that he would be the only one to stand between Joanna's willfulness and the king's temper. Whether she liked it or not, he was her only ally at court.

There was no conversation as they rode the scant mile to Ely Abbey. Rylan scanned the place with narrowed eyes, scrutinizing it closely in the event he be required to beat a hasty exit. The abbey at Ely was a vast complex. Under an earlier series of bishops the abbey had built a chapel, dormitories, and the few requisite buildings. But the abbey had grown considerably since then. Cathedral, refectory, bake house, brew house, millhouse, and more gardens, fishponds, and accommodations for visitors of all ranks. The encircling walls had grown ever wider, like the series of rings in one of the ancient oaks that marked the entry gate. But despite the accommodating walls, the abbey sprawled beyond them, hemmed in only by the bustling town that had grown up beside it.

King John and his vast entourage required just such expansive living accommodations. The court had not been to Ely in three years. No doubt John would stay as long as the bishop's storehouses could provide the generous feasting a king's presence demanded. Rylan grimaced to himself. The people of Ely most certainly faced a lean winter this year.

The two squires tended the horses once the party dismounted. The men-at-arms, knowing their duty, melted into the bustling activity in the abbey. They were to keep their eyes open and their wits about them. Rylan brought only Kell with him to the bishop's great parlor.

While he did not discount the king's treachery, he understood John well enough to know that today at least he would want to gloat. The king would want every baron and noble in the land to know of his victory over Lord Blaecston in the matter of Oxwich Castle and the Lady Joanna Preston.

"Blaecston!" A surprised voice called out to him as he strode across a marble-floored antechamber. "By the rood, man. Hardly thought to see you at court."

Rylan paused to greet Sir Guillaume of Reislip, conscious that the man's booming voice had caused several heads to turn in his direction. As the murmurs quickly began, he knew he was well and truly announced. The quick scurrying of Sir George Gaines into the hall beyond guaranteed that the king would very soon hear of his presence as well.

"Good to see you, Reislip," Rylan answered, not betraying his thoughts by even a wry twist of the lips. He took the hand Sir Guillaume offered then gestured to his silent companion. "May I present Kell Farstad."

Sir Guillaume's eyes widened at the sight of the towering Norseman, and Rylan had to stifle another grin. Kell usually struck most people that way. His excessive height and apparent strength coupled with his perpetual reserve were enough to give any reasonable person second thoughts.

But he'd not frightened Joanna, the aberrant thought came. She'd discovered Kell's one weakness right away —his overpowering fear of water. And she'd used it to her advantage.

Had she since guessed his own weakness—his disturbing weakness for her? Rylan wondered distractedly. A tug at his sleeve brought his attention back to the effusive Sir Guillaume.

"The king's been in a mood," the man whispered confidentially. "You presence here ain't likely to appease him much."

Rylan observed the frank curiosity on Sir Guillaume's face, then glanced around to see several other barons drifting his way.

"I'd like to believe that," he murmured more to himself than to Guillaume. "However, I would not be surprised if for once the king is most pleased to entertain me at court."

There was no time for anyone to question or even wonder at Rylan's words, for a sudden commotion was raised at the entrance to the bishop's parlor. People fell back to make way even as others leaned closer to see. But Rylan did not have to see to know who approached. The king was too anxious to flaunt his victory—his possession of Lady Joanna—to wait even the time it took for Rylan to reach the bishop's parlor. He came now to taunt Rylan, to reveal to everyone who now held the upper hand. Though Rylan had expected no less and had prepared himself for the public humiliation the king would force, he nonetheless did not like it. Though he was flanked by Sir Guillaume and Kell, he did not acknowledge either of them. He only clenched his jaw and steeled himself for what was sure to come.

But even Rylan's self-control was not proof against the sight that met his eyes. He was right that John himself had created the stir in his haste to confront him. But he had not expected Joanna to be at his side.

A part of him knew he should not be surprised, yet he felt the impact of her presence as profoundly as a blow to his stomach. She was more beautiful than he recalled —slender, elegant, with her hair long and flowing down the back of her gown as was appropriate for a maiden.

For one insane moment he recalled how that luxurious length of hair had appeared against the pale skin of her bare breasts. But he immediately choked back that memory. She was on John Lackland's arm now, not his. And if he were to change that fact, he must keep his wits about him. But he nevertheless rebelled at the very idea. King John had no right to clutch her arm so! Nor to draw her nearer with his beringed hand! It did not matter that she was legally a ward of the court now. She belonged only to him—

That mad thought sobered Rylan's fury at once.

She did not belong to him—nor did he want her to. Yet the distinct tautness in his loins made it very difficult to accept that truth. He wanted her wed to a trusted Yorkshire lord. That was what he'd wanted from the beginning, and what he wanted now, he told himself. Yet he could not deny that their time together on Isle Sacré had sorely tested his intentions.

Even now he was torn by the conflicting requirements of duty and honor, of political gain and morality.

Around him murmurs of curiosity began. People shifted for a better view of the king and the unknown beauty on his arm. But Rylan was oblivious to all. Although the king plainly sought out his adversary in the sea of faces, Rylan did not notice.

He saw only Joanna.

She was pale and clearly frightened by the strange surroundings and crush of people. Yet she was lovely beyond his every memory. Beyond all imagining.

"Christ and bedamned," he swore softly—viciously. She was here because of his reckless fascination for her. Had he but kept his wits about him instead of becoming distracted by her innocent beauty, they would both now be safely ensconced at Blaecston Castle, safe from the king's machinations.

Then her darting gaze moved past him and swiftly returned, to lock firmly with his own. Her surprise at his appearance was obvious. But after that was it relief he saw flare? Or was it fury?

He did not have time to determine an answer, for at the same moment the king also spied him. With a smug smile John halted his progress, then patted Joanna's hand, drawing her attention away from Rylan.

"I see Blaecston is here," the king remarked with studied nonchalance to the man at his elbow. His voice was just loud enough to carry throughout the hushed crowd in the antechamber. "Do invite him to join us at the noon meal, Sir George." Then he turned with regal confidence and headed back into the bishop's parlor, his grasp firm on Lady Joanna's arm.

Joanna was in a state of shock as she paraded beside the king back into the chamber they'd exited only moments previously. Rylan was here!

In the past hour since she'd been in the king's presence, she'd felt herself more an object of barter than ever before. The king had scrutinized her as a horse buyer might, and smiled at the queen as if to convey his pride in a bargain well made. Joanna's courage had been sorely tested, and her only defense had been to close her feelings off, to retreat into a shell of frozen emotions. But at her first unexpected sight of Rylan, her heart had leapt with joy. He had come for her, she had thought with enormous relief.

But now she was beset by a far less pleasant thought. If he was here in the lair of his avowed foe, it could only be for one reason. He had come to redeem whatever he could of his foiled plot. She'd ruined his scheme to marry her to a baron friendly to his cause. But he clearly hoped somehow to undo the damage. Could he actually expect to abduct her once more, and from beneath the king's very nose?

Despite her best attempt to restore her composed expression, Joanna felt desolation rise in her throat. She swallowed hard and forced back the tears that burned for release, but she could not help but peer over her shoulder to where Rylan stood. Though the noisy crowd surged behind the king, Rylan's powerful silhouette was easy to discern. His formidable height, his long dark hair, and his piercing gaze captured her gaze. But more than that, his aura of power even in this moment of his apparent defeat was unmistakable.

She stared helplessly at him, overcome with the futility of her position until a sharp pinch on her arm drew her attention away.

"You are new here, so I will forgive your lapse this time," the king murmured for her ears only. "In the future I suggest you ignore all men save those to whom I specifically direct your attention."

His narrowed gaze bored into her wide, frantic eyes. Then he patted her arm and smiled benignly. "Actually, I may wish you to pay particular interest toward Sir Rylan Kempe. Though your distaste for the man who so cruelly attempted to abduct you is understandable, his greatest flaw is only that his little scheme failed. Though brilliantly conceived, he was not able to see it through to fruition. So do not judge him too harshly, my dear. Now—" He broke off as they approached the queen and directed his words to his wife. "We are satisfied to dine. However, I would have Lord Blaecston attend us. And the Lady Joanna as well."

Isabel smiled at her husband, then with a negligent

gesture sent one of her ladies scurrying with instructions to the chamberlain to adjust the seating arrangements accordingly.

For a moment Joanna was left alone, standing in the midst of too many people with too many ulterior motives for her to cope with. Laughter floated in the air. Talk was constant. The scent of mint and lavender rose from the rushes, competing with the fragrance of various perfumes and the odor of unwashed bodies. Myriad braces of candles flickered, as did numerous torches, for the dim hall was well lit for the entertainments. The cry of a hunting bird startled her, and her distracted glance sought out the hooded bird that sat on the back of the king's hide-covered chair.

As she eyed the hunting bird, she felt a sudden rush of kinship with it, for she was in much the same way: hooded and chained. Blind to what was happening around her and unable to free herself. She clutched her hands at her waist and bit down on her lower lip, desperately willing her trembling to cease.

Then one of the ladies-in-waiting tugged at her elbow, directing her toward the high table where she was to sup in the king and queen's company. She moved forward a bit, but her eyes remained focused on the magnificent falcon.

She might indeed be in the same dire straits as the king's prized hunting falcon, she consoled herself, but she was not the only one. Like that fleet bird of prey, Sir Rylan Kempe was also chained, his hunting curtailed by the king's own hand. Still, that did not remedy her situation, for no matter who was the hunter, Oxwich was nevertheless the lure.

And she was still the prey.

15

Joanna stood behind her chair waiting, as did the others, for the king to progress to his place and be seated. Her hands clenched the chair back as if it were a lifeline, and indeed, she was certain her legs would have buckled and she would have collapsed had the solid oak chair not afforded her its support. She stared blindly ahead, refusing to meet any eye—most certainly not Lord Blaecston's. But she was nevertheless acutely aware of the numerous inquiring stares sent her way.

What in heaven's name was the king up to? He and Rylan were quite obviously political adversaries. If she'd doubted Rylan's word on it, the king's smug behavior now confirmed it. This invitation for Rylan to dine at the high table was meant as a means to gloat, but Joanna found it unnecessary and most unbecoming to a monarch. Yet John's behavior mattered to her only insofar as it affected her. And it was clear that he saw her as a method to goad Rylan.

The question she could not answer was why Rylan was cooperating with the king. Why was he at court, allowing himself to be humiliated in so public a manner? Though a fanciful part of her wished to believe it was guilt and shame for his wretched behavior toward her that had brought him here, she quickly squelched that foolish notion. More than likely, it was only that he still disbelieved that his prize had slipped through his fingers so easily.

"The king would have you sit beside the queen," a young serving lad murmured politely. Joanna moved dutifully to the chair he indicated, then nearly stumbled when she spied Rylan waiting just beyond the king's own chair.

Despite all the reasons she had for despising him, Joanna's strongest emotion at that moment was a dark and painful yearning. Like a wound that lingered near the edges of her consciousness, the pain of it leapt until her heart fairly ached from the intensity.

His face was closed against any display of feelings, but not so his eyes. They were dark, glittering with emotion as they ran swiftly over her. Joanna swallowed, then took a shaky breath as she lifted her chin bravely against his consuming gaze. But no words came. Her mouth was too dry, and her mind was a blank. Their gazes met and clung another long moment. Then he shifted slightly and cleared his throat.

"I knew court life would agree with you," he murmured as his eyes once more ran over her elegant appearance. "But I never suspected how well."

That arrogant comment, ill-disguised as a compliment, brought Joanna's anger bubbling to the surface. "You 'knew'! You 'suspected'! 'Tis more than clear that you know nothing at all of me!" she hissed furiously. She started to advance upon him, prepared to vent all the anger, frustration, and confusion that seethed within her, but the timely appearance of the queen at her elbow prevented her further outburst.

"Now, now, Lady Joanna. This is not the place to vent your feelings toward Lord Blaecston. Such discourse is better served in more private surroundings."

Joanna fought down her bitter words, unaware that the queen's clear tone carried to the first row of tables beyond the dais. Then the king also moved between her and Rylan, and with a broad smile on his face addressed Isabel.

"Do not be too hard on her, my dear wife. 'Tis only natural that she feel this antipathy for the man who sought to abduct her so cruelly." He sent Rylan a deliberately forbearing look. "Were it not for Lord Blaecston's high regard among my barons, I would feel compelled to exact a severe punishment from him for such a dishonorable act."

He raised one hand to forestall any interruption from Rylan. "As it is, since no real harm was done—my own guards rescued her in a most timely fashion—I think an apology from Lord Blaecston shall suffice." Once more he smiled, well aware that every ear in the vast bishop's parlor strained to hear. "What say you, my dear Joanna? Shall you accept his apology with the graciousness of a true lady?"

Joanna stared at her king, unable to fathom his motives. Was that all he would exact from his errant lord, an apology? Her gaze moved to Rylan's implacable face, so hard and menacing even in this, his public humiliation. Yet what she saw there was not repentance. Far from it. He seemed almost to dare her—and the king—to cross his will. Could he truly be so foolish?

But perhaps it was not foolishness. Perhaps he was even more powerful than she suspected. After all, the king's men *had* hesitated to kill him when they might easily have done so. And now the king did not demand any punishment from him beyond a public apology to her.

Her eyes narrowed thoughtfully as she stared at the man who had stolen her maidenhood. Powerful he might be, and intimidating even to kings. But he could no longer hurt her. She, however, could at least enjoy seeing him squirm.

She raised her chin a notch and sent a faint smile to King John. "If he should make apology to me—sincere apology," she quickly amended. "Then I shall accept it."

Rylan stared at her. "Graciously accept it?" he asked with a sardonic curl to his lips.

She had to clench her teeth against a furious retort. "Graciously accept it," she repeated, although her glittering stare said otherwise.

The king's gaze veered from Rylan to Joanna and then back to Rylan. "How pleasant. We are all in agreement. I do so prefer harmony to discord." His smile broadened to show his long teeth and his eyes shone with triumph. But it was more than merely triumph over a baron who plagued him. Joanna recognized the light in the king's eyes for what it was: hatred. A shiver of apprehension swept down her spine. She knew with a sudden certainty that the king was hardly likely to let a simple apology end this cat-and-mouse game he had embarked upon.

"Well, Blaecston," the king prodded. "Shall you make your apology or not?"

As Rylan stared coolly at the king, Joanna was convinced he would far rather strangle John than accede to his demand. But he steadfastly turned his icy gaze on her.

Beneath his unwavering stare, Joanna felt as if he shut out everyone else in the crowded hall—king, queen, nobility, and servants alike. He stepped nearer and reached for her tightly clasped hands, taking them between his own warm palms.

"Lady Joanna," he began quietly, all the while staring deeply into her wary eyes, "I profoundly regret the circumstances of our previous association. Had I the power to change the past, I would most certainly do so."

Joanna's pulse had more than doubled at the initial touch of his hands. Her first instinct had been to pull away, for self-preservation was a powerful motivation. But with his tender touch and intense gaze he compelled her to remain. Even more so, the husky quality of his voice started an unwelcome quiver of longing somewhere deep within her.

Was it true? she could not help but wonder. Did he indeed wish they had met under different circumstances? Did he mean what he said—and all he left unsaid, save for the potent look in his eyes?

"I . . . You . . ." Joanna stumbled over her words. "Thank you, Ryl—Lord Blaecston," she finally managed to say. Then he disengaged her hands from their rigid grasp upon one another, so that her fingers lay very naturally within his hands. He bent over to kiss her knuckles, displaying the most correct and courtly of manners. But as his lips caressed the back of one hand, she felt his fingers move in a warm circle against her palm. Then his tongue stole out to stroke across the ridges of her knuckles and she had to stifle a gasp of shock.

"Milady," he murmured with every appearance of humble respect as he straightened up. Only the burning heat of his eyes gave away his real feelings.

"Mi—milord," she barely was able to stammer.

As Rylan released her hands and stepped back from her, the king smiled his satisfaction at Rylan's obeisance to his will. A ripple of gossip swept through the hall as the story of Sir Rylan's attempted abduction of the Lady Joanna of Oxwich spread like wildfire. Everyone knew of Rylan's antagonism toward the king. Now they had witnessed how their king had brought him to heel. John's complacent expression indicated most clearly that he was well pleased with this, the first round of humiliation for Rylan Kempe.

The only observer who seemed less than satisfied with the little scene was Queen Isabel. Her perceptive gaze flitted from John to Rylan, and she tapped one long, manicured fingernail against her pursed lips. She did not speak, however, but only moved regally to her chair, then waited for John to sit. But during the ensuing shuffle of feet and scraping of chairs and benches, her doe-like eyes were bright with speculation. And anticipation.

Rylan ate the meal before him with studied nonchalance. Spring lamb in sauce on a trencher of fine-grained white bread was a particular favorite of his, and a part of him recognized the talent of the king's cook. But today his enthusiasm for the meal was forced. King John denied himself nothing. Not the finest food and drink, nor jewels and fine garments and furs. He taxed his people to the point of penury, yet lived as if his treasury would never empty.

Yet Rylan well knew it was not the king's excesses that caused the food to stick in his throat. Not this time. His appetite had abandoned him because Lady Joanna Preston sat so near and yet was denied him. She ate not five feet from him, but he could neither speak to her nor touch her.

His entire body tightened at the thought of simply touching her, even as he knew it was madness.

Squelching a particularly vicious oath, he reached for his goblet and swiftly quaffed the fine red wine it held.

"You approve of the wine?" John asked in dulcet tones. He stabbed a well-done slice of lamb and brought it to his mouth before he turned to look at Rylan.

"'Tis good," Rylan muttered.

"I have it from Lord Fulton. In lieu of increasing his knight service, I accepted four casks of his finest wine." He laughed at Rylan's stony expression. "I see you disapprove. Perhaps you will not frown so to hear that Sir Harold of Gimsby provided me with two cartloads of the finest fabrics from France. Bolts upon bolts of chaisel, flurt silke, and branched velvet. He wishes license to enlarge his castle on the River Wye, and courts my goodwill in this manner." He stabbed another piece of the lamb. "Though I have not yet decided in the matter of his castle, I have decided to make a gift of several bolts of cloth to Lady Joanna."

At the sudden tension in Rylan's bearing John's smug grin broadened. "She will need a fine gown for her wedding. I think celadon green." He looked past Isabel to where Joanna sat, hardly eating at all. "With those lovely green eyes of hers, a gown of green silk would be most pleasing indeed. Of course, such a beauty as she will look her very best bare and stretched out upon sheets of white linen." He laughed coarsely and reached for his goblet. "No doubt any number of our randy young lords shall flock to her side, hoping to be the one to see her in just such a lack of clothing."

Joanna gasped out loud, and it took every ounce of Rylan's willpower not to silence John's vulgar laughter with a fist to his face. Isabel, however, needed no such restraint.

"Your crudity is better suited to the stables," she hissed, though not so loud that those below the salt could hear.

John did not apologize, but he did have the good grace to stifle his humor under the guise of a fit of coughing. When Isabel was reassured that he would behave, she turned her gaze upon Rylan.

"So, Lord Blaecston. You have eluded the king's wrath once more. How fortunate for you that he receives more pleasure in besting you than in casting you into the donjon."

"Yes. How fortunate." Rylan took a bite of the lamb.

"I must say," the queen continued, "that it is far more pleasant for us to meet in this quiet harmony than has been the turmoil of the recent months—nay, years—of discontent. Discontent, I might add, that you seek ever to foment."

"I seek only to ensure a lasting prosperity—and peace —for England."

Isabel's gaze swept over him with a woman's eye for detail. Had her husband not sat between them, Rylan might have thought by the speculative gleam in her gaze that she contemplated some clandestine meeting between them. But her next words dispelled that notion.

"I should think you would concern yourself first and foremost with the prosperity of Blaecston and your other holdings. As it now stands you are without wife, and therefore without an heir." Her finely plucked brows arched high in question. John also waited for Rylan's answer.

If the circumstances had been different, Rylan would gladly have revealed the advantageous arrangement he'd so recently concluded with Sir Egbert Crosley regarding his daughter, Marilyn. But Joanna's averted profile beyond the king and queen somehow forced him to hold his tongue.

"I assure you, I will not long ignore that situation."

"We are most interested in any such negotiations you should embark upon," John inserted. "Of course, there are certain maidens quite hopelessly beyond your reach." Here he glanced pointedly at Joanna, then smirked at Rylan.

Rylan met the king's scrutiny with a carefully blank expression. To the queen's intent look he offered a faint smile. But then his gaze moved beyond them both to Joanna, and his composure slipped. She too was looking at him, but her emotions were far more difficult to read than John's and Isabel's.

The king hated all who opposed him. He wished to humiliate Rylan and therefore effectively strip him of all influence with the other barons. The queen, though not so vindictive as her husband, nonetheless knew that any lord who was powerful threatened the kingship. She was extremely sly beneath her sweet and smiling exterior.

But Joanna . . . Joanna was an enigma to him.

Her face was pale and somber, her expression not unlike it had been that first day at St. Theresa's. As it had then, only the light in her startling green eyes gave any indication of the emotions that stirred within her. But what those emotions were he could not say. Their eyes met and clung. Clashed was a better description, he decided ruefully. His clung. Hers clashed. He sought to know her very thoughts. She sought to repel his every try.

But she did not turn away. Only the interruption of the queen's favorite confessor, the Bishop of Ely, ended the silent sparring of their eyes.

"A wedding at court. 'Twould be a most welcome break from the routine, would it not?" His round face and balding pate shone with ruddy vitality and his quick darting eyes jumped back and forth among those at the high table. "You recall, milady, the gaiety when Fitzpatrick wed at Christmastide? And what of the festivities at harvest when Lady Helen wed that northern lord, Sir Kendrick? Ah, but that was a time. Such feasting. Such games and sport. And the wines that flowed!" He broke off his ecstatic recitation to grab up his cup and drink deeply. "Yes, a wedding would be a great diversion. Shall it be Lady Joanna's? Or perhaps Lord Blaecston's? Or better yet, two weddings. A double wedding!" he pronounced.

"Neither Lord Blaecston nor Lady Joanna have contracted their unions yet," the king observed dryly. He lifted his goblet to his mouth to sip, then paused as if a thought had only just occurred to him. "Lord Blaecston's contract for marriage is in his own hands. Lady Joanna's future, however, is entrusted to me. What say you, Isabel? Shall we turn our thoughts more quickly to settling our ward's affairs, and thereby add some gaiety to our visit at Ely?"

Rylan's eyes went quickly to Joanna. She, in turn, had darted her gaze to him. Her fear was apparent, yet he did not think her fear could be any greater than his own. For one instant he was certain he divined her thoughts. Then she averted her eyes to stare at her hands. But that solitary moment was enough to decide him once and for all on the course he must take. He'd ridden to Ely in a fury, yet for all his haste, he'd not come with any firm plan save to somehow prevent the king from using her badly. How he could manage the deed he did not precisely know, but guilt and the shredded remnants of his honor demanded that he try.

Now, however, the solution was clear, and he felt a stab of pure relief. He could hardly believe he'd not recognized it before. He was chagrined anew to realize that it was only the desperate plea for help he'd seen in Joanna's eyes for that fleeting moment that had brought him to the logical solution.

He must marry her himself.

He reached for his wine with a hand that shook. He would marry her and thereby save her from the vulgar clutches of any of the king's favored lords. That lot was, to a man, low-minded and selfish, completely undeserving of such an innocent as Joanna.

Conversation went on around him but it barely registered in Rylan's mind. Bishop Ferendi burbled on about weddings and feasts. The queen reminded the king that she and her ladies would require new gowns for the festivities. John laughed, for he had seen the tremble in Rylan's hand, and he gloated already at besting his longtime adversary.

But Rylan did not care, for he was too filled with the wonder of his reckless decision. He was already committed to the Lady Marilyn. Her father would not take his change of heart very well at all, and Rylan had no wish to embarrass either Lord Egbert or his daughter. Thank the Lord that news was still unannounced. Then there was the seemingly insurmountable problem of the king's consent. Joanna was now a ward of the court, and Rylan was the last person John would wish wed to the heiress of Oxwich. Yet none of that truly mattered to him now.

Rylan drank deeply, then turned his head to stare at Joanna. His Joanna, he thought as a fierce sense of possession filled him.

Though his decision altered his political plans enormously, he refused to dwell on it. He'd find some other way to jell the barons' disparate opposition to the king's policies. He'd find the means to appease Sir Egbert. But most of all, he'd find a way to coerce the king into granting him the Lady Joanna's hand in marriage. The king would not be willing, but that would only make his eventual capitulation more enjoyable.

But what if Joanna was not willing?

At that moment she lifted her downturned face and met his gaze directly. Once more he saw her fear and her silent plea for help. Though it cost him a supreme effort, he remained seated, giving no sign of his agitation save his tightened grasp on his goblet. Inside, however, he fought the overwhelming urge to leap up, pull her to his side, and fight off anyone who attempted to intercede.

Her eyes widened slightly at his intent gaze, and he reluctantly tore his eyes from her to once more pay attention to the royal conversation. But his mind spun with determined schemes. He drank again and this time made a silent vow—a vow on the cornerstone of Blaecston Castle itself. He *would* have the Lady Joanna Preston to wife.

She and none other.

16

Though her head pounded with a dull ache, and her stomach roiled against the meal she'd tried her best to eat, Joanna forced a pleasant smile to her face. Was there anything else that could possibly go wrong?

She moved slowly down the steps of the dais, imitating Marilyn and the other ladies-in-waiting who trailed the king and queen as they made their way regally through the crowded bishop's parlor. Bad enough to be at court, when all she wished was to return to the priory. To make things worse, no one would listen to her at all. The queen had deftly turned aside her request for passage back to St. Theresa's, saying that she was simply homesick and would soon recover. The king had patted her hand, then assessed her worth with his bold scrutiny. But he too had not listened. He'd told her to convey her conversation to the queen. Clearly he expected his wife to silence any of his new ward's objections.

Joanna had considered the bishop as a possible ally. After all, he was a man of the church and would surely understand her desire to take up the veil. And he seemed to be the queen's confidant. But then Rylan had appeared, and in her shock, her plans had disappeared.

Joanna concentrated on the trailing hem of Isabel's marten-trimmed gown, refusing to search even briefly for Rylan. Yet even without seeing him she knew he was not far away—and that he was watching her.

Her stomach tightened, but this time it had nothing to do with the food she had consumed so listlessly. The certainty that Rylan Kempe was staring at her caused a heightened awareness to tingle through her body—even unto her most private places. It was that which dismayed her most, for despite all her reasons to hate and distrust him, that one intimate act they'd shared haunted her.

How could a man provide her with such all-consuming pleasure and yet be the cause of all her discontent? Worse, how could she—who knew how hard and relentless he was—still yearn for his touch? It was perverse and yet it was nonetheless true.

Steeped in her own miserable thoughts, Joanna was unaware that the royal couple had halted until she nearly trod on one of the royal garments.

"Careful," Marilyn whispered as she stopped Joanna just in time.

"My thanks." Joanna glanced guiltily at the king and queen, then swallowed hard when John's speculative gaze landed upon her.

"I would have music," he announced with a careless flick of one beringed hand. At once Sir George, the king's ever-present shadow, scurried off to see his liege's command done.

"Let us have some entertainments," King John continued. "Games. No." His eyes remained fixed on Joanna. "Not games, but dancing. Yes." He smiled at Isabel as if he were well pleased with himself. "Music and dancing is the thing."

The musicians summoned by Sir George were hurrying up, and in a matter of seconds their strings and horns rose in metered harmony. Lords and ladies, servants and holy people all fell back, leaving an open space in the huge parlor. Joanna fell back as well but made certain to remain near Marilyn.

Dancing, she thought with undeniable curiosity. She'd never seen dancing before.

"The king is partial to dancing," Marilyn whispered to her. "He is most proud of his skill." Then she giggled. "Even the bishop joins in!"

Even as she said the words, the queen took Bishop Ferendi's hand and proceeded to the center of the room. The king tapped one finger thoughtfully against his chin as his sharp eyes scanned the room. When they lighted on her, Joanna tried to shrink back farther into the crowd, but it was a useless ploy.

"Ah, yes. Our fair ward. Come, my dear. Let us gauge your grace in a musical step. No, no. Do not pretend to such unseemly reticence," he added when she stepped back even farther.

Despite Joanna's clear reluctance, numerous hands shoved her forward until she stood before the entire court. She took the king's extended hand and curtsied as she knew was proper. But when she raised her face to John, her hesitance was even greater than before.

"I know no dances, your Highness. At the priory we did not . . ." She trailed off under his frown.

"Then you shall learn. Come now," he continued in a more pleasant tone. "'Tis not so hard."

So saying, he placed her hand above his and stood her at his side. At once there was a flurry among the spectators, and as the music swelled louder, numerous couples fell in behind the two royal couples. Joanna glanced around in panic to see the other ladies-in-waiting join the growing line of dancers as well. Even the reticent Marilyn had been drawn forth by a tall red-haired man. But Joanna's attention was swiftly drawn back to her own royal partner, and amid several false starts, she tried gamely to follow his lead.

Three steps forward, pause and dip. Twice more they followed the same step. Turn and bow, then draw away. Join hands and start anew.

To his credit, the king moved smoothly, and Joanna had little trouble accustoming herself to the courtly dance steps. But when they had progressed almost to the far end of the hall, she looked to him for guidance. At that point she was prodded into a circular step and somehow, without her being quite aware of it happening, she was suddenly partnered with the bishop as John and Isabel paraded down between the parted rows of dancers.

"My . . . my lord," she stammered to the sweating bishop as he took her hand onto his fleshy one.

"Lady Joanna," he said with a dip of his head. "Here we go again. Now look lively, for the next pass this way shall be yours."

Joanna quickly determined his meaning. The long line of dancers followed the same dance step back across the hall, but this time she was turned into the arms of the man behind her, then paraded through the parted couples. By the time they took their places at the end of the line she understood the moves. *Le Beau Troc* was a dance of switching partners. The king had begun with her but ended up with his queen. So could any careful dancer position himself to eventually escort his partner of choice. Especially when the long line of dancers formed into three shorter lines.

As Joanna watched John and Isabel smiling and laughing together, she felt an unexpected stab of jealousy. No matter what aspersions might be heaped upon King John, no one could deny that he adored his beautiful young wife. Marriage might not be so terrible a thing if your husband felt that way about you, she admitted sadly.

When Joanna and her current partner, a tall slender young lord, reached the end of the dance, she was swiftly whirled about. By now she knew what was to come. She lifted her long skirts with one hand as she spun and reached to grasp her new partner's hand with the other.

To her vast confusion, however, it was Rylan Kempe's hand that closed about her own. For a moment she faltered, but his grip was steady and with barely a misstep they paraded down the long allée of arms. When they reached the end of the column of dancers, they turned to face each other. He bowed, but she did little more than bob her head, for her tumultuous emotions far outstripped her ability to be polite.

But Rylan ignored her obvious distress and took up her hand once more for the dance.

"You look quite beautiful today," he murmured quietly.

Such words were hardly what she expected of him, and Joanna was momentarily silenced. More than anything she would like to have appeared aloof, to cloak her resentment in an icy show of manners. But her anger was clouded by too many other feelings toward him, and she was an utter failure at hiding her emotions.

"I look precisely like what I am become: a prize pet to be awarded to he who will pay the highest cost."

They made their dip in unison but his eyes never left hers. "I will not let that happen."

Joanna lifted her chin and tried to swallow the lump

that had formed in her throat. How dare he pretend to help her now when it was he who had caused all her misery. "It appears to be too late, even for your interferences."

He smiled then, very faintly, and let his thumb rub over her knuckles. "It is not too late, Joanna. You must trust me in this."

"Trust you!" she cried, then abruptly lowered her tone. "Trust you who have proven to be as trustworthy as the serpent in Eden? I trust you to abduct me. I trust you to ignore my wishes completely. I trust you to ruin—"

She broke off when he yanked her into another dip so low that she tripped upon her own gown. He quickly pulled her upright, but his grip remained rock hard on her arm.

"Perhaps you should rest your weakened ankle," he said with a meaningful glare. Then his voice lowered so that only she could hear. "Else your indiscreet babble shall ruin your reputation."

"Ruin yours, you mean!" But as Joanna recognized the curious gazes of the couples nearest them, she was forced to admit the futility of arguing with him in this company. Besides, she rationalized as he quite firmly led her toward a stepped alcove, she had no interest in dancing. Not with him nor any other of John's courtiers.

Restored by her righteous anger, Joanna jerked her hand from his too-intimate grasp. "Thank you for the dance, Lord Blaecston. I believe I shall join several of the queen's women now."

"They're all dancing," he pointed out as he deftly blocked her way. "What better time for us to speak than during this hubbub when no one may overhear?"

"We have nothing to speak about. Our association is

quite finished." For emphasis she turned away from him, intending to depart his company.

"I'm afraid, my love, that our association is only just beginning."

Those few words, murmured in such low, confident tones, halted her departure. *My love.* For an instant she was beset by memories of the other time he'd murmured endearments to her, and a disarming warmth rushed through her. The anger fled her face, and for a moment their eyes met in honest appraisal.

"I am . . . I am not your love," she whispered in a voice that shook only a little.

A shadow seemed to cross his face and he did not immediately respond. When he did speak his voice had taken on a bitter edge. "You *have* been my lover." Then he sighed, seeming to shrug off some darker emotion. "I wish to help you out of this coil, Joanna. I would not have you wed against your will."

Had he not just referred to their shared moments of passion, Joanna would have been quick to castigate him for his abrupt about-face on the matter of her marriage. But she was too overcome by the memories of what they'd done together and too bewildered by the unbidden thrill that went through her to think coherently. Once more she tried to escape their intimate discourse, but this time it was not anger that drove her. The truth was, she feared him. He exercised some unearthly power over her—some hold she could neither explain nor control. But it was undeniably there, and he was no doubt as aware of it as she.

"Don't run away, Joanna." He caught her arm then let his hand slide down until he held her hand. "I want to help you." He tugged her hand, forcing her to face him. "I'm the only one who *can* help you."

Joanna looked away from him to the crowd of dancers, musicians, and spectators beyond them. "No one can help me," she countered very softly. For a moment she understood her mother's desperate decision in the face of hopelessness, and she felt a rush of sympathy for her long-lost parent. But just as quickly she knew that she was nothing like her mother. She could never choose so cowardly a solution.

Yet faced with the nightly assault of a husband she despised . . .

Joanna shuddered and her gaze returned to Rylan. She despised him, she told herself. Yet she had not despised the intimacy they had shared. Hardly.

As if he sensed her mounting confusion, he took a step nearer. "I can help you," he repeated. His eyes were dark as midnight, compelling her to hear him out.

Joanna bit her lip, uncertain what to think and whom to believe. But before he could continue or she could respond, the music ended and they were joined by a number of others. The first person to intrude upon their conversation was the king's confidant, Sir George.

"It shall not work," the man said to Rylan with a smug smile. "You have lost the quarry this time, Blaecston. Best to concede gracefully."

Rylan released Joanna's hand, but his face showed no emotion at the other man's goading. Then John and Isabel strolled up, both somewhat breathless from the vigorous dancing.

"It appears that our ward has well and truly forgiven Lord Blaecston his several trespasses, does it not, Isabel? They seem positively chatty. What say you, Joanna?" the king continued, clearly in a good humor. "Does Blaecston impress you with the sincerity of his apology? Or is he plotting some new mischief?"

Several ladies tittered behind their hands, and the king and his favored barons grinned to see John's chief adversary made sport of. But Joanna found no humor in the moment, for if Rylan was presently at the mercy of the king, she was even more so. She'd not even had an opportunity to present her case to John. But now he waited on her answer and she knew she must make whatever advantage of it she could.

"I trust that Lord Blaecston is as sincere as any man may be. For myself, however, I place my trust in our heavenly Father that He will see me back to St. Theresa's and the holy life I have chosen."

It was obviously not the sort of response John had expected, and his brow creased at the implied directive in her words. Everyone's eyes swiveled to him, awaiting his response. But it was Isabel who spoke first.

"Five years you spent preparing for the holy life. You have been at court but one day. I hope, my dear Lady Joanna, that you will grant us more time than that before you speak again of taking up the veil." Her smile and her pleasant tone kept the rebuke mild. But Joanna caught the glitter in the queen's dark eyes.

Isabel continued. "Once you have met a few of the gallants who already clamor for an introduction, you will no doubt be more than eager to abandon your previous plans. You were but twelve when you made that choice. Now you are older—and wiser," she added with a meaningful glance.

Joanna had a ready retort. She was not twelve now, that was certain. She was old enough and knew well enough that marriage was not a beneficial arrangement for most women, and she was prepared to say as much. But she was prevented speaking by a sharp pinch on the back of her upper arm. She winced, then spied Marilyn's earnest, imploring face. At once Joanna realized that she would not aid her own cause in this manner. Arguing with the royal couple before such an avid audience was worse than useless. It would only harden them in their opposition to her wishes. If she were to succeed, it must be through private conversation and reasoning with them.

She sighed softly and assumed the same patient expression she had learned in her long years at the priory.

"Yes, milady," she murmured with an obedient bob of her head.

The queen smiled, content with Joanna's response. The king, however, had not yet had his say. "The religious life is more suitable for some than for others, wouldn't you agree, Ferendi?"

"Oh, quite. Quite," the florid-faced bishop responded readily. "We all do our duty to God, but He calls to each of us differently." He nodded his head and patted his fingertips together across his wide belly in a gesture everyone knew preceded a lengthy discourse.

"Our king rules his subjects at God's will. Those of us called to the holy life of the church tend to the souls of those very same subjects. Young, healthy noblewomen, however, have their own responsibility, which is to go forth and be fruitful. Yes," he continued under the king's satisfied smile, "your duty to God, Lady Joanna, most clearly falls into that area. I have no doubt our heavenly Father will help our king select the very best husband for you."

"And for Lady Marilyn as well," John prompted.

"Our Father guides all your decisions," the holy man pronounced. Then he looked pointedly at Rylan. "Though some endeavor to dispute the law of divine right, those of us who have a closer communication with our God know that mere human decision—based as it is on a weak and self-serving nature—can never be allowed to triumph over God's will."

There were murmurs of approval and nods of agreement by those who hung upon the king's robes. Privately Joanna thought the bishop a pompous fool and the king probably as selfish and grasping as gossip painted him. But she buried her resentment beneath a humbled mien and kept her eyes appropriately downcast.

It was the queen who changed the tenor of the conversation. "Do not be perturbed by Lady Joanna's honest expression of her feelings, dear husband. I shall make it my duty to ease her into her new life. No doubt she finds court more than a little overwhelming. Shall we start with a stroll around the grounds?" Her eyes sparkled as she glanced around the circle of ladies and courtiers. "Ah, Sir Guy. Will you accompany us?" She patted her husband's hand and gave him a fond smile. "You will excuse us, my lord?"

Joanna could do nothing but follow along as the queen and several of her women drew her away from the dancing. She glanced back once to meet Rylan's smoldering stare. But she was uncertain whether it was anger or frustration she read there.

Or perhaps desire?

She quickly dismissed that foolish notion, however, for she well knew he desired one thing only: to win his game with the king. Any desire he felt for her was merely part and parcel with the manipulative games he played. Yet she could not deny the unwonted flutter that rose from low in her belly and sent warm tremors through her. Frowning, she tried to banish such unseemly emotions. She was not cognizant that someone had fallen in step beside her as the queen's party made its circuitous way from the parlor until a large male hand curved around her elbow.

"Oh!" Joanna let out a gasp of surprise, and a sharp thrill went through her. But when she looked up, the smiling countenance she met was not the one she hoped for.

You are a fool, deserving to wear the jester's cap, she rebuked herself sternly. Though her heart's pace slowed to normal, she cursed the disappointment that welled within her.

"I know we have not been formally presented, Lady Joanna. However, I am hoping you will nonetheless forgive my forwardness, for I have already heard so much about you that I feel as if we are already well acquainted. Allow me to make my own introduction." The fellow managed an abbreviated bow without missing a step. Then he turned his fair-complected face to her with a wide smile. "I am Sir Guy Bosworth. Of Barnstaple in Devon. May I say that never has court glittered so magnificently as it does since your arrival."

Joanna took in this long-winded speech with a mixture of irritation and amusement, of which neither emotion seemed appropriate to reveal. After a quick perusal of Sir Guy's fashionable person, she averted her eyes to watch the trailing hem of Queen Isabel's aqua ferret-silk surcoat.

"Such a sentiment may not be very well received by the queen and her other ladies," she commented acerbically.

Her words had the desired affect, for he glanced warily at Isabel then lowered his voice. "I only meant to say how pleased I am to have such a fair maiden in our midst."

Joanna did not answer, hoping to discourage his attention. Unfortunately, he took her silence for encouragement.

"I shall undertake to make your time at court a pleasure. Once you have met everyone and learned how to get on, you shall wonder at the dullness of your life before now." He beamed at her, showing his wide brow, strong jaw and even teeth to advantage. "So fair a creature as yourself should not be shuttered behind priory walls."

Once more Joanna had to suppress her annoyance. Did he truly think to impress her with words that flattered her face while completely ignoring her deepest wishes? But though she held back her angry retort, her scathing glare made her feelings clear. Or at least it should have. Sir Guy's attention, however, was focused on a bit of twisted braid on the sleeve of his handsome tunic. He then adjusted the brooch that held his short cape open before he looked up with a self-satisfied smile.

"We plan a hawking expedition come the morn. You shall come, of course. Have you a falcon? But no, you arrived quite bereft of baggage, I am told. Then you shall ride with me, for my peregrine is a masterful creature. If you like, I shall let you stroke her."

Through the abbey gardens his prattle continued. Hawks, horses, hunting—he kept the conversation going without the least assistance from her. Only when the queen halted in a neat walled garden did his chatter subside.

Isabel looked over her entourage. "Dearest Guy, would you and Sir Robert be so good as to put out the wickets? We would appreciate a quick game of *jeu du mail.*" Then her quick gaze looked over her ladies. "Pair up, my pretty butterflies. Matilda with Henry. Adele with Roger."

Joanna instinctively sidled toward Marilyn. She most certainly did not want to be paired with Guy or any other of the various court buffoons as she had swiftly counted King John's circle of barons.

"Marilyn and Robert—" the queen began once more. But she was interrupted by the entrance of a young page, who made a hasty bow and murmured something in Lady Matilda's ear. She promptly passed the message on to the queen.

A faint frown clouded Isabel's beautiful face, but in a moment she recovered. Her eyes sought Marilyn out once more.

"Marilyn, my dear, we have a message that your father has just arrived. He asks to see you and awaits your company even now in Bishop Ferendi's private solar. You may go along to greet him." With a gracious dip of her head Isabel indicated the page waiting to escort Marilyn. "You will, of course, convey my regards to your father. I shall anticipate hearing from you any news that he may carry."

Marilyn was silent, only bobbing her head in assent as she curtsied to Isabel. For an instant Marilyn's eyes seemed to search for someone else in the crowd. But before Joanna could ascertain who, the girl turned away, her face two shades paler and her eyes huge with dread.

Why so fearful of her father's summons? Joanna wondered for a moment. But just as quickly she knew the answer. Marilyn had said that her father was negotiating a marriage contract for her. Perhaps his presence signified that the arrangements were now settled.

A shiver of sympathy went down Joanna's back. Poor Marilyn. Yet she knew she was in just as unpleasant a situation as her new friend, and with no one to aid her.

At once Rylan's reassuring words came back to her. *I*

will not let that happen, he'd said so confidently. Yet she knew, to her vast disappointment, that *his* help would be little more than no help at all. No, she was quite alone in this matter. Her only chance was to convince the king to release her from her inheritance.

"Now, where were we?" The queen's soft yet commanding voice interrupted Joanna's dark thoughts. "Oh, yes. The pairings for *jeu de mail*. Joanna, have you met our Sir Evan? He's quite good at games, and he's always a most charming companion. You two shall get on very well, I'm certain."

To Joanna's surprise, it was the very man who had danced with Marilyn. "You are too generous with my reputation, my queen," he averred. Though his smile seemed strained, he bowed to Isabel. Then his gaze turned toward Joanna, and she sensed his curiosity about her. "My Lady Joanna," he said with a sweeping bow. "Allow me to introduce myself properly. Evan Thorndyke, Lord Manning, at your service."

Joanna was prepared to be as put off by this new court gallant as she had been by Sir Guy. When he straightened from his bow over her hand, however, his face reflected only a friendly interest and nothing more. He did not take advantage and kiss her hand. Neither did he squeeze it or attempt to keep it within his grasp too long. Instead he took a small step backward and met her gaze directly.

"No doubt you find court—and all who gather here— a curious lot. If I can ease your discomfort in any way, I would be most pleased to do so. Have you ever played *jeu du mail*?"

Joanna released the anxious breath she'd been holding. Sir Evan actually seemed a rather pleasant sort. He neither leered nor scrutinized her as if she were an oddity never before seen. No wonder Marilyn had seemed at ease with him. Though her returning smile was hesitant, for some reason Joanna felt this Sir Evan might actually be a man she could learn to like. "No, I've never played."

As the game got under way, Joanna's instincts proved correct. Sir Evan was a most affable fellow, quick to laugh, but at himself as much as anyone else. He instructed Joanna in the use of the mallet and balls, and as the competition progressed she found her ill humor lifting.

"Oh, good shot. Good shot!" Sir Evan commended when Joanna's red-striped ball bumped a purple one away from one of the wickets. Joanna smiled her pleasure at him, but her triumphant expression quickly faded. The purple ball was Isabel's, and the queen looked most annoyed.

If she could have called back the shot, Joanna would have. The last thing she wanted was to provoke Isabel's ire. Quite the contrary. But like a fool she had become caught up in the sport and completely forgotten her plan to solicit the queen's goodwill.

Sir Evan took his shot, which went a little wide of the mark, much to the good humor of several other players. On the next play Joanna's ball was nudged by Lady Matilda's blue-striped ball, but it only helped her position. Then the queen and her partner played their shots.

When it was again Joanna's turn to approach her ball, long mallet in hand, her brow was creased in concern. One well-aimed shot could place her directly before the end post; Sir Evan's ball could then bump hers in for their win. But that did not seem very wise. Her hands trembled slightly as she aligned the mallet and ball, but she did not feel the least hesitation when she took her swing. The ball ran straight and true across the closely cut lawn, directly toward its goal. As Joanna's ball clipped the purple ball, an excited murmur went up. She tried to look disappointed as her ball careened off to the side and Isabel's rolled even nearer the final wicket.

Then it was Sir Evan's turn. He approached his red-striped ball thoughtfully, judging all the angles from bended knee. As he arose he glanced up at Joanna. For a long moment their eyes held, and Joanna had the distinct feeling that he knew her shot had been deliberate. But he was still in a position to stymie the queen's victory. He could send her ball spinning away, or perhaps block its path to the end post. He had the skill to do either, and no apparent reason to resist the opportunity.

When he finally stood over the ball, Joanna caught her breath, praying that he would not make the shot and thereby provoke the queen's animosity toward her. The mallet hit the ball with a dull *thwack*. It ran straight at the end post. Clearly he wished to block the queen's final shot. But as the ball approached the post it curved slightly, glanced off, and rolled to a stop in a harmless position.

A small cheer went up from the queen's supporters, and Isabel herself tapped Sir Evan's arm chidingly. "Shall you pass off your poor shot as gallantry, Lord Manning?" She laughed. "Best that you do not, for I shall not allow it."

All eyes then turned to follow the next play—all eyes but Joanna's. Had he missed his shot apurpose?

As if he sensed her question, Sir Evan moved to stand beside her. "Perhaps we shall win another time," he said with a casual shrug.

She stared up into his serious eyes. "You did that deliberately. You might have made that shot but did not."

He smiled but she could not mistake the curious expression on his face. "I did no more than you had done."

Joanna looked away guiltily. "'Tis only a game."

"Yes. Only a game," he concurred after a pause. "'Tis better to lose when the stakes are no more than a moment of triumph. Especially when it might ensure a greater victory."

Joanna had no chance to question him on that vague remark, for a loud shout went up from the onlookers when the queen's ball found the end post. Sir Evan moved away to congratulate Isabel, and in the chattering crowd Joanna could not catch his attention. Sir Guy, however, had no trouble insinuating himself next to her, and as the queen and her entourage made their slow way back to the bishop's parlor, Joanna was subjected to an endless discourse on his every shot and strategy during the game.

She was near to snapping at him in frustration when she saw Sir Evan ahead of them. For a moment he looked up from his conversation with Lady Adele and met Joanna's gaze. Then he winked at her—a friendly conspiratorial wink—and she forgot Sir Guy's presence entirely.

What did he mean by that wink?

Joanna continued to stare at Sir Evan's handsome red head even after he returned to his conversation with the queen's first lady in waiting. What did he mean by that wink? she wondered.

He did not mean to court her. Somehow she was certain of that. But he *was* up to something. Though she had no idea what it might be, Joanna was nevertheless certain that beneath Sir Evan Thorndyke's agreeable surface far deeper currents ran.

17

Marilyn lay upon her bed fully clothed. Her face was pale and her eyes were dry, yet Joanna knew at once that she had been weeping. She eased the door closed behind her, forgetting her own troubled thoughts in the face of Marilyn's obvious distress.

"What is it, Marilyn? Have you seen your father? Does he bear bad news?" Joanna sat on the bed beside the girl and took her cold hand in her own. "Are you all right?"

Marilyn swallowed then took a labored breath. "I am behaving most foolishly," she managed to whisper. "'Tis no more than I expected. And yet . . . and yet . . ." She trailed off once more, swallowing the sob that rose in her throat.

A stab of sympathy for Marilyn washed over Joanna, along with a shiver of fear for herself. She and Marilyn were both caught in the same hopeless trap. Before long she too would face this same fate.

"Has your father selected a husband for you?"

Marilyn nodded. Her eyes swam with tears as she stared up at Joanna. "The contract is made and though I should be glad, for the man is at least not old and ugly—" She broke off and turned away, crying in earnest this time.

Joanna was overcome by Marilyn's consuming sorrow. Was there no way to help her avoid this marriage she so clearly abhorred?

"Perhaps it will not be so terrible as all that," she began weakly.

Marilyn shook her head. "He scares me! He is so dark and . . . and so angry."

"Your father?"

"No. No, Lord Blaecston!" the distraught girl cried. "My father says he is a powerful man and that as his wife I shall be one of the most powerful ladies in the land, but—"

Joanna did not hear the rest. Marilyn was to be the wife of Lord Blaecston? Rylan Kempe was promised in marriage to her?

The shock of that revelation sent her senses spinning, and she stared disbelievingly at the weeping girl on the bed. It could not be true!

And yet, it most clearly was.

A black emptiness welled up from the vicinity of her heart—a hollow ache she could not bury. All the other times in her life when she'd felt abandoned seemed as nothing compared to the overpowering sense of loss that shook her now. Of all the men in England, why must it be Rylan?

Tears started in her eyes but she swiftly dashed them away. It would be worse than foolish to cry for him, she told herself. Who *he* wed mattered nothing to her. She forced back the tears and fought to be logical. It was Marilyn her concerns must be for now. Sweet shy Marilyn was being forced to wed that selfish, hard-hearted scoundrel! The girl was barely more than a child, Joanna thought with rising indignation. Yet she would be subject to the same physical assault she herself had endured from him.

That thought brought Joanna up short. Rylan and Marilyn. She took a quick breath and tried to compose herself, for an emotion closely akin to jealousy had sprung unexpectedly upon her.

But it was not jealousy. She was certain of that. Though the man had a certain winning way about him— though he could kiss a woman and caress her until her will was no longer her own—he was nevertheless a blackguard. Lord Black Heart he was, and not worthy of an innocent such as Marilyn.

She gazed down at the miserable girl and stroked her hair comfortingly. Marilyn should be handed in marriage to a far more deserving man than Rylan Kempe. She needed a well-mannered fellow. Someone gallant and charming, pleasant and mild of manner. Someone like . . . like . . .

Joanna smiled, albeit sadly when the name came to her. Marilyn needed someone like Evan Thorndyke. He was young, nice-looking, and pleasant in the extreme. He was no lecher and appeared to have no particular political aspirations.

There had been that wink, however.

Joanna frowned, then determinedly thrust thoughts of Evan Thorndyke and Rylan Kempe—thoughts of all men—from her mind. Marilyn was her chief concern at the moment.

"Come now, Marilyn," she began anew in a firm tone. "This weeping avails you of naught. What is needed now is a clear head if we are to overthrow your father in this matter."

Marilyn's sobbing subsided a bit at that, and after wiping at her eyes with her fists, she rolled onto her back and stared up at Joanna. "What . . . what do you mean, overthrow him in this matter?" she asked through her hiccups.

As Joanna stared down into Marilyn's young and innocent face, she suddenly felt old and far too wise in the ways of the world. "It is a hard thing to have no one to rely on but yourself," she began, picking her words slowly as she collected her thoughts. "Bishop Ferendi believes that a young noblewoman does her duty to God when she marries and bears the fruit of that union, and that may be true for some. But I do not believe it's true for all. Certainly not for myself. But even if it is, 'tis not for someone else to say who that husband should be. Nor is it right for that husband to treat his wife poorly. Certainly our Lord Jesus loved and cared for the women of his time."

She took a deep breath as she considered that novel idea. It had been forming for some time in her mind, yet not until now had she attempted to fit words to it.

"I am fully capable of selecting my own husband—if I indeed wanted one. So are you. The decision is taken from us only because of the property attached to our hands." She lowered her voice to a secretive level. "I am prepared to renounce my inheritance in order to avoid an unwise marriage. Perhaps you should do the same."

Marilyn pushed up to lean against the high board at the head of the bed. Her face reflected amazement at Joanna's words. "My father would never allow it." She wiped a tear that yet clung to her chin. "No, never. Nor will the king easily allow you to abandon your duty either."

"Perhaps. Perhaps not. But I shall nonetheless try to convince him of it. After all, he would still have what it is he truly wants: Oxwich in the hands of one of his own followers."

Marilyn shook her head. Her voice gained confidence and she spoke now as if *she* were the wise one and Joanna the naive child. "You do not know the king, Joanna. He wants most what he is denied. If you deny him your obedience, then he will demand it all the more."

"He cannot make me say the words. I will not take the wedding vow!"

"Lady Clara, widow of Lord Moreland, tried as much. When the king demanded that she wed Sir Cuthbert, she refused. King John had her children removed from her care and she was kept a prisoner in her own keep the winter through with no fire for warmth. On the Feast of the Annunciation when she still refused he had food withheld from her. By St. Mark's feast day she was wed to that vile old man who has lain four wives to rest already." Marilyn stared intently at Joanna. "Gossip holds that despite her frail condition, he got her with child at once."

Disconcerted by this new proof of the king's cruelty, Joanna sat back. How could anyone be so unfeeling? But she could not let this deter her. Though she preferred not to do so, she could still reveal her unchaste state. That ought to give the king pause. But she would hold that bit of news private until she had no other recourse.

She met Marilyn's resigned gaze. "Be that as it may, I do not see how my situation is made any the worse by an attempt to sway the king. He may ignore my wishes, as you predict. But he might not. If I am careful and present my case well—if I select my words and time them wisely—who knows how he may decide?" Joanna lifted her chin and folded her hands in her lap. "I only know that I cannot be complacent when it is my life that is being decided."

Joanna clung to her brave words the whole night long, but it was not easy. To her chagrin, it was not the threat of marriage to some baron of the king's choosing that caused her the most disquiet. Rather, it was Marilyn's unsettling news about her own betrothal.

Rylan Kempe was to wed Marilyn. It was not fair! She punched the soft featherbed in frustration, then rolled onto her back and tried to calm herself. In the darkness above her, the ceiling could not be seen. No sound came to her save the soft sigh of Marilyn's breathing. She was entirely alone with her thoughts—and extremely uncomfortable with them.

What a fool she was to feel so desolate at Marilyn's news. Her sympathy should be for poor Marilyn, who was to be bound over to the hard-hearted Lord Blaecston. Yet all she felt was anger. Anger and jealousy.

Why had he not offered for her instead? If Oxwich were so precious to his political aims, why did he not wish to wed her himself?

Yet just as quickly she vowed that she would never agree to wed such a blackguard as he had proven to be. She would never wed any man, for they were all of a lot: selfish, greedy, and unfeeling.

He had not been so when they'd lain together, however.

That unwelcome memory sent a heated shiver through her. A knot seemed to unfurl in her stomach as she recalled his sultry kisses and unhurried caress. For that short span of time he'd seemed almost to worship her, so assiduously had he addressed her own pleasure.

In a fit of frustration Joanna curled onto her side, pulling the bed linens over her head. She was so confused she could scarcely think straight, and to make matters worse, even her own body betrayed her. The briefest recollection of the intimacies they'd shared on Isle Sacré caused her nipples to tighten and her nether regions to grow wet and warm.

She clenched her eyes closed, willing herself to recall how hateful he'd been, how persistent. Those hands of his had tossed her over his back as if she were no more than a peasant's sack of turnips. His mouth had uttered taunts and cruel threats. Yet even during her fitful hours of sleep, it was the heated stroke of his fingers and the murmured endearments that stayed with her. Midnight brought her dreams of passion, not of dread.

Morning found her cross and exhausted. Marilyn too was pale, as if her sleep had not brought her much rest, and the pair of them prepared for the day with little conversation. Marilyn donned a close-fitting tunic with full trailing sleeves. The muted blue color flattered her well, yet her glum expression and listless gaze once more dimmed her natural beauty.

Joanna dressed in a gown of pale green shot through with silvery threads. The style was simple and she wore her hair loose and flowing, as the queen had told her befitted an unmarried maiden. Only *she* knew that she was not the pure maiden everyone took her for. That thought stirred once more the disparate emotions Marilyn's announcement had generated.

"I pray you will not divulge anything of which we spoke last night," Marilyn began. "About my betrothal contract."

Joanna looked over at her with troubled eyes. "'Tis a secret then. But it cannot remain so forever."

"No. But my father and . . . and Lord Blaecston

would select the proper moment to announce their agreement."

Joanna was silent a moment. "Their agreement. Not yours."

Marilyn sent Joanna a pleading look. "What would you have me do? I have prayed on it during the night, and I accept my father's judgment in this matter."

"Has he even listened to your feelings on the subject of husbands?"

Marilyn bit her lip and shook her head. "The contracts are already made. Besides, 'tis not for me to interfere."

"If not you, then who?" Joanna exclaimed in frustration. "Surely there are other men who would be acceptable to your father and not so repugnant to yourself. Even now at court there are several."

"The king would see me paired with Sir Robert of Short, but my father mislikes him. He is overfond of gaming."

"What of the others I've met? What of Sir Guy . . . Sir Guy of . . ."

"Sir Guy Bosworth of Barnstaple." Marilyn smiled at that. "He is a fool, more concerned with his fur capes and jeweled brooches than with crops and defenses. *I* could manage our lands better than he."

With a reluctant smile Joanna conceded that point. "All right, then. What of Sir Henry? Or Sir Robert? Or —I know. What of Sir Evan Thorndyke?" Joanna knew at once that she had struck a nerve, for Marilyn's pallid complexion was quickly suffused with color, and a becoming glow lit her eyes. "I . . . I hardly know him."

"You know even less of Rylan Kempe—save, of course, that he is hard-hearted and evil-tempered," Joanna added caustically. Then she sighed. "Can it hurt to question your father on this matter? Sir Evan seems a pleasant fellow. The queen especially favors him."

"I fear that may not influence my father overmuch."

"'Tis certain he will anger the king and queen when he aligns himself with Sir Rylan," Joanna mused. Then her gaze sharpened. "Your father is not an ally of King John's, is he? No, of course he is not," she answered her own question. "For he plots to marry his only child to the king's avowed foe. Tell me, Marilyn, how is it that you come to be in the queen's entourage?"

The younger girl sighed, then sat wearily upon the bed. "My father does not confide in me, not when it pertains to matters of property. However, I am aware that the queen keeps me here to help influence my father's choice of husband." She tried to smile but it was more a grimace. "When I asked my father to allow me to return to Lawton Castle, he admonished me to make the best of my situation. To smile pleasantly at whomever the queen or king directed toward me, but not to become overly friendly with anyone. I am to strictly keep my distance from any man who might aspire to my father's properties through a marriage to me."

Joanna digested that with a faint frown. "When will he announce your betrothal?"

"Not until after we have left the royal court."

Joanna thought a moment, all the while pacing the meager length of their chamber. Then she turned to face Marilyn. "Is there a chance the king might not let you leave court—I mean, if he knew?"

Marilyn's eyes grew large and round as the truth of that possibility struck home. "He could not . . . Oh, but he could. And he *would*."

Joanna sat down next to Marilyn who was now visibly trembling in fear. "If you fear marriage to Rylan Kempe, that is one way to avoid it," she said ruefully. "Of course, there's no promising the king's choice would be any better." Then she remembered the name that had brought a glow to Marilyn's face, and she was gripped with a sudden determination. Neither she nor Marilyn—nor any other propertied woman—should be bargained away to the highest bidder. A gleam lit her clear green eyes as she patted Marilyn's hand.

"Tell me everything you know about this Evan Thorndyke."

Joanna identified Egbert Crosley, Lord Lawton, at once. He was a heavyset fellow, hale and hearty, yet with a cautious frown settled upon his brow. He stood a little to one side of the bishop's parlor, conversing with Sir Guy and two other younger noblemen.

No doubt every unmarried swain at court would sooner or later approach Lord Lawton regarding his very marriageable daughter. Sir Egbert was clearly disinterested in the conversation, for his eyes anxiously scanned the chamber. When Marilyn trailed Joanna into the room, however, his gaze quickly fastened upon his daughter.

Another pair of eyes also watched Marilyn's reluctant entrance, and Joanna did not miss that fact. Evan Thorndyke stood in casual conversation with Lady Matilda, seemingly unconcerned with the constant comings and goings around the royal couple. But his eyes swerved repeatedly to Marilyn, and Joanna felt a surge of hope. Could Evan already have a soft spot for Marilyn? But then, it made so much sense. They were both pleasant, gentle souls, not meant for the devious ways of court. Joanna decided to discount that odd wink of Evan's after their game of *jeu du mail*. It had only been friendliness on his part, nothing else. But the way he observed Marilyn now, why, it was clear he already favored her.

Feeling far more optimistic than she had since she'd arrived at court, Joanna plucked at Marilyn's sleeve. "Introduce me to your father, will you?"

Marilyn hesitated when she spied the small smile playing at the corner of Joanna's mouth. "You will keep silent, won't you? What I spoke of last night, that was in the strictest confidence."

"I shall not divulge your little secret, Marilyn. Though why you should wish to cooperate in a scheme so repugnant to your own wishes is quite beyond my ken. Nevertheless, I assure you that I only wish to converse with your father on the most mundane of subjects."

Marilyn did not look convinced, but with a reluctant sigh she led Joanna forward. In passing they made their curtsies to the king and queen, and paused to greet Bishop Ferendi. But otherwise they avoided speaking to anyone else. Sir Egbert appeared greatly relieved to be saved from conversation with the self-important Sir Guy and two others of similar ilk.

"Good morrow, daughter," he burst out, turning his back on the fawning trio.

"Father." Marilyn gave him a brief kiss on the cheek then stepped back to Joanna's side. "You have not yet met my friend, Lady Joanna Preston of Oxwich."

"Of St. Theresa's Priory," Joanna corrected her, but mildly, for an idea had just come to her.

"Oh, yes. Aslin's girl." He gave her a quick appraising look. Not lecherous at all, but more as if he weighed the value her appearance brought to her already enticing inheritance. Joanna fought down a wave of impatient anger. Was property all a man saw when he looked at an unmarried female? Arpents and chains, sheep and water rights, castles and politics? Did she hold no value at all simply for herself?

She deliberately looked away from his scrutinizing stare only to meet another even more intense pair of eyes. Rylan Kempe stood in the same stepped alcove where he'd spoken to her last night. He was conversing with a well-dressed man she'd met the day before but whose name escaped her. Despite his company, however, Rylan was staring directly at her.

Suddenly unnerved, Joanna turned her attention back to Sir Egbert.

"So sorry to hear he succumbed to that blasted ague," he was saying. "We lost no less than a score at Hurley village and near to twice that in Aldbourne. Only the strong sea winds saved us at Selsey and Shoreham. Blew the illness away, it did." He nodded his head sagely, as if it were his own good planning that had protected his people in the seaside villages from the terrible fever that had taken so many lives. "Aye, 'tis sorry I am for you, girl, though I cannot claim to have known your father well."

"I had not seen him in years, milord." *And anyway, he was neither a good father nor a good husband,* she added silently. But she clamped her mouth against that admission and instead stole a quick glance at Rylan. He was another one who had no business being either husband or father. Yet Sir Egbert surely intended to make him just that to the innocent Marilyn.

She caught Marilyn's nervous stare at Rylan and the guilty return of his interest to the man speaking to him. Then Joanna looked for Evan Thorndyke. He was not staring at Marilyn, however, but at Rylan. And he was frowning. Did he know too? With strengthening resolve she turned her glittering gaze back on Sir Egbert.

"I have long been at St. Theresa's Priory, you see," she began, forcing a humble tone into her voice. "It was my wish to take up the veil and my father did consent. But then I was most rudely abducted from my home and am at a loss now to return."

"The king only exercised his rights in ensuring the orderly disposition of your properties," Egbert replied with an admonishing stare. Then he glanced briefly at Rylan Kempe and his words became less vehement. "Politics are beyond the ken of a girl like yourself."

Joanna gave him a bitter smile. "But it seems I am forced to learn more than I wish of politics, for it was not the king who abducted me from St. Theresa's. No, it was that most black-hearted of all villains, Sir Rylan Kempe. You are no doubt acquainted with the wicked Lord Blaecston?" she added as a final jab.

The expression that took over Sir Egbert's face approached the comical, but Joanna dared not laugh. His florid cheeks grew even more so; his eyes widened in a mixture of disbelief and fury; and his jowls began to quiver. Joanna felt Marilyn's sharp tug on her sleeve, but she did not acknowledge it.

"I do hope he is not a particular friend of yours," she continued as if she did not notice his reaction. "For I can well attest to his lack of manners, decorum, and honor. I was rescued only by chance when a few of the king's men happened upon us."

As Sir Egbert continued to stare at Joanna, aghast, it was Marilyn who spoke up. "Never say that is so, Joanna. Surely Lord Blaecston would not so dishonor a lady."

Joanna glanced at her friend, who already knew the

tale—as did most of the court. But Marilyn's earnest expression of dismay confirmed Joanna's hopes: Marilyn was doing her best to aid Joanna in trying to subvert her unwelcome betrothal.

Sir Egbert's flustered gaze swerved from Joanna to his seemingly distraught daughter, then back to Joanna. As she had hoped, his innate sense of gallantry toward noblewomen and the importance of protecting them was squarely at odds with his political alliance with Rylan Kempe.

"Lord Blaecston is an important man," he finally began in an almost placating tone. "There is much you cannot know of these matters."

Joanna lifted her chin stubbornly. "I doubt my father would have let such a vile deed toward his daughter go unanswered. Would you sanction such behavior toward *your* daughter?"

Once again Joanna had to stifle a laugh, for Sir Egbert appeared close to apoplectic.

"But . . . but . . . but that is precisely the point, you see. If your father were living, there would have been no need for Lord Blaecston to abduct you—"

"So you're saying you approve of such a vile deed?" Joanna asked with an innocent, wide-eyed stare.

"Father!" Marilyn cried, adding to Sir Egbert's confusion.

"No, no. That's not what I said! It's just that women cannot comprehend such things."

"I comprehend well enough how terrified I was of Lord Blaecston and his unholy band of thugs," Joanna threw back at him. "I pray Marilyn is never subject to such vile treatment as that!"

To Joanna's complete surprise—and secret delight—Marilyn proceeded to burst into tears. Before either

Joanna or Egbert could react, she fled the room. Several heads turned at her passing, but she did not care in her headlong flight. Joanna sent Sir Egbert a fulminating glare, then began to follow her friend. But when she saw Evan Thorndyke shoulder his way past a group of three nobles to follow discreetly in Marilyn's wake, Joanna promptly changed her direction.

If Marilyn's timing was perfect, Evan's was even more so. He could do more to ease Marilyn's distress and support Joanna's plan than ever she could herself. She had done all she could for now. Best to lay low for a while.

18

When Isabel and her ladies retired to the solar that the queen had taken over as her own, Marilyn was noticeably absent. Joanna sat quietly at her stitching, thinking of Marilyn as she worked a particularly complicated border pattern onto a gossamer-thin length of veiling, a piece the queen would wear with a magnificent gown Lady Adele was embroidering. Several others of the women worked at a tapestry table, just beginning a large piece that would eventually depict the king at several victorious moments of his reign. As always, talk buzzed softly, gossip interspersed with advice and passed-on bits of news. Joanna paid little attention, for she was too caught up in her own thoughts. But when Marilyn's name was mentioned, her ears perked up.

"She was crying in earnest," Adele said, all the while frowning down at a bit of knotted thread.

"She was speaking with her father just before she fled. And with Joanna."

Several heads swiveled to stare at Joanna.

"What were you speaking of?"

"Was it something her father said?"

"Yes, Joanna." Queen Isabel's imperious voice cut

through all the other chatter. She was sitting a little apart from the others, idly stroking a large white cat that was settled in her lap. "You were with our sweet and innocent Marilyn. Her father must have said something most disturbing for her to make so hasty and undignified an exit. Come, do tell us why she was so distraught."

Joanna's eyes veered from the queen to the cat and back to Isabel. Suppressing a shiver of distaste—whether for the queen or the cat was debatable—she searched for a safe answer. How she wished she could simply blurt out the truth. If the queen knew of Marilyn's betrothal to Rylan Kempe, Isabel would take decisive action to prevent their union. But Joanna had promised to keep Marilyn's secret, and no matter how much she wanted to, she knew she could not renege on her vow.

"Marilyn did not sleep well last night, milady," Joanna began cautiously. "Then, when I explained to her father the particulars of how I came to be at court—he had not heard the tale of how the arrogant Lord Blaecston abducted me from the priory—well, she became upset with her father's inability to understand how a woman might feel under such distressing circumstances."

When Isabel's gaze remained fixed on her, clearly doubting her response, Joanna rushed on. "Evan Thorndyke followed her from the hall, however. No doubt he comforted her. If you do not object, I would seek her out now and reassure myself that she is recovered from her upset."

"Evan Thorndyke?" the queen mused as Joanna put her stitching aside and stood up. Several of the other women shared knowing glances. "How long has Evan been widowed?" Isabel asked the room at large.

"Three years and more," someone answered.

"And he has but the one child?"

"Yes, milady. A young son."

A small smile curved Isabel's full lips and she airily waved Joanna along. "Yes, do see to Marilyn. Men can be so unthinking, especially fathers. My own father would have wed me to that lummox Hugh the Brown. Go see to Marilyn and bring her back to us once her spirits are restored."

Joanna's own spirits were so high that she almost skipped down the shaded arcade that led to the women's quarters. Her half-formed plan was succeeding beyond her wildest expectations! Sir Egbert was, she hoped, having second thoughts about Rylan Kempe as a son-in-law. Evan was consumed with Marilyn's distress. But best of all, the seed she had planted in Isabel's mind about Evan and Marilyn had clearly taken root!

She turned into a low, arched entrance and walked absently across a vacant hall and up a narrow stone stairway. Nothing was certain, of course. Sir Egbert had not renounced Rylan, and even if he had, Rylan was not likely to take such a change of plans easily. Rylan Kempe was nothing if not selfish and determined. In the matter of property and power he was as single-minded as King John, only far more crafty.

She approached the passage that led to the chamber she shared with Marilyn still lost in thought. But a sudden movement in a shallow doorway and a firm hand upon her arm brought her to an abrupt halt.

"At last you come," Rylan Kempe said as he forced her into the sheltering door alcove. Before she could think he had her backed up against a solid wooden door, with one hand clasped on each of her upper arms.

"You!" Joanna eyed him with deliberate distaste, but it was hard, for her heart was pounding with frantic speed. So many emotions crowded her chest that she could hardly breathe. She was afraid. She was thrilled. She was completely confused.

"Yes, me, my little dove. Or were you expecting some other swain?"

Joanna stared up into his shadowed face, all the while completely aware of the heat of his hands through the linen of her gown and kirtle. His eyes were dark and glittering. His jaw was tensed and he seemed unaccountably angry with her. Could he know so soon what she was up to?

"I . . . I was expecting no one. And even if I were," she added as she recovered her composure, "it would be no concern of yours."

His eyes narrowed at that, and his gaze flicked swiftly over her. Then he sighed. "Do not push me, Joanna. I warn you, do not push me. I told you to trust me to set things right. Yet something tells me you have already begun to dabble in matters beyond your ken."

"And I told you that I trust you only to do what's best for you, with no regard for my wishes or my well-being."

To her surprise, he smiled at her words and his taut grip loosened. With a sharp twist she slipped out of his grasp, but she was still backed up to the door with him squarely between her and escape.

"Joanna, hard as it may be for you to believe, I truly *do* have your well-being uppermost in my thoughts."

"And what of my wishes? I wish to return to St. Theresa's, but you will never allow that, will you?"

He stared down at her for a long moment, then unexpectedly reached up to finger a wayward strand of her curling hair. "That has never been possible, Joanna, though you refuse to admit it. But I promise you, you shall soon be very glad you did not take up the veil.

Wait." He placed a finger on her lips before she could argue back. "There are things I cannot tell you. At least not yet. But if you will simply be patient—"

"And trust you?" Joanna interrupted. She meant her tone to be scathing, but the unnerving touch of his finger to her sensitive lips had driven the fire from her words. Instead, there was now an unsettling coil of warmth heating in her belly.

"Yes, trust me," he murmured in a low, husky tone.

Joanna felt his breath against her cheek. She felt his hand curve into her hair and around her neck. His eyes were very dark, yet their midnight blue seemed lit from deep within. Then his face lowered and his lips touched hers, and everything else was lost to her.

His mouth was warm and firm, yet his kiss was gentle, no more than a questing taste of her lips. A small, rational part of her mind knew that she must end the kiss now, before it could go any further. But another stronger voice told her to kiss him back. Just kiss him back and revel in the heavenly sensations he roused in her. Then he moved nearer until his chest brushed her breasts.

At once a rush of heat washed over Joanna, and she gasped at the quick response of her body to his. Rylan deepened the kiss, slipping his tongue along the slight parting of her lips. This time Joanna let out a soft moan of desire, for the silken stroke of his tongue on her inner lips was a pleasure almost beyond bearing.

"You must stop," she managed to whisper. But Rylan's answer was to seek out her tongue with his own, to draw her into an erotic dance that fused their mouths as well as their bodies.

Joanna felt the demanding pressure of his hard masculine form against her legs. Chest, loins, legs—they embraced, firing her to heights that were wicked, yet wonderful. Her arms wrapped around his shoulders. Her fingers curled into his thick shoulder-length hair. When one of his knees slid between her thighs, she pressed herself wantonly against it, feeling the damp heat that had risen so suddenly in her.

"Christ and bedamned, but you are a fire in my blood," he muttered thickly as he moved his kisses to her cheek, her ear, her throat. One of his hands slid down her side and around to cup her derriere. Then he pressed her urgently to him until she was burning as fiercely as he was.

"Rylan," she whispered as her head tilted back to rest against the heavy door. His hungry lips searched out a heated trail down her throat and along her collarbone to where the neckline of her bodice barred him further access to her skin. But he continued anyway, pressing his kisses on the linen gown, searing the upper swells of her breasts through the fabric.

"You are mine, Joanna. No one else's," he murmured in her ear, breaking the pattern of his kisses.

Up to now Joanna had been too disoriented by his drugging nearness to think straight. But his words, claiming her as his and his alone, brought a welcome measure of sanity back to her—and a considerable measure of anger as she remembered his betrothal.

"Yours?" she snapped. She turned her face away as he sought to capture her lips once more.

"Yes, mine, Joanna. No matter how things may appear at court, never doubt that fact." He cupped her face and forced her to look up at him. When he saw the fury in her eyes, however, he hesitated, and it was that moment of his bewilderment that caused her anger to explode.

"How can I be yours when you already claim another!"

No sooner were the words out than Joanna profoundly regretted them. For one thing, she sounded too much like a jealous shrew for comfort. Plus, she had broken her promise to Marilyn. But worst of all, she realized as his brows came together in a frown, she had lost the one advantage she had. Without the advantage of secretiveness, she would be hard-pressed to undermine his betrothal to Marilyn.

"What, by all that is holy, does that mean?" He began furiously. "What do you know of these things?"

"I know that King John will oppose you at every turn, both with me and the Lady Marilyn." She glared defiantly at him, daring him to deny his betrothal to Marilyn. To her frustration, however, he ignored the subject.

"King John shall not hand you over to anyone but me."

Joanna shook her head and laughed out loud, though without any trace of mirth. "Oh, but you are truly the fool. He hates you. And I . . ."

"And you—despite whatever you think you know—you most obviously do not," he finished for her.

As arrogant responses went, this was truly his worst. "You are the . . . the . . . the most odious and dishonorable wretch—"

"That you have ever kissed?" he broke in on her tirade. "Come now, Joanna. You can surely leave off this pretense of outrage after all that has passed between us." He leaned forward, placing his palms on the door on either side of her shoulders, and ensnared her with his mocking gaze. "Let us return to our previous communion. I much prefer kissing to arguing."

"But I do not!" She planted her hands against his chest and tried to force him back, but it was to no avail.

"What a wicked little liar you are," he murmured as he tried to capture her lips. "You're going to have to start telling the truth, you know. And stop interfering in things that don't concern you."

In frustration Joanna moved one of her hands up from his chest to clap over his mouth and glared up at him. "Why? So you can ruin that poor girl as you have ruined me?"

"Ahem."

Joanna jumped at the sound of someone else clearing his throat. Rylan jerked upright as well and had the presence of mind to hide her face against his shoulder in a rough, smothering embrace.

"I'll thank you to move along," he growled at the intruder beyond the doorway.

"This is not a wise place for a tryst, my friend."

As quickly as Rylan had pulled Joanna against his chest did he set her free. "By Christ, Evan!" he barked as he turned to face the man. "Your timing is damned inconvenient."

"That would be a matter of opinion," Evan snapped back. "I wonder if the Lady Joanna feels as you do. I most certainly do not."

With no need to hide her identity any longer, Rylan turned around to face the glowering Evan. "What has you so bedeviled?" he began.

"'Tis bad enough she fears you. Must you now dally with the one maiden she considers her friend?"

"What?" Rylan exclaimed in confusion. But Joanna understood at once.

"Dally!" she snapped. "God preserve me from all wooden-headed men. I was not dallying with him. Indeed, the truth is he lay in wait for me and accosted me even as I made my way to Marilyn's side!" She jerked her hand from Rylan's lingering grasp and gave him a withering glare.

As quickly as Evan had accused her, so now did he swiftly come to her defense. "My God, what ails you, Rylan? You were foolhardy enough to abduct the Lady Joanna. Then doubly so to pursue her here. Would you now bed her within hailing distance of your own betrothed? Not to mention within the confines of a holy house, and while she is a ward of the king's!"

He gestured for Joanna to come to his side, but Rylan stopped her with a steely hand on her arm.

"There are things I have not told you, Evan."

"How enlightening this is. It appears you keep different secrets from different people," Joanna said sarcastically. "Evan apparently knew of your betrothal. I did not learn of it until yesterday."

"I would you had not learned of it at all," Rylan muttered. But he kept his eyes trained on Evan. "My plans are somewhat altered. But this is not a place to talk." He indicated Joanna with a jerk of his head.

Evan's initial anger seemed to cool somewhat and the hot color in his face faded. He gave Rylan a curious look, then directed his attention to Joanna.

"Perhaps you should go to Marilyn. She is calmer but nonetheless unnerved by her outburst before her father and all of the royal court."

Joanna was more than happy to escape from Rylan's angry presence; however, he was not quite finished with her.

"You will hold your tongue on all matters pertaining to me and the Lady Marilyn. The subject of betrothals is forbidden you, no matter who brings it up. Is that clear, Joanna?"

"What is clear," she began with a smug smile on her lips, "is that the exalted Lord Blaecston may threaten and storm, but in the end I shall do as I see fit—"

He jerked her around so fast that she nearly fell. "Don't force my hand, Joanna. For 'tis only you who shall suffer for it." Then he thrust her past Evan and into the passageway beyond. "Go to Marilyn. But I warn you to do or say nothing at all."

Despite her recent brave words, Joanna was only too willing to flee. Rylan's threat had shaken her more than she cared to admit. She knew instinctively that he would not physically harm her. Yet the warning in his words had been distinct. He meant what he said.

But what *could* he do if she should say something to disrupt whatever new plot he had devised? she wondered as she slowed her headlong pace and strove to calm her racing pulse. And besides, Marilyn's future depended on it. Evan was the man for Marilyn, not Rylan.

Rylan was . . . Rylan was . . .

Joanna pressed her palm flat against her stomach, trying to calm the quiver inside her and push the traitorous thought away. Yet no matter how she tried she could not deny, at least to herself, that Rylan was the man for her.

It made no sense. It went against everything she believed and wanted for her future. Yet the evidence was there. His touch, his kiss, his very presence stirred something deep within her—something she'd never even known existed. It was wicked and sinful. But it was true.

With an unhappy sigh she slumped against the cold stone wall. What a terrible mess she was in. Rylan wished to wed Marilyn for the enormous political advantages her inheritance offered. If he'd wanted to wed

Joanna and gain her Yorkshire properties, he would have done so at the outset. But he did not want her for a wife. He only wanted her for his *fille de joie*.

She would not be at all surprised if he wished to save her from marriage to one of the king's followers so that he himself could have easier access to her! Perhaps his altered plan was to establish her at Oxwich, where he could freely visit her and partake of the same pleasures they'd shared at Isle Sacré.

The pity of it, she realized as a shiver of remembered passion shook her, was that she knew all this and yet still yearned for him.

Joanna took a deep breath then pushed herself away from the wall. Lifting her chin, she made her way toward the chamber she shared with Marilyn. Rylan Kempe was a selfish rogue with no thought for anyone's desires but his own. What *he* wanted, however, could simply go to the devil, she decided with a comforting jolt of anger. There was no reason why his grandiose political aspirations should be allowed to make Marilyn and Evan miserable. Her own plan to match them up was well under way, and she was not about to let him ruin it now.

No, Rylan Kempe was not going to marry Marilyn. Evan was. And even though Rylan might never turn to her—indeed, he would hate her if she foiled his plans, and she would probably be wretched wed to such an arrogant, hard-hearted knave as he—she was nevertheless going forward as planned. All she needed was a way to undo Rylan's betrothal to Marilyn.

"Sweet mother of God, but I do believe you mad!" Evan burst out when he and Rylan were safely alone. Evan had strode impatiently at Rylan's side through the abbey's busy quadrangle past the well and fountain, then beyond the vegetable gardens and physic garden, all the while growing more and more angry with his friend. But now, on the open banks of the River Ouse, upstream from the abbey's mill, he felt no need to restrain his words.

"You are betrothed to the one, yet pant after the other! Lady Joanna is no merry widow nor loose woman that you may make free with. She is a sheltered girl, a noblewoman whom you should protect, not attempt to ruin!" Then his face grew even redder as a terrible thought seemed to occur to him. "You cannot mean to prevent John from arranging her marriage by destroying her reputation?"

"Christ and bedamned, Evan! Have you so little faith in me as that?" Rylan grabbed at a tall reed, ripping it from its roots.

"When a man is consumed with a woman he does not think with his head. His cods pulls him in directions his brain would never take."

Rylan's irritation with his friend cooled somewhat at that, for despite the crude wording, there was an undeniable truth to Evan's remark. "The mistakes I made with Joanna Preston are in the past. 'Tis my plan to correct them in the only honorable manner I can." He grinned crookedly at the still-bemused Evan, feeling curiously awkward. "I shall wed her."

The emotions that raced across Evan's face caused Rylan's grin to increase. Evan was shocked at first, then obviously relieved. But then horror and anger returned. "You are betrothed to Lady Marilyn but intend to marry Lady Joanna? What of your contract with Egbert? What of the king's objections? What of the Lady Marilyn's reputation?"

With an exasperated sigh Rylan flung down the mutilated reed and ran a hand through his windblown hair. "'Tis a complex situation, I'll grant you that. But not an impossible one."

"Oh, aye, let us just go and bend an elbow with John and Egbert. Enough wine shall see everything aright!"

Rylan laughed at his friend's sarcasm, and his own composure returned. "I admit it will not be easy. Egbert will be furious, and his enmity is something I would avoid at all costs."

"Do you think he will go over to John?" Evan asked. Having vented his emotions, now that the talk had turned political, he quickly grew serious.

"Of that I cannot be certain. On the one hand, he has resisted all of King John's suggestions for a likely son-in-law. However, his temper is never easy, and in a fit of anger at me he may capitulate to John's pressure. Damn, but I wish we could get Marilyn away from court and the hold that gives the king over her—and thereby Egbert. 'Twas a poor day when he let her come under the king's rule."

"Egbert agreed to that only to placate John and to buy some time," Evan replied. "Also, he felt his daughter should learn something of the ways of court and the royal couple. After all, he has kept her secluded in Lawton Castle most of her life. Her vast properties make her the most valuable heiress in England. She must learn how to comport herself in high places."

Rylan grimaced at that. "The most valuable heiress in all of England. And she was almost mine."

"She still could be," Evan responded to Rylan's words in a guarded tone.

Rylan smiled ruefully. "I never thought to say this, nor even less to believe it. But there are some things more valuable even than properties such as Marilyn's."

With an understanding chortle Evan clapped a hand on Rylan's shoulder. "Some things? Perhaps some Yorkshire heiress?"

It was Rylan's turn to become serious. "I would have her even without Oxwich," he admitted with uncharacteristic candor. "Though she came to me bare of foot and with no more than the priory garb I first spied her in." Then, responding to Evan's speechless stare, he grinned. "First, however, I must find a way to placate Sir Egbert and salvage the Lady Marilyn's pride."

Evan's face broke into a smile. "Perhaps we can turn up another bridegroom for her. One acceptable both to her father as well as herself."

"That's the second time you've implied that Egbert's girl is unhappy with our match. Before you said that she feared me."

"Aye, she does that. She is very young, you see. And quite shy."

"You concern yourself most generously with the girl, Evan. You purport to know her temperament. You are privy to her fears at being wed to such a blackguard as I am said to be. And most damning of all, you are clearly fresh from seeing her—calming her, I would venture to guess." At his friend's reddened face Rylan let out a laugh of comprehension. "Why did you not tell me of this long ago?"

Evan shifted his stance, staring determinedly down at the muddy shore of the river. "'Twas pointless. You were already betrothed to her. I could see it was a wise match, and certain to bedevil King John."

"As would a match between you and Marilyn. Your properties and hers would make a formidable showing against the king." Rylan grinned at the hopeful expression dawning on Evan's face. "'Twould mean the end of your playful days at court, of course. Your opposition to the king's unwise reign could no longer be hidden."

"I chafe at it every day already. To wed Marilyn and throw off this disguise would be a greater blessing than I ever would have hoped for."

"Well, the bridegrooms are agreed. Now it's the father and guardians we must address."

"What of Joanna's consent? I know Marilyn will not object, but the Lady Joanna clearly has a mind of her own. She appeared none too kindly disposed toward you when she left us," Evan added, though with a suppressed smile.

Rylan's dark gaze narrowed speculatively as he thought of Joanna. She would most certainly object. She would harangue him about taking up the veil—as if such a passionate woman could be allowed to waste herself within the confining walls of a priory! But he knew ways to silence her arguments. It would not take long to turn her into a most biddable wife.

"Just leave Joanna to me," he replied with a determined glint in his eyes. "Just leave the fiery Joanna Preston to me."

19

When she slipped into her bedchamber, Joanna gave every appearance of being completely composed. She was resolved not to let Rylan Kempe and his wicked kisses deter her from her goal. When she closed the door and turned to face Marilyn, however, she was taken aback by the beatific expression on her friend's face.

"He is truly remarkable, is he not? So unlike any other man at court. Gentle. Kind." Marilyn sighed in complete contentment. But then the glow in her eyes dimmed. "Oh, if only he had offered for me right away. My father would surely have welcomed his suit. But now he can say nothing. Oh, Joanna, why did Evan not speak up before?"

"Because he is Rylan Kempe's friend, and he knew of the betrothal contract long before you did," Joanna retorted, plopping down upon her half-curtained bed. She knew her tone was unnecessarily short, but she couldn't help it. The sight of Marilyn's dreamy expression had roused the most dreadful feelings of envy in her chest. Why couldn't she be loved as Marilyn was—by a man who loved her as she loved him?

But then, Evan Thorndyke was a rarity, quite unlike

the other arrogant men she'd had the misfortune to be- come acquainted with. First her father. Then King John and the heartless Lord Blaecston. If only she could have been drawn to Evan. Why must she be so perverse as to be attracted to Rylan Kempe? With a sigh of her own she rolled onto her back.

"Forgive me my foul temper, Marilyn. 'Tis only that I am fresh from . . . from conversing with your be- trothed."

"Lord Blaecston?" Marilyn went pale and sat down on a leather-slung stool.

"The same. When I left he and Evan were having rather sharp words."

"About . . . about me?"

Joanna nodded slowly as a disingenuous idea sprang unbidden into her mind. It would be very bad of her to deliberately mislead Marilyn, she tried to tell herself. Yet if it achieved the desired goal, Marilyn would be truly happy. And if it failed . . . even if it failed, no real harm would be done. Resolved at once, she rolled to a sitting position.

"Evan was angry with Rylan."

"I never should have spoken to him about the be- trothal. Oh, but you said he already knew. That's why he never approached me." Marilyn's face clouded with con- fusion. "But if he already knew about everything, then why is he angry at Lord Blaecston at this late date?"

Joanna smiled at Marilyn—a heartfelt smile yet edged with wistfulness. "He is angry because you are unhappy. He followed you here to comfort you—" She broke off then and gave Marilyn a purposefully assessing stare. "And how precisely *did* he comfort you?" she asked with raised brows.

The color that flooded Marilyn's face told the tale

more clearly than did her flustered words. "He . . . he helped me to stop crying. I . . . my . . . my face was wet. We . . . we talked a little while . . ."

"Just talked? Nothing else?" Joanna interrupted, trying hard to keep a serious expression.

"We . . . he . . . that is, I . . . yes, I let him put his arm about me. I shouldn't have, I know. But . . . you see . . ."

"And then he kissed you?" Joanna asked softly. Marilyn bit her lip and stared at Joanna with eyes gone very round. Then she swallowed hard and slowly nodded.

This time Joanna couldn't restrain her smile. "And was it a very nice kiss?"

Again Marilyn nodded. "It was sweet and very . . . very thrilling," she admitted in a wondering voice. "He was so gentle and kind. It was like being in heaven, Joanna. It was truly like heaven. I thought I might faint from the very joy of it."

Yes, she knew that feeling well, Joanna thought, remembering the sultry, drowning sensations Rylan so easily roused in her. Then she steeled herself to initiate her devious plan. "It may have felt like heaven, Marilyn. However, you are betrothed to another. In the eyes of the church, what you did demands repentance. If you are to overcome these feelings for a man not yours to have, then you must pray for forgiveness."

Marilyn's crestfallen features came close to breaking Joanna's resolve. The last thing she felt toward Marilyn was censorious, yet if Marilyn's betrothal to Rylan were to be broken, she must use whatever opportunities came along.

"Perhaps we should go to the chapel and pray. No." She paused for effect. "No, I think the cathedral would be better."

Marilyn did not say a word on the long walk across the abbey grounds to the cathedral. Joanna peered around, hoping to spy the one man who could best see her plan take root. To her enormous relief, the Benedictine monks were just filing out after the None services. Bishop Ferendi and his entourage were still in the apse when the two women slipped down the dimly lit nave of the cathedral.

"A word with you, my lord bishop," Joanna called softly as she hurried up to the well-fed bishop. "If you please," she added with bowed head when he turned to look at her.

"Ah, our own little nun," he mocked her in a patronizing tone. "I wondered when you would seek me out. Ready to confess your sins, my dear? Ready to repent your bold words and disrespectful manner?"

It took every bit of Joanna's willpower to nod her head. It was not her own confession but Marilyn's that she wished the bishop to hear. She was more than certain the vainglorious old busybody would run straightaway to the royal couple should Marilyn's confession reveal the name of the man she was meant to marry. But as for herself, Joanna did not wish to confess any of her many sins to Bishop Ferendi. Least of all those connected with one Rylan Kempe. Some other more pious priest, perhaps, but even then she could hardly confess and ask forgiveness when she did not know if she truly repented. In a moment of desperation she looked over at Marilyn.

"Perhaps Marilyn should go first. I . . . I needs must compose myself." She smiled grimly. "Surely you understand."

"Indeed I do, my child. Indeed I do. Very well then. You first, Lady Marilyn." He waved on the several monks who lingered yet for him, then bustled importantly to the red-curtained confessional that was set into a thick stone side wall.

Marilyn sent Joanna one last sorrowful glance before she too disappeared behind the penitent's portion of the damask hangings.

When Marilyn left the confessional she was pale and obviously upset. She did not look at Joanna but went straight to a niche with a shrine to St. Etheldreda, fell to her knees, and with bowed head began to pray her penance.

Joanna approached the confessional reluctantly. It occurred to her that since she'd left St. Theresa's, she had spent far less time at her prayers than was her custom. Certainly she should not resent whatever the bishop should demand of her now. But she did resent it. Even as she knelt on the hard stone floor behind the curtain, she felt irritation at the pompous fool who sat in judgment of her beyond the pierced-work screen. Though she reminded herself that it was God who judged her—that Bishop Ferendi was only a handservant to the heavenly Father—she could not help but wonder at His choice of servants. Certainly Sister Edithe was far better suited to carrying out the Lord's word than was this conceited, self-important fool.

"Bless me, Father, for I have sinned," she began the litany she knew so well. She was ungrateful, she told him, and impatient. Quick-tempered and far too willful.

They were all shortcomings she had suffered as long as she could remember. Joanna suspected she would continue to suffer them all the many years of her life. But Bishop Ferendi seemed barely concerned as he hurried her through the remainder of her confession. She did not tell him of her more recent failings—the wanton thoughts that so often afflicted her, the wicked sensations she fought to deny, yet secretly relished. Instead, she vowed in silent prayer to amend her ways and do twice the penance he demanded. And all the while she wondered what Marilyn had told him.

The cathedral was silent by the time Joanna finished her penance. Her knees ached and she shivered in the lingering chill from the cold stone walls. Bishop Ferendi had long since departed, hurrying on his way with his rich gowns flapping at his haste. Now only Joanna and Marilyn remained in the dim silence of the vast cathedral, and Marilyn was still at her prayers. Suppressing her impatience as best she could, Joanna waited nervously for her friend to finish.

"The bishop kept you overlong at your prayers," she remarked nonchalantly to Marilyn when they finally made their way toward the squat tower that housed the queen and her ladies.

"I had much to confess, as you well know," Marilyn murmured listlessly. They walked on without further conversation, though Joanna burned all the while to question the subdued girl about what she'd admitted to the bishop.

When they entered the solar, the other women all peered curiously at Marilyn. But when she barely responded to their thinly veiled inquiries, they soon lost interest. Isabel was not there, but before very long she returned. With an imperious flick of one hand she signaled all her women to leave the room. Then as the women scurried to obey, her hard stare landed on Marilyn and Joanna knew immediately that her plan had worked.

"Could I have a word with you, Lady Marilyn?" Although it was worded as a question, there was no mistak-

ing the command in the queen's tone. "The rest of you
may see to your own interest. I shall not have a need of
you until the bells ring for dinner."

Compelled to leave, Joanna nonetheless did not go
very far. A part of her was thrilled to know her little plot
had succeeded so easily. The bishop was most assuredly
a spineless wretch to run straight to the king and queen
with the private confessions of his flock. Joanna was almost sorry she had read him so well, for now she had to
worry about the ramifications of it all. What if the king
kept Marilyn hostage? What if he forced her to wed not
Evan, but some other truly disagreeable fellow? Someone even less acceptable than Rylan Kempe. At least Rylan was handsome and fit, and Marilyn would not suffer
physically at his hands.

But Marilyn feared Rylan and dreaded their union.
Surely this was for the best. But then, there were so
many uncertainties, primary of them being the king's
erratic nature.

Back and forth did Joanna's hopes and fears pummel
her. The minutes passed as hours until she could no
longer bear the suspense. With a muttered curse that she
knew she would later have to confess, she dashed
through a low arch and out into the weak afternoon sunlight. She could do nothing about Marilyn's audience
with the queen. But she *could* seek out Evan Thorndyke.
He was calm and levelheaded, and might know something. Besides, this affected him also.

Joanna found Evan perched on a segment of wall that
looked out over the only bit of undrained fens left
around the abbey. He was so lost in thought that he did
not look up until she was almost upon him and a pebble
skittered noisily beneath her shoes.

"Lady Joanna?" His face creased in worry as he rose to his feet. "What brings you here?"

Staring into his troubled eyes restored Joanna's confidence that she had done the right thing. "There is something afoot of which you should be aware," she began without preamble. "I believe the queen has received word of Marilyn's betrothal contract. Even now she questions her. I do not know what the king will do, but I am certain he will not allow the marriage to go forth as planned."

At once Evan's gaze sharpened. But he did not look overly alarmed by the news, and Joanna was considerably heartened. "It but hastens the inevitable. But I wonder how they learned of it," he added with a suspicious glance at her.

"It was not through my lips that the secret was revealed," she defended herself hotly. "Anyway, that is not the point. I fear the king's reaction to the news. You know the royal court. What do you think shall occur now?"

"She will remain King John's prisoner," he answered flatly. Then, seeing her alarmed expression, he added, "She will be kindly treated, do not fear for her safety. But her father will not be able to remove her from court."

"Will he—the king—force her to wed another?" she asked, watching him closely.

"Without a doubt," he said, but with no hint of either anger or alarm.

Joanna stared at him in confusion. "But why aren't you—that is, I thought . . ." She trailed off then sent him an exasperated look. "You *do* wish to wed her, don't you?"

Evan let out a great bark of laughter. "Yes. If the truth

is to be told—and only between the two of us—I most assuredly do wish to wed the Lady Marilyn. But I confess not to understand at all your concern in this matter. Rumor has it that you are resisting the king's plan to find a politically appropriate husband for *you*. Why trouble yourself over Marilyn's betrothal? Rylan says you have no interest in politics whatsoever, so what—"

"Rylan says!" Joanna snapped. "Rylan says this or that and everyone within hearing must jump? If it weren't for Rylan Kempe neither Marilyn nor I would be in such dire straits. Both of us are at the mercy of the king due to Rylan's selfish plotting!"

At his shocked mien Joanna immediately lowered her voice, then glanced around to see if anyone had overheard her rash words. When she again met Evan's gaze he had an odd expression on his face.

"There is some truth to what you say, milady, but methinks there is even more that you leave unsaid." He straightened up from where he had leaned against the wall and, with a grin on his face, held out his arm to her. "Come, let us go and mingle and see what we may learn. If you will seek out Marilyn, I will find her father. Such a storm as is brewing now can hardly help but soon erupt."

Evan's quiet confidence did much to calm Joanna's unease. If he who wished to wed Marilyn was not too dismayed by the situation, then surely things would come out all right. However, Rylan Kempe's involvement in the whole messy affair continued to trouble her. There were things Evan was privy to which she was not, things about Rylan. The two men were well acquainted, perhaps even friends. Yet Evan did not think twice about thwarting Rylan in the matter of Marilyn Crosley. Though Joanna did not hesitate to trust Evan regarding the matter of Marilyn's betrothal, she was not completely confident about his other alliances.

What a devious, confusing place the royal court was, she decided, not for the first time. Everyone smiling and polite, hiding their true faces from one another. But the most devious of all the players was one Rylan Kempe, Lord Blaecston. Arrogant. Calculating. A man intent on having his own way.

And the tenderest of lovers.

Something warm and unwelcome stirred in her belly at that traitorous thought. Though she tried to squelch the memory, she nonetheless vividly recalled the stirring pressure of his lips on hers and the taste of him. The way he'd felt against her.

Oh, but it was too unfair, she silently protested. Why did he continue to plague her thoughts so? Then, as if her very thoughts conjured him up, she spied Rylan.

She and Evan had just entered the walled garden where they'd played *jeu du mail* together. A number of people were assembled in loose clusters. The king, queen, and bishop, however, were nowhere to be seen.

Likewise, Marilyn was absent. But it was Rylan who drew Joanna's attention. He was just pulling Egbert Crosley away from conversation with two other men, much to the older man's obvious surprise. No doubt the two had previously agreed not to mingle in public, she thought. But with Marilyn in the royal clutches, Rylan was clearly forced to rethink his strategy.

Rylan and Sir Egbert headed down a gravel path away from the others. Evan released Joanna's arm and gave her a firm shove toward several of the queen's ladies-in-waiting. He intended to join Rylan and Sir Egbert and leave her out. But Joanna would have nothing of it.

"I have no intention of standing idly by while the

three of you plot poor Marilyn's future," she said as she fell in stride beside him.

"'Tis beyond your ability to help, Lady Joanna. Besides, I give you my solemn promise that I will not allow her to be badly used in any manner whatsoever."

"Oh, Evan. I believe *you* are sincere. But I'm not at all so confident about those two."

As they caught up with the others, Rylan gave Joanna an intense look, then scowled at Evan. When he spoke, however, his annoyance was held well in check. "You have a curious habit of involving yourself in matters not of your own concern, Joanna. Evan, if you would be so kind as to escort Lady Joanna back to the other women."

"I shall not go," Joanna retorted. "Sir Egbert, I would have a word with you. Alone," she added with a smug moue at Rylan.

Egbert looked from her to Rylan and back to her. She could see the confusion on his face, and the annoyance. "If you wish to reiterate your accusations toward Sir Rylan, 'tis unnecessary. I noted well your complaints of his behavior and mean to take him to task for them. No son-in-law of mine shall mistreat mine only child."

"Mistreat her!" Rylan cried.

"Son-in-law?" Joanna whispered with a sinking heart. Could he still mean to get Marilyn for Rylan?

It was Evan who took matters in hand. "I believe, Sir Egbert, that the subject of your daughter's betrothal to Rylan must now be discussed anew. Grave changes in circumstances force a reconsideration of the betrothal contract."

"What in God's name is going on around here?" Sir Egbert thundered.

"The king has her and he knows of our contract."

Egbert stared at Rylan speechlessly. "But . . . but

how? We told no one—" He shook his head then stared at Evan and Joanna. "You both knew," he began in an accusatory tone.

"Evan has been privy to everything. He is the contact at court that I told you of. But as for the Lady Joanna . . ." Rylan's sharp gaze turned on her and Joanna could not prevent the flush that rose on her face.

"I told no one," she swore. "Marilyn bade me keep her secret, and I did." Her guilty gaze flitted to Egbert who did not look nearly so fierce and threatening as Rylan. "If you had but consulted her in this matter—if you had not selected a man who frightened her so, then all this might have been avoided."

"What? But she is only—"

"A woman? Yes, she is. And a very important woman, it would seem."

"We are all well aware of your views on that subject," Rylan broke in. "However, there is still the question of how the king learned of the betrothal contract."

Joanna gave him a smug look, for her sense of righteous anger had restored her courage. "I suspect it was Bishop Ferendi. He heard our confessions this morning. Perhaps Marilyn—being the dutiful daughter she is—begged forgiveness for the rebellious feelings she harbored. If she mentioned her legal betrothal—"

"That pompous ass went straight to the king," Rylan finished for her.

There was a short silence and in the distance they could hear the buzz of conversation from the walled garden.

"We must think this through," Evan said. "The king will not easily set her free."

"He may do to her as he did to Moreland's widow, the

Lady Clara," Sir Egbert fretted. "My Marilyn is but a young and innocent maiden."

"'Tis a shame you did not consider her feelings before," Joanna threw in. Although it was cruel to accuse him now when he already felt so badly, she wanted to be certain he did not change his tune once Marilyn was restored to him.

"I have a plan," Rylan remarked, deliberately ignoring Joanna. At once the other three turned to him. Only Joanna's face was skeptical.

"You *always* have a plan," she scoffed. "But it always benefits only you at the expense of everyone else concerned."

"And you are always interfering in matters that do not pertain to you." He advanced on her angrily but she did not back down.

"Marilyn is my friend and therefore her future must be important to me. I would do anything to prevent her marriage to you!"

Joanna regretted her reckless words at once. But to her surprise, Rylan did not react furiously. At first he looked surprised. Then bemused. Finally, to her complete bewilderment, he grinned.

"You would save her from my clutches, would you?"

Joanna's eyes narrowed suspiciously and she glanced to Evan for help. But he was watching their verbal battle with a most interested expression on his face and was clearly not willing to take sides.

When she did not answer him, Rylan continued. "I wonder if you might have gone so far as to prod her into going to confession." One of his brows lifted and his lips curled in a mocking smile.

"Why, that's . . . that's ridiculous. You . . . you're just looking for someone to blame so your own guilt won't appear so grave. Don't forget," she said, turning to Sir Egbert. "'Twas he who abducted me and treated me so cruelly. You would not want Marilyn subject to such a heartless man as that!"

Rylan also turned to Sir Egbert. Taking the beleaguered man's arm, he steered him back onto the path, effectively shutting Joanna out of the conversation. "Perhaps there is a way to resolve this dilemma to everyone's satisfaction." He glanced over his shoulder at Joanna, who was staring balefully at him, and gave her a smug look. "Take Lady Joanna back to her station, Evan. Then join us as soon as is possible."

In frustration Joanna started after them, but Evan caught her arm and held her fast. "You've done all you can do, Joanna. 'Twould be best to leave things in our hands now."

With an angry yank she freed her arm from his grasp. Then she glared at Rylan. "You shall not get your way this time, Lord Black Heart. For once you shall not get your way!"

Rylan paused briefly and gave her a bold sweeping stare. "You could not be more wrong, my little dove. I intend to get everything I want. Everything." Then he turned and walked away.

20

King John's expression exuded both malice and triumph, Rylan thought as he entered the room. Isabel's gaze was more cautious, but she was not entirely able to suppress her own gloating smile.

By contrast, Bishop Ferendi was rather subdued. Was the old goat ashamed of his part—carrying the private confessions of an innocent girl to the king and queen for their political gain? Rylan scoffed inwardly at the idea, but there was no denying that the bishop looked distinctly uncomfortable.

To Rylan's relief, Sir Egbert appeared completely composed. Rylan had feared the man would not be able to pull off his part in their scheme, but that worry now seemed unfounded. Only the man's whitened knuckles and clenched hands revealed any sign of tension.

Rylan kept his own face carefully blank as he approached the waiting group. John sat behind a table on a high-backed chair that had been draped with a dark-colored rug for his comfort. His favorite falcon perched on the left back corner, hooded and quiet. Isabel sat off to the one side, with a hand tapestry frame in her lap. But her interest in stitching was understandably absent.

Behind her stood the bishop, looking as if he'd rather be anywhere else.

The room was well lit with two large branches of candles and several torches on the walls, and Rylan could clearly see the unfurled parchment that lay before John. His betrothal contract. He had not expected Egbert to produce it for the king's perusal. Rylan's composure must have slipped somewhat at that realization, for John's smile broadened.

"No doubt you know the purpose of this meeting, Sir Rylan, and since that is the case, I will dispense with the preliminaries. This contract is broken as of this very moment." So saying, he lifted the parchment and, with a vicious jerk, ripped it apart.

Rylan's eyes glittered with emotion. How he was going to enjoy undermining John once again. "Destroying the written evidence of my agreement with Sir Egbert cannot negate the vow given between two honorable men."

"Two honorable men!" the king exclaimed. "It can hardly be honorable to circumvent the will of the king. Were it not for the few loyal vassals I surround myself with, vermin of your ilk would quickly destroy my entire kingdom! But you are foiled this time, Lord Blaecston, for I shall not permit this wedding to take place." With one movement of his arm he swept the torn contract from the table and let the pieces drift to the bare floor.

"You cannot do that. You can't stop the wedding," Rylan countered, forcing his expression to darken.

"So long as I keep your bride from you—and her father," he added, shooting Sir Egbert an angry look, "I can very well do exactly that. The Lady Marilyn is in my safekeeping until such time as her father and I can agree on a new bridegroom for her. And that will not be very long," he gloated.

Rylan endeavored to appear thunderstruck. He turned toward Sir Egbert. "But what of our agreement?"

The older man shrugged in apparent resignation. "Your suit is hopeless, Kempe. I would not have my daughter kept this way. Besides, the queen has named a most eligible young man in your stead, and he has already agreed. It remains only for Marilyn to agree."

"Her opinion is of no moment," John snapped.

Egbert stood a little straighter as he looked at his king. "No, my lord. On this one point I must remain firm. 'Twas my error not to consult with her from the first. Had I done so, then all of this might have been avoided." He glanced sharply at Rylan. "She does not wish to wed with you, sir. 'Twas that which caused this matter to come to the king's attention. I will not make the same mistake twice. She must agree," he said, returning his gaze to the king. "Only then will I sign the contracts."

The king started to respond, but Isabel cut him off. "That is completely agreeable to us, my Lord Lawton. You daughter is kindly disposed toward Lord Manning. I foresee no problems on that front."

"They shall marry at court," John stated emphatically. "This very week."

"Agreed—"

"Not agreed." Rylan broke in on Sir Egbert's words. He stared at the older man. "You make an enemy of me this day if you do not honor our agreement. And I warn you, Egbert, I will not forget this slight you do me."

A tense silence ensued as Rylan waited with bated breath for Egbert to broach the most ticklish matter of all.

"My hands are tied, man! What would you have me do?"

In answer, Rylan faced John. "Your gain from this thievery you attempt against me shall be less than nothing should I turn my forces against Sir Egbert and the hapless Manning. For mark my words, if I wage war on them, there shall be no crops for them to reap and therefore no taxes for them to pay the royal treasury. If I must lay siege to every demesne in his farflung holdings, then so be it. But I shall not be thwarted in this manner!"

John appeared taken aback as Rylan's thunderous words echoed in the chamber. Even Isabel frowned, for she well knew that a countryside embroiled in a private war inevitably yielded little to the royal coffers.

The king glared at Rylan. "Perhaps I would be better served by taking you here and now, and demanding a ransom for your release!"

Rylan laughed contemptuously. "And risk having your barons of Yorkshire turn away from you en masse? I think not."

"Yorkshire, Yorkshire!" Sir Egbert cried in seeming frustration. "Damnation, Kempe! If you would be a king in your damnable Yorkshire, then so be it!" He turned away from Rylan and advanced toward John, then leaned forward with his two hands on the table. "If he already holds Yorkshire in his power to that extent, then give him the rest of what he wants. Let him wed that other girl instead of mine. Give him the Lady Joanna and Oxwich Castle in exchange for a promise of peace!"

"What are you saying, man? Are you mad!" John abruptly rose from his chair and anxiously paced the floor. "He'll have no such thing from me."

"In any event, 'tis not enough," Rylan threw in. He caught the surprised look on Sir Egbert's face but ignored it. One thing he knew was that the king would be appeased only if he thought he had Rylan backed into a corner. "One paltry estate is hardly a fair exchange for the vast properties that go with the Lady Marilyn's hand."

"But he will not release her to you," Egbert shouted back. "And I will not allow her to be kept a prisoner here! Either you agree to wed the other girl in trade for my daughter, or I shall do exactly as *you* threatened. I shall wage war upon *you* and all who claim *your* friendship. You will rue the day you set out to cross Egbert Crosley!"

King John stared at Egbert in total confusion, clearly as dismayed by Sir Egbert's threats of war as he was by Rylan's. When Isabel stood up and crossed quietly to her husband, Rylan followed her every move. As she went, so did this entire bluff go, he realized. She had the power to sway her indecisive husband in any direction she chose.

"It does us no good to shout," she began with a warning glance at her husband. "Such critical decisions of state and property should not be made amid threats that we shall all later regret."

"I will not be the one to regret my threat," Rylan muttered, staring grimly at Egbert.

"Actually, Lord Blaecston, Sir Egbert's suggestion is one of considerable merit." She favored him with a smile even as she squeezed John's arm to keep him silent. "You are understandably angered at being thwarted. Had your plan succeeded, you would have held title to a veritable kingdom all your own. The promise of such enormous power is seductive indeed. But you are smart enough to see that we cannot allow such an unfriendly lord as you have proven to be to wield such power." She smiled at the three sullen men and moved back to her chair.

"When you have a chance to cool your temper, I am certain you will understand our position. Furthermore, you will also realize that a war with Sir Egbert does you as much harm as it does him. No one shall benefit and no one shall win. Marilyn will be well wed to another, leaving you nothing to gain. And you will very likely lose the loyalty of some of your own barons should you instigate such a long and protracted private war."

Rylan stared at Isabel's perfectly composed features. She was most assuredly a rarity among women, he thought with no little admiration. Smart enough to analyze a situation correctly and cool enough under pressure to make her points with no hesitation or sign of dismay. The king had been exceedingly lucky that the beautiful face he'd fallen in love with had come with such an astute mind.

For a moment he thought of Joanna, and he recognized that she too concealed a sharp—albeit devious— mind within her comely form. But thoughts of Joanna pulled him back to the moment. If he would win her, he must pick his words most carefully.

"You miss one critical point, my lady, and that is the matter of my honor. I fight Egbert not for the monetary gain, but to avenge myself against one who should stand with me on this. We had an agreement but he has taken the coward's way out!"

"No one calls me a coward!" Egbert started forward angrily. Had not the queen stepped between the men, they would have been forced to grapple in earnest. As it was, Isabel held a hand against each man's chest and glared furiously at them and then her husband as well.

"That is enough!" she cried in outrage. "It should not

fall to me to step between two men in this way! Husband, make them separate!"

John jumped at her furious command and cleared his throat. "Stand back or I shall call the guards," he barked dutifully. Rylan heard the sulky tone in his voice and knew that John would go along with whatever solution the queen devised.

Egbert stared hard at Rylan as the two men stepped away from one another, but he made no sign that might give away his true thoughts to the royal couple. Rylan was careful to keep a scowl upon his face as he belligerently folded his arms across his wide chest.

"Now then," Isabel bit out. "There is little room for debate. Marilyn will *not* be wed to you, Lord Blaecston, so accept that fact. A private war between you benefits no one and hurts everyone—"

"I will not take this insult lightly," Rylan interrupted her.

She fixed an angry stare upon him. "Pray tell me, Sir Rylan. What would it take to soothe your damaged pride in this matter?"

"His head upon a pike."

"I am not in the mood for your petty anger!" Isabel snapped.

"I say slap him in irons," John threw in peevishly.

"Keep still, John," Isabel replied without even glancing his way. "Well, Blaecston? I am waiting."

Rylan gave her a long, cold look, then sent Egbert a baleful glare. Finally he sighed and pursed his lips. "I will consent to wed the Oxwich girl, but her properties must be unencumbered by taxes for three years."

"What!" John leaped forward with a howl. "I will never consent—"

"One year," Isabel responded, ignoring John completely. "One year of no taxes on her properties only. And you will take a solemn vow not to impede upon Sir Egbert or Sir Evan in any way whatsoever. That means no mysteriously burned fields. No fouled waterways. *Nothing* whatsoever. Are you agreed?"

It took all Rylan's considerable willpower not to break into a huge grin. Just to be on the safe side, he bowed low before the queen, hiding his face in a humble gesture. "I am agreed."

"Good. I will send for the scribes and we will make the contracts here and now. As we do not linger much longer at Ely, I would have both marriages solemnized as soon as possible."

"May I see my daughter?" Sir Egbert asked. There was a clear note of relief in his voice.

"Most certainly," Isabel replied. "What of you, Sir Rylan? Would you speak to your bride as soon as the contracts are signed? Or shall I relate the details of our agreement to our ward?"

Throughout the critical minutes of their discussion, Rylan had always felt sure and in control of the situation. He'd instructed Egbert to play the beleaguered and affronted father, while he himself would play the angry and humiliated suitor. Their byplay had been emotional and almost violent, and it had worked even better than he'd hoped. But now, faced with the queen's mild question about informing Joanna of the results, Rylan found himself truly at a loss.

He swept his hair back with one hand, heaved a troubled sigh, then looked frankly at Isabel. "Would you rather she turn her shrewish temper upon you or upon me?"

Isabel laughed at that, and the last of her irritation seemed to disappear. Not so John's, however.

"I should have sent her back to her priory and be-stowed Oxwich upon a more deserving lord," he bit out, staring resentfully at Isabel. But the queen was not in the least ruffled by his ill temper.

"I shall speak to her shortly, Lord Blaecston, after I see to my husband. I daresay, however, that I shall brighten John's mood long before you are able to sweeten Joanna's disposition toward *you.*"

The afternoon hours stretched into evening and still Joanna waited. Court had abounded with speculation and gossip the whole day through, but even now as the long summer twilight lingered, there was no real news.

The queen had apparently retired an hour ago and was closeted with the king. Bishop Ferendi was pur-ported to be departing for the monastic grange for his seasonal letting of blood. Whether Marilyn was still be-ing held away from her father's rule, Joanna simply did not know. Neither Sir Egbert nor Evan had been seen in hours, and as for Sir Rylan—

Joanna slowed in her restless pacing and frowned. At this moment she would welcome even *his* presence if he did but bring word of what was going on.

As she thought of him, Joanna's pacing ceased alto-gether and with a heavy sigh she stared out into the deepening lavender sky. How confusing everything was, she admitted to herself. How unsettled and upside down all of it was turning out.

All she had wanted was to become a Gilbertine nun. Her goal had only been to return to St. Theresa's and to resume the quiet existence she'd enjoyed before Rylan Kempe had so rudely ridden into her life. But then she'd managed to embroil herself in Marilyn's troubles, to the exclusion of her own. One thing had led to another until now the fates of both Marilyn and Evan—as well as the control of all that property—were being determined, and all because she'd meddled in matters not precisely concerned with her. Rylan's fate also was directly influenced by her manipulation of the innocent Marilyn and the not-so-innocent bishop, for not only might Rylan lose all he'd hoped to gain, he could very well suffer at the king's hand for attempting to circumvent the royal wishes.

That possibility, which she'd not heretofore envisioned, started Joanna's heart beating in alarm. She hadn't considered that the king might actually punish Rylan for daring to align his own power with Marilyn's without the royal approval. Was it possible?

That worry was still uppermost in her mind when a sharp rap sounded from the door. Joanna was across the chamber in a moment, filled with both hope and dread all at once. To her dismay, however, it was the Lady Adele accompanied by Sir George Gaines whom she found awaiting her.

"The queen would speak to you, Lady Joanna. In her private chambers," Lady Adele intoned solemnly.

"Me?" Joanna barely got the single word out, so alarmed was she by this unexpected summons.

Sir George gave her a smug look. "Be quick, miss. 'Tis not for you to keep the queen waiting."

Joanna's heart pounded in unreasoning fear as she followed the pair toward the royal chambers. Neither of them spoke to her, but they both sent her frequent speculative glances. She burned to question them, but she was certain they would not reveal anything to her, even if they *did* know what was afoot. Instead she just hurried in their wake and tried discreetly to dry her damp palms in her skirts.

The queen awaited her in an antechamber. She was dressed in a loose robe with her hair down in two long plaits reaching past her waist. Sir George did not enter the room, and Lady Adele departed at Isabel's gesture. Only when the door was firmly closed did Isabel motion Joanna to approach.

"Come, my dear. Sit down here. This will not take long." She watched Joanna closely with her intense eyes, but her expression was friendly. Once Joanna was settled on a wooden bench covered with a small rug, Isabel sighed.

"I know you shall object, but I warn you in advance it will avail you of naught. This has been a troublesome day and I will not condone any tantrums or tears." Then she smiled, belying her stern words. "You shall be wed, Joanna. The arrangements are made and all parties agree."

"What! But that cannot be—"

"Oh, but it *can* be and it is done. I know you will not be happy with our choice, but you must endeavor to make the best of it."

"No!" Joanna cried sharply as she leaped up from her seat. She did not care whether she angered the queen or not. There was no punishment Isabel could mete out that could be any harsher than this one. "I cannot marry anyone! All I want—all I have *ever* wanted is—"

"What *you* want does not matter!" Isabel stood up stiffly, glaring at Joanna. "'Tis for the good of England!"

Joanna could not believe what was happening to her. She'd feared this all along. Indeed, she'd had no real reason to hope for any better outcome to her dilemma. And yet that did not now lessen her shock. Though the queen had not yet named the man, to Joanna it didn't matter. One man was as bad as the next. Save for Rylan—

She stopped short at that thought. Yet in the very same moment she knew that he was the last person the royal couple would betroth her to. Besides, he would never agree. Even if he lost his political prize in Marilyn, he would not want *her*. He would hold her accountable when the truth of her participation in this mess was brought to light. And anyway, she would never agree to marry him either, she told herself bravely.

Her thoughts of Rylan did serve one purpose, however, for she now recalled the one last bit of defense she held in reserve. The one fact she had kept hidden until now.

She swallowed hard and willed her voice to sound strong. "I do not think this fellow you give me to is likely to consider the bargain well met when he learns . . . when he discovers that I . . . that I . . . I am not chaste."

Her brave pronouncement was met with absolute silence. The queen's eyes narrowed and her hard gaze swept Joanna from head to toe, as if she might tell the truth of it in that manner. She shook her head in disbelief, but as she continued to stare, Joanna sensed when her disbelief turned to acceptance. Her reaction, however, was not at all what Joanna expected. Instead of erupting in fury, the queen began to laugh out loud.

"Oh, this is too perfect! Not a virgin?" Wracked with laughter, she collapsed back into her chair, holding her shaking sides with glee. Then, spying Joanna's bewildered face, she tried to compose herself. "This changes naught, my dear. You shall wed him anon. But oh, I would love to see his face when he learns the truth!"

As the queen's meaning sunk in, Joanna's expression

fell. "But you cannot mean to—he will not want . . ." She trailed off in the face of Isabel's smirk.

The queen leaned forward. "Tell me, girl. Who was the fellow? Someone at the priory? Or, no—could it be your father sent you to St. Theresa's only when he learned of what you'd done?"

Joanna clutched her hands at her waist. She was gripped by a sudden sickening knot in her stomach, and she stared wildly about. "This cannot be happening to me. It cannot—"

She turned abruptly and darted toward the door. Although Isabel cried out to stay her, and Adele and Sir George looked up in alarm at her hasty exit, Joanna did not pause. To stay was unthinkable!

She clutched her skirts with one hand as she ran, aware even as she did that flight availed her of naught. She was caught in a trap of her own making, promised in marriage by the king and queen to one of their allies— yet he could not be so dear to them that they could not delight in the man's disappointment at finding his bride not a virgin.

This is all Rylan Kempe's fault, she agonized as she sped past a staring couple. All Rylan's fault.

21

Joanna was not cognizant of her surroundings as she fled the queen's hateful pronouncement. Down the stairs, past the bishop's parlor and the refectory, then beyond through the walled garden she ran as if a devil pursued her. She neither saw nor cared about the people who stared after her. She knew only that she must be alone so that she could cry. So she could think. So she could pray.

Prayer. That was what she needed, she realized in anguish. She would find a level of calm that way, and comfort and strength.

She sped beyond the walled garden through a gate, then along a winding path she'd not been down before. It led into a semiforested garden maintained for the wild herbs and peaceful meditation spots it afforded the monks. Though she would have preferred the high cliffs and strong winds of Flamborough Head, at the moment any darkened glade would do.

When she found a small circle of birch trees—a grouping that reminded her reassuringly of the grotto at St. Theresa's—she came to a halt. Her sides ached with the force of her reckless flight, and she leaned hard against one thick birch as she struggled for breath. Dear God, dear God. What was she to do now?

In desperation she flung herself onto her knees, unmindful of her skirts. A soft layer of the previous autumn's leaves cushioned her knees and the rising call of a night bird serenaded her, but Joanna was oblivious to everything. One thought only consumed her. She was to be wed to some stranger. She would be bedded as if she were some poor beast with no feelings or wishes of her own. It could not be true and yet . . . She shuddered in revulsion as a vague memory of her mother crying in her bed came back to her.

This could not be happening to her, and yet it was. It was.

The tears came then. Hot and hard, streaming down her cheeks in rivulets to drip onto her bodice. Never had she felt so helpless. Never had the hopelessness of her position been so painfully clear. Even her father's tyranny seemed as nothing compared to the horrifying finality of her present predicament.

She remained that way a long while—on her knees with her head bowed over her tightly clasped hands. Only one phrase repeated itself over and over in her head. One prayer. One plea.

Save me. Please, save me.

When she felt a hand upon her shoulder, for one fanciful moment Joanna thought the hand of God had actually descended upon her in answer. The hand was warm and heavy, reassuring in an odd and inexplicable way. Then reason returned and she instinctively flinched away from the unknown touch. Scrambling to her feet, she turned to find Rylan facing her.

At once she was overcome with an unreasoning surge of gladness. He had come! Everything would be all right now. Yet just as quickly did she remind herself that he had not come to help her. Even if he wanted to—and why would he?—he could not help her now. Besides, he was only after power, through Marilyn or whomever else could aid his cause. She, however, was after . . . was after . . . Joanna bit her lower lip, unable to think exactly what she was after anymore.

With her initial reaction faded by the reality of their starkly different goals, she met his even stare. In the dim light of the evening, his face was cast in shadow. Yet Joanna did not need to see his face to know that he was on edge. His cool confidence of the afternoon had been replaced by a distinct air of unease.

But by now he'd probably been told by the king that he could not wed Lady Marilyn. He'd lost Marilyn's properties as well as control over Oxwich. Still, he was at least the master of his own fate, something she could not claim. Gathering her tattered pride about her, she resolved not to reveal her desperation to him.

"Is there news of Marilyn?" she asked in a cool and carefully modulated voice. "Is she yet held hostage to the king's will?"

"'Twas what you wanted, was it not? You sent her to Ferendi knowing he would run to the king with any secrets her confession might reveal. You kept your promise to Marilyn and yet still achieved your goal."

He spoke quietly. He stood calm and unmoving, but his controlled appearance did not fool Joanna at all. He hid some strong emotion behind his tensed jaw and shuttered eyes. It was only a matter of time before it exploded upon her.

She took a nervous step back. A confrontation with Rylan was the last thing she needed. But he stepped forward a pace. "I owe you an apology, it would seem," he continued.

"What?"

A faint smile curved his lips. "I underestimated you, Joanna. From the beginning I underestimated you—your determination; your intelligence. The strength of your feelings."

Her eyes narrowed suspiciously at that. "What has happened? What is going on that you can stand before me now, saying such absurd things?"

"Absurd?" This time he grinned and she saw the gleam of white teeth in his darkened face. "I just paid you a compliment, my little dove. You should be graciously thanking me."

Joanna shook her head slowly. What game did he play with her now? "If you truly thought I was intelligent, you would not be trying to disarm me with this nonsense you spout."

He was silent a moment. "Perhaps you are right. Perhaps I should simply come right out with it. Very well, then. The king has paired Marilyn with Evan Thorndyke. The marriage is agreeable to all parties involved."

"Thank God for that," Joanna muttered. At least those two would have the opportunity to seek happiness together. And Marilyn would not be wed to Rylan. At that reminder of Marilyn's broken betrothal to Rylan, however, Joanna's caution returned.

"Agreeable to *all* parties involved? What of you? I cannot believe that *you* agreed."

"Then you would be wrong. I did most certainly agree, although the king is not aware—" He broke off before he could finish. "'Twould be better, I think, for us to discuss that matter later. Once we are away from court I'll explain everything."

"Away from the court? What do you mean?" A spark of hope flared in her. "Will you take me back to the priory?"

He glanced at her and then away. Then he locked his hands together behind his back and shifted his stance. "If you wish to visit St. Theresa's, Joanna, then I will take you there."

"Visit? But . . ." She swallowed hard, trying to understand.

"We shall depart here as soon as the wedding is done."

Joanna stared at him, completely bewildered. "But how? I mean, the queen told me I must wed, so how may I leave for the priory?"

An odd expression came over Rylan's face. His eyes seemed to burn her with their consuming gaze, yet his rigid stance told her he restrained himself from moving nearer.

"Damnation, you do not yet know whom you shall wed, do you? Sir George told me you'd been informed." He exhaled noisily then looked intently at her.

Perhaps she should have guessed what was coming. But even after his words were out she could hardly comprehend them.

"I am to be your husband, Joanna. You are to wed with me."

She stared at him for a long time, her mouth gaping wide in shock. It was only with a great deal of effort that she was able to close her mouth and draw herself up enough to respond. "You? You are to be my husband?"

During her lengthy silence his face had darkened in a frown. Now he eyed her belligerently. "Yes, me. We shall wed as soon as the arrangements are complete.

Then we shall depart this godforsaken place for Blaec-ston."

Joanna heard everything he said, even the blasphemy. Yet still she could not quite take it in. To make matters even worse, despite the logic that told her she must object to such an unhappy alliance as theirs would surely be, she could not prevent the sudden leap within her chest and the wild beating of her heart. They were to be wed? She and Rylan?

Then she spied his frown and a black cloud seemed to form above her. He had wanted to wed with Marilyn, but she had ruined that for him. So he had settled for a lesser heiress. At least now his precious Yorkshire would be secure against the king. As if her heart had been abruptly wrenched from her breast, a hollow ache began in the depths of her chest.

"Your . . . your news catches me quite by . . . by surprise." She took a shaky breath but still could not meet his eyes. Even her voice, which she tried to make scathing, came out hesitant and faint. "You will forgive me if it takes a moment for me to understand."

"Yes, of course. I, ah . . . As I said, I thought you had been told. Else I would not have put it so badly." He moved forward then, and Joanna lifted her bowed head to face him. "'Tis for the best, Joanna. You will see."

"For the best?" Her eyes filled with unwelcome tears.

"Best for you, all things considered. The king has prevented you gaining Marilyn's vast properties, so you now take the next best choice. Oxwich will be a nice addition to your little kingdom in Yorkshire, won't it? I only wonder that the king agreed," she finished in a bitter voice.

"It doesn't matter *why* he agreed, only that he did."

She brushed away her tears and lifted her chin. "And why did *you* agree? Why not simply marry me to the same lackey you originally had wanted me for? Surely there are other maidens who hold more valuable properties than I."

Joanna was too upset to recognize the patient expression on Rylan's face. When he placed his hands just above her elbows and pulled her to stand before him, she tried to shrug them off. "No. Don't you *dare* touch me now!"

"Joanna, you work yourself into a turmoil for naught. I want to marry you. 'Tis a choice I made freely—"

"But *I* did not!" she cried. "I did not make *my* choice freely. You and the king have decided and agreed, and now *I* must cope with it as best I can."

"We also decided for the Lady Marilyn and she does not object."

"But she is loved! She loves Evan and he loves her. Oh, but you could never understand!" She twisted furiously in his grasp but he only held her tighter.

"Christ and bedamned! If that is all you want—love—then I can easily accommodate you." So saying, he drew her against his chest and tilted her head back with one hand tangled in her hair.

She knew he meant to kiss her and again she felt that unwarranted surge of heated emotion. Yet the very longing she felt only increased her struggles.

"No! This is not what I—" The rest was lost as his mouth crushed down upon hers.

Joanna fought the onslaught of pure physical pleasure that washed over her. She fought it with her body and her mind. It was her heart, however, that finally betrayed her. She steeled herself against his rough caress and reminded herself that here again he only sought to manipulate her. But it was hopeless. His lips demanded a response from her, and he received it. His tongue stroked and probed, and she gave him entrance. When his hand loosened in her hair, then ran down her back, she arched against him in shameless desire, unable to deny the surge of fire in her veins. In response her hands found his shoulders and circled his neck. She rose upon her toes to meet his possessive embrace and searing kiss.

Like a living flame Rylan's tongue ignited her. Sweet and hot, he delved deep, stirring the passionate embers that had been dormant, only waiting for his return. Now it was like a conflagration, a burning heaven that caught her up in its power no matter how unwilling she knew she should be.

Rylan's arms were around her, crushing her against him. One of his hands slid down to her derriere, moving in a slow hot circle and pressing her urgently to the hard proof of his desire.

"God, but I would carry you off to that island this very minute!" he murmured as his lips moved to her cheek and then to her ear.

A shudder of pure longing rippled through Joanna at that, and she felt a damp heat rise in her lower belly. She had fought so hard to forget the impossibly wicked things they'd done in that holy place. Yet his words brought them all rushing back: the way he'd touched her everywhere; the feel of his strong body sliding naked along hers. The wonderous panic he'd inspired within her. Could anything truly have felt that divine?

Then his hand moved to cup her breast, and Joanna knew it had been just as exquisite as she'd remembered. Once again she felt the inexplicable current igniting her body. The callused pad of his thumb rubbed back and forth across the tensed crest of her nipple and she could have swooned.

"Rylan . . ." she whispered as her forehead fell

weakly against his shoulder. "You cannot . . . I must . . . Oh!"

She gasped as one of his thighs slid between her legs to press up against the hot font of her torturous feelings. His hand moved at the same time, cupping lower on her derriere until she was writhing within his grasp.

"I would have you now, my little dove. My bride. My wife." His breath came in harsh gasps. "I would have you beneath me now and always."

Joanna could hardly breathe, she was so overcome with desire for him. The wind sighed in the trees above them. The soft layer of leaves rustled beneath their feet. One solitary night bird cried its evening lament. But she was conscious only of Rylan and the way he made her feel.

She pressed her face against the side of his neck, kissing and tasting the slight saltiness there, nuzzling the place where smooth skin gave way to the rougher texture where he had scraped his beard away. He swallowed hard and she kissed the spot where his throat bobbed, then smiled when he reflexively swallowed again. As he had the power to overwhelm her with passion, she recalled, so did she also have the ability to excite him.

Then his hand moved beneath her raised skirts and up her thigh, to the moist apex where all her longings seemed to be concentrated.

"Ah, damn, woman, but I need you—"

One of his fingers stole into that heated crevice and she unwittingly cried out. He rubbed along the slick folds, and she sagged within his embrace. Then he slid his finger deep into her and she gasped at the power of her reaction.

"Rylan—Oh!"

"My sweet, sweet girl," he breathed hotly in her ear,

all the while stroking deeply into her and then out again. Joanna was near to fainting from the excruciating pleasure of it. She was caught up in a wicked magic and drowning in its sultry seduction. Without even being aware of it, she moved in rhythm with his hand, rising to his touch, blinded by the need he roused in her.

"Rylan," she murmured, panting, clutching frantically at him. "I need . . ."

"I know what you need, my passionate little dove. And you shall have it, just as I shall finally have what I need." His finger slid out to wet the sensitive nub hidden by her curls. "It has cost me much to have you," he murmured, biting at her earlobe. "But I shall be repaid a hundred-fold."

Joanna did not understand his words nor even note them. She was too close to that explosive feeling he'd brought her to before. So close. But then his hand stilled and he groaned in frustration.

"Milord?"

"Damnation," he growled as he hastily removed his hand and jerked her skirts down.

"Milord?" the same deep voice called out from very nearby.

"I am here, Kell, but I warn you to keep your distance else I—" He broke off with a foul oath.

"'Tis the queen. She sends word via Sir George that the marriage contract but awaits your signature. However, I did not think you wished him to follow you here."

Rylan sighed. His eyes closed and for a long moment he appeared to fight for control. Finally he opened his eyes and gave Joanna a pained smile. "We cannot be away from this damnable place too soon, my love."

Joanna had stumbled back to lean upon one of the

giant birch trees, all the while struggling to regain her wits. Her body yet hummed with desire, a feeling far too strong to easily suppress. In the fog of conflicting emotions that still gripped her, she clung to the only constant she had.

"I . . . I must go back to the priory. I cannot marry. I will not."

"You've never had that option, Joanna. Never. Can you not be content that it is I who shall be your husband?"

"But that . . . that cannot be true!"

In frustration, Rylan raked one hand through his long hair. "You would have been wed to another. Better me than John's choice for you."

She shook her head as her senses slowly began to return. "I would not have married his choice either."

"You would have been forced."

"No. No, when they learned I was not pure—" She broke off as she remembered how ineffectual that approach had been with Isabel.

"What?" Rylan crossed to her in three steps and grabbed her arms. "My God, woman, don't you know how vulnerable that would have made you? You would have become prey to every lusty fool—" He broke off at Kell's impatient call.

"I'm coming, damn it!" He stared down at Joanna, and despite the meager light, she could see he was frowning.

"There is no need for you to risk your reputation that way, Joanna. Not now. 'Twould not have worked in any event, for you are far too tempting a morsel for any man to be so easily put off. But 'tis *I* who shall wed you now."

He pulled her to him for a swift, possessive kiss, effectively squelching her opposition before it could begin.

Only when she became pliant and unresisting in his arms did he pull away and take a long shaky breath.

"Let us go now, and do our duty as loyal subjects of the king." He wrapped one arm about her waist and guided her out of the little grove and onto the path. She saw Kell turn and walk back toward the abbey proper, but Rylan hesitated a moment and turned to face her. "The time fast approaches when we shall do our duty only to one another, and I promise you, my sweet, that you shall be very glad of it."

Joanna tried to pull away, for she was beset by too many conflicting emotions to be made sense of. "I do not wish to wed. Not with you nor anyone else!"

His answer was a laugh, low, seductive, and undeniably mocking. "I shall make you regret those words. The day will come—the night—when you shall pander to my every whim and beg for my attention."

Although she wanted vehemently to deny his words, Joanna feared they were much too true. With a furious cry she tore from his grasp and stalked stiffly away. She would have preferred to run, especially when he called out to her.

"You shall beg for my attention, Joanna. And I shall gladly give it."

22

How had things conspired to reach such an improbable end? Joanna bit her lip and focused on the dry seam in the stone wall before her while two maids dressed her. How was it that the unwanted daughter of a relatively minor baron had been bartered in marriage to one of the most powerful men in the kingdom? The last thing she wanted was to marry.

But that was not completely true, a disturbing voice contradicted her. Marriage to Rylan . . . Joanna shook her head, unable to organize her tumultuous thoughts regarding him. He was heartless and self-serving. Yet he was to be her husband. He did not care for her beyond her property. Yet he would this day take a vow to care for her all the days of her life.

And what would she vow?

She leaned her head forward at the subtle pressure of the maid's deft hands. A silver-woven caul was slipped onto her head and fastened by two cords beneath her chin. But as the woman artfully pulled locks of her curls this way and that around her brow and cheeks, and arranged the rest of her hair in a long cape down her back, Joanna worried over that question. What *would* she vow?

Obedience, of course. And faithfulness. To love, honor, and obey. The irony of it almost made her laugh. Almost. Love was not an emotion that existed between Rylan and her—if indeed it existed at all. But then she reminded herself of Marilyn's joyful anticipation of marriage to Evan, and she knew that love *was* possible in a few rare instances. But certainly not in her own forced marriage.

As for honor, how could she honor a man who put political gain above the consideration of people? He was devious in his methods and ruthless in pursuing his goals.

Obedience was equally unlikely, if she was to be completely honest with herself. It was inevitable that she would balk at anything he suggested, for he seemed to bring out the very worst in her character. Her impatience became belligerence in his presence. Her willfulness became inflexibility.

At the behest of the maid, she did a slow pirouette. The wide skirts of her kirtle and super-tunic flared prettily around her ankles, then settled in graceful folds of rose and wine-colored flurt-silke over the fine chaisel undergarment.

"The queen sent her looking glass for you to view yourself, milady."

Joanna took the carved wooden frame the maid offered her and peered cautiously at herself. Her first thought was that she was excessively pale. Her eyes provided the only color on her face. It was due to being indoors too much, she decided. At the priory she necessarily spent more time outside.

But Joanna knew that was not the real cause. The truth was, she was completely terrified by what was to come. Within hours she would be the wife of Rylan

Kempe. Beyond her frustration with his motive for marrying her—the motive for all noblemen in the selection of their wives—she also feared the absolute power he would now hold over her. She would soon be his to command—not just her property, but her physical self as well. She would live where he decided, run his households as he dictated, and perform the wifely duties—

With an abrupt motion she thrust the looking glass into the maid's hands. She felt the heat of color rising in her cheeks and she suddenly was trembling. But this time it was not fear.

She would perform her wifely duties because he no doubt would not allow her to avoid them. But also, though she inwardly cringed to acknowledge it, she knew she would not long be repulsed by his solicitation of her favors. She had succumbed too many times already to his kisses—to his caresses and even more. Should she object to anything he demanded, he had only to command her with kisses and she feared she would comply.

Joanna closed her eyes briefly and pressed her fingertips against them.

"Art aright, milady?"

Joanna straightened with a sigh and faced the maid's concerned expression. "I am . . . I am fine."

"'Tis not a rare thing for a maiden to fear her wedding," the woman ventured with a reassuring smile.

The other maid nodded vigorously as she fastened a tunnel-quilted girdle about Joanna's waist. "At first 'twill be a trial, to be sure. But yer a lucky one. Ye've a bonny lad, not some dour old man to take t' yer bed. He's sure to give ye strong babies."

Babies.

Joanna stopped breathing at the word. They were

summoned with a strident knock and Joanna went along
mildly with the two pages sent for her. But as they made
their way to the abbey cathedral, she was all the while
unaware of her surroundings.

Babies. Somehow she'd not even considered that possibility.

Logic deemed that babies were a natural result of
marriage—of the marriage bed—yet the thought of
bearing a child of Rylan's had not occurred to her. Now
that she'd been forced to confront the subject, her confusion increased tenfold. When the two pages drew her
before the assembled nobles to stand to one side of Isabel's chair, she trembled as violently as did the dry
heather on the wind-whipped cliffs of Flamborough
Head. Her hands were cold as ice; she knew that her face
had gone pallid. Though she tried to shake off her terrible anxiety, she could not. Rylan would inevitably give
her a child. Would she be a better mother to it than her
mother had been to her? Would she be able to protect
her child from the unreasoning demands of its father?
Or would she fail her baby as her mother had failed her?

No, that was the one thing Joanna *was* sure of. She
would never abandon a child of her own. Never. Still,
that was small comfort now. She looked around in renewed panic, but the only friendly face she spied was the
queen's. Despite their abrupt parting the day before, Isabel was watching Joanna closely, and even appeared
sympathetic to the dismay so clear on Joanna's face.

But Joanna did not want the queen's sympathy. She
wanted to be released from this marriage. She knew,
however, that the queen would not relent, and a spurt of
righteous anger helped restore her control.

From the eastern arm of the transept Marilyn and her
father arrived together, the one positively glowing with

happiness, the other beaming proudly. Marilyn met Joanna's troubled gaze with a smile so joyous that Joanna could not help but smile back. At least Marilyn and Evan would be together. She could take some comfort in that.

Then a murmur at the main entrance to the cathedral drew her attention. There, pausing at the door, were the two men who roused such differing emotions in the two women they had come for. Evan stood straight and tall with an unrestrained grin on his face, despite the somber surroundings. His russet hair had been groomed back and he was dressed handsomely in a robe of brown and gold damask, ornamented with gold braid, a huge brooch, and a gold-worked girdle. But for all his fine appearance, it was the man who walked beside him who drew Joanna's eyes.

Next to Evan's lavish costume, Rylan looked almost severe. His dark hair was freshly cleaned and was tied in the back with a wide strip of black riband. His tunic was a dark metal-colored gray, plain in style with the arms of a paler gray undertunic showing through. Both garments were finely made of the best-quality linen, but Joanna was aware—as she'd been the very first time she'd laid eyes on him—that he was a man with no particular need to project his authority with his clothing. The sheer strength of his personality ensured that one and all recognized his power. The way he stood, the direct way he looked at a person, and his arrogant attitude all emphasized that here was a man better left unchallenged. Here was a man to step lightly around.

As if to underscore her fanciful thoughts, King John entered the room directly after the bridegrooms, followed by three priests. He was dressed in his finest robes, purple lined with silver-tipped ermine and banded in silver and gold braid. His hands were bejeweled; his crown was in place. He was groomed and coiffed and outfitted in the finest that English coin could purchase. Yet beside Sir Rylan he appeared insignificant. He forced a smile but his eyes reflected his resentment, and the result was an expression of peevishness ill-suited to a kingly demeanor.

The king wanted this wedding no more than she did, Joanna realized. What had Rylan done that could force a king to agree to a match of which he plainly did not approve?

She had no time to find out. Isabel stood up and signaled Marilyn to approach her. For a moment the two conversed quietly, then the girl bowed her head to receive the queen's kiss on her brow. When Isabel turned to face Joanna, her expression was watchful.

"I know you go into this marriage with more than the normal amount of dread," she began when Joanna had drawn near. Her voice was quiet so that her words carried to no one else. "Sir Rylan has treated you cruelly in the past and may very well do so in the future. But take heart, my dear." She searched Joanna's pale face before continuing. "You have an ally in me. Keep me well apprised of your husband's activities and you shall be rewarded."

"Rewarded?" Joanna stared at Isabel. Did the queen wish her to spy on Rylan?

Isabel smiled when Joanna's face made it clear she understood the implication in her words. "Should he ever be accused of traitorous intent, I can ensure that you and your heirs are held blameless. And *not* deprived of your rightful properties," she added with a confident nod.

She did not seem to expect a response. With a regal inclination of her head she bestowed a kiss upon

Joanna's brow, then reseated herself. But all the while Joanna's mind turned over this strange new aspect of her marriage. Had John and Isabel thought to plant a spy in Rylan's camp when they agreed to this wedding? She lifted her eyes to search out Rylan, but that only increased her turmoil. He and Evan followed the king up the nave, then stood opposite their brides as the king sat down next to the queen. The three priests moved up to the altar, followed by the wispy trails of smoky incense. A choir of monks began a haunting chant, and the entire assembly grew quiet and still as the ceremony began.

Joanna, however, could not concentrate on the mass. She was acutely aware of Rylan beside her and even felt the probing sweep of his sidelong gaze. But she refused to meet his eyes. She was confused enough without adding to it. Experience had proven already that Rylan was well able to muddle her thoughts and dilute her resolve. Between his unconscionable manipulations and the queen's, she felt like a fly caught up in a spider's gigantic web.

Except that one spider's poison was so sweet as to cause her struggles to cease.

She bowed her head lower and closed her eyes in prayer. Spying for the queen was not something she could ever do. Yet who knew what her future would be under Rylan's tight control? All she could do was beg God's grace in guiding her future.

The Latin incantations passed in a blur. The sermon was brief—one of St. Paul's diatribes on the wickedness of women and the husband's responsibility to discipline his wife most strictly. As if that misguided apostle's words counted for more than the kindly instructions of the Savior's, Joanna thought. Her outrage at the entire plight of womankind negated any uncomfortable twinges her blasphemous thoughts incurred. By the time the marriage vows were to be exchanged, she had worked herself into a fine fury.

Evan said his vow and received Marilyn's in return. They exchanged rings and then a chaste kiss. When it was their turn, Rylan faced Joanna.

Perhaps it was the fiery light in her eyes that alerted him, for instead of taking one of her hands to rest lightly on his opened palm, he grasped each of her hands in his, enveloping them in a tight hold.

"I take thee, Joanna Preston, maid of Oxwich, to be my lawful wife. To have and hold you in fair times and foul. For better; for worse. In sickness; in health. Though rich or poor. From this time forward until death us do part. Thereto I plight thee my troth."

Then it was Joanna's turn. She had not planned what she would say. In her anger and pain she wanted only to strike out at him—at all of them. As if he sensed her heightened emotions, Rylan squeezed her hands.

Joanna raised her eyes to his and opened her mouth to speak. But the words would not form on her lips. Rylan's eyes had never been bluer. His gaze had never been more compelling. Although his hold was tight on her hands, he did not give her pain and thereby threaten her to say the words. Instead, he seemed to promise her something. *Say the words and reap the benefits of my goodwill*, his burning gaze seemed to avow.

She swallowed and began in a whisper only Rylan and the foremost priest could hear.

". . . in sickness and in health. Though rich or poor. To be blithe and—" She broke off, unable to promise obedience to him either in the bed or the board. The priest cleared his throat pointedly and she continued. "From this day forward until death do us part."

Rylan smiled then and relaxed, and Joanna realized just how unsure he'd been about her. The ring was hastily produced and slipped upon her finger.

"With this ring I thee wed," he vowed hoarsely. Then he leaned down and kissed her.

Joanna met his lips but briefly, then quickly pulled away. Yet she could not call the kiss entirely chaste. The instant clamoring of her senses at the touch of his lips made it as intense as the lick of a flame.

They knelt for the priest's blessing, then rose once more to hear the closing incantations and the monks' final hymn. But Rylan kept her hand enclosed in his the entire time. She tried once to free herself from his disturbing grasp, but he would not allow it. His face was unexpectedly relaxed, however, when he looked down at her.

"You make me very happy this day," he murmured for her ears only. "I will endeavor to do the same for you."

More so than his marriage vow, those brief words lingered in Joanna's mind. Through the inevitable feasting, toasting, and entertainments that followed, they stayed in her head, almost haunting her with their unaccountable sincerity. I will endeavor to do the same for you. Did he truly mean to make their marriage a good one?

Before the high table a team of jugglers displayed their skills, tossing daggers and burning brands in impossible numbers and incredible speed. A little boy juggled apples. An even younger girl juggled eggs. Tumblers catapulted across a special carpet, flinging themselves about in what appeared the most heedless of fashions. But they always managed to land upright or within the correct person's grasp. Had Joanna not been so preoccupied with her own circumstances, she would have enjoyed their energetic performances enormously.

But Rylan sat on the one side of her, and Isabel on the other. A most unnerving position for her to find herself in. The king was steadily imbibing in the bishop's free-flowing wine stocks until his crown slipped askew upon his head.

"John. Have a care for your dignity," the queen whispered furiously under her breath.

He straightened his crown with one hand while reaching for his jewel-encrusted goblet with the other. "Where's the dignity in being coerced by the likes of him?" He sent a baleful glare toward Rylan.

Coerced? Joanna also peered at Rylan for she had suspected as much, though she could not understand just how he had managed it. But before she could speculate any further, the king shoved his ornamented trencher aside and leaned forward with both elbows on the table. He shrugged off the queen's cautioning hand.

"A less fair-minded king than I would have seen you hanged long ago for your unreasonable ways. Certainly my warlike brother Richard would have skewered you upon his mighty lance for your many presumptions. But I have been patient, as befits a noble king, waiting for all my errant children to end their divisive bickering and line up behind me. Their king. Their one true liege."

He pushed his crown back and took another drink. Then his squinting eyes swung over to Joanna.

"Despite the kingship that weighs so heavily upon me, however, I am nonetheless still a man. Touched by the hand of God, to be sure. But a man nonetheless." He grinned then, a wide smirking grin that put Joanna in mind of a weasel. "And I'll admit on occasion to finding humor in another man's misfortune. You and your bride make a fair couple, Kempe. You shall have the envy of many a man this night when you climb between the thighs of the winsome wench you wed." He belched, then laughed. "The winsome wench you wed. Indeed, the bards do well to heed the poetic words their king doth pronounce."

Joanna frowned and looked to Isabel for help. In the past the queen had not countenanced such unseemly language from her husband. Today, however, Isabel appeared content to let him speak.

"The winsome wench you wed." John chuckled once more. "Yes. Many a man here will envy you. But at least one among them has preceded you, it appears."

Joanna's eyes widened in surprise at his cruel words. She darted an accusing look at Isabel, who had obviously related the information to the king. But that lady was staring pointedly at Rylan with a faint but unmistakably smug smile on her lips. For a moment there was silence. The king and queen waited, obviously anticipating Rylan's humiliation to learn such a thing. Marilyn and Evan turned at the odd silence from the other side of the table. Even Joanna held her breath, wondering what Rylan would do. Of course, John knew only part of the truth, for she'd not named the man who had compromised her. Still, Rylan could not be happy with this revelation by his foe.

Rylan's response, however, was a far cry from anyone's expectations. First he casually turned to Joanna and gave her a reassuring smile. Then he caught her hand in his and lifted it to his lips. He kissed the gold band that now circled her finger, then planted a warmer, lingering kiss on her palm before closing her hand up within his own. Only then did he answer King John.

"You find us out, it seems. But I would not have my

fair wife suffer for my own impetuous nature. She fires my passion to an unholy degree," he admitted with a wide, lusty grin. "Though I abducted her most foully, 'tis I who found myself well and truly caught. But this is a trap I enter willingly and shall never struggle against."

With that startling little speech he stood up, pulling the dumbstruck Joanna with him. "Enough of feasting and these handsome festivities. I have waited long past the limits of mortal man. 'Tis time to take a wife. What say you, Evan? Shall we be freed from this pretty company to woo our 'winsome wenches' as they deserve?"

A great roar of approval went up from the besotted crowd seated below the salt. Joanna flushed scarlet to realize that Rylan's words had carried throughout the hall. Pewter mugs pounded against the long wooden tables. Bone-handled knives banged approval in a hundred hands. Amid much mirth and many cries of advice, Rylan pulled Joanna along, away from the table, through the crowded banqueting hall until they broke free into a wide passageway.

Joanna glanced back once to see astonishment still plain on the king's face. Isabel too was taken aback. But Sir Egbert was grinning in delight, as was Evan, almost as if this were not a surprise to either one of them at all.

Had this somehow been prearranged? she wondered in amazement. Could Rylan have planned to marry her all along?

How Joanna wished to believe that. How she would have preferred that to the terrible doubt she now felt. But as Rylan hurried her through the antechamber, then out into a small paved courtyard, she had no time to think. Horses awaited them, as did a small contingent of guards led by the towering Sir Kell.

"We are off," Rylan called with an exuberant smile.

He lifted Joanna onto his own big-boned destrier, then mounted behind her. "Come greet your new mistress, my lads. The Lady Joanna of Blaecston."

Amid the nervous shuffling of the horses the men made their courteous introductions. Joanna was too confused by all that was happening to do more than bob her head and murmur a polite response to each of them. When Kell pulled his horse beside them, however, she forced herself to focus on him. He was one of her new husband's most important men, it appeared. Yet he and she had not started off very well together.

"Welcome, milady," he murmured, pulling off his hood and bowing his head respectfully.

"Thank you, Sir Kell." She stared at him warily then decided it might be best to clear the air between them at once. "If you would like, I can teach you to swim."

A huge shout of laughter erupted at once, first from Rylan and swiftly followed up by all the other men. Kell turned quite red but did not otherwise react. Clearly he'd taken much ribbing from his comrades since she'd escaped in the flooded beck, and for that she felt even more uncomfortable. She bit her lip, wishing to apologize, but she suspected that would only make things worse.

"Perhaps you should accept her offer," Rylan suggested, still chuckling. He pulled her back against his chest and kept one arm securely around her. "You can never quite tell where you may be led—and what you will be compelled to do—in pursuit of a woman."

This time Kell laughed and his light-blue eyes stared knowingly at Rylan. "I bow to your greater experience, my lord."

The small group of horsemen made their way to the open abbey gate amid much good-natured teasing, but not before they were hailed by Evan. With Marilyn at his side he approached them, and it was clear to all how happy he and his new bride were.

"Safe passage, my friend. I will not long be here myself." Evan gazed down at the radiant woman on his arm. "We shall go to Manning first, then visit all her family estates. Shall we call on you when we reach Chipping Way?"

"By all means. I will delay the Yorkshire courts until you come. Say, four weeks hence?"

"Fine. Should we become delayed I will send you word. Meanwhile, enjoy your lovely bride. I wish you well in all your dealings." He stared pointedly at Joanna and added, "Yours is a good match that will yield peace and prosperity to you and all who look to you."

Marilyn reached up a hand to touch Joanna's knee. "You shall be very happy. We all shall be."

Joanna stared down into Marilyn's shining eyes, wishing fervently that it would be so. When Rylan urged his horse forward, however, she was not convinced. Marilyn was in love and saw all the world in a special rosy light. But what Rylan felt for her was not love; nor should her confused feelings for him be termed such either.

Then his hand slid lower and he pressed her back into the warm vee of his thighs. At once her heart's pace quickened and an unbidden heat rushed through her.

It was all right to feel this rising passion for him, she tried to tell herself. He was her husband now. What she felt for him was no longer a sin.

Yet it was no longer mere lust either, she admitted as they cantered up the dusty road that led through the town and away from the abbey. Somewhere between their interlude in the birch stand, the talk of babies, and the recitation of her vows, her feelings had changed.

No, not changed. Solidified. Despite her anger with the way she had been handed around more as a possession than a person, the fact remained that she had married the man of her heart's choosing. It was just her misfortune that his choice had been made not to his heart's ease but for his political gain.

23

They were not long away from Ely, headed north on the old Roman Road, when they were joined by a dozen more riders. Her new husband seemed to have planned every aspect of their departure from court with great detail, Joanna realized, for these were Blaecston men-at-arms, well provisioned for the ride to Yorkshire. Only when Rylan was thus satisfied with their safety did he allow Joanna to dismount from before him and ride the gentle palfrey the men had brought for her.

But he did not himself see to her comfort on the amiable beast. Upon dismounting in a clearing within the towering beechwood, he turned her over to Kell and without a word strode stiffly into the forest. He was not gone long, but when he returned his hair was wet and his undertunic was damp at the collar and wrists. Several of the men sniggered at his appearance, especially Kell.

"Gone swimming?"

"Found an icy pool to cool your ardor in?" said another with a laugh.

Rylan silenced them with one cold glare. At Joanna's questioning look, however, he softened.

"I . . . ahh . . . I slipped and fell in the water," he

answered her unspoken inquiry. This generated a whole new wave of muffled laughter from his men, but Rylan only frowned and ignored them. "Are you well seated on your horse?"

"Yes. Well enough. How . . . how far shall we ride today?"

"As far and as fast as you can manage. Does riding alone frighten you?" he asked, misinterpreting her anxiousness. "I shall be at your side if you need to abandon riding astride. You can ride before me again if you become uncomfortable."

Joanna swallowed and looked away. It was not the ride that worried her, but the arrival. When night fell and they retired to their beds . . .

"I would have preferred that you rode more comfortably, in a chariot or a horse-chair. But we must make haste."

"Is there danger?" she asked, struck by all his precautions.

"There is always that possibility. But do not be alarmed. Our king is furious and will become even more so as Evan's loyalties are revealed. However, he is not likely to attack such a well-armed party as we."

"Evan's loyalties?" Joanna looked at him even more confused than before.

Rylan let out a laugh. "Evan is no ally to the king, Joanna. He and I have long been in league together. The king and queen think to have thwarted me in the matter of my betrothal to the Lady Marilyn. They believe that all her properties now rest in their camp. However, they will not long suffer that delusion."

"Are you saying that Evan married her just to get her properties?" Joanna exclaimed, with a terrible sinking feeling. She had thought Evan truly enamored of Marilyn.

Sensing the turn of her thoughts, Rylan drew nearer. "Evan would have wed Marilyn with or without her vast holdings. 'Twas the woman he wanted, not all the rest. But he is not adverse to using the new power he has attained to the betterment of our fair country. That they find mutual satisfaction in their match is their good fortune.

"But you . . . I mean, you were to wed her. And I—"

"And you made sure the king and queen found out." He gave her a stern look. "I cannot have my wife dabbling in such important affairs of state, Joanna. You must vow to end such activities as that."

"But you would have wed her," Joanna persisted. "Had I not interfered, you would have wed her."

Rylan ran a hand distractedly through his damp hair. "Joanna, you must understand. At one time I meant to, yes. But after we . . . after you and I . . . Damn," he swore. Then he met her wounded look with eyes that blazed with intensity. "I wed the woman I wanted. Had I wanted Lady Marilyn, our feeble king could never have prevented it. But I wanted you." His voice lowered to a hoarse whisper. "Bedamned, but I want you this very minute."

His hand moved to her knee, tightening upon her tender flesh, and the warmth of his grasp sent a fiery tremor through her. Beneath her the horse shifted as if it were aware of its rider's sudden disquiet. Rylan stilled the animal with a firm hold on its reins, but his burning gaze never wavered from Joanna's face.

It was she who looked away, swallowing a sudden surge of disappointment. He wanted her. Yes, that was clear and always had been. But wanting her in that way was not enough. Not for her. Not anymore.

She took a shaky breath, then looked down into his darkened eyes. When had she become so foolish? How could she expect words of love from him when all he felt was simple lust? A bitter smile lifted her lips. "Shall we be as fortunate as Evan and Marilyn then, and find *mutual satisfaction* in our marriage also?"

He stared up at her and slid his hand slowly along her thigh. "God willing." Then he became aware of his men watching them and suddenly cleared his throat. "We ride for Dunley Abbey," he told her in a lighter tone. "Though it may be well past dark when we arrive. In the morn we rise early and ride long again. I would make Oxwich by tomorrow evening."

"Oxwich!" That startling news overpowered Joanna's other jumbled feelings of yearning and disappointment. They made for Oxwich? "I thought you said . . . That is, I thought you wished to return to Blaecston. Why do we now ride to Oxwich?"

"I would assure myself that it is well defended against my enemies. The seneschal must swear fealty to me, and I would set a few of my own men among the guards."

"But—" Joanna broke off, unable to express the sudden panic she felt. "I do not wish to go there. You can go without me. Leave me at Blaecston."

Rylan's gaze narrowed at the stricken tone in her voice. "You are mistress there now. They are your people and they have suffered much loss from that fever. You need not fear anyone or anything in that place. I will also be there—"

"I don't want to go!"

Several of the men-at-arms looked up at her sharp

words, then as quickly looked away. Rylan lowered his voice.

"We go to Oxwich, Joanna. Once before I asked you about your life there, but you refused to speak of it. You did not trust me enough to tell me. Will you tell me now why you dislike the place so heartily?" At her stubborn silence he frowned. "Very well then, perhaps when we arrive I shall learn the truth myself."

With a cry of impotent fury Joanna jerked on the reins, setting her mount back on its heels. If Rylan had not caught the startled beast's head, Joanna might have tumbled off the flat saddle. But she was far too agitated by his casual statement to care.

He would take her to Oxwich when he well knew she despised the place. Had he no feelings at all? Had he no heart?

But Joanna already knew the answer to that. Rylan Kempe had no heart whatsoever. And any feelings he had were concerned only with property and political power. She glared at him, trying hard not to succumb to tears. Though he possessed a handsome form and ofttimes displayed a winning manner, he was still no more than he'd ever been: a nobleman, and everything selfish which that implied. Her father, King John, and now him. She was tenfold a fool to expect more of him.

She turned her face away from his searching eyes and only sat there trembling, while the others milled awkwardly about. With a foul oath Rylan jerked the reins from her hands and gave them to one of his men. Then he mounted his own destrier, and, after a last hard look at her, he signaled the party to proceed.

Once on the road, the men fell into a formation that included two forward scouts, several of the fiercest warriors flanking Joanna's mount, and the rest following behind. Rylan and Kell rode ahead of Joanna, and she did not hesitate to send several furious glares at her unfeeling husband's broad back. If he sensed her animosity, however, he did not show it, for he did not once turn to look at her. She had to content herself with wishing him cast to the devil.

Yet for all her anger, she was quickly filled with a cold, numbing fear. He was taking her to Oxwich—loathsome source of all her nightmares. As they rode on, drawing ever nearer the place, she veered between hating Oxwich and hating Rylan. Between dreading their arrival and dreading having ever to deal with Rylan Kempe again.

Through the towering beechwood, past a wide open meadow their party continued, then on into the fens upon a road that twisted and turned to follow the higher ground. The low lands were flat and crisscrossed with myriad brooks and slow-moving rivers and lakes. They forded shallow streams, crossed a crude bridge, and once were ferried across a wider river by a toothless old man and his simpleminded son. The land was mostly without trees, but at times the meadow sweet, dock, and bulrushes towered nearly as tall as the riders. Great flocks of widgeons and pintails rose at their passing, crying their outrage to be so disturbed.

Joanna's mood mirrored that of the riled waterfowl, and she could not enjoy the strange beauty of the place. Even the magnificent whooper swans she spied upon one of the dark pools could not lift her mood, for swans ever reminded her of her mother. She simply could not believe that the very man who had implored her to trust him was now dragging her to the wretched home of her childhood!

They spent the night at Dunley Abbey, a tiny cell that survived by the production of its cheeses and rare

honeys. The Cluniac Brothers were grateful for the generous patronage of their guests. But although Rylan's
coins bought the best accommodations available, they
were nonetheless mean indeed. The men and women
were strictly separated by the monks—marriage vows
held no sway with them.

Joanna convinced herself that she was relieved with
the arrangements, for she was exhausted by the grueling
ride and wanted nothing more than sleep. Added to that,
Rylan's unyielding attitude about Oxwich had not en-
deared him to her at all. Yet a small part of her longed
for the comfort of companionship during the sleepless
hours of the night. They would soon reach Oxwich, and
she was filled with unspeakable dread at the prospect.
But there was no one she could turn to.

For a moment when he had escorted her to the small
women's chamber she was to share with two religious
pilgrims, she had felt a glimmer of the comfort she
sought. Despite her coldness toward him, in the dim
light of the waning moon Rylan had pulled her to him
for a swift, hard kiss. Notwithstanding her deep anger
with him, Joanna had been drawn to the warmth and
strength of his embrace, and had risen to meet his seeking lips. But then he'd released her and pushed her
firmly—irritably—into the small stone building, and she
had felt even more forlorn than before.

Their passion was undeniable. It flared despite her
best intentions to suppress it. But passion was a thing of
the body, and what she needed now was a comfort of the
soul. Rylan could never do that for her, she knew now.
He could never understand how she felt about that damnable place he put so much stock in.

But then, why had she ever expected him to? she berated herself as she curled up on a hard pallet and

wrapped a coarse woolen blanket about herself. She knew better than anyone that men did not concern themselves with women's feelings, so why was she so disappointed now? She had no choice but to endure this visit as best she could. But once she was at Blaecston he would not so easily remove her to Oxwich again.

As sleep closed in on her she admitted to herself that she had hoped for more from him. Once their marriage vows had been spoken, her opposition to their union had disappeared. After all, the vows could not be undone. Even the idea of children, which at first had alarmed her so, had grown into a comforting spot of warmth in her heart. Her children—hers and Rylan's. Even now the thought softened her toward him.

Oh, but she was a fool, she told herself. He was her husband, true. But he was not a man to trust. Still, when sleep finally claimed her, she held close to the only comfort she could find: a blue-eyed boy with dark curls; a laughing girl . . .

They were mounted and underway before dawn. Joanna's legs nearly buckled beneath her as she approached the palfrey. How could simply sitting on a horse test her muscles so sorely? As if he anticipated her weakness, Rylan was at her elbow.

"Would you prefer to ride before me?" he asked as he wrapped one strong arm about her waist.

Joanna steeled herself against the solicitous tone in his voice. Easy for him to be kind when her body was sore and hurting. Why could he not be so for her aching heart? Why could he not care that she dreaded—and feared—returning to Oxwich?

"I can ride," she muttered as she eyed the horse awaiting her. Even if it killed her she would ride alone, she vowed. She could not suffer his touch this day of all days.

But that was not precisely true, she admitted as she settled gingerly upon the animal. She could not suffer his touch and the softening effect it always had on her. She wanted to maintain her anger at him, to revel in it. Riding cushioned in his strong embrace would make it too easy to give in to him and go along. And that she could not do.

As they made their way in the misty predawn, riding in the same defensive arrangement as before, Joanna sighed wearily. What she was doing was wrong—holding on to her anger in this way. The church bade that she forgive and forget, that she seek peace and harmony with her husband and submit to his will so long as it did not run contrary to the laws of God. Yet even a lifetime of yielding to the teachings of her church could not overcome the fear that rose in her now. A day's ride from Oxwich and every step bringing her closer. In the shadowy light she could imagine it all over again. The dark space under the bed. The thudding noise. The weeping.

Joanna rubbed the thin white scar on her wrist, unaware of her action. She understood so much more now than she had as a child. About the rhythmic thudding noise. About her mother's monthly distress. There had been more, though. Her father had spoken another man's name, a man he said had been killed.

She shook her head in confusion. Had her mother wept for her father's cruelty, or the loss of this other man? Perhaps both. She frowned. Oh, why could she not just put this all out of her head? she moaned as she rubbed her throbbing temple. It had all happened so long ago. Parts of it were as clear as yesterday while other things were mired in a fog that would not lift.

But despite her confusion, one thing was completely

clear. Rylan was taking her to Oxwich whether she wished to go or not. He was just as untrustworthy as she had suspected. As unyielding and overbearing as her father had been. It boded very ill for the life they now began together.

Dawn did not bring much comfort. The day remained gloomy, overcast with low-hanging clouds. The mist stayed on the land till near midday, only to be replaced by a slow, depressing drizzle. Though provided with a *chape à pluie*, Joanna was nonetheless miserable. The tender skin of her inner thighs was rubbed raw. The muscles themselves ached, and her headache had worsened.

The noontime respite only made remounting worse, for she feared she could not bear it. But she gritted her teeth and ignored Rylan's watchful gaze.

The afternoon passed in a haze of rain, mud, and excruciating pain. When the late twilight finally gave way to night and the familiar scent of figwort and willow herb alerted her to their proximity to Oxwich and the end of their journey, she was almost happy. Anything to be off this horse she rode!

But when the dark form of Oxwich Castle loomed before her, she forgot her physical misery. Faint lights lit the ramparts and pierced the iron gateway. A figure moved—or was it simply a trick of her eyes?—and for an instant she felt her father awaited her. Though she knew it could not be, her heart nevertheless pounded against her chest and her mouth grew dry with fear. She would have lagged behind but the tight cluster of other riders prevented it. Only when they slowed before the dry moat and the closed gate at the end of the wooden bridge was she able to clear her head of the formless terrors that tormented her. It was just a pile of stone, she told herself. The castle at Oxwich was no more than stones stacked high and strong upon an ancient earthwork mound.

"Come forward, Joanna. We shall seek entrance together." Rylan's voice and the touch of his fingers upon her arm roused her. "Take heart," he said as he took the reins from her hand. "We shall soon seek out our beds and recover from this ordeal."

Joanna could not answer. The combination of physical exhaustion and this emotional confrontation with the home of her youth—the source of her nightmares—left her too numb to speak.

"Open the gate and admit your new lord and his lady," Kell called out imperiously. "Sir Rylan Kempe, Lord Blaecston, and his wife, the Lady Joanna Preston of Oxwich."

Joanna heard the excited murmurs that arose from inside the gate. But all she could think was that she'd never before heard Kell speak so many words at one time.

"Does the Lady Joanna ride with you?" an old man's voice replied.

"She does." Rylan urged his destrier forward into the light of several torches which had been thrust through the iron gate. When he and Joanna were within arms reach of the gate, he pulled back her hood and his own.

"'Tis she," a woman's voice cried. "She's her mother's hair."

"But she is a nun," the old man's voice rose in dissent.

"Almost a nun," Rylan retorted. "Our marriage prevented her from taking her vows. But as you can see, she is wearied unto dropping. We left our marriage table to ride straightaway here. Now open this gate and give us a proper welcome."

In a matter of moments the gate began to inch up with

a screech of protesting gears. What little debate there had been had obviously disappeared at the sight of her. Was she so like her mother as that woman had said? No matter how she tried, however, Joanna could not remember her mother's face nor anything else of her appearance. A swan was what came to mind. A serene and distant swan.

In short order they were welcomed into the great hall by the seneschal, Sir Harris Ponder. Upon seeing his narrow face and thinning gray hair, Joanna recalled the old bachelor. One or two other faces did she also recognize, but most remained strangers to her.

"Welcome, milord. Milady," Sir Harris said with a sweeping bow. "Forgive our poor showing, but had we known of your arrival, we would have prepared—"

"'Tis of no consequence, Ponder," Rylan interrupted the man, but with a smile planted firmly on his face. "We do not expect a feast. Bread, cheese, and ale will suffice. There is time enough on the morrow to tour the estates and meet our people. Tonight we seek only our beds. See you that the servants prepare a place for all of my men."

The servants who yet wandered sleepily into the hall to see what the late-night commotion was needed no word from Sir Harris to set them to their tasks. The commanding presence of their new lord and his confidently voiced request were enough to bring ewers of ale in from the alehouse, and platters of cheeses, breads, and broken meats over from the kitchens. Just as quickly were rugs and blankets brought out from the storerooms. By the time Rylan and Joanna had finished their brief meal, arrangements for everyone had been made and the men had begun to head for their beds.

"Direct us to the master's chambers," Rylan said after draining his mug.

"Yes, milord. 'Tis freshly cleaned and awaiting your presence. We had the whole of the castle well washed with quicklime. You've not to fear for the fever here any longer. We've poisoned the spirits that brought it upon us and had every room blessed." The old fellow bobbed his head earnestly.

Rylan nodded absently at the man as he turned to escort Joanna. Joanna, however, peered at the seneschal through eyes that burned with fatigue. "*All* the evil spirits?" she questioned bitterly. "Neither quicklime nor a hundred priests' blessings can rid this place of all its evil—" She broke off as a sob rose in her throat. The old man stared at her in alarm, as if he feared some evil spirit did indeed still inhabit Oxwich's halls. But Rylan saw deeper and Joanna knew it. Her fears trembled perilously on the surface of her control, while he waited for them to break through.

With a low cry of desperation she whirled and ran toward the steep stairs that led up from the end of the hall. Rylan meant to take the master's chambers, but she could not go there. In unreasoning panic she fled to the only place that had ever provided her comfort at Oxwich. Up the stairs she flew, but just part of the way. Then into the wall chamber recessed in the massive stone walls, into the dark enclosure that had been her own.

The space was low and very dim. Her head almost brushed the rough ceiling. But a rug lay upon the floor and a fur throw was folded in one corner. As she'd done a hundred nights—a thousand—Joanna pulled her feet up into her skirts and flung the fur robe over her so that even her head was covered. Then she lay still and silent, fighting down her tears and counting her breaths as she'd done as a child. Waiting for the entire castle to settle into slumber.

It was not long before footsteps signaled someone's ascent on the stairs. All other movement and noises had ceased save for an occasional call from somewhere beyond the hall. The steps came slowly—wearily—then stopped before her little niche. Joanna knew before he spoke that it was Rylan. How could it not be?

When he did speak, however, it was not to berate her or order her out. Instead he sat down within the niche and sighed.

"I would not have us begin our married life with fear between us," he stated quietly. "You have learned enough of me by now, Joanna, to know that in our marriage bed at least we find some harmony. I would not have you flee from me."

Joanna struggled not to weep as his patient words washed over her. "'Tis not—" She broke off, swallowing the sob that threatened to choke her. "I cannot . . . not here . . ."

"Of course not here. This little hole is too small. Too hard." One of his hands reached out to rest upon her hip. "Let's away to the bed upstairs."

"No!" Joanna rolled away from his touch. She ignored the pain in her legs and scrambled away until she felt the cold outer wall against her back. In the entrance to the wall chamber Rylan was faintly outlined by the dim light that came from the hall below.

"Joanna, be reasonable," he murmured, never moving. "We are man and wife, wed in the eyes of both God and man. You cannot think to hold me off—"

Joanna shook her head wildly. "Not up there. I will not go up there!"

In the ensuing pause only her ragged breathing broke the silence. Then he sighed and leaned over. His boots fell one at a time onto the stairs. He peeled his tunic off and then his shirt. Finally he removed his chausses so that he was clad only in his loosened braies. Moving slowly and deliberately—and without speaking at all—he rolled onto the rug beside her. He lay back in the dark as if he were waiting. When she did not move, however, he turned onto his side, propped his head up on one of his arms, and stared at her.

"Why do you fear this place?"

A shiver ran through Joanna. "I . . . I do not fear it." She swallowed and tried to slow her harried breathing. "I do not fear it. But I do hate it."

He seemed to mull that over. "Tell me why."

Joanna stared at him from across the small space that separated them. In the dark of the enclosure he was an indistinct shape, a large shadow that separated her from the freedom she sought. Yet as she crouched there, her thighs aching, her eyes burning, and so utterly weary that she could drop, she knew there was no freedom that way. Not really. Wherever she were to flee—the priory, to court, even to Blaecston—it wouldn't matter. She didn't belong in any of those places. She didn't fit in. But she didn't belong here either. Most certainly not here. She had never felt more alone than she did at that moment.

Without warning she began to cry. Her hands covered her lowered face and she wept, huddled miserably in the corner.

At once Rylan was next to her, pulling her close and cushioning her hard sobs against his chest. Joanna burrowed instinctively into his comforting embrace, welcoming any solace that was offered. Yet his kindness only served to let down the floodgates even further. Every pain from her childhood came back to hurt her again. All the feelings of loss and of being abandoned. Her father's distance. Her mother's death. Then the three years she had been forced to remain within these cold and hated walls.

Her body shook in terrible spasms as the fears she'd repressed so long finally surfaced. She cried hot salty tears against Rylan's bare chest until she had no tears left to shed. Even then, however, her sobs would not cease.

But he held on to her, pulling her onto his lap, folding her in his arms. Her face pressed against his throat as her anguish poured out. His quiet comfort surrounded her throughout her storm of emotions, but she was only marginally aware of it. It was not the soothing caress of his hands she felt, but the reassuring touch of human caring. It was not the strong and reliable beat of his pulse beneath her ear, but the reminder of life—other lives connected still to hers. He was there, living and breathing, holding her as if he meant never to let her go, and she succumbed willingly to the promise of the future he offered.

When her breathing at last came easier, he moved one of his hands from around her shoulder to cup her face. His palm, hard and callused, was gentle as it held her head pressed against his chest. She felt a slight movement of his throat, as if he meant to speak, and then his hesitation. She shifted slightly and let out a shaky sigh. Only then did his words come.

"I'm sorry, Joanna," he murmured against the top of her head. His lips moved upon her wildly tangled hair. Was that a kiss? "I'm sorry I brought you here. I didn't know— No," he broke off. "That's not true. I knew, but

I didn't want to believe how much you hated this place. We'll leave in the morning."

He pulled away from her then tilted her face up to his. In the dark Joanna could see very little, but the look in his eyes was clear, and in that moment she knew he was sincere.

She nodded, then returned her face to the damp warmth of his chest. She didn't want to think or feel or do anything else but just be. She wanted to sit there in the comfort of his embrace and simply be with him.

She must have dozed, for she came awake with a start when Rylan moved.

"Shh," he murmured as he lay her back against the rug. In the dark he found the laces of her gown and loosened them. He pushed her bunched skirts higher, then tugged the gown over her head.

Joanna winced as the muscles of her back tightened against the pain of movement. When Rylan moved one of her legs to better reach her shoes, however, she groaned out loud.

"Sore from the ride, are you? Saddle sore and heart sore as well."

He pressed her back against the rug and shifted his own position so that she would not have to move her legs. The shoes came off and then her hose as well. His hands were warm and very gentle, yet Joanna could not force down the tension that inexplicably gripped her. From the tips of her toes, up through her aching legs to lodge somewhere in the depths of her belly, a sudden warmth engulfed her.

When his hands began to move against her calves, massaging the knotted muscles there, her heart's pace doubled. With every heated pass of his strong fingers up the curve of her calf to the tender place behind her knees, her breathing became more shallow. Then his hands slid up beneath her kirtle to rub the long muscles of her thighs, and she forgot to breathe at all.

"Relax," he whispered as he found the sore spot on the inside of each thigh. "Breathe slowly and try to relax."

Joanna nodded; she could not speak. But a low groan of contentment did escape her lips.

"Here?" He focused the attention of both his hands on one thigh, kneading and stroking, pressing but not too hard on the knotted muscle then working it until it relaxed. He shifted to her other leg and began the same ministrations.

Had it been another set of hands bringing such blessed relief to her, Joanna might happily have succumbed to the soothing rhythm and drifted into slumber's beckoning arms. But sleep was an impossibility, for these were Rylan's hands, and while they eased one portion of her disquiet, they roused a clamor elsewhere.

Her heart pounded an unsteady rhythm, tortured by the indefinable yearning that had overtaken her. Part physical, part emotional, Joanna only knew that she did not wish him to stop. She shifted restlessly and his hands slid higher. But as she caught her breath in anticipation, he paused. His hands rested on the soft fullness of her upper thighs. In the close quarters of her niche she heard the ragged pattern of his breathing. No longer was the stone enclosure cold; his presence had heated it until she was nearly melting with desire.

Then it was Rylan's turn to groan and turn away.

With that one simple motion he destroyed Joanna's tenuous composure. All her feelings of loneliness and rejection rushed to fill the void, and she felt foolish tears sting her eyes once more. She rolled onto her side, turning her back on him, but every muscle in her thighs and back protested. "Ohh . . ." She groaned in sudden pain.

"You must move slower," he bit out as if he were angry with her. But that only caused her to curl into a tighter ball, unwillingly groaning again as she did so.

"Christ and bedamned," he muttered. Then she felt the warm length of his strong body curl around her.

"No!" she cried, trying to elbow him in the stomach.

"Yes, dammit! Just lie still."

With a stone wall at her face and his equally rigid form behind her, Joanna had little choice in the matter. One of his arms curved around her waist and he drew her fully against him. For the span of several heartbeats they stayed thus. Then she felt his lips moving against her hair, seeking out the skin at the nape of her neck, and she could not maintain her show of indifference. She wanted him to hold her. Why must she pretend otherwise?

"'Tis not the way I meant to spend our wedding night." He breathed the words against her hair.

"Last night was our wedding night," she reminded him.

He grunted. "I am cursed, it seems. First those unbending monks and now . . ." He didn't complete his thought.

Joanna swallowed hard. "And now a weeping wife," she finished for him.

She felt his silent chuckle against her back. "No. And now my wife is too sore from riding horseback to provide me the ride I desire above all things." For emphasis he pressed his hips against her derriere, allowing her to feel the rampant need that gripped him.

Joanna instinctively pressed back against him, only to

earn another stab of pain in her back. "Bedamned!" she swore in a low but heartfelt tone.

This time Rylan laughed out loud. "At least we shall suffer together, my sweet little dove. My passionate bride." His voice grew husky and his free hand roamed down her side to rest upon her hip.

"Our time is coming, Joanna. Our hunger shall be fed. Our thirst shall be slaked." His hand slid farther until it met the bared skin of her thigh. Then, like one burned, he yanked it away.

"Sleep now," he told her in a strained voice. "Tomorrow shall see you feeling better. And me, God willing, as well."

24

Rylan was gone when Joanna awoke. For a long quiet while she simply lay there beneath the fur throw, staring up at the familiar stone ceiling above her. She'd not seen those cracks and fissures in five years, yet even in the gray morning light she remembered every one. The ceiling of her wall chamber—her cave, she'd often thought of it—was rough and unfinished, unlike the smooth facing of most of the castle's walls. It was hardly a grand place, but it had been far better than sleeping in the open hall with the retainers, or on the floor of her parents' chamber.

Slowly she stretched, testing her sore muscles. Although stiff at first, they gradually loosened as she flexed them. She had Rylan to thank for that, she realized as she wondered where he was.

The sounds of activity carried up the stairwell from the hall below. Tables were being dragged into place. Benches were moved alongside them. A pot clanged as it was settled onto the hearth to keep warm. A door banged closed. The voices, however, were muffled, and Joanna did not need to wonder why. A new master was arrived. Everyone would step very lightly until they had taken his measure. Would he be harsh or fair? Would he be jovial or grim? Should they learn to fear him or love him?

Joanna pondered that last question. Rylan's men-at-arms did not appear to fear their lord, although they did respect him. They had openly laughed at him when he'd come back wet from his walk in the woods. Of course, the rapport between men of war was considerably different from that between nobleman and servant. Still, she could not envision him as a cruel taskmaster. If he did but smile upon his people and set out to be charming, they would quickly fall into his camp. After all, hadn't she done so despite her determination not to?

Frowning at that admission, Joanna pushed herself to a sitting position. Her gown lay neatly folded. Her shoes were placed side by side in the corner with her hose laying above them. A comb had been left for her use and a shallow bowl of water as well. There was no reason for her to stay abed any longer.

Even as she dressed, however, she could not push aside the fact that Rylan had indeed drawn her into his camp. Though he possessed the arrogance typical of his rank, and then some—witness his initial abduction of her —he nevertheless also had a considerable capacity for kindness. He had been kind to her last night and compassionate as well. He'd held her and comforted her. He'd eased both her troubled heart and aching body. But most surprising of all, he'd restrained his passions even though no one would have judged him harshly had he not.

Joanna twisted to pull the laces of her gown snug down the left side of her waist, ignoring the slight pang of still-sore muscles. Last night she would have welcomed him in her arms, but he had turned away, though she knew he'd done it as a kindness. Through the night he'd held her close and she'd slept soundly in the security of his embrace. Yes, she was well and truly in his camp now. She did not fear her husband. But was what she felt for him love? There was desire between them, of course. But honesty compelled her to admit that there was more. She had turned to him for comfort and he'd gladly given it. If she turned to him in love, would he give her that as well?

She pushed her unbound hair back from her cheek, but before she could consider that new question, she was startled by a half-grown kitten that leaped into the niche. For a moment they stared at each other, both equally surprised by the other. Joanna swallowed hard, overcome with the same abhorrence she always felt for cats. The kitten seemed just as dismayed, however, for it meowed and whipped its tail around as if to say some stranger had invaded its domain.

"Shoo!" Joanna stamped her foot and flapped her skirts at the aloof animal. "Get away from here, you . . . you . . ."

To her agitation, the skinny creature ignored her completely. With a disdainful turn the cat spied the rumpled fur throw, then, shedding its feline reserve, made a wild tackling leap for the coverlet.

Joanna gasped in alarm as the kitten buried its head beneath a fold in the fur, then burrowed in and flopped to its side. The animal's tail twitched in excitement and all four paws came up to scrabble at its imagined playmate. Then it stilled, righted itself, and twisted around so that only its face poked out.

Clear yellow eyes in a plain gray face peered curiously up at Joanna, and for that moment she forgot to be afraid. Another kitten had played these same games with her long ago. It too had been gray with yellowish eyes. Only it had been much smaller. She rubbed her wrist nervously, then looked down at the narrow white scar she yet carried from that day.

As if she had only just recalled where she was, Joanna stiffened in fear. Right up the stairs was the room where her mother had died— No, she had not died there. She had died outside when she'd thrown herself into the dry moat. But she'd been prodded to her death in that room. Abused and berated by a cruel husband who wanted one thing only from his wife: a son.

For a moment Joanna was glad the castle had come to her. She was glad her unfeeling father had been thwarted in the end. For what had any of it gained him? A son or a daughter—even had he died childless—Oxwich was not his concern once he was gone. Why had he seen fit to destroy her mother over it?

The kitten made a crazy leap, then skidded to a halt in one corner. Joanna peered at it with wide, troubled eyes, but she was not as afraid as she had been. Her fear had been replaced by an ineffable sorrow. What would be would be. The last few weeks had proven that to her beyond any doubt. She had only to endure a little while longer at Oxwich. Then she would never come back again.

She turned to leave, but the little cat, as if realizing its audience was departing, made a sudden dash for the stairs. Joanna stumbled back, still ill at ease with cats. But when the creature disappeared up the stairs instead of down, she stared up behind it. Her parents' chamber was up there. She wondered if anyone stayed there now.

Then she shook her head, clearing her foggy thoughts. She didn't care who stayed in that chamber. She didn't care about anything having to do with

Oxwich at all. As if proving that to herself, she made her way downstairs at a determined pace. She would eat. She would meet the various servants and retainers. Then she would leave, never to return.

Rylan's voice carried clearly to her across the subdued murmurs of the others. While a few people broke their fast, others served and cleaned up. A small group waited in a knot to speak to Rylan while he held court at a wide table beneath the hall's three narrow windows. The bands of light fell at a sharp angle, just glancing across Rylan as he bent to make a notation on a parchment with a long quill pen. For a moment the bright sunshine glinted off his dark hair, almost halo-like, and Joanna slowed to a halt on the bottom step. Then he looked up as if he had been waiting for her and smiled.

Everyone's head turned to see what had brought such a look to the new lord's face. Their stares lengthened when they realized it was the old lord's daughter, their new mistress. But Joanna spared no glance for any of them. Her gaze remained locked with Rylan's and she could not look away.

There was something in his smile, something that reached out to her and touched her in a way she'd never been touched before. Her earlier thoughts returned, but where she'd wondered then at her feelings for him, now —in the warm glow of that smile—she knew. It was love she felt, love and trust and a bone-deep need that went beyond mere physical longings. Somehow he'd opened the locked door to her heart and gotten inside. She knew she could never turn him out now.

As if he read her thoughts, Rylan rose and laid his quill upon the table. In the silence of the watching hall he made his way directly to her, all the while holding her within his dark, compelling gaze.

"Good morrow, my lady wife," he greeted her in a warm tone. "If you are prepared, I will introduce you to your loyal people. Then we can break our fast together."

Overwhelmed by the sudden tumult of new emotions, overcome with the consequences of what loving him truly meant, Joanna could only stare at him. How truly magnificent a man he was, she thought, dumbfounded. So tall and handsome though clothed in his typically understated fashion. His long hair was drawn back with a cord, and his only ornament was his finely jeweled girdle. As always, however, his noble bearing stamped him a man not to be ignored.

How could she not have recognized him as her one true love, that very first day at the priory? How could she have ignored all the signs that were now so clear to her? Her heart raced under the impact of her newfound understanding, and a spreading warmth coiled up from her stomach. In confusion she lowered her eyes.

"Is that a yes or a no?" he asked quietly so that only she could hear.

"Oh, um, 'tis a . . . 'tis a yes. Yes, I will meet them now." She took the arm he offered, then moved alongside him as he slowly made a circuit of the room. A heated flush stained her cheeks as her hand rested upon his hard-muscled arm. This was her husband. She was his wife.

And she loved him.

But as yet they had not lain in their marriage bed. Though she tried to drive that inappropriate thought away, she was not entirely successful.

Operating in a bit of a fog, Joanna greeted the seneschal again, and the chief steward, the marshal, the chamberlain, and the cooks. There were several inside maids and the kitchen help also.

"The shepherds, goatherd, dairy maid, and tanner are about their business. As for the guards, Kell is even now with Oxwich's captain, seeing to the regular defenses," Rylan explained, once their circle of the hall was done. "As we leave today, however, those introductions must wait." He gave her a questioning look, as if he thought she might relent.

In truth Joanna had forgotten in the past few minutes how much she abhorred Oxwich. She was on the arm of the man she loved, and the newness of that discovery yet colored her thoughts. Added to that, so many of the faces were familiar to her. So many of them had smiled at her, relieved to have a master and mistress who meant to see to their needs. They were friendly and welcoming, and Joanna had responded in kind. But now she remembered, and the old horror came back. They could not truly start their marriage until they left this hated place. Only then could her love be given without reserve.

She bolstered her courage. "You need not eat the meal with me. I know you have business here. I will see to my own needs and prepare to depart." Her words were poised and controlled. But then her composure slipped. "Do not linger overlong," she implored, staring up into his dark eyes.

His hand tightened on hers, but he did not speak to the fears she could not disguise. "I have fealties to receive and several judicial matters to resolve. If you will see to our provisions, we will be away soon after the sun's zenith."

Joanna consoled herself with that promise. Yet as the morning dragged on and her solitary task was complete, she found herself drawn more and more toward the stairs and the chamber at the top.

That kitten had gone up there, she fretted. She did

not want any cats in her mother's room. Yet though she paced the hall, glancing unwillingly up the shadowed stairway, she could not bring herself to move any nearer. When Rylan left the hall—something regarding one man's milk cow being injured by another man's dog— Joanna wrung her hands in dismay. Would he never finish! Then she heard the piercing yowl of a cat and without warning two more of the animals streaked into the hall, followed just as quickly by a flustered maid.

"Out, ye damnable creatures! Begotten of the devil are ye!" She brandished her broom at the disappearing pair then nearly dropped it when she spied Joanna.

"Oh, milady. 'Tis sorry I am to disturb ye . . ."

"Wait!" Joanna halted her before she could back out of the hall. "Wait. Are there . . ." She gestured in the direction the two cats had taken. "Are there so many cats here?"

The woman straightened from her timid stance. "Oh, aye, milady. We've not a rat or mouse to be found. But now the cats are a pest."

"Why are there so many?"

"Oh, 'twas the Lady Mertice. She liked 'em around 'er. Anyone who hurt a cat caught the rough side of 'er temper."

"Is there . . ." Joanna hesitated, trying to ignore the imp that drove her, but it was no use. "Is there an old cat here? Gray and white. With large yellowish eyes?"

"A tom?"

"No, not a tomcat."

"Well, there's lots of gray ones. In fact, most of 'em *is* gray somewhere or 'nother. But the only one as is gray and white *and* very old that I know of is Minnou."

"Lady Minnou?" Joanna whispered the question.

"Aye—she's old and touchy now, but once long ago

she was the little miss's kitten. Cook says she treated her like a baby, always singin' to her—oh!" The maid's eyes widened as she remembered just who Joanna was. "She was *yours*, wasn't she?"

Joanna did not answer. She only turned to stare up the stairwell once more.

In the uncomfortable silence, the maid shifted from one foot to the other. "If you're lookin' for 'er, 'tis more than likely she's up there."

Joanna nodded and took a shaky breath. She heard the maid mumble something about sweeping the cobbled forecourt, but she didn't care. As if an ice-cold hand drew her forward, she shivered, then stepped nearer the stairs.

It was only a room, she told herself. And only an old cat. Yet she would rather have done anything else than mount those stairs. Still, something greater than her fear drove her on.

When she finally stood before the half-opened door, at first she just peered in. The same bed was there, and a familiar-looking chest. But the hangings around the bed were new and the rug before it was different. She could not see the entire space, however, so with a last spurt of courage, she swung the door wider and stepped inside.

As the sun was high, very little light came directly into the room. But there was a streak of sunlight upon the wide windowsill, and it was there the cat lay. She was seated neatly, her front paws folded back upon her chest, her chin tucked low as if she slept in the lulling warmth she'd found. But her eyes were not closed. Her wide unblinking stare was fixed on the woman in the doorway.

The emotions that rushed through Joanna were far too numerous to count. Fear choked her throat even as an overpowering sorrow consumed her. Yet also did she feel a terrible awareness, as if she'd come across a friend she'd lost so long ago that she'd forgotten her. But now she remembered, and with that memory came an out-pouring of unbearable emotions. Like a torrent they came: the anguish of her terrible loss; the bitter loneliness of abandonment; and worst of all, the years of love that had been held back within her own heart. She'd had no one to love—neither mother nor father. It was the pain of that pent-up desire to love another and be loved in return that brought her to her knees.

The cat started when Joanna sagged to the floor but did not look away. Silent tears coursed down Joanna's face, a storm tide of all she'd held inside for so long. Then from her girlhood came the rhyme she'd sung those many years ago, lulling a favorite pet to sleep.

"Be not 'A' too amorous; 'B' too bold nor—" Her voice failed on a sob but she wiped her tears away with her knuckles, her blurry gaze fixed all the while on the aged cat. The animal came to its feet and arched its body once. Then, still wary, it leaped down from the window and approached Joanna.

"Be not 'A' too amorous," Joanna began again in barely more than a whisper. " 'B' too bold; 'C' too cruel—" She stopped when the cat paused before her. Her hands lay in her lap, clenched in a knot, until she very slowly extended one to the animal. The old pet sniffed Joanna's hand then, as if expressing its approval, turned its head and rubbed against her fingertips.

It was all that was needed to break down the final walls of Joanna's reserve. Fresh tears started in her eyes and she reached for her old cat, caressing her reassuringly. "Lady Minnou, Lady Minnou," she whispered heart-brokenly through her tears. "How could she have done it? How could she have left me?"

Too wrapped up in her private misery, Joanna was not at first aware that Rylan had entered the room. Her hands clung to the now-purring cat and she pressed her damp face into its warm glossy fur. "Oh, Lady Minnou."

Then Rylan's hands gently smoothed across her shoulders and she felt his lips against her hair.

"Don't cry, Joanna." He knelt behind her, holding her against the solid bulk of his chest, folding her into his embrace much as she had pulled her old cat into her own. "I cannot bear it if you cry."

Somehow she was turned and in the process Lady Minnou slipped away. But Joanna had a new comforter now, one that was not tied to an unhappy past but instead promised her a better future.

"You needn't speak of it," Rylan whispered as he cupped her face with one hand and pressed her close to his heart. "We'll leave here and you'll never have to think of it again—"

But the floodgates had been opened. As her tears spilled forth, so did the words—and the hurt she'd bottled up for so long. "Why did she leave me?" she sobbed against his chest. "Why did he have to hurt her that way?"

She felt Rylan's arms tighten and felt his lips moving in her hair. "There's no understanding now what went on between your parents, love. 'Tis best resigned to the past."

Joanna gasped for breath and struggled for words. "He . . . he raped her." She swallowed hard, then shuddered in horror at the memory. "He had wanted a . . . a son. But he only got me."

"My God," he muttered. Then he tilted her face up toward his. "Don't ever fear such from me, Joanna. I want you, but only if you are willing. And I'll rejoice in our daughters as well as our sons." His eyes locked with hers, searing her with the power of his feelings, and that gave her the courage to go on.

"He spoke another man's name. I don't remember what, but the man had died." A sob caught in her throat. "Then after he left . . ." She trailed off and her eyes veered to the window. "After he left, she jumped."

She sat there frozen, remembering every ghastly detail of that day. The sky outside had been a mauve blue. The cry of wheeling grebes echoed in her ears. But her mother's leap had been utterly silent.

Then Rylan turned her face away from the window and forced her to look only at him.

"I am here for you now, Joanna. The past is—" He shook his head, searching for words. "It's past. It's over. We have only our future now. And I promise you, love— I promise you—I'll make it a good one—"

His words ended abruptly when her hands caught his face and brought it down to meet her kiss. Her emotions were too raw for words, too affected by his fervent vow for her to respond in any other way. She held on to him and his promise, searching his mouth with her own, giving herself over to him completely.

As if he gave her a sustenance she'd craved for far too long, Joanna's kiss went on and on. She was starving for his touch, but it was more than a physical need. Her heart hungered for him. Her soul yearned for him. It was a raw need, as basic as her very need to breathe. She could not pretend or hide her emotions any longer.

His mouth broke away from hers, and they both gasped for air. "Joanna?" His tone was both questioning and confused.

Her answer was to move her frantic kisses to his corded neck and farther down to the hollow of his throat. She clutched at the neckline of his tunic, desperate to be as close to him as possible. She needed his love both for her burning body and her aching heart. Could he ever give both to her?

Then he gathered her in his arms and she had her answer. "Ah, my sad sweet girl. I would do anything to put a smile on your face. Let me take you away from this place."

"No, not yet." Joanna stared up into his darkened eyes. Up into the face she had come to love despite her fear to do so. "Will you ever . . . Can you . . . can you love me?"

His brow creased in concern even as his grasp on her tightened. "Here? I am desperate to make love with you. But I thought—"

Joanna shook her head and her eyes filled with doubt. Yet still she forced herself on. "Can you ever *love* me—in your heart? As I love you," she finished in a low voice that trembled with feeling.

His eyes burned into hers, filled with emotions too numerous and too strong for her to name. Then he smiled and hugged her fiercely. "I thought you knew. I—" He shook his head and laughed. Then he pulled a little away so that their faces were on a level with one another. "I traded away a veritable kingdom to have you, Joanna. Did that tell you nothing of how I felt?"

She stared at him through eyes that sparkled with tears. But this time she dared to hope they might be tears of happiness. "I . . . I would hear the words."

His face grew serious at that. Though they yet knelt upon the floor, neither of them was aware of their surroundings. He smoothed her hair back from her face then wiped a tear away with the pad of his thumb. "I love you, Joanna. I need you for my wife. For my life."

Then he smiled faintly. "Will you say the words to me once more?"

Joanna's heart pounded an unsteady rhythm in her throat and her mouth seemed unable to respond. But as the shine in his eyes turned into a heated gleam, she finally mustered her wits.

"I love you," she whispered, as wonder filled her entire being and lifted her up in a cloud of happiness.

"And I love you," he answered back while his eyes wandered her face. "I love to fill my hands with your hair," he continued, doing exactly as he said. "I love the golden glow in your green eyes and the way your brow creases when you would argue a point with me."

"I am not arguing now," she said, tugging on his tunic while a smile took over her face.

"No."

Suddenly the air seemed almost to vibrate with their powerful feelings. She was filled with love and consumed with desire all at one time. Rylan too was clearly swept up in the same strong tide, for he abruptly rose to his feet, drawing her up as well. With one hand he pushed the door closed. Then he swept her up high in his arms.

"I cannot wait, Joanna. Not one minute longer."

With her arms flung around his neck she clung to him. "Nor can I."

Outside the call of birds came through the open window. But within the master's chamber the world beyond was of no importance. Joanna cared only that her husband loved her and that now he would make love to her. Girdle, gown, kirtle, and hose—her garments all were torn away and discarded alongside a pile of his own clothes. Then he lay beside her on the high bed, stretched out in all his male beauty. The creak of the bed ropes brought a vague memory of angry words and a woman's weeping to her mind, but it was quickly dispelled. When Rylan rolled to cover her with the heated length of his body, she knew nothing but him and the fire he stoked within her. But this time it was a fire of both her loins and her heart. And when he kissed her, the two joined in one fiery conflagration.

"I love you, Joanna," He whispered between a blazing trail of kisses. "I love your eyes." He kissed each lid tenderly. "Your skin." He nibbled along her cheek. "Your ears." Here he used his tongue to trace the intricate curves in a most erotic fashion.

"And your lips," he finally whispered as he met her own seeking kisses.

Such a hard man, yet with such soft, sensuous lips, Joanna thought as she succumbed to his questing kisses. "I love your mouth as well," she managed to answer as he traced a searing pattern along her sensitive lower lip. "And other places too." She let her hands move down from his neck along his back. She felt him shiver in anticipation, and she smiled against his mouth.

"I love when you touch me," he breathed huskily as one of her hands slid lightly along his spine.

Joanna opened her eyes to meet his impassioned gaze. "Where? Where would you have me touch you? Here?" She moved both her hands down along the muscled ridges of his back to where his waist became lean. In response he slanted his mouth ferociously across hers, thrusting his tongue deep inside and rubbing her inner lips and tongue until she was in flames. Her fingers dug into his flesh and she was breathless when he broke the kiss.

Yet the success of her foray made her even more bold. "Or is it better if I touch you here?" she whispered as her palms moved lower to his hard-muscled buttocks.

She was answered by the urgent press of his loins against hers. The heavy length of his arousal burned against the naked skin of her belly as he ground against her in a desperate rhythm. Beneath her hands she felt the bunching of his muscles. Without thinking she rose in automatic response.

"Christ and bedamned," he muttered hoarsely. "You play with fire, my beautiful little dove. And you shall surely be burned." Then with a sudden motion he caught both her hands in his and pulled them above her head. "Now we shall see who burns whom." He held both her wrists captive in one of his hands. With his other he smoothed the hair away from her face, all the while staring deeply into her eyes.

"I would burn my mark into you," he said, all teasing gone from his voice. "Brand your heart so that there is no mistaking who it belongs to."

"You have already done that." Fresh tears glistened in her clear green eyes.

"Have I?" He shook his head as if he could not believe it. "But I did everything wrong with you. I blundered from the first. Underestimating you. Not understanding."

Joanna stared up into his troubled face and felt an overwhelming rush of love for him. She freed one of her hands and tenderly cupped his lean cheek. "As long as you love me—" She broke off as emotions formed a lump in her throat, then blinked back her tears. She began again. "As long as you love me, nothing else can matter."

He turned his head and planted a kiss on the palm of her hand. Then he met her eyes with a serious look. "I made you come here, knowing how you hated this place."

"That's past now. I . . ." Joanna searched her heart, wanting to be sure. She was hardly able to believe it possible after all this time. "I don't hate it anymore," she admitted in a wondering voice. Then she laughed, feeling truly free for the first time in many years. "This place—any place—is defined by those who reside within. If my love lives here at Oxwich, then I must love Oxwich as well."

Her heart shone clearly in her eyes as she stared up at her beloved husband. "If you are here, Rylan, then I would rather be here than anyplace else on earth."

There were no words after that, only the soft sighs and quick gasps of their passionate embrace. He captured her lips with a violence that would have frightened her but for the force of her response to it. His tongue thrust deeply within her mouth, rough and possessive, crushing her to the bed.

But Joanna reveled in the frantic passion that erupted between them. Her legs parted to allow one of his rigid thighs to slide between them and press urgently against the hot core of her. She was excited beyond belief. Drowning in desire. Sinking into the sultry sweetness.

When he finally tore his mouth from hers, she clutched at him frantically. But he slid determinedly down along her sweat-slicked body, letting his coarse body hairs further inflame her sensitized flesh. She held on to his arms, feeling the muscles tense as he slid lower still.

At her breasts he paused, cupping each of them in one of his callused hands so that her nipples stood stiff and pointed, aroused in small hard nubs. Then he licked each one, slowly, torturously. She arched off the bed in unthinking response, demanding that he take them fully into his mouth. But he only smiled at this sign of her arousal. He blew on each nipple, then smiled wider when they puckered still tighter.

"You would never have made a nun," he murmured, meeting her impassioned gaze. "I knew it from the first." He bent to kiss her nipples, tugging lightly on each proud peak until Joanna was panting in desperate need. "I was right, was I not?"

Joanna licked her dry lips and pushed her hips higher, trying to find some relief by rubbing against him.

"Answer me, my sweet, biddable wife. I was right about you, wasn't I?"

Joanna swallowed hard, barely able to think, let alone answer him with any degree of coherency. "Yes, yes. Oh, Rylan, please . . ."

"Say it for me, love. I would have the words from your own lips."

"You were right," she said with a gasp. Then she slid one of her hands down to his flat male nipples and rubbed the damp skin there. At his quick intake of breath she opened her eyes. "You were right. I would have been a very bad nun." She groaned as he flicked his thumbs across the tips of her nipples. "You were right and you may . . . you may remind me of it . . . any time you like . . ."

With a groan of his own he lowered his mouth to the two breasts he held before him. First one, then the other did he kiss and fondle, sucking hard then teasing with fleeting passes of his tongue.

Joanna cried out, almost as one in pain might. But it was not pain she felt gripping her entire being. Far from it. He sucked her demanding nipples until they were wet, then pulled away to watch her face. Joanna was caught in the throes of the most exquisite of agonies.

Between each of his thumbs and forefingers he kneaded one of her nipples as she writhed beneath him.

"Come into me," she pleaded as her head tossed wildly about. Her legs wrapped about his waist and she pressed urgently up against him. "Dear God, Rylan, now. Now!"

"'Tis not for the husband to bend to his wife's demands," he answered her through his own heaving breaths. "Nay, 'tis for me to demand and you to respond." Again he lowered his head to kiss and suck each of her burning breasts. "And I shall be very demanding of you, wife. Ahh, damn—" He broke off as his control began to slip.

With a harsh groan he slid down, pressing fervent kisses along her ribs, into her navel, then lower against the heated flesh of her belly. Joanna's hand roamed restlessly over his damp shoulders, up his neck, and into his hair as his mouth burned a fiery trail to the vee between her legs.

When he spread her legs she moaned in helpless anticipation, trembling against the passion that held her now in its thrall. Then his lips found the aching source of all her torment, and she nearly swooned in response.

"No, no." She groaned, afraid and expectant all at one time. Then she dug her heels into the bed as the fine threads of her control began to unravel. "Ohh, Rylan. . . ."

In a violent rush it came, that mindless ecstasy she remembered. Like a terrible, wonderful storm washing over her. Like the German Sea overtaking a little island.

At her sudden tensing and outcry he swiftly moved that most intimate of kisses lower still, filling her as she longed to be filled, and prolonging the sweet agony of her fulfillment.

When the tremors finally subsided—when she was limp and collapsed into the feather mattress in a near faint—Rylan rose above her. Though weak from the effects of his lovemaking, Joanna lifted her eyelids to view the magnificent sight he presented. His powerfully muscled body gleamed bronze with a sheen of sweat on it. Wide shoulders, broad chest that narrowed to a lean flat waist. Then rising proudly from a dark nest of curls, his stiff arousal commanded her attention.

This was her husband, she thought as a shiver of pride and anticipation went through her. He had taken her for his wife when another had been promised to him. But he had wanted her. Only now could she admit how much she had wanted him. She still did.

A smile curved Joanna's lips and love seemed to surge through her until she was fair to bursting with it. "Come to me, my love." She lifted her arms invitingly and met his avid eyes with her own intense gaze. "I love you."

But it was more even than love, she knew as he moved over her. Her hands slid up along his arms. Their lips met in a kiss of unspeakable sweetness. Regret and hope, longing and love, and even more were there in that kiss. As he came into her, filling her completely with his love and his promise for their future, Joanna drew him down, deeper and closer than ever before, down into her heart to stay forever. He began to move in slow yet stirring strokes, building them both up to that perfect harmony of the body, heart, and soul. Joanna met him stroke for stroke, rising to him in glorious abandon. She drew his face down to meet her kiss once more.

His tongue came out to trace the curve of her parted lips. "There is something incredibly exciting about kissing you when you are smiling, my sweet."

A bubble of laughter—pure unadulterated joy—burst

from her lips, then she moaned in pleasure when he stroked her in a particularly enticing manner.

"'Tis happiness that is so exciting," she answered breathlessly, circling his lips with the tip of her tongue. "Happiness and love."

"I want to make you happy, Joanna. Now and always." He paused, resting deep inside her.

Emotions caught in her throat at the sincerity she saw in his serious face. "You do, Rylan. More than you know." Then she slid her hand down to the hard curve of his buttocks. "Give me all of yourself, my one true love. And I'll give you as much back."

She thought of a baby—his child and hers—and tears of joy filled her eyes. "I'll give you even more."

Epilogue

The sea was calm. Only slow rhythmic swells disturbed the gleaming surface. Puffins and kittiwakes wheeled across the bright summer sky, crying, then dipping low as they hunted in the exposed mud flats. Over all lay the heavy scent of salt and sea vegetation, the unique fragrance of the seashore at midsummer.

Joanna removed her slippers and flexed her toes, then drew her gown daringly high so that the sun fell warm upon her legs. From somewhere behind her she heard a burst of childish laughter followed by excited chatter.

"Mama! Mama!"

Joanna smiled at Adrienne's high-pitched call. They'd been at Isle Sacré for two days, yet her youngest child still viewed everything with wide-eyed wonder. Even Graham, who was usually so serious in his role as the older brother, could not hide his own exuberance.

"Mother, where are you?" he called, then giggled at something his sister said.

"Over here, Graham. By the oak tree."

In a trifling they were upon her, laughing and jumping with excitement. Joanna rolled to her side to smile upon her two adorable children. Graham of the dark curls and midnight-blue eyes. Adrienne who with her long flaxen hair and ethereal beauty might be a fairy child. Joanna's eyes pricked with tears of perfect happiness, and her heart swelled to bursting with love. Then, laughing at her silly sentimental nature, she pulled herself to a sitting position.

"What *are* you two about?"

Adrienne's eyes widened. "We found a kitten—"

"Three kittens," Graham corrected her importantly. From within his shirt he drew out two of the tiny squirming kittens while Adrienne revealed another one in the *couvrechef* she held in her arms.

"Oh, my goodness," Joanna exclaimed. "Bring them here. Let me see. Oh." She took the tiny creatures one at a time and nestled them in her lap. At once the three curled up together, seeking comfort from one another.

"Can we keep them, Mama?"

"Yes, can we? Can we?" Adrienne echoed.

Joanna began to gently pet the kittens, then looked up at her children's eager faces. "We have enough cats already at Blaecston. And even more at Oxwich." She fought back a smile at the sight of their crestfallen expressions. "Besides, their mother cat might miss them."

"That's what Nurse said." Graham frowned. Then he knelt down beside his mother. "But I don't think we have too many cats at home."

"I like the gray one," Adrienne said. She stroked the gray-and-white kitten behind its ears, then laughed when it batted playfully at her fingers.

Joanna sighed wistfully. "She reminds me of Lady Minnou."

"She does. She looks just like her," Graham agreed.

"We'll name her Baby Minnou," Adrienne said as she lay down beside her mother in the sun-warmed grass.

"Why don't you both stretch out right here and I'll sing you a song, just like I used to sing to Lady Minnou when she was a tiny kitten."

Lulled by the warm sun, the gentle breeze, and their mother's soft voice, the two children were soon dozing. Joanna too might have taken a nap, but she was waiting. Rylan had been gone for three weeks. His messenger had arrived three days ago with word that King John had finally signed an agreement with his barons. The Magna Charta, it was already being called. The greatest charter of all. But the messenger's best news had been that Rylan would be home in a few more days.

On a whim Joanna had sent another messenger back, asking Rylan to meet them at the island. She'd had a feeling since dawn that he would arrive today.

The shade of the oak crept over them and Joanna carefully extricated herself from the tumble of sleeping children and kittens. As she stared down at them, so dear and peaceful, she decided—a bit ruefully—that perhaps they *could* keep the gray-and-white kitten. Then her attention was inexplicably drawn toward the far shore.

Joanna's heart leapt to see the dark figure of a man on horseback starting across the sandy causeway. Rylan was back! Unable to restrain herself, she hurried across the beach and on into the ankle-deep water.

The tide had started to come in, but she knew that even had a storm driven the waves shoulder high, Rylan would come for her. He had done it before.

He spurred his destrier on, leaving a plume of water in his wake. Then, when he was almost upon her, even before the horse could stop, he flung himself down and into her arms.

"By damn, but I have missed you!" he muttered into

her hair as he dragged her into his embrace. "It's been a year!"

Joanna laughed in complete joy and tightened her arms around his neck. "It's only been three weeks."

"A year," he insisted. Then he silenced her laughter with a hungry kiss. When they broke apart his eyes were alight with a familiar desire. "God, but I have done naught but dream of this moment."

"And I as well," Joanna confessed. "But what of King John and the agreement he made with the barons?"

Rylan once more stilled her words with a kiss, stirring and urgent. "We can speak of him another time. Tell me, did you miss me? Did Adrienne and Graham miss me?"

"Yes. And yes and yes. They're here now, but they're asleep."

With one arm about her waist, Rylan guided her toward their children. She leaned her head contentedly against his shoulder when they stood to look down upon what their love had made.

"They've grown," Rylan said in a voice suddenly gone low and hoarse.

Joanna nodded, for she understood the quick emotions that had caught in his throat. Then she turned and, with a hand on each of his cheeks, drew his head down to hers.

"I love you," she whispered, gazing up into his beloved face. "You can never know just how happy you make me."

Rylan tightened his arms about her. "I know." His dark eyes seemed to plumb the depths of her soul. "My sweet little dove, I know."